J. G. Ballard: Visions and Revisions

Also by Jeannette Baxter

J. G. BALLARD: Contemporary Critical Perspectives

J. G. BALLARD'S SURREALIST IMAGINATION

Also by Rowland Wymer (*published by Palgrave Macmillan)

DEREK JARMAN

SUICIDE AND DESPAIR IN THE JACOBEAN DRAMA

WEBSTER AND FORD*

THE ACCESSION OF JAMES I: Historical and Cultural Consequences (*edited with Glenn Burgess and Jason Lawrence*)*

THE ICONOGRAPHY OF POWER: Ideas and Images of Rulership on the English Renaissance Stage (*edited with György E. Szönyi*)

NEO-HISTORICISM: Studies in Renaissance Literature, History and Politics (*edited with Robin Headlam Wells and Glenn Burgess*)

SHAKESPEARE AND HISTORY (*edited with Holger Klein*)

J. G. Ballard: Visions and Revisions

Edited by

Jeannette Baxter

and

Rowland Wymer

Introduction, selection and editorial matter © Jeannette Baxter and Rowland Wymer 2012
Chapters © individual contributors 2012

All rights reserved. No reproduction, copy or transmission of this publication may be made without written permission.

No portion of this publication may be reproduced, copied or transmitted save with written permission or in accordance with the provisions of the Copyright, Designs and Patents Act 1988, or under the terms of any licence permitting limited copying issued by the Copyright Licensing Agency, Saffron House, 6-10 Kirby Street, London EC1N 8TS.

Any person who does any unauthorized act in relation to this publication may be liable to criminal prosecution and civil claims for damages.

The authors have asserted their rights to be identified as the authors of this work in accordance with the Copyright, Designs and Patents Act 1988.

First published 2012 by
PALGRAVE MACMILLAN

Palgrave Macmillan in the UK is an imprint of Macmillan Publishers Limited, registered in England, company number 785998, of Houndmills, Basingstoke, Hampshire RG21 6XS.

Palgrave Macmillan in the US is a division of St Martin's Press LLC, 175 Fifth Avenue, New York, NY 10010.

Palgrave Macmillan is the global academic imprint of the above companies and has companies and representatives throughout the world.

Palgrave® and Macmillan® are registered trademarks in the United States, the United Kingdom, Europe and other countries.

ISBN 978–0–230–27812–7

This book is printed on paper suitable for recycling and made from fully managed and sustained forest sources. Logging, pulping and manufacturing processes are expected to conform to the environmental regulations of the country of origin.

A catalogue record for this book is available from the British Library.

A catalog record for this book is available from the Library of Congress.

10 9 8 7 6 5 4 3 2 1
21 20 19 18 17 16 15 14 13 12

Printed and bound in Great Britain by
CPI Antony Rowe, Chippenham and Eastbourne

Contents

Acknowledgements   vii

Notes on Contributors   viii

Introduction   1
Jeannette Baxter and Rowland Wymer

Part I 'Fictions of Every Kind': Form and Narrative

1. Ballard's Story of O: 'The Voices of Time' and the Quest for (Non)Identity   19
   Rowland Wymer

2. Ballard/*Atrocity*/Conner/*Exhibition*/Assemblage   35
   Roger Luckhurst

3. Uncanny Forms: Reading Ballard's 'Non-Fiction'   50
   Jeannette Baxter

Part II 'The Angle Between Two Walls': Sex, Geometry and the Body

4. Pornographic Geometries: The Spectacle as Pathology and as Therapy in *The Atrocity Exhibition*   71
   Jen Hui Bon Hoa

5. Disaffection and Abjection in J. G. Ballard's *The Atrocity Exhibition* and *Crash*   88
   Emma Whiting

6. Reading Posture and Gesture in Ballard's Novels   105
   Dan O'Hara

Part III 'Babylon Revisited': Ballard's Londons

7. The Texture of Modernity in J. G. Ballard's *Crash, Concrete Island* and *High-Rise*   123
   Sebastian Groes

8 J. G. Ballard and William Blake: Historicizing the
   Reprobate Imagination   142
   Alistair Cormack

9 Late Ballard   160
   David James

Part IV 'The Personal is Political': Psychology and Sociopathology

10 Empires of the Mind: Autobiography and
   Anti-imperialism in the Work of J. G. Ballard   179
   David Ian Paddy

11 'Going mad is their only way of staying sane': Norbert
   Elias and the Civilized Violence of J. G. Ballard   198
   J. Carter Wood

12 The Madness of Crowds: Ballard's Experimental
   Communities   215
   Jake Huntley

13 'Zones of Transition': Micronationalism in the Work of
   J. G. Ballard   230
   Simon Sellars

Index   249

Acknowledgements

Our biggest debt of gratitude is to the contributors to this volume; we thank them for their commitment, patience and tireless enthusiasm. We also gratefully acknowledge the support of Anglia Ruskin University for granting periods of study leave and the stimulation from colleagues and students with whom we have discussed some of our ideas. Jeannette would especially like to thank Kate and Wallace for the many delightful distractions and Rowland is similarly grateful to Pauline, Elliott, and Imogen.

Working with Palgrave Macmillan has been a pleasure; many thanks especially to Paula Kennedy and Benjamin Doyle for their continued support and invaluable help and advice with editorial queries. We also gratefully acknowledge the Ballard Estate for their interest in and assistance with this collection.

Notes on Contributors

Jeannette Baxter is Senior Lecturer in English Literature at Anglia Ruskin University, Cambridge. She is the author of *J. G. Ballard's Surrealist Imagination: Spectacular Authorship* (2009); editor of *J. G. Ballard: Contemporary Critical Perspectives* (2008); co-editor of *A Literature of Restitution: Critical Essays on W. G. Sebald* (2012), and author of numerous essays in the areas of literary modernism, postmodernism, and contemporary British fiction. She is co-editing a special issue of *Women: A Cultural Review* on the work of Jean Rhys.

Alistair Cormack is Head of English at Gresham's in Holt, Norfolk. He is the author of *Yeats and Joyce: Theories of History and the Reprobate Tradition* (2008) and of essays on Monica Ali and Ian McEwan. He is currently involved in research for a biography of the Irish translator and journalist Stephen MacKenna.

Sebastian Groes is Lecturer in English Literature at Roehampton University. He specializes in modern and contemporary culture and literature, and representations of cities. He is the author of *The Making of London* (Palgrave Macmillan, 2011), and editor of *Ian McEwan* (2009) and co-editor of *Kazuo Ishiguro* (2009) and *Julian Barnes* (2011).

Jen Hui Bon Hoa is a Ph.D. candidate in Comparative Literature at Harvard University. She is currently completing her dissertation, 'Secret Lives of the City: Reimagining Public Space in Twentieth-Century Literature and Theory from Walter Benjamin to François Bon'. Her essay in this volume is part of her next research project, 'The Compulsive Body', which explores the notion of bodily intelligence in contemporary theories of aesthetic experience, affect, and subject formation.

Jacob Huntley is a Tutor in Literature and Creative Writing at the University of East Anglia. His critical work principally explores non-mimetic or genre fiction from a Deleuzian perspective and he has also written on aspects of the Gothic, horror fiction, William Hope Hodgson, John Wyndham and the Saw films.

David James is Lecturer in Nineteenth- and Twentieth-Century Literature at the University of Nottingham. He is author of *Contemporary British Fiction and the Artistry of Space* (2008) and co-editor of *New Versions of Pastoral: Post-Romantic, Modern, and Contemporary Responses to the Tradition* (2009). He is currently completing a monograph on how modernist aesthetics have been reanimated by twenty-first-century novelists, while guest editing with Andrzej Gasiorek a special issue of *Contemporary Literature* on 'Post-Millennial Commitments' for winter 2012. His latest book, for which he is sole editor, is *The Legacies of Modernism: Historicizing Postwar and Contemporary Fiction* (forthcoming).

Roger Luckhurst is Professor of Modern and Contemporary Literature at Birkbeck College, University of London. His publications include '*The Angle Between Two Walls': The Fiction of J. G. Ballard* (1997), *The Invention of Telepathy* (2002), *Science Fiction* (2005), and *The Trauma Question* (2008), as well as a number of co-edited collections of essays, including *Literature and the Contemporary* (1999), *The Fin de Siècle: A Reader in Cultural History c.1880–1900* (2000) and *Transactions and Encounters: Science and Culture in the Nineteenth Century* (2002). His current projects include a study of the curse of the British Museum Mummy.

Dan O'Hara is Lecturer in English and American Literature at the University of Cologne. He was educated at Warwick, and Oxford, where he took his D.Phil., 'Machinic Fictions: A Genealogy of Machines in Twentieth-Century Prose and Art' (2005). His publications include *Thomas Pynchon: Schizophrenia & Social Control* (1994), the ongoing *Concordance to the Works of Deleuze and Guattari* (2009–), and the forthcoming *Extreme Possibilities: Selected Interviews with J. G. Ballard, 1967–2006*, co-edited with Simon Sellars. He has written often for *Ballardian*, and has also published on Pynchon, Beckett, Deleuze, Bourdieu, and Shelley.

David Ian Paddy is Professor of English Language and Literature at Whittier College, a liberal arts college near Los Angeles. He teaches courses in modern and contemporary British literature, drama, creative writing, science fiction and Celtic literature. His current research area is contemporary Welsh fiction. He is the author of articles on Angela Carter, Niall Griffiths, Jackie Kay, Jeff Noon, Samuel Beckett and R. S. Thomas, and the forthcoming book, *The Empires of J. G. Ballard* (2012).

x Notes on Contributors

Simon Sellars is a researcher in the Centre for Comparative Literature and Cultural Studies, Monash University, Melbourne, Australia. He is the publisher and editor of the widely read website ballardian.com, author of *Applied Ballardianism: the Philosophy of J. G. Ballard* (forthcoming), and co-editor with Dan O'Hara of *Extreme Metaphors: Selected Interviews with J. G. Ballard, 1967–2008* (forthcoming).

Emma Whiting received a Ph.D. from the University of East Anglia in 2010. Her thesis examined the Kristevan concepts of the abject and abjection and the modes in which they are evoked in and by twentieth-century literature, with particular focus on works by J. G. Ballard, along with Kathy Acker, Elfriede Jelenik, Bret Easton Ellis and A. M. Homes. She continues to research and write in this area and contributes review work to *ABES* and *Women's Cultural Review*.

John Carter Wood is a researcher at the Institute of European History (Mainz, Germany) and in the History Department of the Open University. He is the author of *Violence and Crime in Nineteenth-Century England: The Shadow of Our Refinement* (2004) and *The Most Remarkable Woman in England: Poison, Celebrity and the Trials of Beatrice Pace* (Manchester University Press, forthcoming). His current research focus is on criminality, policing and the culture of inter-war Britain, and he has continuing interests in the longer-term and cross-cultural history of interpersonal violence.

Rowland Wymer is a Professor of English at Anglia Ruskin University, Cambridge. His publications include *Suicide and Despair in the Jacobean Drama* (1986), *Webster and Ford* (1995), and *Derek Jarman* (2005), as well as a number of co-edited collections of essays, including *Neo-Historicism* (2000) and *The Accession of James I: Historical and Cultural Consequences* (2006). He is currently working on a book on science fiction and religion and editing *The Witch of Edmonton* for the Oxford edition of *The Collected Works of John Ford*.

Introduction

Jeannette Baxter and Rowland Wymer

It is difficult to 'introduce' J. G. Ballard for at least two reasons. The author of over 20 novels, nearly 100 short stories, and an extensive catalogue of non-fictional writings, produced over six decades, Ballard was, before his death in 2009, one of the most prolific and well-known writers of the contemporary period. He remains one of the most influential. Writers as various as Martin Amis, William Boyd, Toby Litt and Will Self acknowledge the extent to which Ballard's literary imagination has impacted upon and shaped their own. In a recent tribute to the author, Iain Sinclair singles out Ballard's keen eye for urban and technological landscapes which, to any other writer, may seem peripheral or uninteresting: 'He was very influential on me, particularly his sense of space and the edgelands . . . No other English writers were interested in those kinds of places . . . he wasn't interested in social satire but on things like the effects of advertising on the world, buildings that no one knew what they were being used for and the world of surveillance cameras.'[1] Indeed, this distinctive view of modernity now has its very own term, 'Ballardian'. That J. G. Ballard has officially been accepted into the English language as an adjective is surely a measure of his enduring imaginative presence and significance within contemporary literary landscapes.

Of course, as non-literary artists and cultural commentators are increasingly pointing out, Ballard's imaginative and intellectual influences extend far beyond the realm of letters. Taking 'influence' as one of its organizing principles, the 2010 exhibition '*Crash*: Homage to J. G. Ballard' at the Gagosian Gallery in London paid testimony to the enormous impact of Ballard's work on the visual arts.[2] Its premise was simple: to bring together the work of visual artists who inspired Ballard, such as Salvador Dali, Francis Bacon, and Helmut Newton,

1

and the work of young contemporary artists (painters, photographers, sculptors, filmmakers), such as Tacita Dean, Damien Hirst, and Rachel Whiteread, who have all, in turn, been inspired by Ballard's visionary and visual imagination. Ballard's own visual experiments (including his collage texts for *Project for a New Novel* (1958)) were juxtaposed with, for instance, Hans Bellmer's illustrations for Georges Bataille's *Story of the Eye* (1928), a blown-up photograph of a Boeing 747 undercarriage (Adam McEwan, 'Honda Teen Facial'), and Jake and Dinos Chapman's idiosyncratic *Crash* homage, *Bang, Wallop. By J & D Ballard*. It is an obvious point to make, but what emerges from this exhibition is not only the challenging, frequently disturbing, and always obsessive character of the Ballardian imagination, but also its capacity to initiate a dialogue with other imaginations, creating a shared dream (or nightmare) universe.

And the dialogue, as we can only begin to gesture towards in this brief and inevitably partial sketch, extends to the realms of cinema, TV, music and architecture. Peter Bradshaw observes, for example, that Ballard's influence on cinema is 'elusive, indirect, glimpseable at the margins'. Searching for Ballardian cinema in conventional terms, he suggests, is misplaced: 'we should be looking instead at CCTV footage taken from any shopping-mall security camera, or the Big Brother daytime live feed, or one of the direct-impact 9/11 World Trade Centre plane-crash shots – avidly consumed on YouTube, but now considered too brutal for television'.[3] Ballard himself was very positive about all three film adaptations of his novels, Steven Spielberg's *Empire of the Sun* (1987), David Cronenberg's *Crash* (1996), and Jonathan Weiss's *The Atrocity Exhibition* (completed in 2000 but never released theatrically), but all of them should perhaps be judged as honourably, even heroically, falling short in their attempts to film the 'unfilmable', to capture an idiosyncratic inner landscape and throw 'the nerves in patterns on a screen'.[4] Ballard's chilling and uncompromising visions of sex, violence and the invasive presence of modern technology have influenced some of the most controversial directors of the twentieth century such as David Lynch, Gus van Sant, Michael Haneke, and of course Cronenberg himself, but Bradshaw is probably right to see Ballard's main cinematic presence in less obvious places. It is not so much a matter of direct and conscious influence as of repeated surfacings of the unmistakably 'Ballardian' which bear witness to the collective cultural significance of his very personal set of obsessions. It is quite possible that Haskell Wexler, the director of *Medium Cool* (filmed in 1968, released in 1969), had never read any of Ballard's stories but his brilliant indictment of the media not only succeeds in completely confusing fiction with reality (by involving the actors playing fictional characters in the real riots which were currently taking place in Chicago) but also opens with journalists callously filming the aftermath of a horrific car crash in which an attractive young woman is dying in the wreckage.

According to Mark Lawson, *Empire of the Sun* (1984) was never adapted for television for purely financial reasons. Ballard's other major works, meanwhile, were either 'too sexually or politically explicit' for general broadcasting tastes.[5] Notably, a short film called '*Crash!*' (1971) did appear on BBC Two, two years before the publication of the eponymous novel and twenty-five years ahead of Cronenberg's film. But Harley Cokliss's '*Crash!*', in which Ballard stars alongside Gabriella Drake, and for which he provides the voice-over (reading extracts from his work), can be seen as something of a rehearsal for what was to come. Reworking textual extracts (such as the condensed novel, 'Crash!') and imagined scenarios from *The Atrocity Exhibition* (1970), Cokliss's '*Crash!*' combines footage of crash tests with close-ups of Ballard and the mannequin-like Drake standing silently in empty multi-storey car parks; these images are interspersed with looped images of motorway signs, car interiors, and Ballard driving along the Westway.[6] As Lawson points out, two other Ballard short stories have featured officially on the BBC: 'Thirteen to Centaurus' (1965), adapted from the eponymous short story published in 1962, and directed by Peter Potter for BBC Two; and 'Home' (2003) an adaptation of 'The Enormous Space' (1989), directed by Richard Curson for BBC Four. Given the extent to which Ballard's writings engage with televison images and formats – we need only think of David Cruise, the day-glow 'TV host' with the winning smile from *Kingdom Come* (2006) – it is perhaps surprising that so little of Ballard's work has made it onto the small screen, though the absence of conventional plotting in many of his stories must be a relevant factor. As Lawson notes, however, perhaps Ballard's influence on television is to be found less in 'what' and more in 'how' we watch: 'What is most Ballardian about TV today is the common modern experience of switching on, and being uncertain whether we are watching news or entertainment, or some half-life hybrid.' Indeed, it is Ballard's prescience and his ability to interrogate the slippages between fiction and reality that makes him 'a true televisionary.'[7]

Apart from occasional snippets of *muzak* playing in the Ballardian shopping mall or the lift of an executive high-rise building, Ballard's novels and short stories are conspicuously short on music. In numerous conversations and interviews (including interviews for *New Musical Express*), Ballard even went as far as to insist that he never listened to music and that it had no conscious impact on his work (despite the fact that his first commercially published story, 'Prima Belladonna' (1956), centred on a musically gifted orchid). How can it be, then, that according to many music critics, journalists and contemporary musicians, no other writer has shaped and influenced the music scene from postpunk onwards like J. G. Ballard?[8] Ballardian lines of influence have been drawn between artists as various as Brian Eno, Cabaret Voltaire, The Normal, Radiohead, Joy Division, The Manic Street Preachers, The Klaxons, The Comsat Angels, Burial and Kode9, to name just a few.[9] Some of this 'influence' may amount to little more than the appropriation of some of Ballard's more resonant story titles but, according to Dave Simpson, Ballard's obsessions – 'the collision of sexuality and technology, the human struggle within a consumerist landscape' – have become the preoccupations of songwriters ranging from Thom York to the garage rocker Dan Melchior.[10] The latter obsession is explored rather humorously in Melchior's 2002 song, 'Me and J. G. Ballard' (2002): imaginary competitors at the frozen food section of one of Shepperton's supermarkets, Ballard just pips Melchior to the last packet of peas.[11]

Early short stories such as 'The Concentration City' (1957) and 'Chronopolis' (1960) set the tone for what would prove to be one of Ballard's enduring fascinations: the psychological effects of the built environment on its human inhabitants. Geoff Manaugh, architecture critic and author of *Bldgblog: Architectural Conjecture, Urban Speculation, Landscape Futures* (2009), a text bringing together a wealth of materials from his prominent blog (BLDGBLOG), goes as far as to suggest that: 'We have more to learn from the fiction of J. G. Ballard . . . than we do from Le Corbusier'.[12] This is a view shared by Nic Clear, founder of Unit 15 at the Bartlett School of Architecture who ran the first course – 'Crash: Architectures of the Near Future' – dedicated to exploring the multifarious facets of Ballard's psycho-spatial imagination.[13] In a special issue of *Architectural Design*, which partly explores current economic, technological and environmental crises through Ballard's work, Clear celebrates Ballard as one of the most visionary commentators on architectural design and discourse: '[Ballard's] general description of the cultural landscape is far more accurate than almost anything that has been published in the pages of many recent architectural publications.'[14] And Ballard's influence, as Deyan Sudijc points out, is far-reaching: 'He managed to touch the imagination of architects as diverse as Nigel Coates and Rem Koolhaas, who shared his interest in dystopia. He ushered architects who saw themselves as modernists out of the innocence of hi-tech – as personified by Dan Dare – into a much stranger but more poetic vision of the future.'[15]

The second difficulty of introducing Ballard is that his work resists any straightforward move towards explanation or interpretation. This is something the author himself recognized in the various and often contradictory 'introductions' to his own novels and short story collections that he produced over the years. Take, for instance, the following statements, which form part of the Introduction to the French edition of *Crash*:

> I feel that, in a sense, the writer knows nothing any longer. He has no moral stance. He offers the reader the contents of his own head . . .
>
> Needless to say, the ultimate role of *Crash!* is cautionary, a warning against that brutal, erotic and overlit realm that beckons more and more persuasively to us from the margins of the technological landscape.[16]

So which part of the 'Introduction' do we follow? Is *Crash* an uncensored, provocatively amoral expression of a perverse imagination? Or is *Crash* a cautionary tale, a moral indictment of contemporary culture's insatiable appetite for violence as entertainment, which would seem to suggest that there is, after all, some critical distance in which we can seek temporary refuge? Notably, Ballard later went on to retract the second introductory statement in the most telling of manners: 'I went wrong in...that introduction...in the final paragraph, which I have always regretted...*Crash* is not a cautionary tale. *Crash* is what it appears to be. It is a psychopathic hymn. But it is a psychopathic hymn which has a point.'[17] Wrong-footing the reader every time, *Crash* remains maddeningly, fascinatingly open to various and paradoxical readings.

The impulse of this volume is double: to explore some of the formal and contextual influences of and upon Ballard's diverse collection of writings; and to respond to the different and often contradictory readings which all of these writings invite. The chapters in this volume have been organized around four key thematic headings that address what we perceive to be the distinctive concerns and features of Ballard's work: Form and Narrative; Sex, Geometry and the Body; Ballard's Londons; and Psychology and Sociopathology. Clearly, these categories are by no means discrete; as we would expect, productive points of tension and debate can be found both within and across the essays in the four sections. Also, the volume's critical ambition is inevitably modest: it makes no claim to offer an exhaustive analysis of Ballard's entire literary output. But neither does it concentrate its attention exclusively, as an earlier collection of essays does, on what are often regarded as Ballard's major works. Certainly, texts such as *The Atrocity Exhibition*, *Crash*, *Empire of the Sun* and the novels which form Ballard's final phase – *Cocaine Nights* (1996), *Super-Cannes* (2000), *Millennium People* (2003) and *Kingdom Come* – are discussed at various points, and within various contexts, throughout the volume, but they jostle alongside discussions of works that have, thus far, largely fallen out of Ballardian criticism: *The Unlimited Dream Company* (1979), *Running Wild* (1988), *Rushing to Paradise* (1994), Ballard's non-fictional writings (essays and reviews), and his very first published short story, 'The Violent Noon' (1951). In what follows, we outline the specific approaches of the various contributors to the volume. Each essay has been written in the spirit of stimulating further debate about one of the most engaging, fascinating and challenging writers of the contemporary period.

***

Part 1, 'Fictions of Every Kind': Form and Narrative, focuses on a variety of formal and narrative innovations at work in Ballard's writing from the 1960s onwards. According to William Boyd, 'In the short history of the short story – not much longer than 150 years – very few writers have completely redefined the form.'[18] To the select list of those who have – Chekhov, Hemingway, Borges – Boyd adds J. G. Ballard, 'whose haunting stories are closer to art and music...than to literature'. 'Haunting' was also the word Fredric Jameson used to describe 'The Voices of Time' (1960), the most radical and innovative of Ballard's early stories. Rowland Wymer opens the volume by emphasizing the pivotal role of this story, which retained enough of the characteristics of genre SF to be anthologized by Kingsley Amis in *The Golden Age of Science* (1981) *Fiction* yet was also arguably the first major 'New Wave' story, with its montage of different linguistic registers and 'terminal documents' and its fusing of entropy with depth psychology. The deliberately 'difficult' form of the story, difficult both for readers of genre SF and for those used to the conventions of the 'literary' short story, allowed Ballard to embed within it, in a cryptic form, many of the psychological paradoxes which were to feature in his later work, paradoxes which here draw explicitly upon the ideas of both Sigmund Freud and Carl Jung and implicitly upon the Eastern religious and philosophical traditions which influenced both of them in various ways. Identity and non-identity no longer seem to function as opposed terms or opposed goals but appear to be different ways of looking at the same underlying reality.

Roger Luckhurst turns his attention to what are perhaps the most formally elusive and explosive of all of Ballard's texts, the 15 'condensed' novels that have been collected as *The Atrocity Exhibition*. From 1966 Ballard began to experiment with a new form of avant-garde writing that suppressed the exhaustive context and connective tissue of both the Realist novel and conventional SF. The result, Luckhurst suggests, is a series of texts 'composed/found/collated between 1966 and 1970' that flaunt a density of (counter)cultural references and formal influences. Exploring the critical, filmic and narrative possibilities of the splice (/), Luckhurst contextualizes the 'violent logic of simultaneity/ compression/juxtaposition' enacted within and across the shifting forms of *The Atrocity Exhibition* before going on to analyse them in relation to the assemblage films of Bruce Conner. Extraordinary yet untapped parallels exist between Ballard's avant-garde textual forms, which drew on images and techniques taken from cinema, the visual arts and television, and Conner's avant-garde visual forms (for example, Conner obsessively reworked and manipulated television footage of nuclear tests, Marilyn Monroe and the Kennedy assassination throughout the 1960s). Following Walter Benjamin's method of *critical montage*, Luckhurst attempts an act of creative–critical splicing of his own, one which juxtaposes two experimental projects in order to forge new critical and aesthetic insights.

In the final essay in this section, Jeannette Baxter also employs a (typo)graphic sign to critical ends in her discussion of Ballard's 'non-fictional' forms. Focusing on a selection of essays and review essays written between 1962 and 2005, she re-reads Ballard's 'non-fiction' in the light of Sigmund Freud's 'The "Uncanny" ' ('Das Unheimliche' (1919)), an essay concerned precisely with the troubling nature of definitions. Following Freud's English-Language translator James Strachey's use of single quotation marks around the word 'uncanny' as a way of marking its hermeneutic ambivalence, Baxter places Ballard's 'non-fiction' in single quotation marks in order to interrogate its stability of meaning. Indeed, how usefully or accurately can one talk about Ballardian 'non-fiction'? To what extent do Ballard's 'non-fictional' forms provoke their own set of questions about textual boundaries, generic classification (fact/fiction, biography/autobiography), and the stability of authorial identity. What role does repetition – both formal and contextual – play? And what kinds of textual effects are produced in the act of (re)reading Ballard's 'non-fictional' forms?

Ballard's views on the traditional relationship between sex and the body have always been unequivocal: 'I believe that organic sex, body against body, skin area against skin area, is becoming no longer possible, simply because if anything is to have any meaning for us it must take place in terms of the values and experiences of the media landscape.'[19] The essays in Part 2, 'The Angle Between Two Walls': Sex, Geometry and the Body, respond to the variety of sexual and somatic forms on display throughout Ballard's writings. Jen Hui Bon Hua's wide-ranging analysis of *The Atrocity Exhibition* takes as its starting point a productive tension at work in Ballard's pornographic imagination: his various utilizations of pornography are as much an observation of the relationship between exploitative social relations and solipsistic fantasy as they are a commentary on the far-reaching possibilities of the pornographic imagination. Focusing on what she terms the 'erotics of geometry', Hui Bon Hua considers the intersection of abstract thought and eroticism – abstraction itself as pornography – as the central cultural logic of the spectacular society dissected in *The Atrocity Exhibition*. Drawing on theories of abstraction in, amongst others, the work of Siegfried Kracauer, and the figure of the schizophrenic developed by Gilles Deleuze and Félix Guattari, Hui Bon Hua reassesses the compulsive creation and reassemblage of partial objects which drives the fragmented subjectivity of Travers/Travis/Traven/Trabert. The abstract analytic mode of pornography, she suggests, comes to represent alienated social relation as well as its sublation, a new and highly ambiguous way of making contact with and of understanding the world.

Emma Whiting pursues the tensions between pathology and therapy in her reassessment of *The Atrocity Exhibition* and *Crash* as works of 'abject literature'. According to Julia Kristeva, abject literature is that writing which threatens boundaries – social, psychological, linguistic – approaching an impossible 'beyond' and invoking crises in its readers. However, in what Ballard identifies as an 'all-voracious present', characterized by mass media and proliferating technologies, these boundaries are already collapsed in the perpetual pursuit to render every impossibility possible. It would seem that sociality itself has taken on the work of abjection, giving rise to a 'pathological public sphere' with the wound as its central motif encoding the traumatic openness that constitutes sociality. With their preoccupation with crash deaths and dead or dismembered bodies, *The Atrocity Exhibition* and *Crash* appear to engage explicitly with such discourses. Nevertheless, there is an absence of the expected crisis: these are 'traumas that fail to traumatize'. Is it possible, Whiting asks, that the 'everydayness' of crisis has negated it, that abject literature – an ostensibly appropriate term for these texts – has been rendered redundant, caught up in and testifying only to the pervasive 'death of affect' with which Ballard is so concerned? Whiting explores the possibility that, whilst *The Atrocity Exhibition* and *Crash* may fail to invoke the crisis of abjection, these texts are not merely a celebration of desireless surfaces, but instead use the figure of the car crash to merge these surfaces at the point of the wound, which is re-situated as an erotically charged gateway onto what Ballard terms 'inner space'.

Opening representations of the Ballardian body up to discourses beyond sex and eroticism, Dan O'Hara interrogates the relationship between posture, environment and technology across a selection of Ballard's fiction in order to address one of the enduring accusations levelled at the author: why is Ballard unable to draw convincing characters? O'Hara suggests that the critical consensus judges Ballard's fiction by the wrong formal and contextual criteria; Ballard's innovations cannot be fully appreciated if they are measured against the limited conventions of Realism. The active elements of Ballard's brand of anti-characterization – of gestures, roles and contexts – are systematically organized, O'Hara argues, and any meaning to be found in Ballard's characterization 'resides in the formal system, not the individual agents'. What is damaged or altered in Ballard's fictional worlds is the set of abstract relations between characters, a situation that has required Ballard to devise a method of non-naturalistic characterization. Subsequently, O'Hara posits an experimental reading method, one that turns away from dialogue and which reads, instead, the relationships and geometries between inanimate objects, postures, gestures and contexts. Focusing on *Running Wild*, one of the least discussed of Ballard's works, and *Super-Cannes*, O'Hara develops this innovative re-reading of Ballard according to the psychiatric theories of R. D. Laing and Gregory Bateson, which not only shape Ballard's characterization but also his narrative structure, prose, and ideas.

Ballard is one of the most incisive and compelling literary cartographers of London. A resident of the Thames-side town of Shepperton for over forty years, he has somehow managed to write with equal intensity and facility about the idiosyncratic nature of contemporary life at the centre and the edges of the British capital. Part 3, 'Babylon Revisited': Ballard's Londons, engages with differentiated aspects of Ballard's urban imaginary as it manifests itself across four decades. Adopting a historicist approach to the early 1970s urban trilogy – *Crash*, *Concrete Island* (1974), *High-Rise* (1975) – Sebastian Groes presents these novels as works of 'literary anthropology' that not only criticize utopian forms of post-war town planning and housing schemes, but which also serve as allegories for the spatial impact of these phenomena upon modes of living, revealing late capitalism's brutal reshaping of the social and cognitive processes that determine everyday lives. Drawing specifically on Dante's *The Divine Comedy* (1314–21), Groes goes on to suggest that one way of reading Ballard's urban trilogy is as an attempt to translate postmodern spatiality into classical, human structures by inducing specific sensory reading experiences. He develops this argument by showing that the move into late twentieth-century capitalism expresses itself in the changing configuration of space and place. *Concrete Island*, for instance, operates a 'slum sociology' in order to trace the emergence of Junkspace, the abandoned or dysfunctional spaces (following Rem Koolhaas) that are left behind after modernization has run its course. Ballard's novelistic forms, as usual, form a mirror of the processes that they interrogate, and stretch the genre's usual conventions in order to make visible how the worlds inside the novels relate to the ones beyond the texts.

The Unlimited Dream Company (1979) has been read as something of celebratory novel, marking a dramatic turn away from the brutal urban landscapes of Ballard's so-called 'dark period'. The novel's shift in tone and style has been attributed, in part, to its adoption of a Blakean aesthetic which has been largely understood as a vision of revolution. In his reading of the novel, however, Alistair Cormack suggests that Ballard's use of William Blake is more ambiguous than it first appears and a close reading of Blake's poetry is required to tease out its full implications. The central character in *The Unlimited Dream Company*, 'Blake', far from being a figure of liberation, has much in common with William Blake's cannibalistic and punitive god, named in the prophetic books 'Urizen'. Ballard, it seems, may be examining the limits of the 'counter-culture' as much as exploring its revolutionary potential, and Cormack unearths some rather illuminating proto-punk connections to Ballard's novel in order to tease out its expressions of discontent. He then develops his reading by exploring the ways in which William Blake serves Ballard as a means of reconceptualizing suburban space. *The Unlimited Dream Company* obsessively rehearses the 'lineaments' of Shepperton to reveal the reality beneath just as Blake's *Jerusalem* (1804 (c. 1804–20)) makes of London a potentially visionary zone. Ballard's novel, Cormack contends, is as dark as anything he has written, and his return to William Blake should be read as a serious investigation of post-war cultural history, not a merry-prankster's co-option.

Bringing Ballard's visions of London up-to-date, David James detects something of a paradox in *Millennium People* (2003) and *Kingdom Come* (2006): their prose appears to be too 'anodyne for the task of narrating their stories of urban revolt'. Through meticulous analysis of matters of style and literary technique, James attempts to make sense of the apparent formal and contextual disjuncture at the heart of Ballard's 'late' London writing. He proceeds by suggesting that it would be reductive to read Ballard's 'stylistic moderateness' and 'intermittent banality' as a lapse from form. Instead, Ballard's late style, which risks simplicity (in syntax, vocabulary, narrative perspective) and even tedium (through reserved idiom, recursive plotting), is far more purposive and daring than it might at first appear. At work here is a 'late' aesthetic of disturbance, one which sets out to agitate and unsettle the reader in order to offer a 'counterforce to the endemic social monotony' and territories of inaction that Ballard maps out in his post-millennial Londons.

It was a huge compliment to Ballard when the reader's report for *Crash* landed on his desk: 'This author is beyond psychiatric help. Do not publish!' Had he needed 'help' Ballard would surely have diagnosed himself: when he went up to Cambridge to study medicine in 1949, he always had it in mind to become a psychiatrist. Instead, he quit medicine and immersed himself in Freudian depth psychology and the works of other major controversial figures within psychology, such as C. J. Jung and R. D. Laing. Subsequently, Ballard's fascination with the relationship between individual and social pathology has become one of the defining features of his work, and the essays in the final section in this volume, 'The Personal is Political': Psychology and Sociopathology, attempt to trace and explore some of the contexts which are relevant to this preoccupation.

How to make a case for J. G. Ballard as a post-imperial writer? This is the question driving David Paddy's interrogation of the relationship between autobiography, imperialism and psychology in a selection of Ballard's writings. Although Ballard's autobiographical texts have attracted a good deal of critical attention, it would appear that the scholarly focus has been a bit too narrow. Ballard's attempts to remap the psychological landscapes of the post-war period in 'Which Way to Inner Space?' (1962) and 'Time, Memory and Inner Space' (1963) have largely been discussed within the context of the 'New Wave' transformation of post-war science fiction. Yet a striking feature of these essays is the degree to which they draw attention to the autobiographical basis of Ballard's fiction. In these non-fictional pieces, Ballard reveals the psychological significance of his Shanghai childhood for his imaginative fiction. Building his argument with an analysis of 'The Violent Noon', Ballard's first published story and one which has thus far fallen out of critical view, Paddy illustrates how imperial and postcolonial contexts and issues were an early concern of Ballard's. Going on to explore the development of 'inner space' as a potentially more nuanced literary methodology for an examination of the traumas of Empire and an analysis of the new forms of cultural imperialism manifesting themselves in television advertising and electronic media in the 1960s, Paddy reads Ballard's psychologically inflected science fiction as a critique of what he terms 'psychic imperialism'. The final section of this essay brings Ballard's interests in nation, imperialism and psychology into the new millennium. Reading *Super-Cannes* within its multinational and consumer-capitalist contexts, Paddy explores the ways in which Ballard presents globalization as a new, post-war form of imperialism, one which operates by means of civilized violence, and one which 'makes coolies' of the contemporary human mind.

Ballard's enduring fascination with overlapping models of civilization, violence and human psychology also fuels John Carter Wood's analysis of *High-Rise* and *Super-Cannes*, and he too opens his discussion in interrogative mood: 'How should we evaluate J. G. Ballard's fiction as social commentary?' In an imaginative move to address this question and open Ballard's work up to an alternative set of theoretical and interpretative contexts, Wood proposes that *High-Rise* and *Super-Cannes* might be usefully read in light of a theory that has greatly influenced historical and social analyses of violence: namely, Norbert Elias's 'civilizing process'. Specifically, *High-Rise* and *Super-Cannes* dramatize two characteristics of civilization identified and explored by Elias: firstly, its potential fragility; and secondly, its tendency towards creating psychological dissatisfaction. Whilst *High-Rise* stages a '*de*-civilizing process', whereby internal and external interdependencies are disrupted, the monopoly of force breaks down, and psychological restraint is shown to be relaxed, the sprawling business park of *Super-Cannes* allows Ballard to explore a more chronic and subtle civilizational tension. As Elias observed, the 'quest for excitement in unexciting societies' leads to the 'controlled decontrolling of emotional controls' in contexts such as sport, an analysis that Wood extends to the violent games and exercises in controlled madness that operate so menacingly throughout Ballard's novel.

For Jake Huntley, the communities of willed madness that occupy Ballard's latter fictional phase – *Cocaine Nights*, *Super-Cannes*, *Millennium People* and *Kingdom Come* – are pockets of accelerated culture, where particular, perverse and shared obsessions have caused a kind of crowd fever. Extending from the derangement of individuals to collective psychopathologies, these 'Petri-dish' communities are excused in various ways from regular social restraints although, most notably, conventions of class remain, simultaneously rigid and precarious. Huntley sets out to address the contemporary anxieties explored in these texts, alongside their echoes within Ballard's earlier work, and interrogate the symptoms and idiosyncratic dynamics of the Ballardian crowd. Drawing on Elias Canetti's revisionist theories of the crowd and power, which move away from an assumed, unidirectional model of leadership, Huntley detects a far more ambiguous and fluid set of relations at work in Ballard's crowded micro-communities. He pursues this line of analysis further with reference to Gilles Deleuze and Félix Guattari's concepts of 'order-word' and 'assemblage', the shifting and indeterminate qualities of which have particular resonance for this reading of the psychologies and psychopathologies of the Ballardian crowd.

In the closing essay in this section, Simon Sellars re-reads the psychosocial character and logic of Ballardian space in light of the idiosyncratic, real-world phenomenon of micronations. Tracing parallels between Ballard's physical and psychological spaces or 'zones' of suspension – motorways, airports, supermarkets, shopping malls – and Marc Augé's idea of 'non-place', Sellars tracks the development of Ballard's varied and differentiated micronations across a wide range of short stories, such as 'The Enormous Space' (1989) and 'The Overloaded Man' (1961), and novels, including *Concrete Island*, the much-neglected *Rushing to Paradise*, and *Kingdom Come*. To what extent can the urge to create micronations be attributed to globalization's illusion of connectedness and the failure of political action to spark the mass imagination? What revolutionary potentials are to be found in Ballard's models of micronationalism? Are they spaces of physical and psychological retreat or can they be read as viable models of imaginative resistance and regeneration? Sellars engages with such exigent questions in order to probe new critical territories and to cast a thoroughly contemporary light on Ballard's shifting conceptions of psychology, space and community.

There is one further difficulty with 'introducing' Ballard. Readers of his overdetermined writings are no doubt familiar with the feeling that the author is always one step ahead. Why should it be any different now? By the time this volume is published, the J. G. Ballard literary archive (a collection of manuscripts, letters, papers, notebooks and other miscellanea) will be open to readers at the British Library in London, and a new phase in Ballard scholarship will have begun, one which will engage with some of the discussions in this collection and, inevitably, challenge and extend them. New lines of influence will need to be drawn; new responses to the tensions and contradictions inherent in Ballard's work will continue to be mapped out; and the process of 'introducing' J. G. Ballard will start all over again.

Notes

1. Iain Sinclair pays tribute to J. G. Ballard, *The Guardian*, 29 April 2009, http://www.guardian.co.uk/books/2009/apr/20/jg-ballard-tribute-writer, accessed 15 December 2010.
2. *'Crash*: Homage to J. G. Ballard', 11 February–1 April 2010, Gagosian Gallery, London.
3. Peter Bradshaw, in 'How J. G. Ballard cast his shadow right across the Arts', 20 April 2009, http://www.guardian.co.uk/books/2009/apr/20/jg-ballard-film- music-architecture-tv, accessed 15 December 2010. A version of this multi-authored feature was published under the title 'The poet of modern fears' in the G2 section of the *Guardian*, 21 April 2009.
4. For accounts of the relatively obscure Jonathan Weiss film see the DVD Review in *Sight and Sound* (August 2006), http://www.bfi.org.uk/sightandsound/review/3348; Jonathan McCalmont, 'A Benign Psychopathology: The Films of J. G. Ballard', *Vector: The Critical Journal of the British Science Fiction Association*, 261 (Autumn 2009), 12–16; Roger Luckhurst, 'Found-Footage Science Fiction: Five Films by Craig Baldwin, Jonathan Weiss, Werner Herzog and Patrick Keiller', *Science Fiction Film and Television* 1:2 (2008), 193–214.
5. Mark Lawson, in 'How J. G. Ballard cast his shadow right across the Arts', 20 April 2009, http://www.guardian.co.uk/books/2009/apr/20/jg-ballard-film- music-architecture-tv, accessed 15 December 2010.
6. For an in-depth discussion of various adaptations of Ballard's *Crash*, see Iain Sinclair, *Crash: David Cronenberg's Post-mortem on J. G. Ballard's 'Trajectory of Fate'* (London: BFI Publishing 1999). See also Simon Sellars's visual essay, 'Crash! Full-Tilt Autogeddon', 10 August 2007, http://www.ballardian.com/crash-full-tilt-autogeddon, accessed 10 December 2010.
7. Mark Lawson, in 'How J. G. Ballard cast his shadow right across the Arts'. A complete bibliography of cinema and TV adaptations of Ballard's novels and short stories is beyond the scope of this introductory piece. Let it suffice to mention Sam Scoggins's *The Unlimited Dream Company* (1983), which is now available on the excellent *Ballardian*, http://www.ballardian.com/sam-scoggins-unlimited-dream-company; and Solveig Nordlung's fascinating 'Low-Flying Aircraft' (2002), which was screened on BBC Four in 2003.
8. See Simon Reynolds's cultural history of postpunk, *Rip it Up and Start Again: Postpunk 1978–1984* (2005), which traces a clear Ballardian line of influence across this era.
9. For other excellent discussions of Ballard and music, see: Simon Reynolds, 'Magisterial, Precise, Unsettling': Simon Reynolds on the Ballard Connection, 2 June 2007, http://www.ballardian.com/simon-reynolds-on-the-ballard-connection, accessed 21 December 2010; Ben Myers, 'J G Ballard: The music he inspired' 20 April, 2009, http://www.guardian.co.uk/music/musicblog/

2009/apr/20/jg-ballard-music-inspired, accessed 21 December 2010; Mike Ryan, 'No-One Dances in Ballard': An Interview with Mike Ryan, 15 June 2006, http://www.ballardian.com/ballardian-music-mike-ryan-interview, accessed 18 December 2010.
10. Dave Simpson, in 'How J. G. Ballard cast his shadow right across the Arts'.
11. See Simon Sellars's short piece, 'J. G. Ballard vs Dan Melchior', which includes the lyrics from 'Me and J. G. Ballard', 12 June 2006, http://www.ballardian.com/jg-ballard-vs-dan-melchior, accessed 18 December 2010.
12. Geoff Manaugh, bldgblog-as-soundbite, 3 January 2005, http://bldgblog.blogspot.com/2005/01/bldgblog-as-soundbite.html, accessed 12 December 2010. See also Manaugh in conversation with Simon Sellars: 'The Politics of Enthusiasm: An Interview with Geoff Manaugh', 7 November 2006, http://www.ballardian.com/politics-of-enthusiasm-geoff-manaugh-interview.
13. For further information on Ballard and Unit 15 see Nic Clear and Simon Kennedy, Programme 07-08: Crash: Architectures Of the Near Future, http://www.bartlett.ucl.ac.uk/architecture/programmes/units/unit15_08.htm. Clear elaborates further in conversation with Simon Sellars: 'Architects of the Near Future': An Interview with Nic Clear, 24 December 2008, http://www.ballardian.com/near-future-nic-clear-interview.
14. Nic Clear, 'Introduction: A Near Future', Architectures of the Near Future, *Architectural Design*, Volume 79, Issue 5 (September–October 2009), 6–11 (p. 9). Ballard's literary analyses of the contemporary built environment continue to be the subject of many cultural events. See, for example, the lectures delivered at the symposium, 'Ballardian Architecture: Inner and Outer Space', held at the Royal Academy of Arts, London, 15 May 2010, http://www.royalacademy.org.uk/podcasts/ballard-architecture-inner-and-outer-space-audioc,1248,AR.html; and 'J. G. Ballard and New Brutalism', Institute for Modern and Contemporary Culture, University of Westminster, London, 10 November 2010, http://instituteformodern.co.uk/2010/j-g-ballard-and-new-brutalism.
15. Deyan Sudjic, in 'How J. G. Ballard cast his shadow right across the Arts'.
16. J. G. Ballard, 'Introduction to the French edition of *Crash*' [1974], *Crash* (London: Triad/Panther, 1985), p. 9.
17. J. G. Ballard, 'Conversations: J. G. Ballard' in Will Self, *Junk Mail* (London: Penguin Books, 1995), pp. 329–71 (p. 348).
18. 'Twelve Tales for Christmas', *The Guardian* 12 December 2010, http://www.guardian.co.uk/books/audio/2010/dec/07/william-boyd-gallard-dream-wake-island, accessed 16 December 2010.
19. J. G. Ballard in conversation with Lynn Barber, *Penthouse*, 5:5 (1970) 26–30 (p. 29).

Part I

'Fictions of Every Kind': Form and Narrative

1
Ballard's Story of O: 'The Voices of Time' and the Quest for (Non)Identity

Rowland Wymer

'The Voices of Time' (1960) is the finest of Ballard's early stories, an enigmatic but indisputable masterpiece which marks the first appearance of a number of favourite Ballard images (a drained swimming-pool, a mandala, a collection of 'terminal documents') and prefigures the 'disaster' novels in its depiction of a compulsively driven male protagonist searching for identity (or oblivion) within a disturbingly changed environment. Its importance to Ballard himself was confirmed by its appearance in the title of his first collection of short fiction, *The Voices of Time and Other Stories* (1962), and by the introduction to it he wrote for a 1977 selection of his best short stories:

> If I were asked to pick one piece of fiction to represent my entire output of 7 novels and 92 short stories it would be 'The Voices of Time', not because it is the best (I leave that for the reader to judge), but because it contains almost all the themes of my writing – the sense of isolation within the infinite time and space of the universe, the biological fantasies and the attempt to read the complex codes represented by drained swimming pools and abandoned airfields, and above all the determination to break out of a deepening psychological entropy and make some kind of private peace with the unseen powers of the universe.[1]

It was first published in the October 1960 issue of the science fiction magazine *New Worlds* alongside more conventional SF stories by James White, Colin Kapp, E. C. Tubb, and W. T. Webb. This was three-and-a-half years before Michael Moorcock took over the editorship of the magazine and inaugurated the 'New Wave' by aggressively promoting self-consciously experimental forms of speculative fiction. However, his predecessor, E. J. 'Ted' Carnell, had worked hard to develop a distinctively British science fiction magazine which could challenge the major American publications and had already published several of Ballard's early short stories, either in *New Worlds* or in the sister magazine which he edited, *Science Fantasy*. None of these stories would have fully prepared the typical SF reader in 1960 for the 'modernist' psychological obscurity and lack of conventional plotting (not to mention the typographical oddities) to be found in 'The Voices of Time' and not all readers were appreciative of Carnell's willingness to push beyond the conventions of genre SF.

On the other hand, the extensive and unapologetic use of scientific terminology and concepts in the story (Ballard was currently working as the deputy editor for the technical journal *Chemistry and Industry*) would have been alienating for many readers of mainstream literary fiction, even if they had been able to encounter the story outside the prejudicial context of its publication in an SF magazine. Charles Nicol, in an eloquent account of the literary value of the story, doubted that,

> a mainstream reader can appreciate the subtlety and beauty of such SF works, because his own set of literary values is limited by a tradition that excludes them. It is not the writer but the reader that builds the distinction between science fiction and mainstream fiction into a wall.[2]

As a piece of modernist SF, 'The Voices of Time' risked pleasing nobody in 1960. Since then, of course, Ballard has acquired a large and appreciative mainstream readership but, as Andy Sawyer points out:

> Many current readers of Ballard, while hailing him as the significant writer that he is, seem to either overlook his early stories, or suggest that their appearance in sf magazines is some sort of aberration, or ignore the fact that it was *science fiction* rather than any other form of literature that Ballard wanted to reform and invigorate.[3]

Non-SF readers with a certain amount of literary experience, who refused to be put off by the gestures towards hard SF ('The ribonucleic acid templates which unravel the protein chains in all living organisms are wearing out'),[4] would have recognized and appreciated the story's direct and indirect allusions to writers like Conrad, Kafka, Blake (the sunflower which 'sees' time) and T. S. Eliot (the dead geranium destroyed by the neurotic chimpanzee) and its modernist recourse to different type faces, page layouts, and linguistic registers to create a sense of fragmentation but also a sense of a potential new ordering through some hidden principle of montage.[5]

They would also have recognized the story's affinity with earlier poetic meditations on time, death, and change, such as Spenser's 'Mutabilitie Cantos', Shakespeare's Sonnets, or Donne's 'An Anatomie of the World, *wherein* . . . the frailty and the decay of this whole World is represented'.[6] The comparison with Donne is particularly apt since Donne also paradoxically deploys up-to-the-minute scientific knowledge ('new Philosophy') as further support for his very traditional theme of universal degeneration. Ballard, in a way which runs counter to so much genre SF of the 1940s and 1950s, reverts to the standard pre-Enlightenment perspective of Spenser, Shakespeare, Donne (and most early theologians) that, since the Fall, 'all this world is woxen daily worse',[7] and that as far as humanity is concerned 'the peak has already been reached, and the pathway now leads downwards to the common biological grave' (24).

The modern scientific 'validation' of this melancholy vision was partly provided, of course, in the nineteenth century by the Second Law of Thermodynamics which states that energy transfers within a closed system (such as the Universe) are always imperfect, resulting in an inevitable increase of entropy (the measure of disorder within a system) and culminating eventually in the 'heat death of the universe', when all heat and light have been expended by the stars to become unusable low-level background radiation. From the very beginnings of modern science fiction, this Law acted as a 'hard science' counterweight to the myths of progress which underpin a good deal of popular SF. The strings of numbers derived from intergalactic radio transmissions which punctuate Ballard's story and which reveal a countdown towards the end of the universe were anticipated by the countdown built into the date H. G. Wells chose for his Time Traveller's first voyage into the future – 802,701. The closing vision in *The Time Machine* (1895), some thirty million years further into the future, of a swollen, cooling sun and the disappearance of all but the most primitive forms of life, uses the fate of the solar system as a synecdoche for the inevitable fate of the whole universe.

The Time Machine's other scientifically well grounded form of pessimism – the likelihood of human devolution within industrialized societies in the absence of any other mechanism of natural selection – licensed genre SF writers, who were often more interested in dramatizing successful applications of technology, to indulge in more poetic and world-weary fantasies. 'Twilight' (1934), the most anthologized short story by John W. Campbell Jr., who as editor of *Astounding Science-Fiction* did more than anyone else since Wells to shape the development of science fiction in the twentieth century by publishing the early stories of Heinlein, Asimov, van Vogt, and Sturgeon, is a memorably elegiac glimpse of a dying human race no longer able to understand the great machines which their ancestors had built. When one also remembers the vitality of the 'catastrophe' tradition in British SF and the big rise in 'end of the world' SF stories following the development and use of atomic weapons in 1945 (Ballard's protagonist Powers refers casually to the prospect of World War IV as if, in spite of the near-future setting, World War III has already occurred) one can see that, despite its avant-garde form, 'The Voices of Time' had a distinguished and recognizable ancestry in conventional SF. The consolatory thought which briefly occurs to the doctor treating Powers, whose ever-increasing need to sleep could be read as one of the many symptoms of clinical depression, '*I'm sorry, Robert. What can I say – "Even the sun is growing cooler" –?*' (10), would not have seemed absurd or out-of-place to SF readers.

The link between the fantastic visions of SF and inner psychological states was always an implicit and often unacknowledged part of their appeal, an explanation of why some stories seem to 'work' in ways which have little to do with the logic of their plotting or the scientific ideas put into play. Eighteen months before his famous guest editorial for *New Worlds*, 'Which Way to Inner Space?', Ballard made the link between psyche and cosmos fully explicit in his picture of a man sliding down 'the physical and mental gradients' whilst being presented with evidence that the river of time was also flowing downhill and that '*the life of the universe is now virtually over*' (29). The psychological and figurative use of the idea of entropy was to become a distinctive feature of many *New Worlds* stories to the extent that it could be said to give 'New Wave SF its coherence as a group project'.[8] In addition to Ballard and Moorcock, other writers who exploited the concept effectively included Brian Aldiss, John Sladek, Thomas M. Disch, M. John Harrison, and Pamela Zoline. In Zoline's 'The Heat Death of the Universe' (1967), one of the most important stories ever published during Moorcock's editorship, the mental breakdown of a Californian housewife is counterpointed by coldly neutral explanations of the Second Law of Thermodynamics culled from reference works. By the story's climax, the scientific statements no longer occupy separate paragraphs (marked as 'inserts') but have merged with the developing domestic tragedy to form a continuous howl of despair:

The total ENTROPY of the Universe therefore is increasing, tending towards a maximum, corresponding to a complete disorder of the particles in it. She is crying, her mouth is open. She throws a jar of grape jelly and it smashes the window over the sink. Her eyes are blue. She begins to open her mouth. It has been held that the Universe constitutes a thermodynamically closed system, and if this were true it would mean that a time must finally come when the Universe 'unwinds' itself, no energy being available for use. This state is referred to as the 'heat death of the Universe'. Sarah Boyle begins to cry. She throws a jar of strawberry jam against the stove, enamel chips off and the stove begins to bleed.[9]

The connection between the macrocosm and the 'little world of man' is as close as in the storm scenes in *King Lear*. As Kaldren says to Powers in Ballard's story: 'Think of yourself in a wider context. Every particle in your body, every grain of sand, every galaxy carries the same signature' (35). It is hard to imagine Zoline's brilliant fusion of 'hard' science with 'soft' psychology being produced prior to 'The Voices of Time'.

The pivotal and Janus-faced position of Ballard's story, with its recognizable relationship to classic SF and its even closer relationship to the 'New Wave' journeys into 'inner space' which were shortly to follow, can be demonstrated by the apparent oddity of its inclusion by Kingsley Amis in his misleadingly titled anthology *The Golden Age of Science Fiction* (1981). For Amis, the 'Golden Age' of SF was not the early years of John Campbell's editorship of *Astounding* (as recorded in most reference works) but the 1950s, 'more precisely the period 1949–62'.[10] In Amis's fascinating and polemical introduction, the 'New Wave' is presented as an unmitigated disaster for SF and he endorses the view of E. C. Tubb (an 'old school' SF writer whose story, 'Memories are Important', appeared alongside 'The Voices of Time') that 'the result of bringing highbrow values into what was an essentially popular form or field would be to ruin it' (18).[11] Amis singles out 'The Heat Death of the Universe' as an example of everything he most dislikes about the 'New Wave', claiming that, apart from its title, 'Nothing else about or in the story has anything to do with science fiction however defined' and that, shorn of its technical devices, 'all it amounts to is a women's magazine, day-in-the-life account of a commonplace little woman in Alameda, CA' (24). The close formal and thematic relationship between Zoline's story and Ballard's makes it difficult to see how the one can exemplify all that was wrong with the 'New Wave' while the other can proudly represent the 'Golden Age' of SF. The gendered language ('women's magazine', 'commonplace little woman') may give a partial clue to what is going on here. At any rate, 1960 is specifically singled out by Amis as the year when science fiction began to change for the worse yet he obviously felt Ballard's story had retained a close enough connection with genre SF to continue to be anthologized despite its obviously disastrous influence on the field and the possibility that Ballard 'has never been *in* the genre at all' (28).[12]

Zoline's protagonist Sarah Boyle tries to resist the chaos into which her life is descending by a number of increasingly frantic attempts to impose order:

> Sometimes she numbers or letters the things in a room, writing the assigned character on each object. There are 819 separate moveable objects in the living-room, counting books. Sometimes she labels objects with their names, or with false names, thus on her bureau the hair brush is labelled HAIR BRUSH, the cologne, COLOGNE, the hand cream, CAT.
>
> (53)

She 'writes notes to herself all over the house' and, whereas over the stove she has written 'Help, Help, Help, Help, Help', she has put 'on the wall by the washing machine' Yin and Yang signs and mandalas, symbols associated both with Eastern religious philosophies and the psychological theories of Carl Jung.

If entropy was a defining preoccupation of 'New Wave' SF, there was also a complementary and compensating interest in Jung's theories about how to achieve the psychic order and balance which was the goal of individuation. Writers published in *New Worlds* who had a serious interest in Jung included Michael Moorcock, Brian Aldiss, Roger Zelazny, and D. M. Thomas and this interest was shared by a number of other major writers of science fiction and fantasy such as Ursula Le Guin, Philip K. Dick, and Doris Lessing. Ballard himself had begun a degree in medicine with the aim of becoming a psychiatrist and was familiar with the work of both Freud and Jung, whose ideas were then given rather more respectful attention within the academic and professional discipline of psychology than they are now.

The apparent orientation towards death shown by Powers and other protagonists in early Ballard stories and the increased interest in sexual psychopathology in the later stories might suggest that it is Freud who is the crucial influence, and indeed his complete works form part of Kaldren's collection of 'terminal documents'. If that were the case, Powers' decision to submit himself to whole-body irradiation, like the creatures Whitby was experimenting on, and merge himself with the cosmos would be a pathological surrender to the death drive, the instinctual rival to Eros which Freud (influenced by Schopenhauer) hypothesized in *Beyond the Pleasure Principle* (1920) and which posited an urge in all living things to return to their former inorganic state of being. Although in apparent opposition to the sexual instincts, the death drive could combine with them to produce compulsively masochistic or sadistic behaviour and can hardly be ignored in any analysis of *Crash* (1973). Freud's highly speculative notion was partly prompted by his investigation of the repetitive nightmares of shell-shocked soldiers, but was also a response to Jung's criticism that Freud's account of the libido was too exclusively sexual and can be seen as part of an unacknowledged move back towards some of Jung's ideas.[13] Although the Freudian hypothesis that 'the aim of all life is death'[14] has frequently been dismissed, it has recently received some potential support from biologists who believe that the 'default' mode for all living cells is death; in other words, they are programmed to commit suicide unless they receive chemical signals to the contrary.[15] When this system of control breaks down, the result is cancerous tumours, 'totally disorganized growth' like that shown by the irradiated specimens in Whitby's laboratory (22).

The drained swimming pool which appears on the first page of the story has biographical origins in the abandoned pools which Ballard saw in the Shanghai International Settlement as European families began to flee from the Japanese but it also strongly recalls one of Freud's most famous images for the psychoanalytic project: 'It is a work of culture – not unlike the draining of the Zuider Zee.'[16] This was to become the controlling metaphor of Zoline's second short story, 'The Holland of the Mind' (1969) and also appears in a story by Brian Aldiss, 'Danger: Religion!' which was printed alongside 'The Voices of Time' in an anthology called suggestively *The Inner Landscape* (1969):

> Almost as far as our vision extended, we could see another dyke extending parallel with ours. The sea was being chopped into polders. In time, as the work of reclamation proceeded, the squares would be drained; the sea would dwindle into puddles; the puddles would become mud; the mud would become soil; the soil would become vegetables . . . [17]

When Ballard first saw a drained swimming pool, it struck him at the time as 'strangely significant in a way I have never fully grasped' but he later decided that 'the drained pool represented the unknown'.[18] In Freud's rhetoric of course, the draining of the Zuider Zee figures a process of enlightenment and clarification: 'Where id was, there ego shall be' (112). By contrast, on the floor of Ballard's drained pool are 'strange grooves' cut by the biologist Whitby before his suicide which interlock 'to form an elaborate ideogram like a Chinese character', constituting 'an enigma now past any solution' (9). This 'enigma' is not quite as enigmatic as it appears, since its shape is explicitly described for us a few pages later: 'It covered almost the entire floor of the pool and at first glance appeared to represent a huge solar disc, with four radiating diamond-shaped arms, a crude Jungian mandala' (13). In a story which comes close to overwhelming its readers with an informational overload, forcing them to scrabble for meaning among 'a heap of broken images', Ballard has helpfully, perhaps teasingly, provided a key which promises to explain everything.

The importance of Jung in Ballard's early work was recognized by a number of critics, including David Pringle, Robin Briggs, Gregory Stephenson, and Patrick Parrinder, who wrote that 'the main "scientific" background for these stories is not biology, as it was for Wells, but Jungian psychology . . . Ballard's fiction is a progressive subjugation of every feature of external reality to the demands of the "collective unconscious" '.[19] The advantages and disadvantages of a broadly Jungian approach are most apparent in Gregory Stephenson's 'archetypal' analysis of the Ballard *corpus* in *Out of the Night and into the Dream* (1991) which has some interesting things to say but is handicapped by its decision to leave Freud out of the picture entirely and to see all of Ballard's work as enacting the same redemptive 'quest for an ontological Eden'.[20] In his chapter on the early disaster novels, Roger Luckhurst is sharply critical of what he saw (in 1997) as still 'the dominant critical approach to Ballard', accusing critics who celebrate a repeated movement towards psychic fulfilment and transcendence in these novels of 'homogenizing complex frames of reference (psychoanalysis, analytic psychology, existentialism) into an unrigorous mish-mash of mystical religiosity, which is then – and this is the major concern – offered as *the* interpretation which would unlock the entire chain of Ballard's oeuvre'.[21]

There are many different reasons why a writer or artist might be drawn to Jung, as many were in the 1960s. He gives a much more accurate and sympathetic account of the creative process than does Freud and his notion of a 'collective unconscious' seems to validate the idea that a writer who digs deep into his or her own psyche will encounter 'archetypes' which are communicable to others in a way which bypasses some of the normal obstacles created by historical and cultural difference, so that 'we are all accomplices in the dream world of the soul'.[22] As far as Ballard's writings are concerned, much the most important Jungian idea is that of individuation, the process whereby the conscious and unconscious are brought into a closer relationship to form a new unity, or Self, whose centre is not the ego. A version of this idea was also picked up by the dissident 'existentialist' psychologist R. D. Laing, who was another important influence on Ballard.

Jung's own 'confrontation with the unconscious' began at the end of 1912 and brought him close to a complete breakdown as his dreams of mass destruction began to increase in number and intensity during 1913–14. The outbreak of World War I connected the personal with the historical in the same way that World War II and the prospect of World War III form part of the inner landscapes of so many Ballard stories. Although Jung was reassured that it was not only his own mind which was fragmenting, he continued to be subject to disturbing dreams and fantasies which he recorded in his notebooks and later transcribed calligraphically into the famous 'Red Book' (or 'Liber Novus'), accompanied by his own commentaries and paintings. This deeply personal document, beautifully decorated to resemble a medieval manuscript, underpins all his later work (it is described by its editor as 'nothing less than the central book in his oeuvre') but has only recently been made fully available in published form.[23] In it can be found many examples of the intricate combinations of circles with crosses, squares, or other tetradic shapes which he began painting in January 1916 and called 'mandalas' (from the *Sanskrit* word for circle).

In *Memories, Dreams, Reflections* (1963), Jung wrote, 'My mandalas were cryptograms concerning the state of the self which were presented to me anew each day. In them I saw the self – that is, my whole being – actively at work . . . It became increasingly plain to me that the mandala is the centre. It is the exponent of all paths. It is the path to the centre, to individuation.'[24] Following the example of Whitby, Powers spends most of the story constructing his own giant mandala on the abandoned weapons range out in the desert and, when it is complete, places himself at the centre of it. This makes it easy to see why 'The Voices of Time', like many of the early novels, can be described as a story of 'psychic fulfilment', a successful completion of the process of individuation. The construction of the mandala proceeds in parallel with the lengthening periods of sleep experienced by Powers which are associated with the possibility of psychological development (all the permanent 'sleepers' at the Clinic possess the 'silent pair' of genes and may therefore be 'the forerunners of a massive move up the evolutionary slope' (21)). By contrast, Kaldren, who to some degree functions as the antagonist or 'shadow' of Powers, has been surgically deprived by him of the need for sleep, an idea first explored by Ballard in 'Manhole 69' (1957). This procedure has added twenty years to Kaldren's active life but left him subject to 'periodic storms which tear him apart' as 'the psyche seems to need sleep for its own private reasons' (26).

Jung took his idea of a progression from a deluded conscious ego towards an essential inner Self from Hindu philosophy, where the true inner Self (*âtman*) is identical with the Absolute Reality (*Brahman*). The Self and the Universe cease to be distinct and participate in the same Reality. As the 'endless river' of time washes Powers away and he feels his body 'gradually dissolving, its physical dimensions melting into the vast continuum of the current' (39), the mandala seems to confirm that he has reached the centre of his own psyche which is also the centre of the cosmos: 'Around him the outlines of the hills and the lake had faded, but the image of the mandala, like a cosmic clock, remained fixed before his eyes, illuminating the broad surface of the stream' (39). This positive sense of fulfilment achieved through a mystic union of the Self and Absolute Reality seems to carry quite different connotations from the Freudian death drive, even though Powers' dead body is found shortly after he reaches this psychological centre and Whitby's completion of his own mandala was followed by his suicide. It is also relevant that the 'sleepers' at the Clinic are referred to as 'terminals' and their sleep appears to be 'dreamless'. As in many Ballard stories, the reader feels like asking at the end: 'were we led all that way for / Birth or Death?'[25]

The answer is, of course, both/and rather than either/or since the competing Jungian and Freudian interpretations are simply different ways of describing the same phenomenon, as are the Hindu and Buddhist traditions which are the ultimate sources of their ideas. The Hindu quest for the *âtman*, or essential Self, which is identical with the underlying reality of the Universe was reformulated in Buddhism as a quest to achieve an understanding that the Self is as much of an illusion as all other phenomena. The emptiness of *nirvâna* in Buddhist thought is because, within the flow of time, there *is* no stable, essential Self (this is the Buddhist doctrine of *anâtman*, or no-self). Freud's notion of an inbuilt drive towards extinction derives from the Buddhist elements in Schopenhauer, whereas Jung's theory of individuation is more closely related to core Hindu beliefs. But if a stable centre to the psyche cannot be achieved *within* time, then the longing for one becomes difficult to distinguish from a longing for extinction and the process of individuation begins to closely resemble the death drive.[26]

The mandala which Whitby carved on the floor of the swimming pool was almost wholly obscured by 'damp leaves and bits of paper' (13) and the 'mouldering gullies' were 'half-filled with water leaking in from the chlorinator' (9), all this suggesting a ceaseless flow of time which threatens the achievement of a centred Self. The phrase which concludes the story's first paragraph, 'an enigma now past any solution' (9) may carry a barely concealed watery pun in its final word. Although the mandala is one of Jung's most important archetypal images of the Self, along with the Philosopher's Stone and Christ, it does not connote, for either Jung or Ballard, an unambiguous fullness of presence, something which can be firmly grasped. For Jung, 'The archetype in itself is empty and purely formal', a structuring principle which is only partially represented by concrete images.[27] When Kaldren's girlfriend, the ironically named Coma, asks Powers what he has been scribbling on a desk blotter, he 'realized he had been unconsciously sketching an elaborate doodle, Whitby's four-armed sun' but what he replies to her is, 'It's nothing' (26). In expressing a doubt that any single hermeneutic key will serve to 'explain' the disaster novels, Roger Luckhurst asks pointedly: 'Could the ciphers which litter Ballard's landscapes merely draw a zero? Could the Jungian mandala, that symbol of wholeness and completeness that Powers builds in concrete in "The Voices of Time" – could its plenitude of suggested meaning actually be empty?'[28]

The circular form can signify wholeness, completion and plenitude or, equally, absence, emptiness and nothingness. Unlike the glass which is either half-full or half-empty, depending on point of view, the mandala is both wholly full and wholly empty. The abandoned swimming pool is also both full of meaning and 'empty' (9), like the drained pool in T. S. Eliot's *Burnt Norton* (1935), the first of the *Four Quartets*, which 'was filled with water out of sunlight . . . Then a cloud passed, and the pool was empty'.[29] In another early Ballard story, 'Zone of Terror' (1960), the desert setting (not dissimilar to that of 'The Voices of Time') had been chosen, we are told, as the location for a 're-creational' centre for tired executives because of its 'supposed equivalence to psychic zero' and the psychologist's internal telephone number, 0, is 'almost too inviting' to ring.[30] In 'The Terminal Beach' (1964), the story which Ballard said 'marks the link between the science fiction of my first ten years, and the next phase of my writings that led to "The Atrocity Exhibition" and "Crash" ',[31] the protagonist Traven is admonished (by a corpse): 'It seems to me that you are hunting for the white leviathan, zero'.[32] In 'The

Voices of Time' Powers speaks of his own 'approaching zero' (14) which he reaches when he places himself at the centre of the mandala he has built on the weapons range.

Ballard was an admirer of the erotic novel *Story of O* (1954) by 'Pauline Réage' (since identified as Anne Desclos, whose usual pen name was Dominique Aury) and, along with Graham Greene, Harold Pinter, and Brian Aldiss, was happy to have his praise of this notorious work included as one of the promotional quotations used by the Corgi paperback edition.[33] An explicit erotic dimension is largely missing from Ballard's own story of simultaneous fulfilment and annihilation, though it is present in 'Track 12', published two years earlier, in which the central character, 'his fading identity a small featureless island nearly eroded by the waves beating across it', drowns to the sound of a massively amplified kiss as the 'island' of his identity 'slipped and slid away into the molten shelf of the sea'.[34] Like the mandala, the name of Réage's character signifies completeness, fullness, and eternity of being and, paradoxically, the 'nothing' or 'zero' to which her masochistic submission has reduced her:

> O is a conventional symbol of eternity, the snake with its tail in its mouth, which has neither beginning nor end. The O of the marriage ring symbolizes everlasting love, a circle that is lifted out of time and mortality. O is the hole, the cunt, female sexuality, which is either the eternal circle or an emptiness – zero – waiting to be filled.[35]

It is not far-fetched to suggest that the 'perverse' sexual psychology of *Story of O* is very closely related to the simultaneous quest for identity and non-identity which we find in 'The Voices of Time', which could perhaps be described as Ballard's own 'Story of O', or rather the first of many such, since the pattern is repeated in so many of his later works, including those with an explicit sexual dimension. In her very influential book on *Fantasy: The Literature of Subversion* (1981), Rosemary Jackson assimilates both erotic and non-erotic forms of fantasy to a bold, psychoanalytically based, general theory. She writes of:

> that goal which lies behind all fantastic art, to a greater or lesser degree, the arrival at a point of absolute unity of self and other, subject and object, at a zero point of entropy. Jacques Lacan has identified the longing for this unity as the profoundest desire of the subject, referring to it as an 'eternal and irreducible human desire . . . an eternal desire for the nonrelationship of zero, where identity is meaningless'.[36]

This seems implausible as a generalization about all fantastic art and, despite her deployment of the term 'entropy' she has little to say specifically about science fiction, where the element of fantasy is both disciplined and apparently validated by an appeal to scientific concepts and the use of scientific terminology. However, it is an uncannily apt comment upon 'The Voices of Time', capturing its longing for a unity of being which can only be completed outside the flow of time and hence only attained in death.

Because the quest for identity takes place within time, because our being is *in* time, we can never reach that 'still point', the centre, the Self, represented by the mandala, because the centre cannot hold. The ceaseless Heraclitean flux carries everything away with it, so that falling leaves and running water obscure the mandala's outlines. It can still be glimpsed, in the way that a religious ikon can be glimpsed on the bed of a flowing stream in Andrei Tarkovsky's film *Stalker* (1979), but it cannot be fully grasped or possessed. This is why the most extreme and mystical of all Ballard's quests for identity, *The Crystal World* (1966), is predicated upon the idea that time is 'leaking' out of the universe, causing matter to replicate itself by crystallization. This confers a kind of immortality on both living things and inanimate objects (the distinction has ceased to be meaningful), and produces a vision of a single atom filling the entire universe 'from which simultaneously all time has expired, an ultimate macrocosmic zero'.[37]

The Self which is found in 'The Voices of Time' turns out to be a no-Self, as Powers dissolves his identity in the vast 'endless river' of cosmic time which flows over him. Except, of course, that the river of time is not 'endless'. The very entropic forces which prevent full individuation and the achievement of a centred Self will eventually bring about what Jackson called a 'zero point of entropy', the reduction of the universe to a state of undifferentiated, changeless, background radiation, the so-called 'heat death of the universe'. At one level, there is an undoubted sense of pathos in the fact that Powers has merged with the *Brahman* or Absolute Reality of a cosmos which is itself dying and therefore not a stable ground of Being, a pathos captured in the poetry of the 'mysterious emissaries from Orion' who spoke of 'ancient beautiful worlds beneath golden suns in the island galaxies, vanished forever now in the myriad deaths of the cosmos' (41). On another level, like Spenser in the 'Mutabilitie Cantos', Ballard gives us a vision beyond mutability of 'that same time when no more *Change* shall be' (VIII.2), when the countdowns in the intercepted radio transmissions have all reached zero and Powers will indeed be 'beyond hope but at last at rest' (40), secure in his (non)identity, the circle or O of his life, as well as that of the universe itself, now complete but also completely empty.

Notes

1. *The Best Science Fiction of J. G. Ballard* (London: Futura, 1977), p. 155.
2. Charles Nicol, 'J. G. Ballard and the Limits of Mainstream SF', *Science Fiction Studies*, 9 (July 1976) http://www.depauw.edu/sfs/backissues/9/nicol9art.htm, p. 8.
3. Andy Sawyer, 'Foundation's Favourites: The Voices of Time by J. G. Ballard', *Vector: The Critical Journal of the British Science Fiction Association*, 261 (Autumn 2009), 50–1 (p. 51).
4. 'The Voices of Time' in J. G. Ballard, *The Voices of Time* (London: J. M. Dent, 1984 [1974]), p. 24. Subsequent page references are given in the main text. This volume is a reprint of Ballard's first British collection, *The Four-Dimensional Nightmare* (London: Gollancz, 1963), with two stories changed, rather than of *The Voices of Time and Other Stories*, which had been published the year before in America.
5. Charles Nicol identifies 'The Waste Land' as the story's most revealing mainstream literary analogue, p. 4.
6. John Donne, *Poetical Works*, ed. Herbert J. C. Grierson (London: Oxford University Press, 1971 [1929]), p. 206.
7. Edmund Spenser, 'Two Cantos of Mutabilitie', VI.6, in *Poetical Works*, ed. E. De Selincourt (London: Oxford University Press, 1969 [1912]). Psalm 102 says both the earth and the heavens 'shall wax old like a garment' (Authorized Version, verse 26).
8. Roger Luckhurst, *Science Fiction* (London: Polity Press, 2005), p. 158. See also Colin Greenland, *The Entropy Exhibition: Michael Moorcock and the British 'New Wave' in Science Fiction* (London: Routledge & Kegan Paul, 1983), ch. 11 'No more, with feeling: entropy and contemporary fiction', pp. 191–206.
9. Pamela Zoline, 'The Heat Death of the Universe' (1967), in *Busy About the Tree of Life* (London: The Women's Press, 1988), pp. 50–65 (pp. 64–5). The unreferenced scientific statements are in fact taken from *The Penguin Dictionary of Science*.
10. Kingsley Amis, ed., *The Golden Age of Science Fiction* (Harmondsworth: Penguin, 1983 [1981]), p. 32. The rather precisely chosen dates 1949-1962 correspond to the founding of *The Magazine of Fantasy and Science Fiction* (seen as a positive development by Amis) and Ballard's guest editorial for *New Worlds*, 'Which Way to Inner Space?'. The cover of the Penguin edition features a rock-jawed spaceman wielding a ray gun, a reassuring image for many readers of genre SF but unlikely to attract 'the general reader' (to whom Amis says he was trying to reach out).
11. Nevertheless Tubb continued to have stories published in *New Worlds* after Moorcock had taken over the editorship.
12. Kingsley Amis had earlier included 'The Voices of Time' in the third volume of the influential *Spectrum* anthologies of SF which he edited with Robert Conquest (London: Gollancz, 1963). Ballard himself reviewed *The Golden Age of Science Fiction* for the *Guardian* and wrote that 'Amis's contempt for

post-1960 science fiction seems bound up with his growing hatred of almost everything that has happened in the world since then'. See J. G. Ballard, 'New Means Worse', *A User's Guide to the Millennium: Essays and Reviews* (London: Flamingo, 1997 [1996]), pp. 189–91 (p. 190).
13. See note 26.
14. Sigmund Freud, *Beyond the Pleasure Principle*, in *On Metapsychology: The Theory of Psychoanalysis*, trans. James Strachey, *The Pelican Freud Library* vol. 11 (Harmondsworth: Penguin, 1984), p. 311.
15. See, for example, Martin Raff, 'Cell Suicide for Beginners', *Nature*, 396:6707 (12.11.1998), 119–22.
16. Sigmund Freud, Lecture 31 'The Dissection of the Psychical Personality', in *New Introductory Lectures on Psychoanalysis*, trans. James Strachey, *The Pelican Freud Library* vol. 2 (Harmondsworth: Penguin, 1973), p. 112.
17. Brian W. Aldiss, 'Danger: Religion!', in Mervyn Peake, J. G. Ballard, Brian W. Aldiss, *The Inner Landscape* (London: Corgi, 1970 [1969]), pp. 127–90 (p. 128). The third story is Mervyn Peake's 'Boy in Darkness', which is developed out of the world of the *Gormenghast* novels.
18. J. G. Ballard, *Miracles of Life* (London: Harper Perennial, 2008), pp. 26–7.
19. Patrick Parrinder, 'Science Fiction and the Scientific World-View', in Patrick Parrinder, ed., *Science Fiction: A Critical Guide* (1979), pp. 82–3.
20. Gregory Stephenson, *Out of the Night and into the Dream: A Thematic Study of the Fiction of J. G. Ballard* (New York: Greenwood Press, 1991), p. 148.
21. Roger Luckhurst, *'The Angle Between Two Walls': The Fiction of J. G. Ballard* (Liverpool: Liverpool University Press, 1997), Ch. 2 'J. G. Ballard and the Genre of Catastrophe', p. 48.
22. Derek Jarman, *Kicking the Pricks* (London: Vintage, 1996), p. 108. This autobiographical work was first published under the title *The Last of England* in the same year (1987) as his film of that name.
23. C. G. Jung, *The Red Book: Liber Novus*, ed. and intro. Sonu Shamdasani, Philemon Series (New York: Norton, 2009), p. 221.
24. C. G. Jung, *Memories, Dreams, Reflections*, recorded and ed. Aniela Jaffé, trans. Richard and Clara Winston (London: Flamingo, 1985 [1963]), pp. 221–2.
25. T. S. Eliot, 'Journey of the Magi', in *Collected Poems 1909-1962* (London: Faber, 1974 [1963]), p. 110.
26. It has been argued (by Bruno Bettelheim among others) that the close relationship between the two ideas can be traced back to a more recent source, some speculations by Sabina Spielrein, who was a patient and lover of Jung's before becoming a Freudian analyst. In a 1912 paper she argued 'that the sexual instinct contains both an instinct of destruction and an instinct of transformation', giving us the origin of 'both Freud's dual-instinct theory *and* Jung's theory of individuation!' (Elio J. Frattaroli, 'Me and my anima: through the dark glass of the Jungian/Freudian interface', in Polly Eisendrath and Terence Dawson, eds, *The Cambridge Companion to Jung* (Cambridge: Cambridge University Press, 1997), p. 182). See also Aldo Carotenuto, *A Secret Symmetry: Sabina Spielrein between Jung and Freud*, trans. Arno Pomerans, John Shepley and Krishna Winston (London: Routledge, 1984); Rowland Wymer, 'Freud, Jung, and the "Myth" of Psychoanalysis in *The White Hotel*', *Mosaic* 22:1 (Winter 1989), 55–69; John Kerr, *A Most Dangerous Method: The Story of Jung, Freud, and Sabina Spielrein* (London: Sinclair-Stevenson, 1994).

27. C. G. Jung, 'Psychological Aspects of the Mother Archetype', trans. R. F. C. Hull, in *The Archetypes and the Collective Unconscious*, vol.9 part 1 of *The Collected Works* (London: Routledge and Kegan Paul, 1959), par.155.
28. Luckhurst, 'The Angle Between Two Walls', p. 70.
29. T. S. Eliot, *Burnt Norton*, in *Collected Poems 1909–62*, p. 190.
30. J. G. Ballard, 'Zone of Terror' (1960), in *The Complete Short Stories*, 2 vols, (London: Harper Perennial, 2006 [2001]), vol. 1, pp 184–201 (p. 185).
31. *The Best Science Fiction of J. G. Ballard*, p. 370.
32. J. G. Ballard. 'The Terminal Beach' (1964), in *The Complete Short Stories*, vol. 2, p. 49.
33. Pauline Réage, *Story of O* (London: Corgi, 1976 [1954]). Ballard is quoted on the back cover as saying: 'Here all kinds of terrors await us, but like a baby taking its mother's milk all pains are assuaged. Touched by the magic of love, everything is transformed. STORY OF O is a deeply moral homily.' When Anne Desclos/Dominique Aury confirmed in 1994 that she was the real author, she also explained that she wrote the book for her lover Jean Paulhan as a way of ensuring his continued sexual interest in her. See Joan Smith, 'Love letter', *Guardian*, 8 August, 1994.
34. J. G. Ballard, 'Track 12' (1958), in *The Complete Short Stories*, vol. 1, p. 95.
35. Maurice Charney, *Sexual Fiction* (London: Methuen, 1981), p. 69.
36. Rosemary Jackson, *Fantasy: The Literature of Subversion* (London: Methuen, 1981), pp. 76-7. The Lacan quotation is from *The Language of the Self*.
37. J. G. Ballard, *The Crystal World* (London: Triad/Panther, 1978 [1966]), p. 85.

2
Ballard/*Atrocity*/Conner/*Exhibition*/ Assemblage

Roger Luckhurst

The fifteen 'condensed' novels that form J. G. Ballard's *The Atrocity Exhibition*, prose experiments composed/found/collated between 1966 and 1970, work by such a violent logic of simultaneity/ compression/juxtaposition that any critical exposition feels inevitably partial and incomplete. If the book overflows you, it also overflows itself: Ballard added four allied pieces and extensive marginalia in a new edition in 1990. It will take decades to decompress Ballard's brutal paragraphs, to trace out the wiring diagram of this fiendishly booby-trapped device. It was William Burroughs no less, that master of the splice, who called *The Atrocity Exhibition* a bomb: 'This is what Bob Rauschenberg is doing in art – literally *blowing up* the image. Since people are made of image, this is literally an explosive book.'[1]

To begin to grasp the meanings of Ballard's text/s, scholars have explored the avant-garde project of *New Worlds* under the editorship of Michael Moorcock between 1964 and 1970, the figure who opened an SF pulp magazine to the synaesthetic possibilities of art across multiple manifestations of London's counter-culture in the mid-1960s. For a brief moment, it seemed as if SF might do more than escape the ghetto, becoming instead the privileged mode of cultural representation for its era. The text/s that were assembled into *The Atrocity Exhibition* were the flag-ship for *New Worlds*, dismantling the redundant machinery of dominant novel forms, junking the moral framework and tiresome formal necessity of accumulated mimetic detail required by social Realism. The text/s acted like an echo-box of literary experiment and cultural commentary of the 60s: concepts were spliced in from Marshall McLuhan, R. D. Laing, Herbert Marcuse. The text/s appeared to incorporate their own theoretical commentary on the 'death of affect', a phrase embedded as a paragraph title that returned as a central thesis of Fredric Jameson's

Postmodernism, or the Cultural Logic of Late Capitalism.[2] *The Atrocity Exhibition* was even prophetic enough to contain an explicit critique of that counter-culture, the recognition that Thanatos was intertwined with Eros, and thus that the revolutionary moment would shortly end. Literary and science fictional histories have worked hard to grasp the very temporary but significant fusions of avant-garde/popular modes typical of the *New Worlds* 60s experiment.[3]

The extent to which *The Atrocity Exhibition* was entwined with visual arts has always been a significant way of opening up these provocations. Three principal networks of association and convergence suggest themselves in the various forms of citation used in Ballard's prose experiments: Surrealism, American Pop Art, and the London-based Independent Group. *The Atrocity Exhibition* is saturated with references to European Surrealism, most persistently the 'paranoiac-critical' method of Salvador Dali and a small group of 'decalomania' works by Max Ernst. Citations in chapter and paragraph titles as well as in method and form prompt Jeannette Baxter to term Ballard's text/s 'interchangeable documents within a Surrealist narrative collage'.[4] A similar cluster of citations to American Pop Art and an uncanny parallelism between Ballard's and Andy Warhol's obsessions shifts the aesthetic locus in a different direction, away from subjective desire towards technological externalizations of empty traumatic repetition. The mechanical reproduction and modulations of Warhol's silk-screens in portraits of Monroe or Jackie Kennedy or in the *Death and Disaster* series seem to explore the same hollowed out, mediatized subjects in Ballard's text/s who ecstatically embrace their deathly/machinic state of being.

Much less overtly, yet just as significantly, *The Atrocity Exhibition* shows profound debts to the Independent Group. This loose grouping was formed in 1952 by a new generation of artists and critics who began meeting at the Institute of Contemporary Arts. It was centred around Lawrence Alloway and Richard Hamilton and went on to stage the important *This is Tomorrow* exhibition at the Whitechapel Gallery in 1956.[5] The impact of Ballard's visit to the show on his writing consistently featured in his autobiographical statements. In the 60s, Ballard described his experimental prose works in much the same terms as the collages constructed by Eduardo Paolozzi, a series begun possibly as early as 1947 and retrospectively named *Bunk!* These had been first shown to the Independent Group in 1952, allegedly to snorts of derision.[6] The collages incorporated tearsheets of lurid covers of SF magazines such as *Amazing Stories*, glamour shots, the sexualized iconography of glossy American magazine advertising, juxtaposed in provocative layouts with

B-17 bombers and adverts for hand-guns. Ballard later wrote a preface for a book of Paolozzi's collages, *General Dynamic F.U.N.*, and in a published conversation aligned their projects:

> You've got to use, I think, a much more analytic technique than the synthetic technique of the Surrealists. Eduardo does this in his graphics. He's approaching the subject-matter of the present-day exactly like the scientist on safari, looking at the landscape, testing, putting sensors out, charting various parameters. The environment is filled with more fiction and fantasy than any of us can singly isolate.[7]

At this juncture, Ballard and Paolozzi were seeking the same density of information overload and violent discursive wrenching and compression in their text/s. 'I'd love to have a tickertape machine in my study constantly churning out material: abstracts from scientific journals, the latest Hollywood gossip, the passenger list of a 707 that crashed in the Andes, the colour mixes of a new automobile varnish ... I regard myself as starved of information. I am getting a throughput of information in my imaginative life of one-hundredth of what I could use.'[8]

These layers of reference and association don't yet exhaust *The Atrocity Exhibition*. It is only very recently that the architectural spaces of Ballard's project have begun to be considered. Nic Clear has called Ballard 'one of the most important figures in the literary articulation of architectural issues and concerns',[9] and he reinforces Ballard's significance in the Introduction to a special issue of *Architectural Design* partly devoted to the author's work.[10] The work, Simon Sellars argues, 'is about nothing but the built environment', Ballard's focus remaining on 'urbanism and spatial dynamics'.[11] Ballard's sly critique of the psychopathologies that lurk in Le Corbusier's Modernist utopias, the murderous violence that erupts when volumes attempt the erasure of history, is the substratum of much of Ballard's fiction from the earliest days. *The Atrocity Exhibition* adds in the terminal irony of the Independent Group critic Reyner Banham, whose book on Los Angeles perversely celebrated the Californian 'autopia', the freeway system as 'a single comprehensible place, a coherent state of mind, a complete way of life, the fourth ecology of the Angeleno' which he suggested was breeding new kinds of being.[12] Ballard's texts share the same busy surface density as a lot of the output of the radical 60s architectural practice, Archigram, founded in 1961, who also produced magazines and booklets using a collage aesthetic that sliced up image, text, architectural theory and u/dys/topian musing. To look at Warren Chalk's *Living*

City Survival Kit (1963), a mix of jazz records, cigarettes, a Norman Mailer novel, washing powder, chocolate bars, hand-guns and a *Playboy* magazine is inevitably to be reminded of the sex and apocalypse assemblage kits that appear in *The Atrocity Exhibition*.[13] We have still yet to put into their proper context Ballard's icy scientific languages that translate disinterestedly between the volumes of cantilevered concrete balconies, instrument binnacles and female bodies.

Yet this still does not complete the barest gestures of the kind of work required to decode *The Atrocity Exhibition*. Although spatial logics of paintings, exhibition displays, architectural volumes and the juxtapositions of collage dominate the text/s in question, it is also a project informed by the temporal axis of cinema too. Film is a constant presence in *The Atrocity Exhibition* from the opening page, when Travis blocks out the noise of 'the cine films of induced psychoses' in order to concentrate on his assemblage of terminal documents.[14] From there, atrocity footage, simulated and real, spools across the pages. Footage from Vietnam and the Congo vies with the pornography of public information films on disaster management or road safety. The Zapruder footage of the Kennedy assassination becomes a modulus for decoding the obscene visibility of sex and death in a media landscape that McLuhan and others were theorizing in terms of neural transformation. The auratic quality of dead or dying film stars invests the early researches in *The Atrocity Exhibition*, a logic of what Guy Debord termed the 'spectacle' that in the later sections of the book comes to understand how Hollywood sheen translates into political power in the menacing figure of Ronald Reagan, B-movie star, conservative Hollywood activist and, after 1968, governor of California. Experimental film is also integral to the very form of *The Atrocity Exhibition*. It is a work that hinges on the possibilities of the splice.

Given that Ballard sampled many areas of aesthetic experiment in the 60s, his interest in film is unsurprising. The 'New Wave' in SF named itself after the revolution in French cinema which began in 1958. In *New Worlds*, Ballard praised Chris Marker's *La Jetée* (1962), the short photomontage film about time-travel and nuclear catastrophe by the Left Bank documentarist, as an exemplary form of SF that disposed of redundant rocket ships: 'Not once does it make use of the time-honoured conventions of traditional science fiction. Creating its own conventions from scratch, it triumphantly succeeds where science fiction invariably fails.'[15] *La Jetée* constructed its science fictionality, like Godard's *Alphaville* (1965), from the materials of the contemporary world and in the energy of the edit. Marker later produced *A Grin without a Cat* (1977), a vast montage of diversely sourced film footage of the wars and revolutionary struggles in the conjunctural moment of 1968, which is a kind of visual analogue to *The Atrocity Exhibition*. From the early *Vermilion Sands* (1971) stories, the landscapes of Ballard's fictions share the same radical use of space as the films of Michelangelo Antonioni, where enigmatic women are eclipsed in the harsh angles of architectural modernism and blasted natural landscapes. In a very different filmic register, Ballard later recalled underground showings of *Mondo Cane* (1962), shown in England only after extensive cuts demanded by the Board of Censors, that were important to the development of his aesthetic in the mid-60s. *Mondo Cane* spliced together apparently true documentary materials of atrocities/animal killings/scenes of cruelty, in a frenzied montage. Ballard claimed that they were 'an important key to what was going on in the media landscape of the 1960s'.[16] It is clear that the revolutionary practice of cinematic montage was also crucial to the form of the text/s of *The Atrocity Exhibition*.

To underline this, I want to add to this 60s frame of reference the experimental films of the San Francisco assemblage artist Bruce Conner. Conner's obsessions in his key works of the 60s and 70s are uncannily similar to Ballard's, perhaps even more so than Warhol's work. In introducing Conner's assemblages to Ballard scholarship, I make no big claim about lost or recovered influence, since it is unlikely that Ballard saw these works. Following Walter Benjamin's method of *critical montage*, however, if we splice these allied projects together the act of juxtaposition can provide critical insights about the conjunctures of experiment in the 60s.

Bruce Conner (1933–2008) was a central figure in the San Francisco Beat and counter-cultural scene.[17] He arrived in the North Beach from art school in 1956, in time to be part of a sub-culture that suffered police intimidation that included the prosecution of Allen Ginsberg's *Howl* in 1957. In the same year, the artist Wallace Berman was jailed for obscenity for his sexualized crucifix sculpture. Conner's early work involved fragile, temporary constructions that threw together abstraction with pop cultural sources involving an obsession with Marilyn Monroe, images torn from pornographic magazines and the covers of pulps like *Weird Tales* and *Dime Mystery*. These accumulations of material were often bound together with ripped nylon stockings. For these constructions which combined painting, sculpture, found objects and collage, the curator coined the term 'assemblage'. In 1961, William Seitz proposed that it could be defined by two principal elements: '(1) They are predominantly *assembled* rather than painted, drawn, modelled, or carved. (2) Entirely, or in part, their constituent elements are pre-formed natural or manufactured materials, objects, or fragments not intended as art materials.'[18] Precursors were Marcel Duchamp and Jean Dubuffet; Seitz's principal contemporary artist of assemblage was Bruce Conner.

The abiding theme of Conner's early work was sexual violence: he produced assemblages around the 'Black Dahlia' case, the notorious unsolved sexual murder in Hollywood in 1947. Here, a pornographic image is veiled in swathes of nylon and torn fragments of a sequin dress. The image has nails driven through it with a sadistic energy. Conner's confrontational assemblage art caused a scandal when he exhibited *The Child* in 1959–60, a protest piece at the impending state execution of alleged rapist Caryl Chessman (the Chessman case was a rallying point for campaigners against the death penalty throughout the 50s). *The Child* was a small figure, endowed with an outsized penis, bound to a chair with nylons, fried beyond recognition by electricity, the limbs burnt away, the mouth a rictus of death agony. Early reviewers tended to read through the work to speculate on the artist's psychopathology (but perhaps revealing more of their own):

> 'I would hate,' said a woman at one of his openings, 'to be his wife.' One can appreciate her uneasiness: could he not transform her most enticing postures into a 'Black Dahlia', with its nail pounded manically into the heart of the matter? What must he see as she draws on those nylons, those silken underthings, those bangles and geegaws which he discards into his works like a skid-row bargain store? Looking at his work, one conceives a mentality which must obsessively re-cast all it observes into the imagery of the most unutterable horrors of our times.[19]

Conner remained a restless artist throughout his career, shifting between sculpture, drawing, photography and film, fighting with the rigid art branding of 'Bruce Conner', even to the extent of attempting to exhibit his work under Dennis Hopper's name. The refusal of a signature style and a life-long suspicion of art-world marketing was partly inspired by Duchamp, whom he met in 1963, at a lecture given the day before Kennedy was assassinated. This rather ornery refusal was mainly because Conner's fame came to rest very early in his career on two short films which for a long time eclipsed his other work, *A Movie* (1958) and *Cosmic Ray* (1961).

These were not the first films to re-cycle and re-signify found footage in collage form, but they were the most influential. Found-footage films begin with Sergei Eisenstein's political investment in montage as 'the collision of various cinematic modifications of movement and vibration', but extend the notion to splicing together a multitude of film sources: they are assemblages in time.[20] They extended assemblage art's fascination with modern detritus, with 'soiled, valueless, and fragile materials' into the junk resources of popular culture's reservoir of the moving image.[21] With this extension of collage into assemblage films, 'Conner would almost single-handedly redirect the materialist perspectives of late modernism onto cinema', it would later be claimed.[22]

A Movie is a twelve-minute epic that edits together materials from a range of appropriated sources, 'scavenged news-reel, scientific, soft-core porn, leader, and other types of film'.[23] Scored in three movements, the film starts with sight gags, exposed leader heads counting down, interrupted by inter-titles that read 'End of Part Four' and 'The End', before splicing in a teasing glimpse of a striptease from a stag film. Frenetic intercutting of cowboys and Indians with drag-racing pileups moves towards a blank screen and a prolonged return of the title cards A/MOVIE. In the second movement, a joke collage puts a narrative together: a submarine captain looks through a periscope/spies a reclining beauty in a bikini/launches a torpedo/unleashes a sex-bomb that culminates in an atomic mushroom cloud. Yet this sequence is fenced around with images of dramatic technological failures: the Hindenberg in flames/the Tacoma suspension bridges filmed collapsing/tightrope walkers/boats clattered by surf. Jaunty images of failure darken in the third movement, which is dominated by war imagery: aerial dog-fights/disintegrating bombers/parachute failures/sinking ships/mournful black-out screens/the body of Mussolini strung from a lamp-post/bodies of hundreds of dead East Asian civilians/ another atomic mushroom cloud. The study fuses the frenzy of sexual voyeurism and generic tropes of technological speed with the orgasmic rush of the military-industrial arms race reaching for apocalyptic climax.

A Movie has been canonized as a pioneering form of avant-garde cinema, the exemplary instance of what David Bordwell and Kristin Thompson call the 'associational form', where narrative is displaced by 'repeated motifs to reinforce associational connotations'.[24] It feels like a post-war form, moving far beyond the oneiric associations of Surrealist film, cranking up the speed of edits between diverse orders of visual discourse and foregrounding the materiality of film passing through the sprockets. Conner later said:

I got involved in playing with the camera and getting more information for the same length of time. There are 24 frames per second, so you've got thousands of single photographs for every hundred feet of film. To work with that kind of information, with multiple exposure and fast-cutting and subliminal images and stroboscopic light-and-dark patterns, you've got to educate your audience; that kind of movie didn't exist before I made *A Movie*.[25]

Cosmic Ray is only four-and-a-half minutes yet intensifies this education in information overload even further, using multiple exposures and faster, near subliminal cutting. The visuals pulse between countdowns/leaders marked TITLE/HEAD/SOUND/fireworks/public information diagrams/and erotic dancers culled from soft porn. Conner filmed some of this material himself. Again, as the film progresses, the military images merely glimpsed in the opening sections come to dominate. The striptease dancers now have skulls for pudenda/soldiers march/the flag is raised on Iwo Jima/the atomic mushroom cloud rises again. The rhythm of the edit is tied to the ecstatic soundtrack of a Ray Charles live performance, which also dictates the length of the piece. As several Conner obituaries suggested, *Cosmic Ray* was the precursor for the frenetic editing style that several decades later came to be associated with MTV.[26] One didn't need to see Conner's original films to be saturated in his influential assemblage style of editing. Music soundtracks would dictate many of his later films, including *Mea Culpa* (his last film in 1981, using music from Brian Eno and David Byrne's found-sound collage *Life in the Bush of Ghosts*) and *Looking for Mushrooms* (made in 1969, which used the Beatles' *Tomorrow Never Knows*).

As a result of these early forays in experimental film, Conner became active in the film-maker collective Canyon Cinema with Stan Brakhage and others, created to build an alternative distribution network for 16mm avant-garde film and meant to feed rental fees directly back to the directors. Canyon was a utopian collective, with an archive regarded by one director, Robert Nelson, as inherently political: 'The hundreds of screens glowing with this twentieth century folk art represent an extraordinary communications feat, because of the mounting resistance, repression and censorship that exists in all the public media.'[27] Like most avant-gardes, it was continually rocked by internal strife over aesthetic and financial questions, arguments to which Conner contributed enthusiastically for nearly forty years before withdrawing his films. All experiments need fractious and contentious frameworks to find their path: Ballard had *New Worlds*, Conner Canyon Cinema.

Aside from this new method of assemblage, thematically there are three key films by Conner that bring him into direct overlap with the matrix of *The Atrocity Exhibition*. The last of these, *Crossroads* (1976), probably requires the least commentary. *Crossroads* is the culmination of Conner's obsession with the image of the atomic mushroom cloud. It is a film constructed from declassified government footage of an underwater detonation of a bomb at Bikini Atoll, an event shot by nearly five hundred cameras. Conner montages these angles into an ambiguous hymn to the psychological effect of living under the threat of the bomb in post-war America and the perverse sexualization of death within the military-industrial complex. It is very beautiful, but then Conner was always 'the master of the ambivalent attitude'.[28]

Marilyn Times Five (1968–73) takes soft-porn footage of the topless Monroe lookalike, Arline Hunter, a grimy masturbatory tease of a film shooting her lounging on a floor in cramped surroundings, and transforms it into an elegiac monument to the dead actress. Monroe's own breathy recording of *I'm Through with Love* plays through completely five times, over footage of the model captured, slowed down and obsessively re-worked and re-played. Stock erotic gestures become elegant structural patterns of light and dark, the degraded body transformed into abstract volumes. Sound and image feel progressively disjunct, the tension 'reveal[ing] more by their difference than if they were matched up'.[29] Pornography's brute framing, cutting off the head to focus on the torso, in *Marilyn Times Five* indicts the murderous sadism of the male voyeur's gaze, although the film does not wish to escape its own fetishistic manipulation of the woman's image. As Art Simon comments about most of Conner's early films, 'the female body is assigned an ontological filmic status, as if like the exposed sprocket holes, frame lines, and academy leader that surround it'.[30] After each repeat there is a mournful fade to black, and these blackouts increasingly intrude into the replays, as if preparing for her final disappearance. The obsession in Conner's working and re-working of the images might suggest that the practice of assembling these materials is either a mournful process of 'working through' the lost loved object or else a compulsive melancholic act that denies loss by monumentalizing the impossible presence of the absent one in the living immediacy of the filmed image.

A similarly fine balance is kept in *Report* (1963–7), Conner's continually reworked film about the assassination of John F. Kennedy. A highly complex and masterful collage of materials, *Report* is a reflection not just on Kennedy's death, but on the circulation of images of Kennedy in an era when access to any footage of the Dallas motorcade was controlled by government and commercial restrictions. The famous Zapruder footage of two bullets hitting Kennedy was only seen in stills after being purchased by *Life* magazine (and then being confiscated by government for the Warren Commission report) and was not seen as moving film in public viewings until the mid-70s. Conner happened to be in Brookline, Massachusetts, when the assassination occurred, near to the birthplace of John F. Kennedy. He had planned to film the funeral there, before plans switched the burial to the cemetery at Arlington. Instead, Conner filmed 8mm footage of Kennedy's funeral and the on-screen murder of Lee Harvey Oswald off the TV screen, creating an early engagement with Kennedy's death called *Television Assassination* (1963–95). Here the footage of Oswald was looped six times, and 'the alleged assassin materialises and dematerialises slowly and repeatedly over the course of fifteen minutes, just as he would over the next thirty years in the assassination literature'.[31] For *Report*, Conner relied on images taken from an annual News Parade summary reel, stitched in with other found footage.

Report begins with a stuttering crowd shot of the motorcade, JFK and Jackie briefly in centre frame before the car speeds by. The footage is repeatedly pulled back to start again, as if willing a temporal reversal to save Kennedy from his fate. The soundtrack is the banal chat of TV or radio news commentators, which shifts into panic when they realize 'something has happened' in the motorcade. The screen fades to black/then white/and into an epileptic fast strobing that lasts for nearly three minutes, as the panicked commentators switch between locations trying to gather news on the condition of the injured president. Strobing is succeeded by very short, repeated splices of footage: the assassin's rifle paraded above the head of the press/a reversed scene of Jackie Kennedy reaching for the door of a locked ambulance which carries her husband's body. Representational footage is replaced by a long sequence of exposed leader countdowns (Conner punning on every element of that technical term), the circle and cross behind the numbers now transformed into cross-hairs. The countdown can be stalled or repeated only for so long (although it cycles through thirty looped repeats), before the announcement that the president is dead/and the screen fades to black. The second half of the film moves from the affective to the analytic, using a diverse range of sources for a critique of media representation. Conner increasingly regarded the death of the president as exploited by the media, mourning transposed into a brisk commemorative trade. Kennedy's daily round of presidential meetings/intercut with the ritualized performances in the bullfighting ring/starts an argument that situates the assassination inside a sacrificial logic. Banal voice-over reportage now chimes visually with materials from glossy advertisements for refrigerators and shopping powders/whilst splices from *The Bride of Frankenstein* key Kennedy to the manufacture of life and death, and his ungodly afterlife as a walking corpse. Kennedy's idealized televisual image is cut across by precognitive flashes of the Texas Book Depository/his state funeral/fragile lightbulbs shattered by bullets/troops swarming over entrenched enemy positions (taken from *All Quiet on the Western Front*)/Oswald's shooting frozen in press flashbulbs/the ubiquitous mushroom cloud. The film ends with an informational film for an IBM device, a woman pressing the button SELL. This final section, sound-track moving in and out of synchrony with the assembled images, has been called 'one of the most innovative and sustained experiments in Eisensteinian vertical montage...in the history of the medium'.[32]

Conner made and re-made this film eight times between 1963 and 1967, the material re-worked as theories about the assassination swirled and transformed, successive inquiries drawing radically different conclusions. 'I was obsessed', Conner confessed, 'I didn't want to stop the changes.'[33]

Ballardians will not need much prompting to translate either the substance of *Report* or Conner's obsessive reworking of materials into the matrix of *The Atrocity Exhibition*, its text/s performing a parallel project of moulding and re-moulding the traumatic media landscapes of the 60s:

> The start of the show was J. F. K., victim of the first conceptual car crash. A damaged Lincoln had been given place of honour, plastic models of the late President and his wife in the rear seat. An elaborate attempt had been made to represent cosmetically the expressed brain tissue of the President/

> Soon the climax of the scenario would come, J. F. K. would die again, his young wife raped by this conjunction of time and space/

> 'He wants to kill Kennedy again, but in a way that makes sense.'[34]

The text/s of *The Atrocity Exhibition* are thoroughly driven by the promise that an epistemological and/or aesthetic resolution of the open wound of the Kennedy assassination will somehow stop the shattering effects of trauma, ramified by dulling media repetition. Cross-contaminating Kennedy with Vietnam, the Congo, James Dean, Biafra, the violence sexualized through the 'conceptual murder' of female objects, the crescendo moving towards apocalyptic, atomic explosion, all echo between the works. But parallels occur not just in content, but in form too. Ballard's lists of random objects, the tension between proliferating information sources and the formal rigidity of the paragraph-grid, follow not just Surrealist juxtaposition or Cubist collage, but are saturated in the logic of assemblage art, particularly as envisaged on/with film:

> Endlessly, the films unwound: images of neuro-surgery and organ transplants, autism and senile dementia, auto-disasters and plane crashes. Above all, the montage landscapes of war and death: newsreels from the Congo and Vietnam, execution-squad instruction films, a documentary on the operation of a lethal chamber. *Sequence in slow motion: a landscape of highways and embankments, evening light of fading concrete, intercut with images of a young woman's body. She lay on her back, her wounded face stressed like fractured ice. With almost dream-like calm, the camera explored her bruised mouth, the thighs dressed in a dark lace-work of blood. The quickening geometry of her body, its terraces of pain and sexuality, became a source of intense excitement.*[35]

'At the moment,' the art critic Brian O'Doherty commented in 1967, 'assemblage as a technique is permeating all the arts with extraordinary vigor.' It was, he suggested, 'a new way of coping with the environment'.[36] That environment, Marshall McLuhan argued in 1964, had experienced a technological step-change in the 60s that prompted catastrophic overloads: 'It could well be that the successive mechanizations of the various physical organs ... have made too violent and superstimulated a social experience for the central nervous system to endure.'[37] This was the core subject of Ballard's experimental text/s and Bruce Conner's films, and dictated their radical form.

One last word. It was perhaps inevitable that one day a film version of *The Atrocity Exhibition* would appear, with some ambitions to use the appropriate found-footage aesthetic. If only the film had been directed by Bruce Conner rather than Jonathan Weiss. Weiss's willed ignorance of the avant-garde tradition of assemblage cinema left him with few resources.[38] Yet everything he might have needed was already there, waiting in the archive. In fact, he might have discovered that *The Atrocity Exhibition* had already in effect been filmed, was filmed into being, in the crucible of 60s assemblage art.

Notes

I want to express my thanks to Michelle Silva of the Conner Family Trust for providing me with copies of the Bruce Conner films I examine in this essay.
1. William S. Burroughs, 'Preface' in *The Atrocity Exhibition* (San Francisco: Re/Search, 1990), p. 7.
2. These echoes are explored in an excellent chapter on *The Atrocity Exhibition* in Andzrej Gasiorek, *J. G. Ballard* (Manchester: Manchester University Press, 2005).
3. See Rob Latham, 'The New Wave' in D. Seed, ed., *A Companion to Science Fiction* (Oxford: Blackwell, 2005), pp. 202–16. See also Roger Luckhurst, *'The Angle Between Two Walls': The Fiction of J. G. Ballard* (Liverpool: Liverpool University Press, 1997), pp. 73–117.
4. Jeannette Baxter, *J. G. Ballard's Surrealist Imagination: Spectacular Authorship* (Farnham: Ashgate, 2009), p. 60. See also Dawn Ades, 'J. G. Ballard and Surrealism' in *Crash: Homage to J. G. Ballard* (London: Gagosian Gallery, 2009), pp. 31–4.
5. The standard history of the group is Anne Massey, *The Independent Group: Modernism and Mass Culture in Britain 1945–59* (Manchester: Manchester University Press, 1995). Ballard's association is discussed in Eugenie Tsai, 'The Sci-Fi Connection: The I. G., J. G. Ballard and Robert Smithson' in B. Wallis, ed., *Modern Dreams: The Rise and Fall of Pop* (New York: MIT Press, 1988), pp. 71–5.
6. John-Paul Stonard, 'The "Bunk" Collages of Eduardo Paolozzi', *The Burlington Magazine*, 150 (2008), 238–49.
7. 'Speculative Illustrations: Eduardo Paolozzi in Conversation with J. G. Ballard and Frank Whitford', *Studio International*, 183 (Oct. 1971), 136–43 (p. 136).
8. 'Speculative Illustrations', 143.
9. Nic Clear, 'Crash: Architectures Of The Near Future', http://www.bartlett.ucl.ac.uk/architecture/programmes/units/unit15_08.htm.
10. Nic Clear, Introduction: A Near Future, *Architectures of the Near Future: Architectural Design*, Volume 79, Issue 5, (Sept.-Oct. 2009), 6–11.
11. Simon Sellars, 'Stereoscopic Urbanism: J. G. Ballard and the Built Environment', *Architectures of the Near Future: Architectural Design*, Volume 79, Issue 5, (Sept.–Oct. 2009), 82–7 (pp. 85 and 86).
12. Reyner Banham, *Los Angeles: The Architecture of Four Ecologies* (Harmondsworth: Penguin, 1971), p. 213.
13. For discussion, see Simon Sadler, 'The *Living City Survival Kit*: A Portrait of the Architect as a Young Man', *Art History*, 26: 4 (2003), 556–75 and his history of the group, *Archigram: Architecture without Architecture* (Cambridge: MIT Press, 2005).
14. J. G. Ballard, *The Atrocity Exhibition* (London: Panther, 1979), p. 7.
15. J. G. Ballard, *A User's Guide to the Millennium* (London: HarperCollins, 1996), pp. 28–9 (p. 29).
16. J. G. Ballard, 'An Exhibition of Atrocities', in M. Goodall, *Sweet and Savage: The World through the Shockumentary Film Lens* (London: HeadPress, 2006), pp. 13–15 (p. 15).

17. Conner's career is considered in most detail in *2000 BC: The Bruce Conner Story Part II*. There is no Part I, incidentally.
18. William C. Seitz, *The Art of Assemblage* (1961), cited by Diane Waldman, *Collage, Assemblage, and the Found Object* (London: Phaidon, 1992), pp. 264–5.
19. Philip Leider, 'Bruce Conner: A New Sensibility', *Artforum* I (1962), 30. This piece and Conner's place in the San Francisco Beat scene is discussed in John P. Bowles, ' "Shocking 'Beat' Art Displayed": Californian Artists and the Beat Image', in S. Barron, S. Bernstein and I. S. Fort, eds, *Reading California: Art, Image and Identity 1900–2000* (Berkeley: University of California Press, 2000), pp. 221–46.
20. Sergei Eisenstein, 'Methods of Montage' (1929) in *Film Form: Essays in Film Theory*, trans. J. Leyda (London: Dobson, 1963), pp. 72–83 (p. 79). For discussion of the movement, see William C. Wees, *Recycled Images: The Art and Politics of Found Footage Films* (NY: Anthology Film Archives, 1993). I have written about this cinema in my essay 'Found-Footage Science Fiction: Five Films by Craig Baldwin, Jonathan Weiss, Werner Herzog and Patrick Keiller', *Science Fiction Film and Television*, 1: 2 (2008), 193–214.
21. William C. Seitz, 'The Realism and Poetry of Assemblage', collected in K. Hoffmann, ed., *Collage: Critical Views* (London: UMI Research Press, 1989), 79–90 (p. 89).
22. Bruce Jenkins, 'Explosion in a Film Factory: The Cinema of Bruce Conner', in *2000 BC*, p. 186.
23. Rob Yeo, 'Cutting through History: Found Footage in Avant-Garde Filmmaking' in S. Basilico, ed., *Cut: Film as Found Object in Contemporary Video* (Milwaukee: Milwaukee Art Museum, 2004), pp. 13–27 (p. 17).
24. David Bordwell and Kristin Thompson, *Film Art: An Introduction*, 8th edn (Boston: McGraw Hill, 2008), p. 386. *A Movie* also receives extensive discussion in P. Adams Sitney, *Visionary Film: The American Avant-Garde 1943–78*, 2nd edn (Oxford: Oxford University Press, 1979).
25. Conner, cited in Jerome Tashis, 'Bruce Conner is Not "Bruce Conner" ', *Art News*, 76 (Jan. 1977), 80–7 (p. 86).
26. See, for instance, Manohla Dargis, 'An Artist of the Cutting-Room Floor', *New York Times* 12 July 2008, http:www.nytimes.com.
27. Robert Nelson, 'Letter', *Canyon Cinema News*, anthologized in Scott MacDonald, ed., *Canyon Cinema: The Life and Times of an Independent Film Distributor* (Berkeley: University of California Press, 2008), p. 143.
28. Sitney, *Visionary Film*, p. 310.
29. Peter Gizzi, 'Out of Time' (review of Bruce Conner's *2002BC* DVD), *Modern Painters* (Autumn 2002), 90–3 (p. 92).
30. Art Simon, 'Bruce Conner' in *Dangerous Knowledge: The JFK Assassination in Art and Film* (Philadelphia: Temple University Press, 1996), p. 133.
31. Simon, *Dangerous Knowledge*, p. 136.
32. Bruce Jenkins, 'Bruce Conner's *Report*: Contesting Camelot' in T. Perry, ed., *Masterpieces of Modernist Cinema* (Bloomington: Indiana University Press, 2006), pp. 236–51 (p. 243).
33. Conner, cited in Bruce Jenkins, 'Bruce Conner's *Report*', p. 237.
34. Ballard, *The Atrocity Exhibition*, pp. 30, 34, 45.
35. Ballard, *The Atrocity Exhibition*, p. 89.

36. Brian O'Doherty, 'Bruce Conner and His Films', in G. Battcock, ed., *The New American Cinema: A Critical Anthology* (NY: Dutton, 1967), pp. 194–6 (pp. 195, 196).
37. Marshall McLuhan, *Understanding Media: The Extensions of Man* (London: Ark, 1987 [1964]), p. 43.
38. See my 'Found-Footage Science Fiction' essay for a reading of this film. Weiss's film was made between 1996-8, and released on DVD by Reel23 in 2006. His rejection of all film prior to his own work (other than Tarkovsky) is asserted in his interview with Simon Sellars, 'Thirsty Man at the Spigot: An Interview with Jonathan Weiss,' *Ballardian* May 2006, www.ballardian.com/weiss-interview, accessed 16 Nov. 2007.

3
Uncanny Forms: Reading Ballard's 'Non-Fiction'

Jeannette Baxter

The publication of *A User's Guide to the Millennium: Essays and Reviews* (1996) has gone a long way to establishing J. G. Ballard's reputation as a writer of 'non-fiction'. Bringing together nearly one hundred essays and reviews written between 1962 and 1995 in publications as various as *Playboy*, the *Sunday Telegraph*, and *Time Out*, this collection exhibits Ballard's cultural and literary commentary in all of its diversity: reviews of biographies (Marlon Brando, Robert Searle, Salvador Dali) and films (*Blue Velvet*, *Alien*, *La Jetée*) jostle alongside essays on Coca-Cola, Adolf Hitler, and the photography of Robert Capa. Ballard continued to publish essays and reviews into the new millennium, revisiting familiar topics such as Surrealism, modernist architecture, and film noir, and penning incisive, and often humorous, responses to the politics and personalities of post-millennial history and culture: 9/11 and the rise of al-Quaeda; Tony Blair and New Labour; neo-fascism and the politics of Premier League football.

Given Ballard's prolific 'non-fictional' output – he also wrote prefaces and introductions to his own and other people's work, and articles and captions for art exhibition catalogues – I limit my reading to two forms of 'non-fiction': the review and essay.[1] Yet, even to attempt a discussion of these writings as examples of 'non-fiction' is far from straightforward. For the negative prefix – 'non' – sets up an immediate sense of opposition: Ballard's 'non-fictions' must, by definition, differ formally and contextually from his fictional writings. But is this really the case? A consistent feature of Ballard's work, as Roger Luckhurst has argued, has been its insistent interrogation of discursive and aesthetic divisions: 'Ballard renders visible the space *between* frames, exposes the hidden assumptions behind the secure categorizations of literature and literary judgement.' 'The Ballard oeuvre', he concludes, 'is nothing other than a prolonged meditation on the question of protocols, boundaries, frames and the evaluations they set in train.'² If this is so, how can one talk usefully about Ballardian 'non-fiction'? With its focus on the troubling of definitions, Sigmund Freud's 'The "Uncanny" ' ('Das Unheimliche' (1919)) is a useful starting point for this discussion. Even though Freud begins his essay by trying to pin down the meaning of the 'uncanny', what emerges from his anxious etymological investigations is a linguistic exercise rich in ambiguity. Starting with the opposite term, 'heimlich', meaning 'belonging to the house, not strange, familiar', Freud traces its shifting histories and contexts only to find that, somehow and at some point, 'heimlich' exhibits a meaning which is its opposite, namely 'kept from sight . . . secretive . . . deceitful'.³ Freud concludes: 'Thus *heimlich* is a word the meaning of which develops in the direction of ambivalence, until it finally coincides with its opposite, *unheimlich*' ('U' 347). Familiar and unfamiliar, knowable and unknowable, visible and concealed, the 'uncanny' gestures repeatedly to what it is and to what it is not, frustrating every move to locate a fixed and final meaning. Furthermore, as Freud's own anxious readings of E. T. A. Hoffman's 'The Sandman' demonstrate, the uncertain nature of the uncanny cannot be explained away by reducing it to a theme or object in a text. This is because the uncanny is an *effect* of reading, an experience which is unpredictable, strange, and sometimes unnerving.

This essay focuses on the uncanny effects of reading Ballard's 'non-fiction'. My move to place 'non-fiction' in single quotation marks echoes Freud's English-Language translator James Strachey's own use of single quotation marks around the word 'uncanny' as a way of signalling its uncertain and unstable meaning. Ballardian 'non-fiction' provokes its own set of questions and anxieties about the stability of textual boundaries, generic classifications (biography/autobiography, fact/fiction), and the security of textual meanings. Divided into three sections, this chapter begins with a reading of Ballard's essays and reviews on the work of William Burroughs, which, over the course of their textual histories, have undergone significant revisions. How is one to respond to the formal and contextual differences across these texts? What role does repetition play in their reception? And what relationship exists between the original documents, which have largely fallen out of view, and their more visible anthologized versions? Next, I read a selection of Ballard's writings on China, his home from 1930 until 1945. Having experienced an expatriate lifestyle in the International Settlement of Shanghai, a period of internment in Lunghua Civilian Camp (1943–45), and subsequent years in England, Ballard's sense of home is freighted with uncertainty. I explore the tensions between the 'homely' (*heimlich*) and the 'unhomely' (*unheimlich*) as they manifest themselves across Ballard's 'non-fictions'. One notable aspect of these writings is their drive to tell stories which have been concealed from official narratives of Chinese history and culture: the 'non-fictional' space provides an alternative form of storytelling for Ballard. Furthermore, I explore how these unfamiliar stories impact on that most familiar of stories – the story of J. G. Ballard – only to emphasize its resistance to notions of completion. Finally, I pursue this tension between endings and beginnings in a selection of Ballard's post-millennial 'non-fictions'. If these essays and reviews go some way to forming Ballard's *User's Guide to the [New] Millennium*, they do so with a keen recognition of the uncanny presence of the past within contemporary history and culture.

Invisible literatures

Ballard's book-reviewing career began on the pages of *Chemistry and Industry*, the Journal of the Society of Chemical Industry, where he worked as assistant editor from 1958–1964, whilst simultaneously developing his career as a science fiction writer. Although Ballard's editorial duties immersed him in so-called invisible literatures – 'press releases, conference reports, annual bulletins from leading research laboratories'[4] – his writing was mostly confined to 'straight production'.[5] This is nowhere more evident than in the short book reviews which appeared from the early 1960s onwards under the signature: J.G.B. Titles under review included: *Dictionary of Commercial Chemicals* (1962); *Technical Market Research* (1962); *Roget's Thesaurus of English Words and Phrases* (1962); *Committees: How they work and how to work them* (1963).[6] Reading through J.G.B.'s reviews, one is struck by their prosaic nature: the content is descriptive and instructive; the tone is formal and matter-of-fact, and at no point does the reader recognize the authorial voice of contemporaneous stories such as 'The Man on the 99th Floor' (1962) and 'End-Game' (1963).[7] Take the following:

> This dictionary [*Dictionary of Chemistry and Chemical Technology*] contains some 12,000 terms from all branches of theoretical and applied chemistry, chemical engineering, chemical and related technologies, and essential scientific terms frequently encountered in chemical literature.[8]

The formal constraints of a technical review of this kind, combined with audience expectations, stifle authorial personality. Indeed, this might be one way of interpreting the condensed, not fully visible, identity of the author: J.G.B. At the same time, however, a certain familiarity resides in these initials and in the materials under review. For what we see is evidence of the assimilation of the technical language and scientific terminology which would become a Ballardian aesthetic.

It is in subsequent literary reviews that the full authorial identity – J. G. Ballard – surfaces. I use the term 'literary' broadly to 'embrace a wide range of contributions to those cultural and intellectual discussions'[9] that take place in newspapers, periodicals and magazines. The term 'review' should also be expanded in the context of Ballard's literary reviews. Indeed, the hybrid term 'review essay' might be more appropriate. As Theodor Adorno observes in 'The Essay as Form' (1958): 'In the essay, concepts do not build a continuum of operations, thoughts do not advance in a single direction, rather, the aspects of the argument interweave as in a carpet.'[10] Ballard's review essays proceed in this manner, reading less like closed accounts of discrete works and more like interventions which, in their 'mosaic-like' relation to other review essays, are provisional and resistant to the idea of origins and endings: they 'are neither deduced from any first principle nor do they come full circle and arrive at a final principle'.[11]

Take Ballard's review essays on the work of William Burroughs, which respond to each other in fascinating ways: 'Myth Maker of the 20th Century' (published initially in *New Worlds* in 1964); 'Myth Maker of the Twentieth Century' (a revised version of the earlier essay, published in *A User's Guide* in 1996); and 'Terminal Documents' (published in *Ambit* in 1966). All three texts celebrate Burroughs's work for its representation of the twentieth century 'in terms of its own language, its own idioms and verbal lore'.[12] For Burroughs's fiction constitutes: 'the first definite portrait of the inner landscape of our mid-century, using its own language and manipulative techniques, its own fantasies and nightmares'.[13] That these (and many other) phrases repeat verbatim across all three texts might be accounted for by the ephemeral nature of book-reviewing: writing 'to the moment, whatever the moment supplies', the reader-reviewer responds 'on the run, in the present tense'.[14] Certainly, as a developing author and single parent, Ballard was not immune to the material pressures of writing, and the recycling of ready-made documents would have been a particularly efficient methodology for meeting deadlines.

At the same time, though, repetition manifests itself as a signature of Ballard's review essays, and its effects are uncanny. The recycling of phrases across 'Myth Maker of the 20th Century', 'Myth Maker of the Twentieth Century' and 'Terminal Documents', creates a sense of readerly *déjà vu*; the texts are, in part, already read, and the process of reading becomes a process of re-reading. Clearly, this experience of *déjà vu* is intensified when Ballard's writings on Burroughs are read collectively. Yet, even when read as individual pieces, these texts chime with other Ballardian 'non-fictions'. Pronouncements on Burroughs's experimental post-war aesthetics echo aspects of Ballard's own literary agenda as they are mapped out in essays and reviews such as 'Which Way to Inner Space?' (1962), 'The Coming of the Unconscious' (1966), and 'Notes from Nowhere: Comments on Work in Progress' (1966).[15] A further effect of textual repetition, then, is the recognition of a discursive and aesthetic continuity between Ballard's and Burroughs's literary projects. The unsettling feeling of *déjà vu* which we experience when we read 'Myth Maker of the 20th Century', 'Myth Maker of the Twentieth Century' and 'Terminal Documents' is bound up with a process of doubling, with 'the impression that the present reality has a *double*'.[16] In other words, Ballard's review essays of Burroughs's fiction are uncannily duplicitous in as much as they presuppose 'a kind of double talk, double reading, double writing'[17] in which Ballard's own fiction is a haunting presence.

There is another instance of doubling worth noting here. 'Myth Maker of the 20th Century' appeared as a review of *The Naked Lunch* [sic], *The Soft Machine*, and *The Ticket that Exploded* in 1964. By the time it was renamed and reprinted, however, 'Myth Maker of the Twentieth Century' had been streamlined and recast as a response to *Naked Lunch*. Textual omissions included: musings on Burroughs's 'difficulty'; his literary links to Franz Kafka; and the following, closing dedication to Burroughs:

> William Burroughs,
> *I'm with you in Rockland*
>   *where we wake up electrified out of the coma by*
>   *our own soul's airplanes*
> *I'm with you in Rockland*
>   *in my dreams you walk dripping from a sea-*
>   *journey on the highway across America in tears*
>   *to the door of my cottage in the Western night*
>
>   (47)

This ending adds a performative dimension; it is a 'maddening supplement, something unpredictable and *additionally strange* happening in and to what is being stated, described or defined'.[18] For readers familiar with Ballard's writing on Burroughs, strangeness lies in the unfamiliar tenderness with which Ballard expresses a sense of literary affiliation. Even though Ballard had a life-long admiration for Burroughs, one evidenced in his Introduction to *Naked Lunch* (1993) and reviews of *Literary Outlaw: The Life and Times of William S. Burroughs* (1991) and *The Letters of William Burroughs, 1945–1959* (1993), his response is unusual in its tonal and formal qualities, initiating as it does an odd switch from a critical to a creative discourse. Of course, the poetic voice which concludes 'Myth Maker of the 20th Century' is not straightforwardly Ballard's, for this textual fragment is intertextual, repeating almost verbatim Part III of Alan Ginsberg's 'Howl' (1955). Furthermore, 'Howl' is a richly allusive poem, one haunted by voices of the Beat Generation, and its inclusion raises the question of who, exactly, is speaking. With this uncanny (inter)textual fragment, Ballard's review essay performs a concluding move that remains ambiguously open: indeed, it does not even attempt to convey the sense of an ending by means of a full stop. And even the later process of editing brings no sense of closure. For, in its excision from 'Myth Maker of the Twentieth Century', this uncanny (inter)textual form survives, returning in the process of reading, to haunt a text which is an incomplete, or ghostly, version of itself.

But the processes of doubling do not end there. Some of the excised sections of 'Myth Maker of the 20th Century' resurface in 'Terminal Documents' (1966), a review essay which updates Ballard's reading list to include *Nova Express* (1966). Repeating himself verbatim, Ballard resituates Burroughs in relation to Joyce: 'to whom he bears more than a passing resemblance – exile, publication in Paris, undeserved notoriety as a pornographer, and an absolute dedication to the word'.[19] Similarly, he restates how Burroughs's 'difficulty' 'resides in the fact that he is a writer, systematically creating the verbal myths of the mid-century at a time when the oral novel . . . holds almost exclusive sway'.[20] Amongst these repetitions, however, there are some notable modifications:

> Whatever his reservations about some aspects of the mid-20th century, Burroughs accepts that it can be fully described only in terms of its own language, its own idioms and verbal lore. Dozens of different argots are now in common currency; most people speak at least three

or four separate languages, and a verbal relativity exists as important as any of time and space.

'Myth Maker of the 20th Century' (122)

Whatever his reservations about some aspects of the mid-20th century, Burroughs accepts that it can be fully described only in terms of its own language, its own idioms and verbal lore. Dozens of different languages are now in common currency, from the sinister jargon of Rand Corporation 'think-men' to the non-communicating discourses of politicians and copy-writers, and a verbal relativity exists as important as any of time and space.

'Terminal Documents' (46)

By 1966, Ballard's general observation about linguistic currency across and within cultures returns, with difference, to form a critique of the concealing powers of contemporary discourse. The provisional nature of Ballard's review essay allows for intellectual shifts of this kind. But what are the effects on the reader? On the one hand, the reader who has not read 'Myth Maker of the 20th Century' is none the wiser; the early text remains unfamiliar, and so all modifications are assumed to be original statements. The reader familiar with Ballard's writings on Burroughs, however, is all too aware of these repetitions, phrases restated insistently, almost mechanically, though sometimes with difference. Repetition, then, reveals itself to be as much of a thematic focus and aesthetic drive of Ballard's 'non-fiction' as it is of his fiction. Yet these repetitions, 'whilst being read, are also . . . unreadable in that they give no access to interpretation but merely reinforce the enigma'.[21] Familiarity leads, frustratingly, to unfamiliarity; and we, the knowing readers, are left feeling all the more uncertain as we continue to navigate our way through these uncanny textual forms.

(Un)homely memories

As Freud's etymological enquiries into the word 'heimlich' reveal, the 'uncanny' is intimately bound up with the home. Meaning 'belonging to the house or the family', 'heimlich' connotes a sense of being-at-home; it arouses 'a sense of agreeable restfulness and security as in one within the four walls of his house' ('U' 342). Of course, by the time Freud has finished consulting his dictionaries, the ostensible security of the 'heimlich' has somehow ruptured: 'what is heimlich . . . comes to be unheimlich' ('U' 345). The home, and with it one's sense of self and family, is shown to be unstable; a site of unfamiliarity and unease, it is a place in which one does not at all feel at home. This is a useful starting point for a discussion of Ballard's writings on China, his home for fifteen years. Here, I focus on the effects of Ballard's memories of home as they surface throughout two review essays – 'Survival Instincts' (1992) and 'Sinister Spider' (1992) – and two autobiographical essays, 'Unlocking the Past' (1991) and 'The End of My War' (1995). Ballard's reviews of other people's lives exist in an uneasy relation with the narration of his own life stories: (un)homely memories return to pose disquieting questions about origins and identity.

'Survival Instincts' is a review essay of Jung Chang's memoir, *Wild Swans* (1992), an unofficial history of twentieth-century China, which was originally banned.[22] Beginning in Manchuria in the 1920s and finishing with the demise of Maoism in the late 1970s, *Wild Swans* reveals a clash of personal and political histories as told through the lives of three generations of women: Yu-fang (grandmother); De-hong (mother) and Jung Chang (daughter). 'Survival Instincts' is alive to the resilience and resourcefulness of the women involved: sexual slavery (Yu-fang was the concubine of a Manchurian Warlord at the age of 15); underground political activity leading to arrest by the Kuomintang (De-hong survives a firing squad when the prisoner next to her was shot and killed); and banishment to the Himalayas (where Jung Chang worked as a barefoot doctor) are just some of the extraordinary stories which make up the lives of these ordinary women.

For the most part, 'Survival Instincts' reads like a straightforward account of Jung Chang's memories. Straightforward, that is, except for those odd moments in which Ballard's own memories of home intervene. In relation to Yu-fang, he recalls:

> She herself was the daughter of a woman so unvalued, like all female children, that she had never been given a name and was known simply as 'number two girl' – like the servants of my own childhood whom I addressed for years as 'number two boy' and 'number two coolie'.
>
> (9)

This moment of recollection produces a readerly jolt. Although Ballard alludes to his unwitting complicity in an imperialist discourse founded on racial discrimination in his autobiographical fictions, he does so

58   *'Fictions of Every Kind': Form and Narrative*

through the fictional doubles of Jim/Jamie. In 'Survival Instincts', however, Ballard does not distance himself from this aspect of his historical and cultural make-up. Instead, he situates himself firmly in a colonial discourse that, amongst other things, reduced human beings to numerical variations of one another. Even though 'Survival Instincts' goes some way to countering the dehumanizing discourse of colonialism by paying tribute to the female characters of *Wild Swans*, Ballard's memory remains troubling. This is because it opens up a tension between official and unofficial versions of history that haunts Ballard's *oeuvre*. Written into an imperialist narrative in 1930s Shanghai, Ballard's response has been to resist and complicate this story of origins, and to practise a sustained interrogation of narrative constructions of history.

We see this in 'Sinister Spider' (1992), a review of *Dragon Lady: The Life and Legend of the Last Empress of China* (1992) by Sterling Seagrave.[23] The enigmatic lady in question is Tzu Hsi, the Empress of China from 1861–1908, and one of the most 'maligned women in history'. The source of Tzu Hsi's maltreatment, according to Ballard, is repeated misrepresentation. For Tzu Hsi is the product of fictions of every kind: court reports, press dispatches, rumours, and stories told to young boys:

> During my Shanghai childhood in the 1930s I listened spellbound to strange tales about the Dowager Empress told by old China hands who had lived in Peking during the last years of her reign. Virtually entombed within the Forbidden City for fifty years, she had presided like a sinister spider over the Manchu empire. Only her closest courtiers had ever set eyes on her, and even her doctors were never allowed to touch her . . . whenever she was ill, so the story went, silken cords were tied to her wrists and unwound to a curtained anteroom where the royal physician would make his diagnosis from the faintest tremblings.
>
> (x)

In this moment of remembering, the reader – ever hungry to know more about Ballard's Shanghai childhood – is gifted a fragment of the author's past. As Ballard's 'non-fictional' form of story-telling stresses, however, the act of narration is not innocent, but politically-motivated and partial: 'What I was not told as a child was that Tzu Hsi was widely believed to be a monster of depravity'(x). Tales of sexual perversion are kept from young ears. But, as Ballard reveals, this portrait of Tzu Hsi as a sex-crazed monster is yet another political fiction, one created by Edmund Backhouse, the unofficial editor of the Shanghai publication of the *Times*, whose form of reportage was well-known for effacing the boundaries between fact and fiction.

Sterling Seagrave's biography of Tzu Hsi attempts to redraw these boundaries. Unearthing long suppressed reports by western visitors who had found the Empress to be kind and genial, Seagrove attempts to rescue the ordinary facts of Tzu Hsi's life from a *mélange* of extraordinary fictions. Although Ballard has some sympathy with Seagrave's revisionist project, his closing remarks identify this biography as just another version of events, and one which has come a little late:

> [F]iction, though not as strange as truth, can be far more potent and self-justifying, and the Dowager Empress's supposed depravity seemed retrospectively to vindicate the gunboats and raiding parties of the European powers as they set about their ruthless exploitation of her nation.
>
> (x)

Suggesting that fact and fiction cannot be readily distinguished from one another, Ballard tests Freud's assumption that 'an uncanny effect is often and easily produced when the distinction between imagination and reality is effaced' ('U' 367). For Ballard, uncanny effects are born precisely out of the inability to identify, and therefore efface, the difference between fact and fiction. Furthermore, the inherent ambiguity of language, one which manifests itself in Ballard's adjectival and verbal choices – 'supposed', 'seemed' – means that stories and histories, whether one's own or someone else's, can only ever be rendered knowable in the very moments in which they are rendered unknowable.

This is certainly the reader's experience of 'Unlocking the Past' (1991) and 'The End of My War (1995), two autobiographical essays that chart Ballard's return to China in 1991. A supplement to 'Shanghai Jim', the BBC Two *Bookmark* documentary of Ballard's home-coming, 'Unlocking the Past' opens on an anxious note: 'One can never go home . . . everything changes, the past and one's memories of it. Since coming to England . . . I had kept alive my precious memories of Shanghai . . . But what if my memories are false?'.[24] Ballard's return to Shanghai after an absence of forty-five years is freighted with a tension between a past which is remembered and familiar, and a radically unfamiliar present that threatens to efface the past: 'My great fear was that, far from evoking new memories, the visit might erase the old ones that had sustained me for so many years' (1). But whose memories are under threat? Who, precisely, is speaking in this autobiographical essay?

Just as Ballard employs doubles throughout his autobiographical fictions, in 'Unlocking the Past', he explores his journey of physical and psychic return through the persona of 'Jim', who is identified at the end of the essay. Up until that point, however, the reader is never entirely sure as to who is speaking. Whilst the essay invites the reader to assume a seamless identity between Ballard, the essayist, and Jim Ballard the author/character, it also, at multiple junctures, stresses the performative nature of identity: the narrator rehearses introducing himself as Conrad's 'Mr Kurtz'; he refers to his lost suit as the ' "costume" for the film'; and, 'Jim' arrives in Shanghai to discover that the director of 'Shanghai Jim' also happens to be called James (James Runcie). Of course, the repetition of names is coincidental, yet the *effect* of this coincidence is uncanny. The reader's faith in the narrative is immediately shaken by this curious process of doubling, one which recurs when 'Jim' meets the young actor in the *Bookmark* production: 'He would play my younger self in the film, and James had misguidedly told him that he resembled me' (1). The effect of this sentence is dizzying: the density of pronouns – all of which exist in some relation to the proper name 'James' – confuse any straightforward sense of self and origin.

The uncertain nature of subjectivity is compounded further by an uncertain sense of home as 'Jim', and his doubles, return to 31a Amherst Avenue, the Ballard family home, which had not only been turned into the library of the Shanghai Electronic Industry Information Bureau, but also into a temporary 'location' for the shooting of 'Shanghai Jim'.[25] Walking around his childhood home, 'Jim' admits: 'I had the weirdest sense that I was exploring a ghost' (1). That the house is described as a ghost (rather than 'Jim', who is a sort of revenant) is significant; it gestures to the way in which 31a Amherst Avenue haunts the Ballard *oeuvre* as a physical and psychological presence. Indeed, 'Jim's' home-coming echoes those passages in *Empire* and *Kindness* in which the Jim/Jamie doubles return home after the war. It is not the transformation of 31a Amherst Avenue that unsettles, but the way in which residues of the past continue to live on in the subtlest of ways. 'Jim's' childhood bedroom still has its original pale blue paint and bookshelves, for instance, even though these shelves now house scientific journals and text books. The coexistence of physical and psychic remnants of a familiar past and an unfamiliar present render 31a Amherst Avenue a *locus suspectus* or 'uncanny place' ('U' 341–2): feelings of 'homeliness' and 'unhomeliness' emerge out of one another in disquieting ways.

Of course, the 'unhomely' nature of 31a Amherst Avenue is accentuated by the fact that, for two-and-a-half years, Ballard's 'home' was a small room in Block G of Lunghua C.A.C. (now the Shanghai High School). In 'The End of My War', 'Jamie' (another authorial double) couches his return in nostalgic terms: 'Standing between the bunks, I knew that this was where I had been happiest and most at home'.[26] In 'Unlocking the Past', 'Jim' reveals the further significance of this particular home-coming:

> Going back to the camp had been, without my realising it, my main reason for returning to Shanghai, and visiting Lunghua again had opened a door that I thought was sealed for forty-five years . . . I had . . . confirmed that my memories of Shanghai had been clear and accurate.
>
> (2)

But are these memories as reliable as 'Jim' insists? 'The End of My War' concludes, for instance, with a striking error: 'In 1992 [sic], nearly fifty years after entering Lunghua camp, I returned for the first time. To my surprise, everything was as I remembered it' (2). What are we to make of this mistake? Is it an example of the fallible nature of the essay, a provisional form which is open to error because it 'lacks security'?[27] Or, is the unstable nature of memory manifesting itself? Has 'Jamie' misremembered this most significant of events? Given the ambiguous nature of Ballard's autobiographical fictions, this latter explanation seems unlikely. It might be more helpful to read Ballard's error as a move to set these autobiographical 'non-fictions' apart from claims to veracity. 'Unlocking the Past' and 'The End of My War' refuse to be read as closed statements on Ballard's life; rather, they are uncanny autobiographical forms, possessing 'a sense of strangeness given to dissolving all assurances about the identity of a self',[28] and ensuring that the story of J. G. Ballard remains incomplete.

Post-millennial hauntings

Towards the end of *Specters of Marx* (1994), a text manifestly indebted to Freud's 'The "Uncanny" ', Jacques Derrida suggests that any response to the complexity of contemporary history is haunted by the past: 'everyone reads, acts, writes with his or her ghosts'.[29] Although the past, by virtue of its passing, cannot exist as such, it does return in the present as an uncanny presence, as something which is simultaneously known and unknowable: 'If the readability of a legacy were given, natural, transparent, univocal, if it did not call for and at the same time defy interpretation, we would never have anything to inherit from it. One always inherits from a secret – which says "read me, will you ever be able to do so.?"'[30] Derrida's call for a form of historical response, which rejects ontological certainty and embraces 'hauntological' uncertainty, provides a way into thinking about Ballard's post-millennial 'non-fictions'. Violent histories, and specifically the ghosts of World War Two, return as uncanny, spectral forms throughout Ballard's review essays, forging unexpected and unwanted connections between the past and the present.

Commentators have noted the uncanny nature of the al-Quaeda terrorist attack on the World Trade Centre on 11 September 2001: 'As the twin towers collapsed, "live" on television, and the images of this collapse were repeatedly screened over the hours that followed, a sense of the uncanny seemed all-pervading. Is this real?'[31] In 'The Ultimate Sacrifice' (2002), a review essay of *Kamikaze: Japan's Suicide Gods* (2002) by Albert Axell and Hideaki Kase, Ballard also discusses the events of 'September 11' in uncanny terms, only he does so to forge a connection between images of the al-Quaeda attack and images of Japanese suicide missions during World War Two: 'The wartime newsreels that show waves of suicide pilots . . . diving into aircraft carriers near Okinawa uncannily evoke the images of al-Qaeda terrorists flying their hijacked Boeings into the World Trade Center.'[32] The strange process of doubling which Ballard identifies has, in turn, a double impulse: historical violence repeats actually and virtually. The recycling of catastrophic images, a contextual and formal feature of Ballard's own fictions, leads to a blurring of ontological boundaries. In each moment of repetition, the dead are reanimated, brought back to life only to be killed over and over again: death is conceptual.

In 'The "Uncanny" ', Freud remarks on the 'constant recurrence of the same thing - the repetition of the same features or character-traits or vicissitudes, of the same crimes, or even the same names through several consecutive generations' ('U' 356). This compulsion to repeat is bound up with the death drive, an inward-directed drive that manifests its tendency in self-destruction, and subsequently turns to the external world in the form of destructive behaviour. As Freud outlined in *Civilization and its Discontents* (1930), however, death and life instincts are not diametrically opposed: 'the two kinds of instinct seldom – perhaps never – appear in isolation from each other, but are alloyed with each other in varying and very different proportions'.[33] Ballard traces the unnerving co-existence of Thanatos and Eros in the actions of the Japanese suicide pilots, noting that: 'Far from seeking heroic death, the kamikaze pilots saw the suicide attacks as their only means of delaying the American advance.'³⁴ The pilots' dedication to the preservation of the nation through a form of self-destruction, he notes, is 'a mystery to the western mind, but all too close to the behaviour of the al-Qaeda flyers on 11 September. At a certain intensity, the will to suicide becomes a deranged affirmation of life'.³⁵

Kamikaze: Japan's Suicide Gods is an 'unsettling and draining' textual experience for Ballard because he sees Japan's suicide missions as uncanny anticipations of al-Quaeda's response to American military power: 'one dimly senses that the fightback may have already begun, launched more than 60 years ago when Japanese carrier planes bombed Pearl Harbor'.³⁶ Historical atrocity returns, in Ballard's formulation, as a kind of *déjà vu*. Furthermore, the very form of *Kamikaze: Japan's Suicide Gods* is uncanny: it is a strange, collective suicide note written by those who plummeted to their deaths and those who did not; namely, 'former suicide pilots who finished their training but were never sent on missions'.³⁷ Ballard recalls how, as a boy roaming the abandoned airfields of Shanghai following the 'end' of the war, he frequently encountered these living dead: 'They knew what was in store for them ... I realised that in a sense, they were already dead.'³⁸ This memory, one which echoes Ballard's fictional accounts of war, makes manifest the unsettling coincidence of beginnings and endings, life and death, fact and fiction. But it also allows Ballard to formulate a response that calls for an awareness of the psychological and political complexities of each historical event: 'bravery' and 'cowardice' are, contrary to popular belief, inadequate terms for analysis. The World Trade Centre 'may have gone', Ballard argues, 'but the shadows of the twin towers seem to lengthen, pointing to the coming war in Iraq, and beyond that to Saudi Arabia and even, who knows, to an unco-operative European state'.³⁹ Of course, 'the coming war in Iraq' has been and gone for the contemporary reader in the West (for whom the war was a virtual event in any case). But, beyond this uncanny textual effect, the point remains that historical violence will repeat. What is truly terrifying about this process of repetition with difference, however, is that no-one can quite anticipate what form the difference will take.

Another violent presence that haunts the popular historical imagination and Ballard's 'non-fictions' is Nazism: 'Why are the British ... so gripped by the Nazi era?' This question fuels 'The Day of Reckoning' (2005), a review essay of *A Woman in Berlin* (Anonymous, 1960 [sic]) and *Germany: Jekyll and Hyde* (1940) by Sebastian Haffner, two texts which, Ballard believes, might just serve as antidotes to 'the spectral glamour of the Nazi epoch'.⁴⁰ Beginning at the end of the War, *A Woman in Berlin* is a diary account of the final Russian assault on the Capital city and its civilian population, most of whom were women and children. With the withdrawal of the defeated German soldiers, the civilians are left to the mercy of the Russians, and what ensues in this time of 'peace' is a period of relentless sexual brutality. First published anonymously in 1954 and translated into English in 1955 (not 1960, as Ballard claims), *A Woman in Berlin* generated a storm of controversy, but this had less to do with the catalogue of sexual crimes documented in it than, as one reviewer argued, the author's 'shameless immorality'. What unsettled German readers was the revelation that, in order to survive, the author and other women allowed their Russian captors to 'revive' them with 'parcels of bread and herring': ' "What does it mean – rape?", the author asks, "It sounds like the absolute worst, the end of everything, but it's not " '.[41] This account of the immediate post-war experience challenged official, amnesiac narratives of economic and social recovery by bringing to light that which 'ought to have remained hidden' ('U' 364). Subsequently, the book went out of print and the author (later identified as Martha Hillers [not Martha Hiller, as Ballard claims]) requested that it only be republished posthumously. Historical silence takes many forms, however, and, towards the end of his review essay, Ballard gestures to one such silence: 'There are no references to the mass murder of Russians, Poles and Jews, to the inhuman brutality of the German armies.'[42] Falling silent at conspicuous moments, *A Woman in Berlin* operates its own form of repression. Yet, as Ballard's readerresponse demonstrates, that which is repressed has an uncanny capacity to return; the ghosts of historical violence persist as absent presences.

According to Ballard, *Germany: Jekyll and Hyde* is remarkable for its prescience. First published in 1940, it is 'an alarm call trying to awaken the British to the unique nature of Hitler and the Nazi regime'.[43] Key to Haffner's thesis is an understanding of the psychology of Nazism. Ballard notes: 'Hitler, [Haffner] maintains, is an out-and-out psychopath, who plays successfully on the age-old tendency of Germans to see themselves as persecuted, slighted and ill-treated.'[44] *Germany: Jekyll and Hyde* and Ballard's reading of it are haunted by a ghost text; namely, Adolf Hitler's *Mein Kampf* (1924), which Haffner read and Ballard reviewed for *New Worlds* in 1969. Indeed, Ballard's review essay, 'Alphabets of Unreason', echoes Haffner's study as it comments on the 'remarkably strong paranoid structure' of *Mein Kampf* and Hitler's dubious biological interpretations of history: 'By dispensing with any need to rationalise his prejudices, he was able to tap an area of far deeper unease and uncertainty.'[45] A further observation, one which is edited from the reprinted version of 'Alphabets' in *A User's Guide*, is particularly chilling. Comparing Hitler's generalizations about human behaviour with those of Desmond Morris, Ballard notes: 'Both are writing for half-educated people whose ideas about biology and history come from popular newspaper and encyclopaedia articles' (26). Ballard begins 'The Day of Reckoning' by taking a swipe at Channel Five's relentless coverage of the Nazi era: historical viewing is compulsive, but it is also uncritical. Is some connection being forged between the consumers of Nazi rhetoric and modern-day consumers of Nazi history in its commodified forms? If so, Ballard recognises that he, too, is somehow ensnared; not only as a self-confessed viewer of Channel Five, but also as the reviewer of two books which were reissued to coincide with the sixtieth anniversary of the end of World War Two. Even if *A Woman in Berlin* and *Germany: Jekyll and Hyde* are antidotes to the unthinking consumption of history which contemporary media and publishing industries promote, their timely reappearance suggests that they too are, inescapably, part of those culture industries.

No sense of an ending

Ballard's 'non-fictions' resist any sense of an ending. By exploring their shifting textual histories, their troubling of textual boundaries and disruption of generic classifications (fact/fiction, biography/autobiography), this reading has shown Ballard's 'non-fictions' to be curiously repetitive, oddly inconclusive, always open to re-reading and to re-thinking. Any study of these uncanny textual forms is, therefore, itself inevitably incomplete: indeed, this final reading is haunted by what has fallen out of the discussion; it is all too aware of what has not (but might have) been said. The processes of reading and writing about Ballard's uncanny 'non-fictional' forms are themselves uncanny: the production of unsettling textual effects combined with the constant generation of questions, rather than the imposition of answers, leaves the reader-writer feeling somewhat vulnerable. However, as Freud (recalling Jentsch) recognised, feelings of uncanniness are born precisely out of 'intellectual uncertainty', the uncanny is always something 'one does not know one's way around in' ('U' 341). Disorientation and hesitation are necessary, and not wholly unappealing, consequences of engaging with Ballard's 'non-fiction'. Operating somewhere *in-between*, these uncanny forms immerse the reader-writer in intellectual territories that are at once familiar and unfamiliar, knowable and unknowable, calling for forms of readerly and writerly negotiation which, in the absence of all that we regard as certain, are alive to the potential risks and rewards of uncertainty.

Notes

1. For a useful, if at times erroneous, survey of Ballard's essays and reviews see, Dominika Oramus, *Grave New World: The Decline of the West in the Fiction of J. G. Ballard* (Warsaw: Warsaw University Press, 2007), pp. 25–36.
2. Roger Luckhurst, *'The Angle Between Two Walls': The Fiction of J. G. Ballard* (Liverpool: Liverpool University Press, 1997), xiii.
3. Sigmund Freud, 'The "Uncanny" ' [1919] in *Art and Literature*, The Pelican Freud Library, vol. 14, trans. James Strachey (London: Penguin, 1985), pp. 339–76 (p. 342, p. 344). Emphases in original. All subsequent references are given in the main body of the text.
4. J. G. Ballard, *Miracles of Life: Shanghai to Shepperton* (London: Fourth Estate, 2008), p. 190.
5. J. G. Ballard, 'From Shanghai to Shepperton' in V. Vale and Andrea Juno, eds, *RE/Search #8/9: J. G. Ballard* (Re/Search Publications: San Francisco, 1991), pp. 112–24 (p. 120). For a fascinating reading of the influences of *Chemistry and Industry*, and its sister journal, *Chemistry and Engineering News*, on Ballard's fictions, see Mike Bonsall, 'J. G. Ballard's Experiment in Chemical Living', http://www.ballardian.com/jg-ballards-experiment-in-chemical-living, accessed 12 August 2010.
6. **Dictionary of Commercial Chemicals.** 3rd edn. By F.D. Snell and C.T. Snell. Pp. viii+714. *London: D. Van Nostrand Co. Ltd.* 1962. 97s., in *Chemistry and Industry*, 8 September, 1962, p. 1607. **Technical Market Research.** By R. Williams. Pp.118. *Geneva: Roger Williams Technical & Economic Services, S. A.* 1962., in *Chemistry and Industry*, 3 November, 1962, p. 1900. **Roget's Thesaurus of English Words and Phrases.** Revised and modernised by Robert A. Dutch. *London: Longman, Green and Co, Ltd.* Pp. lii+1309. 30s., in *Chemistry and Industry*, 1 September 1962, p. 1566. **Committees: How they work and how to work them.** By E. Anstey. Pp. 116. *London: George Allen and Unwin Ltd.* 963. 15s. *The Flash of Genius.* By A. B. Garrett. Pp. ix+249. London: D. Van Nostrand Co. Ltd. 1963. 30s., in *Chemistry and Industry*, 19 October, 1963, p. 1680.
7. Ballard's review of *The Science of Dreams* (1962) by Edwin Diamond is a notable exception that Bonsall links to Ballard's short story, 'Manhole 69' (1957). Bonsall, 'J. G. Ballard's Experiment in Chemical Living'.
8. J.G.B., **Dictionary of Chemistry and Chemical Technology.** In four languages: English, German, Polish and Russian. Edited by Z. Sobecka, W. Biernacki, D. Kryt and T. Zadrozna. Pp. 724. *London: Pergamon Press*, 1962. 200s., in *Chemistry and Industry*, 13 October, 1962, p. 1787.
9. Stefan Collini, 'The Critic as Journalist: Leavis after Scrutiny', in Jeremy Treglown and Bridget Bennett, eds, *Grub Street and the Ivory Tower: Literary Journalism and Literary Scholarship from Fielding to the Internet* (Oxford: Oxford University Press, 1998), pp. 151–76 (p. 153).
10. Theodor Adorno, 'The Essay as Form', trans. Bob Hullot-Kentor and Frederic Will, *New German Critique*, 32 (Spring–Summer, 1984), pp. 151–71 (p. 161).

11. Adorno, 'The Essay as Form', 164, 152.
12. J. G. Ballard, 'Myth Maker of the 20th Century', in *New Worlds*, 48:142 (May–June 1964), 121–7 (p.122); J. G. Ballard, 'Myth Maker of the Twentieth Century', reprinted in *A User's Guide to the Millennium*, pp. 126–30 (pp. 262,126); 'Terminal Documents', in *Ambit* (Special Review Number – The Contemporary Scene), 27 (1966), 46–8 (p. 46).
13. J. G. Ballard, 'Myth Maker of the 20th Century', 121; 'Myth Maker of the Twentieth Century', 126; 'Terminal Documents', 46.
14. Lorna Sage, 'Living on Writing', in Jeremy Treglown and Bridget Bennett, eds, *Grub Street and the Ivory Tower*, pp. 262–75 (pp. 262, 266).
15. 'J. G. Ballard, 'Which Way to Inner Space?', *New Worlds*, 40:118 (1962), 2–3, 116–18; 'The Coming of the Unconscious', *New Worlds*, 50:164 (1966), 141–6; 'Notes from Nowhere: Comments on Work in Progress', *New Worlds*, 50:167 (1966), 147–51.
16. Havelock Ellis, *The World of Dream* (London: Constable, 1911), p. 252 (emphasis in original), quoted in Nicholas Royle, *The Uncanny* (Manchester: Manchester University Press, 2003), p. 183. Royle's excellent study is an uncanny presence throughout my reading of Ballard's 'non-fiction'.
17. Royle, *The Uncanny*, p. 16.
18. Royle, *The Uncanny*, p. 16.
19. Ballard, 'Myth Maker of the 20th Century', 121. 'Terminal Documents', 46.
20. Ballard, 'Myth Maker of the 20th Century' 121. 'Terminal Documents', 46–7.
21. Luckhurst, '*The Angle Between Two Walls*', p. 169.
22. J. G. Ballard, 'Survival Instincts', *Sunday Times*, 1 March 1992, 9.
23. J. G. Ballard, 'Sinister Spider', *Daily Telegraph*, 27 June 1992, xix.
24. J. G. Ballard, 'Unlocking the Past', *Daily Telegraph*, 21 September 1991, 1.
25. The Ballard family home has undergone various transformations. Currently it is an up-market restaurant called SH508, which is situated on Xin Hua Road (formerly Amherst Avenue). For an account of Ballard's physical and virtual returns to his former home see Rick McGrath's excellent essay, 'Empire of the Son: Exploring J. G. Ballard's Shanghai Home and Haunts', http://www.jgballard.ca/shanghai/jgb_shanghai_home.html, accessed 14 September 2010.
26. J. G. Ballard, 'The End of My War', *Sunday Times*, 20 August 1995, 1–2 (p. 2).
27. Adorno, 'The Essay as Form', 161.
28. Royle, *The Uncanny*, p. 16.
29. Jacques Derrida, *Specters of Marx: The State of Debt, The Work of Mourning, and the New International*, trans. Peggy Kamuf (London: Routledge, 1994), p. 139.
30. Derrida, *Specters of Marx*, p. 16.
31. Royle, *The Uncanny*, vii-viii.
32. J. G. Ballard, 'The Ultimate Sacrifice', *The New Statesman*, 9 September 2002, http://www.newstatesman.com/200209090032, accessed 25 September 2010.
33. Sigmund Freud, *Civilization and Its Discontents* (1930 [1929]), in *On Metapsychology: The Theory of Psychoanalysis*, The Pelican Freud Library, vol. 12, trans. James Strachey (Harmondsworth: Penguin), pp. 251–340 (pp. 310–11).
34. Ballard, 'The Ultimate Sacrifice'.
35. Ballard, 'The Ultimate Sacrifice'.
36. Ballard, 'The Ultimate Sacrifice'.

37. Ballard, 'The Ultimate Sacrifice'.
38. Ballard, 'The Ultimate Sacrifice'.
39. Ballard, 'The Ultimate Sacrifice'.
40. J. G. Ballard, 'The Day of Reckoning', *The New Statesman*, 4 July 2005, http://www.newstatesman.com/200507040040, accessed 27 September 2010.
41. Ballard, 'The Day of Reckoning'.
42. Ballard, 'The Day of Reckoning'.
43. Ballard, 'The Day of Reckoning'.
44. Ballard, 'The Day of Reckoning'.
45. Ballard, 'Alphabets of Unreason', *New Worlds*, 53:196 (1969), 26.

Part II

'The Angle Between Two Walls': Sex, Geometry and the Body

4
Pornographic Geometries: The Spectacle as Pathology and as Therapy in *The Atrocity Exhibition*

Jen Hui Bon Hoa

J. G. Ballard's *Atrocity Exhibition* (1970) elaborates a conflicted and fetishistically obsessive relationship to the human body. Throughout, the body is repeatedly exhibited in various states of fragmentation, sometimes subject to careful descriptions of mutilation, sometimes sectioned by the pornographic gaze or by the cropped frame of an extreme close-up into partial objects. Paradoxically, at the same time as it appears under a fragmented and fatalistically exhausted aspect, the body also emerges as the potential medium of affectively rich, subconscious communication. In *The Atrocity Exhibition*, Ballard invests the pop-psychology notion of 'body language' with an almost mystical exactitude, suggesting that the geometry of bodily postures and features can both accurately reveal a subject's affective states and influence, in precise and quantifiable ways, those of onlookers. The body is thus posited as the agent of an intelligence beyond reason: an emitter and receiver of subconscious cues, and a powerful channel for shaping consciousness.

As its point of departure, this essay considers the tension between the conceptions of the thoroughly objectified body on the one hand, and the intelligent, communicative body on the other, in order to approach a provocative proposition that resurfaces throughout Ballard's fictional and non-fictional work. The idea finds its most direct articulation in the following programmatic statement: 'Rather than fearing alienation, people should *embrace* it. It may be the doorway to something more interesting. That's always the message of my fiction. We need to explore total alienation and find what lies beyond.'[1] In the notion that we have arrived at the possibility of 'total alienation', and that there might be a – presumably unalienated – mode of experience and social relation beyond it, Ballard's gnomic commentary straddles the dystopian and the utopian, and seems to offer a dialectical move beyond their opposition. The proposition that 'total alienation' cannot be reduced to the foreclosure of human possibility – that it also opens up new possibilities – is the ultimate expression of what *New Worlds* editor Michael Moorcock has dubbed an attitude of 'acceptance' and identified as a distinguishing characteristic of Ballard's approach to social commentary. Moorcock observes that, while other science fiction writers have tended to depict contemporary society in a satirical mode that was premised on 'a conventional distaste for the modern world' Ballard 'accepted the world and celebrated its wonders'.[2] According to Moorcock, such a willingness to find ways of adapting creatively to the dangerous aspects of modernity permits a deeper engagement with contemporary reality. By substituting a pragmatic approach to critique for the moralizing resistance of his peers, Ballard was ultimately better able to explore the developmental possibilities available to the modern subject.

While it may have been rare among his peers, Ballard's attitude of acceptance as a mode of subversion emerges from an established history of avant-garde cultural politics. From Surrealism's courtship of irrationality and Futurism's worship of the machine to Pop Art's ambiguous embrace of commercialism, contestatory gestures throughout the twentieth century have tarried with extremes of alienation. It was often with the hope of dialectical advancement, rupture, or transformation that the avant-garde tried to appropriate, rather than reject outright, the dysfunctional limits of alienated existence. Judging from the abundant references to such avant-garde movements in *The Atrocity Exhibition*, Ballard clearly situates his own intervention in dialogue with them. Many scholars have considered the implications of Ballard's homages. Jeannette Baxter explores Ballard's numerous allusions to titles of Surrealist paintings.[3] Roger Luckhurst and Andrzej Gasiorek discuss the sadistic treatment of the female body in relation to Hans Bellmer's dolls, and the affinity to Pop Art of *The Atrocity Exhibition*'s deadpan regurgitation of mass culture.[4]

Perhaps the idea of a redemptive moment beyond 'total alienation' is foundational for any project of raising rebellious consciousness through parody or rousing subversive energies through shock. In its most general formulation, then, the posture of 'acceptance' within the context of critique might simply denote the attempt to appropriate the weapons of the enemy, to outwit the system at its own game. This strategy, as Luckhurst argues in his reading of *The Atrocity Exhibition*, is fraught with an undecidable political valence, teetering on 'the knife-edge of complicity and critique'.[5] Walter Benjamin's appraisal of photography is thus also true of any kind of subversive repetition: as a technique of representation, it possesses the power to reveal the underlying structures of reality, but 'captions become obligatory' to deploy this revelatory power.[6] In other words, if an attitude of 'acceptance' is truly a tactical position – if it identifies with critique, rather than complicity – it requires, like the photograph, explicit directives for interpretation. This essay seeks to offer directives, not for reaching any final verdict on the politics of Ballard's novel, but for considering how its exploration of alienation illuminates a critical tradition based on the belief that, in Friedrich Hölderlin's formulation, 'where danger threatens / That which saves from it also grows'.[7] Staking out a privileged vantage point on this idea, *The Atrocity Exhibition* poses the question of 'total alienation and what lies beyond' in its most basic and urgent form – in terms, on the one hand, of the experience of compulsion and the attendant loss of rational agency and, on the other, of a powerful, untapped resource beyond rationality, in the form of unconscious processes of perception and cognition rooted in the body.

'Science is the ultimate pornography': the mass ornament and the pathological spectacle

As has been more frequently discussed with regard to *Crash*, *The Atrocity Exhibition* is driven by deep anxieties about the way that new technologies shape human ecology and, in particular, the way they affect the relationship to the body. Developed out of an eponymous chapter in *The Atrocity Exhibition* and published three years later, *Crash* considers the automobile in terms of the physical vulnerability that it introduces into everyday life and the libidinal energies that are awakened by this vulnerability. *The Atrocity Exhibition*, on the other hand, examines the visual technologies of the spectacle and the *psychological* vulnerabilities that they generate. With worry as well as with curiosity, Ballard contemplates the circulation of sensationalist imagery of the human body in the mass media: 'What actually happens on the level of our unconscious minds when, within minutes on the same TV screen, a prime minister is assassinated, an actress makes love, an injured child is carried from a car crash?'[8] Regarding the spectacle as a dominant instrument of socialization, he asks: What neural patterns of dread and desire are forged – what instincts and habits are formed, what kind of subject is produced – by repeated exposure to juxtaposed images of sexualized and damaged bodies?

Ballard experiments with a number of answers to this question. The most predictable of his hypotheses is almost arithmetic in its simplicity: the intermingling of erotic and violent imagery develops into sadistic forms of desire, such that mutilated bodies elicit a sexual response, and eroticized bodies a violent one. In both *The Atrocity Exhibition* and *Crash*, characters make love while watching atrocity footage and fantasize about violence enacted on iconic bodies (Elizabeth Taylor and John F. Kennedy repeat throughout *The Atrocity Exhibition* and *Crash*). A second theory suggests that overexposure to sensationalist imagery causes a waning of sensation. Recalling early twentieth-century diagnoses of psychological numbness as an adaptive response to overstimulation in the urban environment and to the trauma of World War I, Ballard's notion of 'the death of affect' adapts neurasthenia for the society of the spectacle. Drawing on both of these first two theories, a third, more complex response is acted out by Traven, the protagonist of *The Atrocity Exhibition*, who undertakes a series of 'bizarre but . . . logically constructed' projects in order to overcome trauma sustained by exposure to spectacular culture.[9]

Responding to the spectacle in its own language, Traven orchestrates a series of vast murals and billboards featuring highly magnified segments of Elizabeth Taylor's body, turning the surfaces of the city into a giant replica of her anatomy. Perceived by Traven to be pornographic, these images are so hugely magnified and tightly framed that, when taken individually, they fail to evoke the integral body and thus any potential sexual agent: 'Only an anatomist would have identified these fragments, each represented as a formal geometric pattern' (15). And yet the logic at work is still recognizable; Traven is simply multiplying the power of magnification of the already larger-than-life images of body parts shown on movie screens and billboards. His images reveal the structuring paradox of spectacular culture: the closer you get to the image, the further you get from the referent.

Ballard's reflections on the obsessive scopophilia generated by the indexical power of the photographic image recall Michelangelo Antonioni's roughly contemporaneous *Blow-Up* (1966). In Antonioni's film, the equation of magnification and explosion evoked in the title is emblematized by the reduction of image to the grain of the photograph – to the asignifying mechanics of photographic technology. In *The Atrocity Exhibition*, the scopophilic will to magnification similarly dissolves the image's ability to evoke any relationship to lived reality:

'Fossilized into the screen, the terraced images of breast and buttock had ceased to carry any meaning' (51). The oversized partial object of the erotic close-up and the broken body of the violent image converge in the abstraction of a body reduced to geometrical fragments that, bearing little recognizable relation to the organic world, are no longer differentiated by affective charge or significance. 'Cinemascope of breast and thigh' (64) becomes an abstract assemblage of lines and curvatures.

Reduced to the probing attention to surface and shape that defines them, geometry and pornography merge in an aggressively estranging combination of sensationalist content and affectless, mathematical language: 'Her breasts and buttocks illustrated Enneper's surface of negative constant curve, the differential coefficient of the pseudo-sphere' (40). Dr. Nathan, a fellow psychiatrist and exegete of Traven's behaviour, explains the logic driving this convergence: ' "[F]or Traven science is the ultimate pornography, analytic activity whose main aim is to isolate objects or events from their contexts in time and space. This obsession with the specific activity of quantified functions is what science shares with pornography" ' (36). By Dr. Nathan's diagnosis, Traven's sexualization of geometry means that the erotic is no longer simply produced by the 'analytic activity' of fetishization but equated with it; it is no longer the body or the sex act that holds any erotic charge but rather the process of abstraction itself. Passing through the reduction of lived experience in the society of the spectacle from being to having, and then further from having to appearing, the structure of the fetish becomes entirely recursive in a way that resonates with Fredric Jameson's definition of Postmodernism. Mirroring an economy based on 'the consumption of sheer commodification as a process',[10] Traven's abstract pornography stages the erotic enjoyment of the very process of fetishization.

The drive to recode the body in terms of abstract shapes in *The Atrocity Exhibition* revisits Siegfried Kracauer's commentary on the hybrid spectacle of burlesque dance and military drill performed by the Tiller Girls. Describing the troupe's precise formations as the merging of individual dancers into 'indissociable girl clusters whose movements are demonstrations of mathematics', Kracauer considers the Tiller Girls' exhibition of female bodies to be more evocative of assembly-line production than of sensual experience.[11] The reduction of the human organism in the factory to the partial objects of labour – hands that pull levers, feet that press pedals – finds its aesthetic correlate in the appearance of dismemberment in the assemblage of '[a]rms, legs, and other segments' that compose the formations of the dancers.[12] At the same time, the appeal of the Tiller Girls to mass audiences indicates, conversely, how sensual experience is being reshaped in the form of efficiently industrialized capitalist production; it reveals that the disciplining of the body in the assembly line has itself become fetishized into an aesthetic, a figuration of desire and, moreover, one enthusiastically received by the very same masses who mechanically perform specialized and repetitive tasks in the fragmented process of industrialized production. Recognizing the irony of a situation where the worker spends his wages earned at the factory to be entertained by other wage labourers performing movements derived from the very same assembly line, Kracauer completes the mapping: 'The hands in the factories correspond to the legs of the Tiller Girls.'[13] The circle closes: the worker seeks distraction from his dehumanizing labour in the spectacle of dehumanized bodies.

Guy Debord has suggestively dated the origins of spectacular society to the time of Kracauer's article – 'in 1967 [when Debord published *The Society of the Spectacle*] it had barely forty years behind it'; Kracauer wrote 'The Mass Ornament' in 1923.[14] While still principally focused on a lived experience of capitalism defined by Taylorist production rather than by the consumption of images, Kracauer's commentary does beckon towards Debord's notion of spectacular society, principally in its analysis of the relationship between the individual social agent to the overarching structure of social relations. For Kracauer, the 'mass ornament' of the Tiller Girls exemplifies the way that popular culture offers spectators an aestheticized reflection of themselves as a mass formation, stripped of independent subjectivity and agency, and organized according to principles and ends that are ultimately opaque to them. Just as the individual dancers that make up the Tiller Girls' abstract formations neither design their own movements nor experience their overall effect, in factory production – as in any mass social formation – the individual subjects that reduce themselves to 'mere building blocks' of a larger social organism forgo both self-determination and a sense of the whole: 'Everyone does his or her task on the conveyor belt, performing a partial function without grasping the totality.'[15]

Traven's billboard images diagram a relationship of spectators to the spectacular exhibition of the body in advertisements and entertainment media that rehearses the formation of the mass ornament: 'They were equations that embodied the fundamental relationship between the identity of the film actress and the millions who were distant reflections of her. The planes of their lives interlocked at oblique angles, fragments of personal myths fusing with the commercial cosmologies' (16). The fetishized body of the cultural icon becomes a medium of unification, but one that retains the quality of fragmentation. For those who recognize their fantasies in it, the contours of her body are the medium through which 'the planes of their lives' intersect. However, these intersections occur only at 'oblique angles' and within a solipsistic framework – commonality lies in the incorporation of the same 'commercial cosmologies' into the individual realm of 'personal myths'. For Kracauer, the mass ornament establishes a form of unity that is impoverished because it is constituted by an externally imposed homogeneity, rather than conscious self-organization: 'Although the masses give rise to the ornament, they are not involved in thinking it through.'[16] In terms resonant with Ballard's analogy of the magnified and fragmented body to the broken mirror of the 'millions who were distant reflections of her', Kracauer says of the geometrical formations of the mass ornament: 'As linear as it may be, there is no line that extends from the small sections of the mass to the entire figure.'[17] A very similar figure would later surface in Debord's description of the relationship of participants to each other through the spectacle: 'Spectators are linked only by a one-way relationship to the very center that maintains their isolation from one another. The spectacle thus unites what is separate, but unites it only *in its separateness* [il le réunit *en tant que séparé*].'[18]

The most captivating trait of the characters that drive the action in *The Atrocity Exhibition* and *Crash* is that they refuse the irreversibility of the 'connection to the center' – the condition of passivity that Debord considers to be constitutive of the spectacle. Vaughan, the prophetic-psychotic organizing principle of *Crash*, devises the 'optimal' mass media event of a car crash, based on data collected from questionnaires about preferred victim, wound patterns, vehicle, and manner of collision. Vaughan explains: 'With a little forethought she [Elizabeth Taylor] could die in a unique vehicle collision, one that would transform all our dreams and fantasies.'[19] In a culture where a select number of celebrities function as deities, accessible only through mass-reproduced iconography and personal fantasy, Vaughan's extreme act of fetishism carries a defetishizing quality. His desire to interact with the spectacle as an active participant rather than a passive spectator can be understood to stem from a democratic impulse, a drive to intervene in the production of the conditions of collectively shared reality.

Vaughan's project is clearly prefigured by Traven's 'therapeutic' restagings of John F. Kennedy's assassination, and his strategy of transforming collective 'dreams and fantasies' through manipulation of the media environment finds its most literal expression in Traven's billboards and murals. As Ballard's often anecdotal commentary in the margins of the RE/Search re-edition of *The Atrocity Exhibition* serves to underscore, the latter project carries an autobiographical resonance; it recalls Ballard's own attempts to work within mass media channels. Ballard's *Project for a New Novel* (1958) was intended for publication on a series of billboards; the five full-page 'advertisements' that he published in *Ambit* magazine from 1967 to 1971 all featured images of the female body and no product for sale. The symmetry suggests that, through Traven's psychotic behaviour, Ballard is working out – at an urgent and practical level, for the purposes of his own cultural interventions – the problem of agency in spectacular society. Traven does not simply serve to expose the madness inherent to the domination of lived experience by mass media images; he also gestures towards a madness that may be necessary to overcome this domination. Unlike Kracauer's Taylorist workers applauding the Tiller Girls, Traven gravitates towards an aesthetic of the fragmented body not for distraction from his own experience of fragmentation, but for the promise of meaning and transformation that it holds. In the context of a search for new, more powerful avenues of cultural production – for more direct ways of communicating with the mass public – the second part of this essay considers Ballard's conception of an unconscious, embodied intelligence.

The surgeon, the magician, and the acupuncturist: Walter Benjamin and Antonin Artaud on the therapeutic spectacle

In a short story published several years prior to *The Atrocity Exhibition*, Ballard entertains an openly paranoid vision of the psychological workings of the spectacle. Offering a standard dystopian account of life under one-dimensional capitalism, 'The Subliminal Man' chronicles characters whose lives follow a compulsive cycle of miserable labour and insatiable consumption. The cause of the irrational behaviour is revealed to be ubiquitous giant billboards through which corporations emit subliminal commands. ' "They're trying to transistorize our brains!" ' warns the prophetic figure of the story.[20] Bluntly formulated in 'The Subliminal Man' (1963) as a loss of rational autonomy in the face of conspiracy ('they') and an engineered environmental determinism ('transistorize'), the question of how mass media affect the unconscious mind is more subtly posed in *The Atrocity Exhibition*, yet still quite recognizable. There is, nonetheless, one structural difference between these two iterations of the problem: whereas the effects of the spectacle in 'The Subliminal Man' are limited to a single-tracked commercialism, the decentered model of the spectacle in *The Atrocity Exhibition* deploys visual strategies of shock and titillation in a more chaotic fashion and to much more uncertain effect.

The character of Traven functions to perform a theory about the logical structure of spectacular culture and the psychological tendencies that it promotes. For this reason, the question posed by Traven's wife about his role at the psychiatric institute – ' "Was my husband a doctor, or a patient?" ' (12) – is never quite decided. The clinical interpretations of his fellow psychiatrist, Dr. Nathan, present Traven's schizophrenic response to the environment as keenly diagnostic; his delusions, free of the regulatory capacities of repression, make explicit in an extreme form the psychological conflicts generated by contemporary culture and experienced on a collective scale. Just as Kracauer finds an unselfconscious and therefore uncensored mirror for the dominant cultural logic in kitsch, Ballard presents Traven as a mimetic instrument, similar to the 'recording surface' of Gilles Deleuze and Félix Guattari's schizo.[21] With only the scantest biographical information and no character development, Traven is defined solely by his madness. Traven is the faceless embodiment of a static set of cultural coordinates, as abstract and desubjectivized a presence as the fragmented bodies and geometrical figures that he sees everywhere around him.

The schizo, for Deleuze and Guattari, embodies the deterritorializing drive of capitalism, epitomized by its reduction of value to a language of quantification: money. According to Georg Simmel's phenomenology of money: 'To the extent that money, with its colorlessness and its indifferent quality can become a common denominator of all values it becomes the frightful leveler – it hollows out the core of things, their peculiarities, their specific values and their uniqueness and incomparability in a way that is beyond repair.'[22] Taking one step further Simmel's analysis of the homogenizing effect of money, Deleuze and Guattari suggest that the capitalist reduction of everything to exchange value unleashes at the same time the potential for singularity by freeing phenomena for an unlimited number of significations and configurations. In other words, capitalism tends towards the anarchic dissolution of all institutional stability (schizophrenia), and only survives through non-capitalist regulation (repression). The schizophrenic serves to make visible this tension and to push capitalism to its extreme limits: 'The schizophrenic deliberately seeks out the very limit of capitalism: he is its inherent tendency brought to fulfillment, its surplus product, its proletariat, and its exterminating angel.'[23]

In Traven's case, the language of universal exchange is geometry. The fetishistic isolation of anatomical detail and reduction of objects to geometrical form introduces the abstraction necessary for the work of resignification and redeployment. It enables the perception of homologies between the human body and its material surroundings, such that the angle between two walls can take on the same significance as the junction between two legs, and, as *Crash* explores more single-mindedly, the fashioning of new composite entities through dismemberment and prosthetics. Deleuze and Guattari claim a world of pure sensory receptivity for the schizo; Traven's substitution of a spatial language for the entirely abstract calculus of money enables a more focused engagement with embodied experience. Familiar modes of sense perception are still relevant to questions of spatial organization, whereas money has severed all meaningful and systematizable relation to the organic world. For this reason, Kracauer's approach to abstraction through the Tiller Girls is an especially important precursor for *The Atrocity Exhibition*. By discussing social relations in terms of the individual body and its mode of relation to other bodies, Kracauer retains a sense of the material and organic specificity of the individual as a counterweight to the object of his study – the will to abstraction.[24]

Having described alienation as imprisonment within an impoverished language, Ballard goes on to consider the new possibilities afforded by fluency in that language. Traven's rapt attunement to the psychological impact of geometry demonstrates not only autistic imperviousness to other structures of meaning but also a savant's sensitivity to subliminal prompts. His madness explores the idea of environmental determinism through the idea that visual stimuli not only provoke affective responses but reshape the very patterns governing these responses. Ballard's ambivalent evaluation of the technologies of the spectacle – as productive not only of dysfunction but also of new adaptive capabilities – recalls Walter Benjamin's assessment of the effects on consciousness of the new visual technologies of photography and film in 'The Work of Art in the Age of Mechanical Reproduction' (1936). Laying the groundwork for Traven's fusion of pornography and science in the magnified image, Benjamin discusses the convergence of art and science in the ability of photography and film to magnify and slow down the visual field. Such a heightening of visual acuity reveals previously unnoticed aspects of the world and thus 'extends our comprehension of the necessities which rule our lives'.[25] At the same time that it identifies determining forces on behaviour, photography also points to new possibilities of action by indicating the unfamiliar dimensions of an over-familiar world; new visual media 'burst this prison-world asunder by the dynamite of the tenth of a second . . . With the close-up, space expands; with slow-motion, movement is extended'.[26]

Following an exploration of the promising capabilities afforded by emergent technologies, the epilogue to the 'Work of Art' essay abruptly changes tack, evaluating the political *problems* supported by the introduction of new possibilities of perception and action. Citing at length from F. T. Marinetti's Futurist Manifesto in the essay's epilogue, Benjamin suggests a connection between the new sensibility produced by visual technologies and the aestheticization of war: 'Fascism . . . expects war to supply the artistic gratification of a sense perception that has been changed by technology.'[27] The success of this fascist strategy of social control indicates a situation where: 'Its [Mankind's] self-alienation has reached such a degree that it can experience its own destruction as an aesthetic pleasure of the first order.'[28] By 'self-alienation', Benjamin means that an abstract understanding of the self as 'an object of contemplation' has supplanted an embodied self of subjective experience. In a situation where people regard each other as images and where the scopophilia trumps the sensations of lived experience, even violence can be enjoyed in the same way as any other spectacle – as in the idea of an 'atrocity exhibition'.

For Benjamin – as, later, for Debord – self-alienation appears to be a part of the new cognitive wiring native to a popular culture dominated by the pursuit of increasingly powerful visual stimulation. Out of this seemingly exitless situation, Benjamin offers a solution in the famous final sentence of the essay; to disrupt the fascist aestheticization of politics: 'Communism responds by politicizing art.'[29] Susan Buck-Morss provides a helpful reading of this programme. The politicization of art, she explains, cannot be reduced to the communication of political messages through the medium of art. Rather, Benjamin evokes an aesthetics that strives 'to *undo* the alienation of the corporeal sensorium, to *restore the instinctual power of the human bodily senses for the sake of humanity's self-preservation,* and to do this, not by avoiding the new technologies, but by *passing through* them'.[30] *The Atrocity Exhibition,* too, sets itself the riddle of how to resolve the problem of alienation from embodied experience (which Ballard calls the 'death of affect') and to 'restore the instinctual power of the human bodily senses' by embracing and exploring the potential of the very technologies that generate the experience of alienation.

In answer to the practical question of how new technologies might be used to liberate subjects from a state of sensorial alienation, Buck-Morss concludes her essay with an analysis of photographs displaying Hitler's range of facial gestures. She suggests that disalienation is ultimately a question of breaking unreflective libidinal attachments (to figures perceived as 'auratic', for example). By using the advanced visual technologies to slow down and magnify footage of the charismatic figure's performances, viewers can gain a demystifying comprehension of the techniques by which he elicited powerful emotional responses, as well as insight into the overarching affective structure of fascism. This reflexivity about how the spectacle affects individuals on an immediate, even instinctual, level permits them to interrogate, recontextualize, and ultimately reject that initial unconscious reaction. In other words, it allows them to regain rational control over their sensory responses.

Like Benjamin and Buck-Morss, Ballard is interested in the 'unconscious optics' of spectacular technology – in its ability to reveal determinants of behaviour that fall outside of rational agency.[31] Ballard's interest, however, stems from a rather different vision of its application. Benjamin discusses the efficacy of new technologies in the service of greater knowledge and mastery of the self, as expressed in the Freudian slogan, 'Wo Es war, soll Ich werden'. Ballard, on the other hand, seems to find something salutary in the very ability of stimuli to elicit instinctive responses – that is, in the faculty of unconscious cognition itself. He wonders, 'Will modern technology provide us with hitherto undreamed-of means for tapping our own psychopathologies?'[32] Ballard is concerned not with 'understanding' but with 'tapping' the psychological tics generated by exposure to the spectacle; he points not to the resolution of psychopathology but to its potential utility. In the quest 'to explore total alienation and find what lies beyond', *The Atrocity Exhibition* suggests that the very mechanisms of psychological manipulation learnt from the media might be harnessed for a therapeutic project.

In a striking structural parallel with Buck-Morss's essay, Ballard, too, concludes his text by turning to the scientific study of the human countenance and its psychological impact upon an audience. Styled after case studies, the final chapters of *The Atrocity Exhibition* include an analysis of the psychosexual appeal of Ronald Reagan's facial features. 'Why I Want to Fuck Ronald Reagan' advances a theory about 'Presidential figures being perceived primarily in genital terms; the face of L. B. Johnson is clearly genital in significant appearance – the nasal prepuce, scrotal jaw, etc. Faces were seen as either circumcised (JFK, Krushchev) or uncircumcised (LBJ, Adenauer). In assembly-kit tests Reagan's face was uniformly perceived as a penile erection' (107). The other 'case studies' monitor the psychological reception of violent spectacles – footage of car accidents and war atrocities. The responses of test subjects suggest that the composition of these violent images can be engineered for 'maximum arousal,' applied in the manner of a drug to regulate 'blood pressure, pulse and respiratory rates to acceptable levels,' or to create 'an optimum environment . . . [for] work-tasks, social relationships and overall motivation' (93).

With the idea of a therapeutic 'atrocity exhibition', Ballard's novel enters squarely into the realm of Artaud's theatre of cruelty. Written contemporaneously with Benjamin's 'Work of Art' essay, Artaud's 'An End to Masterpieces' (1936) similarly denounces a cultural situation where a society seems to be abandoning itself to its own destruction, resigned to a state where it is 'no longer good for anything but disorder, famine, blood, war, and epidemics'.[33] As a corrective for the domination of affect by 'neurosis and petty sensuality' and an aesthetic norm 'that petrifies us, deadens our senses,' Artaud suggests that the technologies of the spectacle be used systematically, as a means of administering psychological treatment.[34] Sharing Ballard's consternation over the chaotic juxtaposition of sensationalist images and its possible psychological effects, Artaud complains about art 'in which exciting shapes explode here and there but at random and without any genuine consciousness of the forces they could rouse'.[35] In its place, he proposes an art that is fully cognizant of its power to shape mood and behaviour, and that exercises this power in a scientific manner.

Like Ballard, Artaud insists that therapy cannot take place in a detached, intellectual register, as it does in the process of self-understanding proposed in Buck-Morss's reading of Benjamin. On the surface, the denunciation of an overly worshipful attitude towards artworks in Artaud's 'An End to Masterpieces', appears to mirror the democratizing disappearance of aura that Benjamin reluctantly champions. For Benjamin, auratic presence is defined by 'the appearance of a distance, however close the thing that calls it forth' – a magical distance from which the thing commands a cultish authority that 'takes possession of us'.[36] By doing away with the elevated stature of the original artwork through the proliferation of copies, 'mechanical reproduction emancipates the work of art from its parasitical dependence on ritual'.[37] Artaud moves in precisely the opposite direction. What Benjamin calls auratic distance, Artaud experiences as emotional detachment, for the reason that an awestruck appreciation of the artistic representation inhibits a subjective confrontation with the lived experience that it represents. In response to this idolatry, the theatre of cruelty seeks to revive 'a religious idea of the theatre (without mediation, useless contemplation, and vague dreams)'.[38]

The problem that Artaud identifies, therefore, is not too much immediacy, but too little. A curative project, he maintains, must engage a primarily physiological response; it must operate through compulsion, not contemplation. Such an aesthetics will draw on a 'physical knowledge of images' in order to produce a spectacle capable of 'directly affecting the organism . . . of attacking this [petty] sensuality by physical means it cannot withstand'.[39] Artaud offers two analogies to clarify what it might mean to 'directly affect the organism'. He refers first to acupuncture, and its precise manipulation of the nervous system 'in order to regulate the subtlest functions'.[40] Anticipating Roland Barthes's idea of the *punctum* – the powerful affective charge located in the details of the photographic image – Artaud's acupunctural spectacle also conceives of the visual (and sonic) detail as an 'element which rises from the scene, shoots out of it like an arrow, and pierces' the spectator with an immediacy that circumvents rational cognition.[41] Explaining further how the theatre of cruelty communicates with its audience, Artaud goes on to evoke the snake charmer, who controls the movements of the snake through the vibrations in the ground produced by his music. Artaud explains: 'I propose to treat the spectators like the snakecharmer's subjects and conduct them *by means of their organisms* to an apprehension of the subtlest notions.'[42] Although Artaud's diction often signals a brutality that seems incongruous with his references to precision and subtlety – he speaks of violent images that 'crush . . . the sensibility of the spectator' and 'shake the organism to its foundations and leave an ineffaceable scar' – the theatre of cruelty does not seem to operate through terror.[43] Suggesting a possible reading of the monotone seriality of Ballard's prose, Artaud speaks instead of hypnosis and inducing a trance-like state. The theatre of cruelty elicits a state not of defensive reaction or heightened analysis but of unconscious receptivity. Correspondingly, the therapeutic power of the 'physical image' stems from its capacity to bypass conscious thought and interact with an unconscious, somatic intelligence.

It is perhaps unsurprising that, in a text similarly about cultural pathology, we should also find allusions to therapeutic figures in Benjamin's 'Work of Art' essay. Distinguishing between two modes of representing reality, Benjamin compares two approaches to intervention in the organism: 'The magician heals the sick person by the laying on of hands; the surgeon cuts into the patient's body.'[44] The difference between the two methods of healing analogizes the opposition of the painter's presentation of a coherent vision of reality to the cameraman's dissection of the visual field through fragmentary images that are later reassembled in montage. Artaud's acupuncturist theatre presents a third, non-representational alternative to the expressive means of the cameraman and the painter. Opposed to the tradition of 'a purely descriptive or narrative theater' dominant since the Renaissance, the theatre of cruelty, 'far from copying life, puts itself whenever possible in communication with pure forces'.[45] While clearly tongue-in-cheek in their formulaic oversimplification, the final chapters of *The Atrocity Exhibition* rehearse Artaud's provocative, even practical, hypothesis – that, by developing a map of our psychosomatic responses to our environment and administering these cues to ourselves, we can make our unavoidable psychological implication in the media landscape work in our favour. Through the attunement to mechanisms of automatism and compulsion, Ballard too suggests that, a new resource might emerge, beyond the 'total alienation' of the body in fragments, in the form of an acephalic intelligence.

Notes

1. Quoted in Iain Sinclair, *Crash: David Cronenberg's Post-mortem on J. G. Ballard's 'Trajectory of Fate'* (London: British Film Institute, 1999), p. 42.
2. Michael Moorcock, Introduction to *New Worlds: An Anthology* (New York: Thunder's Mouth, 2004), xix.
3. Jeannette Baxter, *J. G. Ballard's Surrealist Imagination: Spectacular Authorship* (Surrey: Ashgate, 2009), pp. 59–98.
4. Andrzej Gasiorek, *J. G. Ballard* (Manchester and New York: Manchester University Press, 2005); Roger Luckhurst, *'The Angle Between Two Walls': The Fiction of J. G. Ballard* (Liverpool: Liverpool University Press, 1997).
5. Luckhurst 1997, p. 105. Similar arguments have been made compellingly by Jonathan Crary with regard to the Futurist embrace of technology in Fernand Léger's essay, 'The Spectacle,' and Susan Rubin Suleiman with regard to the estrangement-effect of misogynist excess in Alain Robbe-Grillet's *Project for a Revolution in New York*. See Jonathan Crary, 'Spectacle, Attention, Counter-Memory' in *October*, 50 (1989), 96–107; Susan Rubin Suleiman, 'Reading Robbe-Grillet: Sadism and Text in *Projet pour une révolution à New York*' in *Subversive Intent: Gender, Politics and the Avant-Garde* (Cambridge, Mass.: Harvard University Press, 1990), pp. 51–71.
6. Walter Benjamin, 'The Work of Art in the Age of Mechanical Reproduction' in *Illuminations: Essays and Reflections*, trans. Harry Zohn (New York: Schocken, 1988), p. 226.
7. Friedrich Hölderlin, 'Patmos' in Eric L. Santner, ed., *Hyperion and Selected Poems* (New York: Continuum, 1990), p. 245.
8. J. G. Ballard, *The Atrocity Exhibition* (San Francisco: RE/Search, 1990), p. 89. All subsequent references are given in the main body of the text.

9. Interview with David Gale, BBC Radio 3, 10/11/98. The transcription can be found at http://www.jgballard.com/gravenewworld.htm, accessed 06 July, 2010.
10. Fredric Jameson, *Postmodernism or, the Cultural Logic of Late Capitalism* (Durham, NC: Duke University, 1991), x.
11. Siegfried Kracauer, *The Mass Ornament: Weimar Essays*, trans. and ed. Thomas Y. Levin (Cambridge, MA; London, England: Harvard, 1995), p. 76.
12. Kracauer, *Mass Ornament*, p. 78.
13. Kracauer, *Mass Ornament*, p. 79.
14. Guy Debord, *Comments on the Society of the Spectacle*, trans. Malcolm Imrie (London and New York: Verso, 2002), p. 3 (§2).
15. Kracauer, *Mass Ornament*, p. 78.
16. Kracauer, *Mass Ornament*, p. 77.
17. Kracauer, *Mass Ornament*, p. 77.
18. Debord, *Comments*, p. 22 (§29).
19. Ballard, *Crash* (New York: Picador, 2001), p. 130.
20. Ballard, 'The Subliminal Man' in *J. G. Ballard: The Complete Short Stories* (London: Flamingo, 2001), pp. 412–25 (p. 413).
21. Gilles Deleuze and Félix Guattari, *Anti-Oedipus: Capitalism and Schizophrenia*, trans. Robert Hurley, Mark Seem and Helen R. Lane (New York and London: Continuum, 2004), pp. 13, 17.
22. Georg Simmel, 'The Metropolis and Mental Life', trans. and ed. Kurt H. Wolff (Glencoe, Ill.: The Free Press, 1950), pp. 409–24 (p. 414).
23. Deleuze and Guattari, *Anti-Oedipus*, p. 35.
24. Kracauer's peers, most famously Theodor Adorno, also analyzed high Modernism for its mimetic quality, drawing comparable conclusions: 'New art is as abstract as social relations have become,' comments Adorno in *Aesthetic Theory*. Kracauer's intervention is distinguished, however, by its insistence on the ways in which individual bodies are disciplined into mass formations and, for this reason, it opens most seamlessly onto a vocabulary that we recognize in *The Atrocity Exhibition*.
25. Benjamin, 'Work of Art', p. 236.
26. Benjamin, 'Work of Art', p. 236.
27. Benjamin, 'Work of Art', p. 242.
28. Benjamin, 'Work of Art', p. 242.
29. Benjamin, 'Work of Art', p. 242.
30. Susan Buck-Morss, 'Aesthetics and Anaesthetics: Walter Benjamin's Artwork Essay Reconsidered', *October*, 62 (1992), 3–41 (p. 5). Italics in the original.
31. Benjamin, 'Work of Art', p. 237.
32. Ballard, Introduction to the French edition of *Crash*, in *Crash* (New York: Picador, 2001), p. 6.
33. Antonin Artaud, 'An End to Masterpieces' in *The Theater and Its Double*, trans. Mary Caroline Richards (New York: Grove, 1958), pp. 81, 80. The text can be dated approximately by the first time it is mentioned in Artaud's correspondence, in a letter to Jean Paulhan on 6 January 1936.
34. Artaud, 'An End to Masterpieces', p. 78.
35. Artaud, 'An End to Masterpieces', p. 79.

36. Walter Benjamin, *The Arcades Project*, trans. Howard Eiland and Kevin McLaughlin (Cambridge, Mass.; London, England: Harvard, 1999), p. 447 (M16a, 4).
37. Benjamin, 'Work of Art', p. 224.
38. Artaud, 'An End to Masterpieces', p. 80.
39. Artaud, 'An End to Masterpieces', p. 81.
40. Artaud, 'An End to Masterpieces', p. 80.
41. Roland Barthes, *Camera Lucida: Reflections on Photography*, trans. Richard Howard (New York: Hill and Wang, 1981), p. 21.
42. Artaud, 'An End to Masterpieces' p. 81. Italics in the original.
43. Artaud, 'An End to Masterpieces', pp. 83, 77.
44. Benjamin, 'Work of Art', p. 233.
45. Artaud, 'An End to Masterpieces', pp. 76, 82.

> # 5
> ## Disaffection and Abjection in J. G. Ballard's *The Atrocity Exhibition* and *Crash*
>
> Emma Whiting

In the 1974 introduction to the French edition of *Crash* (1973), J. G. Ballard locates science fiction as a 'casualty of the changing world it anticipated and helped to create. The future envisaged by the science fiction of the 1940s and 1950s is already our past'.[1] Ballard describes an all-voracious present, which has produced an 'almost infantile world' in which 'any demand, any possibility ... can be satisfied instantly' and even the future, he argues, is 'merely one of those manifold alternatives open to us' (8). The result is stagnation, inertia and a pervasive 'death of affect' (5). If everything is perpetually available, what remains to aim towards and to inspire any passion? He speaks of his own consequent intention to move away from the themes of earlier science fiction writing – 'outer space, and the far future' – towards a 'new terrain' yet to be colonized. Ballard calls this terrain 'inner space': 'that psychological domain ... where the inner world of the mind and the outer world of reality meet and fuse' (7) to produce 'a heightened or alternate reality beyond and above those familiar to either our sight or our senses'.[2] In 'inner space', that is, new crossings and intersections reveal the presence of undiscovered, latent energies and meanings that should revitalize the disaffected, aimless and sterile world and this, for Ballard, confers upon inner space a 'redemptive and therapeutic power'.[3]

The persistent disintegration of boundaries at the root of inner space has led Victor Burgin to describe it as a space of 'abjection'.[4] In *Powers of Horror* (1982), Julia Kristeva situates abjection as a horrific blurring of boundaries, primarily between subject and object, that should remain always beyond our knowledge but which, in a controlled encounter, may constitute a restorative, boundary re-affirming experience, re-asserting what I am and what I am not. It is arguably just such a shocking but also restorative 'power of horror' that Ballard draws upon in his deployment of the boundary-blurring terrain of 'inner space' and its far more visceral and abject incarnation in the blurring of corporeal boundaries, in order to disrupt the 'death of affect'. Many critical readings of Ballard's writing address inner space, but it is this relation to abjection that I believe best offers a means of understanding not only why the unnerving, destabilizing and ostensibly shocking terrain of inner space in Ballard's texts might also offer a redemptive experience but, moreover, why many readers find it fails as a redemptive or even shocking experience. For if abjection is a question of boundaries, is it not, also, subject to the 'all-voracious' boundary crossing Ballard identifies: assimilated and neutralized as another alternative in the perpetual present? Focusing on *The Atrocity Exhibition* (1970) and *Crash*, I consider whether Ballard's inner space is a victim of the very death of affect he seeks to resist or if it is possible that his texts do offer a kind of abjection that might still serve a disruptive but also therapeutic purpose.

Inner space

The intersections and fusions of inner space are the dreams of the protagonist of *The Atrocity Exhibition* who is himself a confusion of identities: Traven, Travis, Talbot, Trabert, Tallis, Talbert and Travers. Throughout *The Atrocity Exhibition* he seeks out points of intersection between such seemingly unconnected domains or 'planes', as Travis refers to them, as the wall of his room, his own and others' bodies, natural landscapes, buildings, but also between events, time and space, past, present and future, and between his own psyche and the world around him. Dr Nathan states that Travis is reacting against the ' "the specific and independent existence of separate objects and events" ' in order to form ' "a distinctive type of object relation based on perpetual and irresistible desire to merge with the object in an undifferentiated mass" '.[5] The crossings that Tallis draws out include an enlarged photograph of Elizabeth Taylor's punctured bronchus perceived as 'mimetising' Vietnam and the Congo, or a close up of her right eye and cheekbone as an 'equation' through which the actress and her audience could be linked: 'The planes of their lives interlocked at oblique angles, fragments of personal myths fusing with the commercial cosmologies' (16). He perceives 'the equivalent geometry of the sexual act with the junctions of this wall and ceiling' (53), the breasts and buttocks of his lover, Karen Novotny, 'illustrated Enneper's surface of negative constant curve' (40) and '[i]n the perspective of the plaza, the junctions of the underpass and embankment, Talbot at last recognized a modulus that could be multiplied into the landscape of his consciousness' (23).

Throughout the texts, planes are mapped onto and conceived in terms of each other in such a way that they become almost interchangeable. Such fusions also pervade *Crash*. The car crashes which fuse body and machine produce in James a 'growing sense of a new junction between my own body and the automobile' (47). These new junctions are evident in, for example, James' fascination with 'the conjunction of an air hostess's fawn gabardine skirt on the escalator in front of [him] and the distant fuselages of the aircraft, each inclined like a silver penis towards her natal cleft' (36). Here the corporeal appears to extend into the machine, just as in Vaughan's photo of a sexual act between James and his lover Renata where the chromium window sill of James' car and Renata's bra strap seem to form 'a single sling of metal and nylon from which the distorted nipple seemed to extrude itself into my mouth' (81).

James' fascination with these collided planes is augmented by his relationship with Vaughan. Vaughan compulsively repeats and reconceptualizes other collisions, particularly crash deaths, during his sexual exploits which he uses to mimic crash positions and the symmetries between mechanical and corporeal bodies that the crashes invoke. James, too, uses his sex acts with Helen Remington to re-imagine Helen's husband and his death in a series of bodily and mechanical postures. In both texts, then, as well as collisions taking place between bodies, between bodies and cars, and between bodies and geometries, each collision is itself rendered equivalent to other collisions. Sex acts repeat car crashes, the collision of facial angles repeats the Apollo crash. Moreover, the equivalencies drawn out between these collisions also suggest a further equivalency between the crash wound and the point of intersection of any other 'planes' – the 'angle between two walls', for example, or the intersection between a skirt and an airplane fuselage.

Abject literature

These recurrent crossings and intersections lead the terrain of inner space to dominate the landscape of both texts. This space constitutes what Burgin identifies as a 'post-modern geometry' wherein 'spaces once conceived of as separated, segregated, now overlap'[6] and which he likens to a return to the origins of geometry which, '[i]n so far as geometry is a science of boundaries', may be said to lie 'in *abjection*'.[7] Julia Kristeva describes the abject as that which is neither subject nor object but which lies beyond these boundaries and those of the social order: the disturbing meaninglessness of the 'in-between, the ambiguous, the composite': the very terrain of Ballard's texts.[8] As such, the abject is intrinsically related to the Lacanian real, that radical alterity beyond social reality or the symbolic order that consists of the horrifying undifferentiation from which each individual originated but which must be left behind for the speaking subject to be established. The abject threatens a return to this undifferentiation. Though its existence is necessary to establish the borders of the subject – what I am not – if it comes too close, these borders may collapse, bringing about the destitution of the subject which Jacques Lacan calls the 'second death'.[9]

This ambiguous relation to the abject is at the root of Kristeva's insistence on the restorative and renewing function of a controlled encounter with the abject wherein the boundaries of the subject may be tested but ultimately, through the act of expelling the abject, are re-asserted and strengthened: ' "subject" and "object" push each other away, confront each other, collapse and start again – inseparable, contaminated, condemned, at the boundary of what is assimilable, thinkable: abject'.[10] Kristeva sees some literature performing this function, which I will call the literature of abjection. I believe Ballard's own deployment of inner space is intended to offer such a restorative encounter with an alterity that he believes still lies beyond the static, sterile boundaries of the twentieth-century socio-symbolic order; an encounter that will allow the subject to 'start again' by perceiving there is still a boundary yet to be crossed.

However, some responses to the novels suggest that Ballard may exceed this restorative function. Following legal advice, the first US edition of *The Atrocity Exhibition* was pulped by Doubleday prior to publication, the review of *Crash* in *The Times* called the novel 'repellent'[11] and a publisher's reader responded to Ballard's original submission of *Crash* with the verdict: 'This author is beyond psychiatric help. Do Not Publish!'[12] Rather than a literature of abjection, Ballard's texts might be considered to tend towards what Kristeva identifies as 'abject literature'. This is the literature which draws the reader too close to the abject. It allows no room to expel the abject and instead submerges the reader in its full power of horror. For Kristeva, this power is most concentrated in the representation of death, the image of the corpse or the wounded body, which recalls Lacan's own elision of the real with the flayed body, for this is the body completely stripped of its boundaries, radically opened and so ceasing to exist, just like the subject in the encounter with the abject real. With their prolific crashes of bodies, cars, angles and 'planes' and fetishization of the wound, *The Atrocity Exhibition* and *Crash* ostensibly produce precisely such a direct and disturbing encounter with the abject.

Traumas that fail to traumatize

Nevertheless, there is an absence of the expected crisis in these supposedly abject texts. Discussing David Cronenberg's film adaptation of *Crash*, Parveen Adams observes that it is pervaded by 'traumas that fail to traumatise'.[13] This seems also to be true of the texts. Despite apparently bringing the reader into direct contact with the epitome of abjection, the texts seem strangely devoid of horror. The crashes and crashed bodies provoke little affect either within or without the text and are often presented as merely elaborate, stylistic poses. The failure of these traumas to traumatize may have something to do with the fate of the abject in our 'all-voracious' culture.

Mark Seltzer has observed that: '[n]othing is more visible across the range of recent cultural studies than "the return of the body" and "the return of the real" '.[14] Recalling once more Lacan's description of the real, this visibility is registered in the current fascination in popular culture with images of the collapsed, gaping body in, for example, plastic surgery shows, hospital and crime dramas, reality shows with their rhetoric of 'laying bare' and 'opening up', or in the film industry trend towards 'ultraviolence' in franchises such as *Hostel* (2005) or *Saw* (2004). This urge towards the real of the body via the media is symptomatic of a larger-scale turn to, and visibility of, the real itself: Ballard's 'all-voracious present' taken to its absolute extreme in the quest to break down every boundary and to gain absolute knowledge and access, even to what should be the most radical of impossibilities.

Slavoj Žižek identifies this voracious exposure as our 'passion for the real'[15] which has caused inside and outside, body and world, psychical and social to collapse into each other, placing a great deal of tension upon the borders not just of the socio-symbolic order but also of our sense of subjectivity. The very subjective destitution of abjection appears now to constitute the experience of sociality and subjectivity. This gives rise to what Seltzer calls the 'pathological public sphere' wherein the subject is perpetually opened and gaping towards all that had been impossibly beyond them: an 'uninterrupted interface', to use Jean Baudrillard's phrase.[16] The images of the wounded, haemorrhaging body that pervade popular culture therefore not only gauge the increasing visibility of the real but also provide a means of representing to ourselves the ensuing re-conceptions of sociality and subjectivity in terms of abjection. It is for this reason that Seltzer places the wound within a series of mimetic relays that are used by the subject of the pathological public sphere to understand itself and attempt to come to terms with its trauma. This, Seltzer argues, is 'wound culture', of which, he also states, Ballard is one of the 'compulsive cartographers'.[17]

Yet, in these mimetic relays it is the trauma of the real – the height of abjection and impossibility – that is not only exemplary of, rather than antithetical to, subjectivity and sociality, but is also being endlessly circulated through the media in the image of the wound, and this ubiquity of abjection can only serve to dilute its power of horror. As an article in *The Times* observes, 'ultraviolence' has become 'a critical and accepted part of the mainstream'.[18] Indeed, *Hostel Part II* (2007) was likened to: 'a torture garden where you can run through the thorns, scrape your skin off and not feel a scratch'.[19] Kristeva herself acknowledges this fate of abjection when she asks: 'And yet, in these times of dreary crisis, what is the point of emphasizing the horror of being?'[20] Abjection, in other words, presents no new crisis but only emphasizes or mimics a crisis already being experienced as everyday sociality. Is this perhaps also what Ballard's own abjection has been subjected to? Has the terrain of inner space been made victim to the very 'death of affect' from which it had been intended to offer redemption?

For Baudrillard, *Crash* is always already a novel that fully participates in, even celebrates this affectless present. In his somewhat controversial essay 'Ballard's *Crash*' (1991), Baudrillard describes an 'intense initiatory power' in the novel originating from a particularly extreme ambivalence: a 'violently sexualized world totally lacking in desire, full of violent and violated bodies but curiously neutered'.[21] Bradley Butterfield attributes Baudrillard's fascination with the world Ballard creates in *Crash* to the fact that Ballard appears to be depicting in his fiction and initiating the reader into the 'world of total absorption into simulacra' that Baudrillard theorizes as a model for the twentieth century.[22] A world where everything has already been mediated or reproduced and where, following the blurring of such distinctions as conscious/unconscious or real/imaginary, it is the 'law of reciprocity' that governs.[23]

One might certainly argue that Ballard's inner space already contains within it the disaffection of the redemptive encounter with abjection it had ostensibly aimed at, for in the various collapses Ballard describes, all planes, whether corporeal, technological, or geometric, are brought into a radical equivalency with each other and each collapse is made reciprocal to all others. The crash wound, for example – the 'flayed body' that should bear the power of horror of the real – is made equivalent to all other intersections of planes such as the angle between two walls or sexual intercourse. If everything is equivalent to everything else, nothing holds any specific power of horror, hence the traumas that fail to traumatize in Ballard's texts. Rather than projecting a future, Ballard's radical 'new terrain' of inner space has apparently been reduced to reflecting the experience of late twentieth- and early twenty-first-century sociality and subjectivity wherein the corporeal, technological, psychical, and social overlap and collapse, and bodies and machines, wounded subjectivities and wounds, abjection and sociality are undifferentiated in an 'uninterrupted interface'.[24] The violence is disappointingly rendered, like the 'Festival of Atrocity Films' in *The Atrocity Exhibition*, and the wounds that populate our television screens, little more than 'sophisticated entertainment' (20), and instead of performing encounters with the abject, whether redemptive or crisis-laden, these novels have seemingly become exercises in the very pervasive inertia and death of affect Ballard had intended to resist.

On the other side of the mirror

It does not seem to me, however, that this is the whole story. Indeed, responses to the republication of Baudrillard's essay in *Science Fiction Studies* in 1991 criticized his reading for missing a fundamental dimension of Ballard's writing that does allow for some form of transcendence.[25] In Ballard's own response, the author states that he has 'not really wanted to understand' Baudrillard's reading of *Crash*.[26] Butterfield sees in this evasion 'a sense of dread or *Unheimlichkeit*' which he attributes to Baudrillard perhaps hitting 'too close to home'.[27] Benjamin Noys also perceives parallels between the two writers but attributes them to a shared belief that there still remains a 'radical alterity beyond representation' that can be accessed by truly 'radical crime' or transgression.[28] Certainly in Ballard's case, both *Crash* and *The Atrocity Exhibition* attest to this possibility of a remaining 'real'. In these novels, Ballard does not simply wallow in the exorbitance of the mass-mediated present, and his deployment of 'inner space' resists merely describing a return to, and reiteration of, the banalization of the space of abjection in the pathological public sphere. Instead he offers a way out of this inertia; the possibility of something that still has yet to be assimilated and simulated. In Ballard's texts a different kind of abjection looms with which he uses his writing to imagine a productive encounter in the mode of what I have termed the literature of abjection, in order to counter rather than succumb to the death of affect.

Though seeming to flatten everything out, the 'equivalent geometry' proposed in *The Atrocity Exhibition* is also described as 'renascent' and 'transcendental' and as a 'seismic upheaval', a rhetoric which suggests that the collision of planes does not simply produce a radical and affectless equivalency, but also gives birth to something (24, 41). Dr Nathan states that ' "[w]here these planes intersect, images are born, some kind of valid reality begins to clarify itself" ' (47). It is this birth and not simply the fusion of planes that Travis has been searching for. Something is missing from him – '[p]erhaps his soul, the capacity to achieve a state of grace' (36) - and his experimental collisions, reconceptualizations and 'alternate deaths' offer a 'measure of hope' (36) for they may redeem this grace for him. For example, the motorcade of crash cars he assembles 'recapitulates' the Apollo disaster not as simply another anaesthetizing equivalency, but with the intention of liberating or resurrecting the men who were trapped in the capsule (44, 48). Similarly, in *Crash* each of the sexual acts between James and Helen is not simply symptomatic of the deadening symmetries between crashes, sex acts and bodily geometries for they also: 'recapitulated her husband's death, re-seeding the image of his body in her vagina in terms of the hundred perspectives of our mouths and thighs, nipples and tongues within the metal and vinyl compartment of the car' (67). Likewise, the sex acts Vaughan uses to recapitulate the positions of crash victims are carried out because: 'the translation of these injuries was the only means of re-invigorating these wounded and dying victims' (146).

Here in my car . . .

Vaughan's, James' and Travis' obsessions with the car crash are therefore not simply for its potential to represent *in extremis* the collision of planes that constitutes contemporary sociality and subjectivity, but rather to provoke this re-invigoration. The interface invoked by the car crash collision is given particular significance because, as Ballard observes, the car is something most of the population will own and many will fetishize in some way. In *The Atrocity Exhibition*, Ballard scribbles an authorial note that describes the car as: 'an iconic entity that combines the elements of speed, power, dream and freedom within a highly stylized format that defuses any fears we may have of the inherent dangers of these violent and unstable machines' (97). The car is, in other words, the icon of the affectless mediated landscape of contemporary sociality and subjectivity, entirely stylized and embodying both absolute possibility and violence and the absence of any sense of the horror at this. Moreover, it is yet another point at which humans and technology intersect: the paradigm, as Baudrillard suggests, of the body as 'uninterrupted interface'.[29]

The car crash brings together the body and this paradigmatic form of technologized, mediated and interfaced existence, and, as such, it constitutes the most potent means of realizing the possibility of rebirth or re-invigoration held within these interfaces. This is why Ballard posits the car crash as: 'the most common dislocation of time and space the rest of us ever know' (44), why Dr Nathan observes that the car crash is ' "a fertilizing rather than destructive event" ' (23) and why, in *Crash*, James believes that a fatal crash for his wife, Catherine, would be 'the one event which would release the codes waiting within her' (139). Vaughan's persistent search for the perfect crash scenario is also motivated by the dream of this release for himself, and his ideal death is in a car crash with Elizabeth Taylor, for the celebrity – like the car – epitomizes contemporary sociality, intersecting public and private, the human and the media, to produce a highly stylized surface that is repeated over and over again in affectless, iconized images. A celebrity car crash would then offer the optimum conditions for the release Vaughan seeks. Indeed, James is convinced that Vaughan 'could never really die in a car-crash, but would in some way be reborn through those twisted radiator grilles and cascading windshield glass' (160). The last paragraph of the novel describes remnants of Vaughan's semen being carried by aircraft to 'the instrument panels and radiator grilles of a thousand crashing cars, the leg stances of a million passengers' (171): another act of fertilizing collision which, with its allusion to flight, also suggests the car crash offers up the possibility of rising above or transcending socio-symbolic restrictions – the very 'grace' Travis seeks. The crash with Miss Taylor would, Vaughan believes, 'transform all our dreams and fantasies. The man who dies in that crash with her...' (102). With this ellipsis Ballard leaves the exact nature of this future to the reader's imagination, purposefully refusing to articulate it in order to avoid its assimilation into the 'all-voracious present'. Nevertheless, something, as Adams argues, 'creeps and crawls out of' the crash;[30] something that enables the crash to take up a central place in a 'benevolent psychopathology' propounded in the texts whereby the car's 'deviant technology' – the possibility of a transcendent alterity – provides 'the sanction for any perverse act' (107).

There are some tentative allusions made to what might crawl out of the crashes in, for example, James' LSD-fuelled vision of wounds flowering into 'paradisial creatures' in a 'metallized [sic] Elysium' (152). Travis' 'presiding Trinity' of Xero, Coma, and Kline – 'personae of the unconscious' who 'run hot with a million programmes' (45) – also offer some kind of model for these 'paradisial creatures' as do the ghostly, elusive bomber pilot and radiation-scarred woman who follow Travis and who may be 'couriers from his own unconscious' (11). These latter two figures seem to be lingering remnants of past disasters – Hiroshima or Nagasaki – or of the past lives of Travis who himself was an H bomber and briefly dead 'in a technical sense' (36) which is what caused something to 'vanish' from him. The ghostly figures may also be echoes of a future as the pilot is described as a 'projection of World War Three's unknown soldier' (12). These figures evoke a sort of secularized immortality which is not simply that of living through the destitution of a subjectivity founded in abjection, but one in which there is a sort of excessive, obscenely replete life where all planes – temporal, spatial, technological, corporeal – have collided, releasing all codes or possibilities to produce a second life rather than second death. Apart from these ephemeral possibilities, however, whatever is generated by the crash collisions remains only implicit in the rhetoric of re-seeding, re-invigoration and fertility in both texts and is thereby retained as an impossibility or future towards which to aim. The collapsed boundaries therefore fail to traumatize in these novels not simply because the horror they once held has been made banal, but because this weight of abjection has been transferred onto something else which has yet to be revealed and subjected to the 'passion for the real'[31] and so still holds some sort of transcendent power or intensity.

With Ballard's newly formulated alterity, then, there is a degree of ambiguity for it is both abject in the sense that it lies beyond the borders of the subject, delimiting what it is not, but is also imagined as transcendent, almost sacred. This ambiguity emerges in Kristeva's own discussion of abjection and its relation to religion. For Kristeva, religious purification rites function to expel a particular element of the socio-symbolic system as filth or defilement – abjection – in order to maintain 'the "self and clean" of each social group if not of each subject'.[32] This act of expulsion founds a realm that transcends the socio-symbolic order and so, Kristeva argues, not only positions the 'filthy object' as abject, but also 'lines it at once with a sacred facet' so that '[a]s abjection – so the sacred'.[33] With Ballard, too, by ensuring the abject element is approached but ultimately excluded by his texts, this element is rendered simultaneously abject and sacred, and it is the crashes that facilitate this ritualized encounter with the abject. Gregory Stephenson compares them to sacrificial 'ancient fertility rites' that are catalysts to 'mystical experience and transcendence . . . a shamanistic release of fertilising, creative energy into the physical world and the spirit'.[34] It is Travis and Vaughan who sacrifice themselves through their ritualistic rehearsals of crashes (and of course Vaughan's own crash death) in order that this extraction of the abject/sacred can be performed. In doing so, both Travis and Vaughan position the loss of boundaries afflicting the twentieth-century socio-symbolic order not as an end but as an opening onto a space that is profane but also sacred and that offers purpose, meaning and redemption; a kind of secularized religiosity of which they, Christ-like, are the centre. Indeed, to compound this analogy, Dr Nathan observes that 'in twentieth-century terms the crucifixion, for example, would be re-enacted as conceptual auto-disaster', and Koester imagines a crash death for Travis which would constitute 'some kind of bizarre crucifixion' (26, 27). Vaughan's death is precisely such a crash crucifixion through which he expels himself into a transcendent alterity that establishes the order of both the abject and the sacred without allowing either to cross into the social order; the crash also paves the way for his 'disciples' – James, Catherine, Gabrielle – who, through their own crashes, have been, as Stephenson suggests, 'baptised' into the new faith.

Consequently, Ballard's texts do not simply mirror or photograph a sterile, disaffected subjectivity and sociality. If they photograph at all, it is in the mode of the chronograms Travis produces in *The Atrocity Exhibition*. Whilst E. J. Marey's chronographs captured several phases of movement on one photographic surface such that the two-dimensional, flat surface would seem to become almost three-dimensional, Travis' 'brilliant feat' was, Dr Nathan states, ' "to reverse the process" ':

> 'Using a series of photographs of the most common-place objects – this office, let us say, a panorama of New York skyscrapers, the naked body of a woman, the face of a catatonic patient – he treated them as if they already were chronograms and *extracted* the element of time. . . . A very different world was revealed'.
>
> (12)

In other words, Travis treats one photograph as if it already contained a multiple exposure or several phases of movement. For example, his close-ups of Elizabeth Taylor's face focus on the intersections of contours, angles and surfaces of her face and body which are conceived as 'the primary act of intercourse, the first apposition of the dimensions of time and space' (56); a fertilizing event rather than a static image. Travis' photography of collisions is therefore not intended simply to emphasize the deadening and inert equivalencies of the socio-symbolic order, but, rather, to draw out the movement latent in this order towards some other, transcendent form of being such as that which is found by going through the crash collisions. This is precisely what Ballard's minimalist, stylized 'photography' of the present day is intended to achieve. His texts can be understood as multiple exposure chronograms, capturing all stages of the collisions between bodies, architecture, geometries and machines to reveal what he perceives to be the movement held within them towards one more remaining alterity.[35]

The wound as a gateway

The possibility of some remaining form of intensity or impossibility beyond the intersections of planes accounts for the sexualization of the wound in Ballard's texts. Here the wound – whether a bodily one or a conceptual one where planes intersect – is not limited to Seltzer's mimetic relays where it would simply represent the collapses of the already everyday abjection that has come to constitute subjectivity in the pathological public sphere. Ballard brings an alternative significance to the 'mimetization' in which the wound is engaged in his novels, bringing it to denote, as Vic Sage suggests, more than simply Baudrillardian simulation or virtualization where a loss (of the object) is masked or disguised. It is also, or instead, 'what is self-consciously presented as simultaneously subjective fantasy and "historical event" '.[36] That is, part of a generative rather than degenerative process, where something new is imagined to arise each time the wound is repeated or reconceived. Consequently, though Baudrillard may be quite justified in stating that there is no desire for the bodies in the texts, this does not mean there is no desire at all or, indeed, that the bodies are simply affectless, alienated ciphers. Vivian Sobchack is critical of Baudrillard's interpretation of the body in *Crash* which, she argues, denies the *'lived', 'felt'* and 'real' body in favour of one that is only imagined and thought.[37] Writing her response to Baudrillard's essay whilst recovering from major cancer surgery on her thigh, Sobchack stresses the *'scandal'* of this dissociation from the reality of the body and particularly the wounded, pain-ridden body.[38] Roger Luckhurst also emphasizes the significance of the opened body but views it as indicative of the 'obsessively phallic' nature of *Crash* where the wound, as a fetish, 'disavows and displaces – but also affirms – the lacking phallus'.[39] He perceives a particular focus in Ballard's texts on the wounded woman and even an underlying aggression towards women, particularly in *The Atrocity Exhibition*. For Luckhurst this is due to Ballard's position as the male avant-garde figure of the 'transgressive son' who 'enacts his violent refusal [of the Father's Law] over the body of the woman'.[40] As the object of the Father's prohibition, the woman embodies some form of truth and so 'she must be *mutilated*, ripped open, in order to reveal it', that is, to reveal the phallus.[41]

Though I would certainly agree that the open body is, in Ballard's texts, the pathway to a truth still missing from the socio-symbolic order which one may well view in terms of the phallus, Luckhurst seems to have placed undue emphasis on the specifics of the body in question. In Ballard's texts it is the collision, intersection or opening of the body to another 'plane' that is desired, and it does not matter whether the intersections are between man, woman, car, staircase, or fuselage, for any combination could potentially generate the emergence of this remaining 'Elysium' (152). This certainly makes the wounded body the focus of a great deal of intensity of feeling as Sobchack calls for, but her own experience of the crash between technology and her body via her surgery explicitly denies any erotic possibilities. In Ballard, however, the wounded body is not just a site of aggression and suffering. Commenting on images of crashed bodies he encountered in his research, Ballard acknowledges the 'enormous price' but suggests nevertheless that these bodies had become 'mythical beings in a way that is only attainable in these brutal acts' for with their wounds the 'skin of reality and convention' had been broken.[42] The wounded body is an essential facet of the 'benevolent psychopathology' his texts propound (107), a gateway to the myriad possibilities generated by the fertilizing collisions: 'In our wounds we celebrated the rebirth of the traffic-slain dead' (155).

Accordingly, Gabrielle's car-crash-scarred, deformed and transformed body encased in its metal framework and Vaughan's scarred, blood- and semen-stained body, as opposed to Catherine's perfect, immaculately clean one, are the central images of the new sexuality propounded in these texts. When James first sees the photographs of Gabrielle, he observes that her crash: 'had turned her into a creature of free and perverse sexuality, releasing . . . all the deviant possibilities of her sex. Her crippled thighs and wasted calf muscles were models for fascinating perversities' (79). And when James has sex with Gabrielle all of the depressions, grooves and markings left by her supports are eroticized into: 'templates for new genital organs, the moulds for sexual possibilities yet to be created in a hundred experimental car crashes' (136). Her position in her 'invalid car' emphasizes these possibilities. Even more stylized than conventional cars, it draws attention to her own new form as a hybrid of body, braces and surgical supports; countless intersections and collisions that will provide a 'readily accessible anthology of depraved acts, the keys to an alternative sexuality' focused round the new possibility of transcendence (80). Similarly, Vaughan's multiple scars act as 'handholds' for James, signs of intersections and wounds that guide James up a 'ladder of desperate excitement' (129), towards the potential that would be released in the full crash wound.

Literature of abjection

The Atrocity Exhibition and *Crash* propose a new passion to replace the exhausted 'passion for the real', a belief in a remaining possibility of transcendence that would provide a sense of hope, purpose and vitality in place of inertia and disaffection. As Ballard himself states, his characters are driven 'by a dream of a perfectible world – a better world, in a moral sense – where everything will make sense', a world in which 'there is some sort of truth to be found'.[43] Or, to re-phrase slightly, a world in which not everything has been found.

It is precisely this vitality that Baudrillard appears to miss in his reading of *Crash* which he seems to position as a historical document of a twentieth century suffering from a loss of the tabooed Other that would confer limits upon the subject and stalled in disaffection. As Sage stresses, however, such a reading takes Ballard too literally, replacing metaphor with metonymy and converting analogy into reflection. Ballard is not describing where we are but where we might go. His crash sexuality consists of 'imaginary perversions', 'the horrific invention of the Other'.[44] It is in this suggestion, that there is still something to be imagined, that the 'initiatory power' of Ballard's fiction lies. The invention of this 'horrific Other' – abjection – and, moreover, the maintenance of its position elsewhere reinstates the possibility of transcendence that Baudrillard, perhaps rightly, presumes to be lacking in contemporary culture but, wrongly, also believes to be lacking in Ballard's writing. It also prevents these novels from being fully abject themselves. Instead, *The Atrocity Exhibition* and *Crash* can be considered as the literature of abjection which is the very mode of writing that Kristeva locates as the 'aesthetic task' in 'a world in which the Other has collapsed'.[45] Ballard's texts approach a re-imagined abject but do not quite expose it. They thereby retrace and re-assert the missing limits of the socio-symbolic order and so are still able to offer that 'redemptive and therapeutic' power Ballard sought.

Notes

1. J. G. Ballard, 'Introduction to the French Edition of *Crash*' [1974], in J. G. Ballard *Crash* (London: Triad/Panther Books, 1985), pp. 5–9 (p. 7). Further page references are provided within the text.
2. J. G. Ballard 'The Coming of the Unconscious' in *New Worlds*, 50:163 (July 1966). http://www.jgballard.ca/non_fiction/jgb_reviews_surrealism.html, accessed 10 June 2010.
3. J .G. Ballard, 'The Coming of the Unconscious'.
4. V. Burgin, 'Geometry and Abjection', in J. Fletcher and A. Benjamin, eds, *Abjection, Melancholia and Love: The Work of Julia Kristeva* (London and New York: Routledge, 1990), pp. 104–23 (p. 115).
5. J. G. Ballard, *The Atrocity Exhibition*, V. Vale and Andrea Juno, eds, (San Francisco: RE/Search Publications, 1990 [1970]), p. 34. Further page references are provided within the text.
6. Burgin, 'Geometry and Abjection', p. 108.
7. Burgin, 'Geometry and Abjection', p. 115.
8. Julia Kristeva, *Powers of Horror: An Essay on Abjection*, trans. by L. S. Roudiez (New York: Columbia University Press, 1982), p. 4.
9. Jacques Lacan, *The Seminar of Jacques Lacan Book VII: The Ethics of Psychoanalysis 1959–1960*, trans. D. Porter, ed. J. A. Miller (London: Routledge, 1992), p. 216.
10. Kristeva, *Powers of Horror*, p. 18.
11. 'The original *Times* review of *Crash* by J. G. Ballard', originally published 28 June 1973, re-printed in *Times Online*, 19 December 2007, http://entertainment.timesonline.co.uk/tol/arts_and_entertainment/books/article3073540.ece , accessed 10 June 2010.
12. S. Sandhu, 'J. G. Ballard: A love affair with speed and violence' *The Daily Telegraph*, 27 April 2009, http://www.telegraph.co.uk, accessed 10 June 2010.
13. Parveen Adams, 'Death Drive' in M. Grant, ed., *The Modern Fantastic: The Films of David Cronenberg* (Westport: Praeger Publishers, 2000), pp. 102–22 (p. 108).
14. Mark Seltzer, *Serial Killers: Death and Life in America's Wound Culture* (New York and London: Routledge, 1998), p. 270.
15. Slavoj Žižek, *Welcome to the Desert of the Real* (London and New York: Verso, 2002), p. 12.
16. Jean Baudrillard, 'The Ecstasy of Communication' in H. Foster, ed., *The Anti-Aesthetic: Essays on Postmodern Culture* (Washington: Bay Press, 1983), pp. 126–34 (p. 127).
17. Seltzer, *Serial Killers*, p. 264.
18. C. Goodwin, 'Sitting Comfortably?' in *The Sunday Times* 15 April 2007, pp. 6–7 (p. 6).
19. S. Crook, '*Hostel Part II*: Is this the end of the road for Gorno?' in *Empire* (August 2007), p. 42.

20. Kristeva, *Powers of Horror*, p. 208.
21. J. Baudrillard, 'Ballard's *Crash*', trans., by Arthur B. Evans in *Science Fiction Studies*, 55 (November 1991), 313–20 (p. 319).
22. B. Butterfield, 'Ethical Value and Negative Aesthetics: Reconsidering the Baudrillard-Ballard Connection' in *PMLA*, 114:1 (January 1999), 64–77 (p. 71).
23. Butterfield, 'Ethical Value and Negative Aesthetics', 72.
24. Baudrillard, 'The Ecstasy of Communication', p. 127.
25. See N. Katherine Hayles et al, 'In Response to Jean Baudrillard' in *Science Fiction Studies*, 55 (November 1991), 321–29.
26. J. G. Ballard, 'A Response to the Invitation to Respond' in *Science Fiction Studies*, 55 (November 1991), 329.
27. Butterfield, 'Ethical Value and Negative Aesthetics', 65.
28. B. Noys, 'Better Living Through Psychopathology' 16 May 2010, www.ballardian.com, accessed 9 June 2010. Noys believes this invocation of a ' "real" alterity' by Baudrillard actually 'steps back from' what he himself perceives to be the radical banality of transgression.
29. Baudrillard, 'The Ecstasy of Communication', p. 127.
30. Adams, 'Death Drive', p. 109.
31. Žižek, *Welcome to the Desert of the Real*, p. 12.
32. Kristeva, *Powers of Horror*, p. 65.
33. Kristeva, *Powers of Horror*, p. 17.
34. Gregory Stephenson, *Out of the Night and Into the Dream: A Thematic Study of the Fiction of J. G. Ballard* (New York, Westport, Connecticut, London: Greenwood Press, 1991), pp. 68–9.
35. Corin Depper also comments on the analogy between Ballard's writing and chronophotography with particular reference to *The Atrocity Exhibition*. However, he argues that Ballard should not be compared with Marey but rather with 'that other pioneer of chronophotography, Eadweard Muybridge'. Muybridge presented motion through a 'decomposition of separate fragments' rather than a 'fluid movement' caught in one photography plate as in Marey. I, on the other hand, would argue that it is precisely in Ballard's desire to merge planes together and draw out fertile combinations that distinguishes him from Muybridge and draws him closer to Marey. The separation of stages of movement Muybridge produced presents a series of figures caught in static poses and, as Depper states, 'destined to live out in perpetuity a time of cyclical movement' and it is this stalling that Ballard is writing against. See C. Depper, 'Death at Work: The Cinematic Imagination of J. G. Ballard', in Jeannette Baxter, ed., *J. G. Ballard: Contemporary Critical Perspectives* (London: Continuum, 2008), pp. 50–65 (pp. 53–5).
36. V. Sage, 'The Gothic, the Body, and the Failed Homeopathy Argument: Reading *Crash*' in Jeannette Baxter, ed., *J. G. Ballard* (London: Continuum, 2008), pp. 34–49 (pp. 48–9, footnote 3).
37. V. Sobchack, 'Baudrillard's Obscenity' in 'In Response to Jean Baudrillard', 327–9 (327). Emphasis in original.
38. Sobchack, 'Baudrillard's Obscenity', 328. Emphasis in original.
39. Roger Luckhurst, *'The Angle Between Two Walls': The Fiction of J.G. Ballard* (Liverpool: Liverpool University Press, 1997), pp. 112–13.
40. Luckhurst, *'The Angle Between Two Walls'*, p. 108.

41. Luckhurst, 'The Angle Between Two Walls', p. 109.
42. J. G. Ballard interview with Graeme Revell in *RE/Search* 8/9, (San Francisco: RE/Search Publications, 1984), pp. 42–52, (p. 47).
43. Ballard, interview with Graeme Revell in *RE/Search* 8/9, p. 45.
44. Sage, 'Reading *Crash*', pp. 34–49 (pp. 45–7).
45. Kristeva, *Powers of Horror*, p. 18.

6
Reading Posture and Gesture in Ballard's Novels

Dan O'Hara

Whatever Ballard's strengths may be, it is a critical commonplace that he cannot produce plausible characters. Critics of all kinds have been less than charitable about his ability to characterize convincingly, largely viewing his characters as either so much dead wood or as mere spokespeople for Ballard's own views. Martin Amis, for example, has always found Ballard's characterization wanting, 'hardly more than a gesture' in *Concrete Island* (1974), whereas in *High-Rise* (1975) 'his characterization is merely a matter of "roles" and his situations merely a matter of "context" '. In reviewing *Hello America* (1981), Amis considers that Ballard's 'eye for the comedy of human variety is non-existent, and this is why landscape naturally dominates his fiction'.[1] It is a view shared by critics: Colin Greenland believes that 'Ballard parades his disregard for characterisation',[2] and even the possibly most sympathetic of Ballard's critics, David Punter, confirms the 'strong erasure of character' in Ballard's fictions, although he sees this absence of 'enclosed and unitary subjectivity', supplanted by 'retailed narratives' of media stereotypes, as one of Ballard's uniquely post-structuralist strengths.[3]

Ballard himself has of course inveighed against the social novel and its concerns, including its method of Realist characterization. By his own criteria, the critical consensus judges Ballard against the wrong yardstick; we cannot fully appreciate his innovations if we measure his fictions against the inappropriate conventions of realism. David Punter's reading places Ballard beyond such criticism, appropriately – yet in practice it seems that Ballard's characters do not merely fit into preformed stereotypes, or 'roles', as Martin Amis would have it, even if his characters appear to aspire to the reduced behavioural spectrum of the movie star, the political icon, or the mass-murderer. The gap between what Ballard's characters actually are and what they desire to be remains unaccounted for in these readings, all of which tend to reduce the characters to mere expressions of pre-determined media-marketed fantasies.

A reading method of initially disregarding dialogue as a means of misdirection from the real action works well in much of Ballard's fiction from the early 1970s onwards. By looking at the interrelations of inanimate objects, postures, gestures and contexts, we obtain a better idea of what shapes not only Ballard's characterization but also his narrative structure, prose, and ideas. The active elements of Ballard's brand of anti-characterization – of gestures, roles and contexts – are systematically organized, and any meaning to be found in his characterization resides in the formal system, not the individual agents. What is damaged or altered in Ballard's fictional worlds is the set of abstract relations between characters, a situation that has required him to devise a method of non-Realist characterization – and once his method is understood, we are in a better position to evaluate the real meanings which lie latent behind each line of dialogue.

But what is this method? Colin Greenland notes Ballard's use of the 'minutiae of Kinesics, the analysis of gesture and posture popularly known as "body language"', but believes that his 'Characters are flat and functional, their humanity subordinated to their values as roles or signs', a view which would preclude any analysis of gestural relation as signification.[4] Greenland's view undoubtedly holds true for some of Ballard's novels: one thinks particularly of *High-Rise*, in which the architect Anthony Royal, the protagonist Dr. Robert Laing, and the television producer Richard Wilder respectively play the roles of the Freudian superego, ego and id of the high-rise itself, 'as if it were some kind of huge animate presence',[5] with these three principal players the embodied hypostatic union of a mental battle raging within the skyscraper's mind. Yet the rest of Ballard's opus does not seem so programmatic, so easily decoded; and to equate 'Laing' with the ego, amid the more obvious and banal associations of *roya*lty with the superego and *wild*ness with the id, suggests that the name 'Laing' has a specific resonance for Ballard – as indeed it does. The evident correspondence with the psychiatrist R. D. Laing has been noted elsewhere: Peter Brigg has suggested that the *High-Rise* protagonist 'may be named in honour of R. D. Laing, who through the 1960's and on into the early 1970's contended that many forms of insanity were socially defined',[6] though he misses the fact that *High-Rise* was not the first fiction in which Ballard invoked Laing's name; a 'Dr Laing' is one of the three central characters in 'My Dream of Flying to Wake Island' (1974), a short story first published the year before *High-Rise*.[7]

More recently, both Gregory Stephenson and Roger Luckhurst have noted rather more substantial parallels between R. D. Laing's radical anti-psychiatric theories and Ballard's own views on the relation of the individual to society. As Stephenson remarks:

> Both share the notion that we are profoundly ambivalent with regard to our individual identities and our collective social identity, that we are clinging determinedly, apprehensively, to an illusion while at the same time forces within our psyches are working to overturn that illusion. Both writers also share the belief that 'breakdown' and 'break-through' are inextricably intertwined, that what may appear to be madness or disaster may be, as Laing phrases it, 'veritable manna from heaven'.[8]

Luckhurst sees a broader connexion between the two, suggesting that Laing's work in psychiatry was part of an existentialist Zeitgeist in the 1950s and 60s, and therefore one of the discourses that, with Albert Camus' novels which 'seem largely concerned with the relation of the central figure to that landscape rather than the affectless relations between humans', and Heidegger's forgotten ' "unthinkable" relation between existence and its inaccessible ground: Being', inform Ballard's own preoccupations.[9]

Certainly to read Laing's *The Politics of Experience* (1967) is to encounter a remarkably Ballardian tone and rhetoric, and Luckhurst quotes from that book to demonstrate the consanguinity:

> We are far more out of touch with even the nearest approaches of inner space than we now are with the reaches of outer space. We respect the voyager, the climber, the space man. It makes more sense to me as a valid project – indeed, as a desperately urgently required project for our time, to explore the inner space and time of our consciousness.[10]

But the correspondence is perhaps even more substantial than mere confluence, and a closer examination of R. D. Laing's writings suggests that Ballard did more than simply borrow Laing's name for his characters, or absorb the air of existentialism in the 1960s. Laing first became notorious in the 1960s for his espousal and promulgation of the concept of the double bind, a psychological theory proposed first by Gregory Bateson in 1956.

The term 'double bind' denotes an unresolvable position in which a person finds him/herself. In any situation where the subject is psychologically trapped, prevented from escape by ties of loyalty, family, employment and the like – in short, in any power relationship – the instigator of the double bind communicates simultaneously two mutually contradictory messages to the subject. One of these messages is verbal, usually an injunction *not* to do something, with an implied or explicit threat. The other message is more abstract, contextual, perhaps an intimation of love, and is non-verbal: 'Posture, gesture, tone of voice, meaningful action and the implications concealed in verbal comment may all be used to convey this abstract message.'[11] Bateson describes these secondary messages as belonging to a class of 'metacommunicative signals',[12] implying an entire category of non-verbal metacommunication (some aspects of which may be understood by the common term 'body language', although this term falls short of an adequate description of the system of metacommunication in Ballard's writings). Bateson's original view in 1956 was that repeated exposure to such psychological *impasses* might be schizogenetic – that is, that the double bind might be the causal trauma in cases of schizophrenia; but by 1961, R. D. Laing was already observing that such situations were rather more ubiquitous than Bateson had suggested, and that the double bind was a banal fact of everyday family life.[13]

Did Ballard read either Bateson's original 1956 paper on the double bind, or one of Laing's papers published in the late 1950s on collusive relationships? Or perhaps Laing's major work, *The Divided Self*, published in 1960? We cannot know for certain,[14] though the incorporation of Laing's name into *High-Rise* and 'My Dream of Flying to Wake Island' indicates at least a familiarity. It's certainly the case that he was reading such matter: he has spoken in interviews of how a friend, Dr. Christopher Evans, a computer scientist at the National Physical Laboratory, sent him a regular parcel of the contents of his waste paper basket, having noticed Ballard's interest in such things. The basket held out-of-date psychiatric journals, case studies, scientific bulletins and the like.[15]

I would contend that the double bind in fact plays a crucial part in Ballard's fiction, generating a clinical style, a method of characterization, a logic of relations, and even providing and determining the type of setting of the earlier novels and short stories. In particular, Ballard's novels from the late 1980s onwards regard the environment of technology as an immense double-bind context. *Running Wild* (1988), in its focus upon the murderous revolt of a group of children against their manipulative and affluent parents, seems specifically designed to provide an opportunity for an examination of the double-bind act. We are all familiar, no doubt, with the predicament of the child whose father insists: 'This is going to hurt me more than it's going to hurt you', a statement that rather contradicts the painful evidence of the child's subsequent experience. The metacommunicative framing which so often accompanies corporal punishment – the parent's expression of sorrow, of loving and sometimes even tearful reluctance – contradicts, from the child's point of view, the act of physical chastisement. In *Running Wild*, it would seem that the conventional requirements for the context – a parent and a child – are absent: the parents are already dead; the children are missing, presumed kidnapped. The psychiatrist narrator, Richard Greville, must piece together the evidence without the aid of witnesses. The traces the inhabitants have left behind – closed-circuit television recordings, home-made videos, computer documents – are, with the exception of the parents' bodies, the only indications of their lives and activities. Yet, even given the absence of parents and children, the novella is replete with instances of the contradictions that characterize the double bind.

This absence of characters in fact permits Ballard to focus purely upon the metacommunicative elements of posture, environment and technology. The first and most dramatic postures he depicts are those of the dead bodies of the parents, as seen through the diegetic eye of a police camera. Greville interprets the video for the reader: he notes how, as one of the murdered fathers, Roger Garfield, sits patiently in his car, 'Perhaps his clouding mind still assumed that he would be driven to his office in the City of London.'[16] His chauffeur, Mr Poole, lies 'cap still held in his right hand'; Mrs Garfield is in the shower stall, 'her yellow toothbrush still in her hand' (8). The physical attitudes of the corpses, lying where they have fallen, should carry no meaning, yet Greville finds that after watching it, he has 'exhausted [his] central nervous system with the police video' (11). The key phrase is the reference to the central nervous system: Greville has not exhausted his emotional response, but has been challenged at a more fundamental level by this postural display, its overload of apparent intentional meaning emphasized by the 'minimalist style of camera-work' (4). Reason tells Greville that these mannequins are corpses; but his nervous system continues to interpret them as intentional objects.[17]

The children themselves are also revealed solely through the traces of their normal activities: Jeremy Maxted's bedroom contains a 'surf board and swimming trophies', the sight of which prompts Greville to reflect that 'He must have swum miles in that pool downstairs. Jeremy was the bedwetter' (36), drawing attention once again to the links Ballard implies between beds, dreams, water and the unconscious. The implication here is that Jeremy Maxted is a child more in thrall to his primordial and unconscious self than to the constructed identity of a teenager who surfs and wins trophies. The hint thus given, Ballard reveals the double-bind act, as on the computer screen in Jeremy's room a message flashes from his parents:

47 lengths today!

There was a pause, and then:

Well done, Jeremy!

(36)

What is apparent from this comment of congratulations is that the children's every action is monitored by cameras, in what Greville describes as 'surveillance of the heart' (22).

According to the logic of the double bind, the status of this message is as it seems: a congratulation and an encouragement. Yet the metacommunicative framing – of posture, gesture, tone of voice – is absent, or rather is filled by the machinic system of computerized surveillance and communication. If the reader is left to 'fill in' the tone of the message upon the screen – as Jeremy himself must – it may be read as kind, but equally well may be read as sarcastic or patronizing. Hence the system is set up to trail the kind of ambiguity that characterizes the double-bind context: the message says simultaneously 'I care' and 'I do not care'; encouragement becomes identical with a warning of punishment: 'I am watching you...'.

In *Running Wild* the specific targets of these mediated double binds are children, yet children are largely absent from Ballard's later novels, as these deal with exclusively adult worlds, the expatriate gated communities and corporate villages where careers take the place of parenthood. As with Ballard's characterization, the sheen of artificiality this lends the later novels is less an attribute of the fiction itself than of the environments the fiction represents. In these worlds Ballard suggests a more general prevalence of such mediated encounters and indeed a nascent preference for them. In *Millennium People* (2003), another of his psychologists, David Markham, helps to develop a new diagnostic system:

Instead of facing a tired consultant eager for a large gin and a hot bath, the patient sat at a screen, pressing buttons in reply to pre-recorded questions from a fresh-faced and smiling doctor, played by a sympathetic actor. To the consultants' surprise, and relief, the patients preferred the computerized image to a real physician.[18]

It would seem that the children of *Running Wild* mature into adults who need all affect carefully contained within the static metacommunicative frame of a computer. Yet, in one of the patients subjected to the new system, the pathology of Bateson's schizophrenic, who absorbs and duplicates the double-bind act, develops as soon as she establishes a relationship with the real doctor behind the screen, Markham. The mimicry, inversion of appearance and reality, and manipulative doubling of the double-bind context are all played out in full as Markham's ploy of presenting himself as a digital avatar rebounds on him, as if he finds himself infected by a virus which he administered to his patient:

> she was amazed to find that I existed. Over the next days her good humour returned, and she enjoyed mimicking my wooden acting. As I sat on her bed she teased me that I was not completely real. We talked to each other in our recorded voices, a courtship of imbeciles that I was careful not to take seriously.
>
> (24)

In actualizing their virtual selves, incarnating their simulations, Markham and his patient Sally take on the constraints of a behavioural grammar defined by the limitations of the diagnostic machine.

A corollary to the inversion of appearance and reality is the further and final Batesonian inversion: that of the metaphorical and the literal. Perhaps the most immediate way to test the applicability of this inversion to Ballard's novels is to look at his presentation of humour, as it is one of Bateson's most prominent and defined metacommunicational 'contexts': not the extra-diegetic irony of the author, who is presumably unaffected by the psychopathologies he describes, nor any situational comedy of plot, all of which must be contrived without any reference to any pre-theorized Batesonian structure, but solely the humour found in character behaviour and dialogue – in other words, that which we could reasonably expect the characters themselves to find amusing. Bateson suggests that the initial effect of the double bind is to make the subject 'respond defensively', and, most often, *literally*:

> An individual will take a metaphorical statement literally when he is in a situation where he must respond, where he is faced with contradictory messages, and when he is unable to comment on the contradictions... This is characteristic of anyone who feels 'on the spot', as demonstrated by the careful literal replies of a witness on the stand in a court trial.[19]

Bateson suggested that the schizophrenic develops a pathology founded upon this literalist strategy, in which the subject confuses the literal and the metaphorical, often not only responding to a joke in an apparently painstaking, analytically literal manner, but also expressing the most literal, mundane sentiments or ideas in an abstruse metaphorical code.

In consonance with Bateson's theory, it seems that by and large Ballard's characters, schizophrenic or not, respond to any joking or humour in a literal manner. No-one laughs in Ballard's novels. Instead, we encounter the occasional 'stage laugh' or 'playful... punch', delivered with 'mocking cheer'.[20] The form of humour which predominates is *teasing*, as shown above: that slightly aggressive form which requires its instigator to simulate shock when calm, disapproval when one approves, callousness when one cares. Casual, joking asides are to be taken literally: when, in *Super-Cannes* (2000), Wilder Penrose says to the narrator, Paul Sinclair, ' "I'll borrow your wife" ' (14), we should expect the truth to be hiding behind the lie of the joke. Elsewhere, Paul Sinclair's wife Jane tells Penrose that she likes Eden-Olympia, the business community which they are joining, ' "Because there isn't any culture. All this alienation... I could easily get used to it" ' (15). Paul himself knows that his wife 'was teasing the psychiatrist' (15), but Penrose's response is either the stoic straight face of the corporate automaton, or the literalizing miscomprehension of the schizophrenic. Ballard makes the two seem much the same thing:

> 'That's misleading.' Penrose pointed to two nearby office buildings, each only six storeys high but effectively a skyscraper lying on its side. 'They're all at their computer screens and lab benches.'
>
> (15)

Penrose typifies Ballard's symmetrical characters with all their apparently reductive contradictions. His actions conform not only to the literalizing habit described above, but also exemplify the kind of double-bind act which Ballard represents as underpinning the social interactions between all his characters. Physical postures and gestures convey distinct and often opposing signals to the messages contained in dialogue; for example: 'Penrose pressed his large hands against the roof, and lazily flexed his shoulders. "I prefer to exercise the mind"' (17–18). This kind of self-contradiction, already implicit in the double-bind act, gives rise to characters of vivid and obvious, almost clichéd contrasts, whose descriptions lend themselves to the neat and easily pastiched epithet: in this case, the muscular psychiatrist. The formula is not complex; Ballard's achievement is to reduce it to an equation, and treat it as such.

This apparently reductive strategy cashes out as a generator of prose that is of necessity unusually shorn of ornament. Every word is purely *functional* in Ballard's best writing: the reader must pay attention, by and large, less to the dialogue than to the precise descriptions of the actions and gestures that accompany it. This is less tractable in practice than it sounds as, in a strange combination of behavioural psychology and dramatic irony, Ballard's diegetic narratives are often concerned with his first-person narrator's *unconscious* perceptions and, as a consequence, we must watch the postural dispositions of the characters in order to discern the thoughts of which *they themselves* are unaware.

In *Crash* (1973), Ballard leaves the prepositional to stand in for the abstract, so that the language of physical, spatial relations – *on, in, under, on top of, behind* – serves as a code for the more metaphysical human relations of love, hatred, desire and so on, all of which are conspicuously absent. Ballard's use of this device, which is common in late Elizabethan poetry but hardly in the modern novel, is suggestive. Where similar prepositional devices occur in John Donne's poetry, as for example in his 'Elegie: To his Mistris Going to Bed' – 'Licence my roving hands, and let them goe, / Before, behind, between, above, below. / O my America! My new-found-lande'[21] – they are evidence, according to T. S. Eliot, of a now-lost 'direct sensuous apprehension of thought, or a recreation of thought into feeling'.[22] Following Eliot, one might describe *Crash* as an attempt to recover this apprehension of thought as an experience in itself; and perhaps even as an attempt at the re-unification of sensibility.

One early episode in *Crash* is particularly suggestive of this attempt. As James Ballard drives Helen Remington to the airport, he orgasms on their approach towards the location at which they first met – the scene of their crash, in which Remington's husband died:

> The arch of the flyover rose against the skyline, its northern ramp shielded by the white rectangle of a plastics factory. The untouched, rectilinear volumes of this building fused in my mind with the contours of her calves and thighs pressed against the vinyl seating.

> Clearly unaware that we were moving towards our original meeting ground, Helen Remington crossed and uncrossed her legs, shifting these white volumes as the front elevations of the plastics factory moved past.
>
> The pavement fell away below us. We sped towards the junction with the Drayton Park motorway spur. She steadied herself against the chromium pillar of the quarter-window, almost dropping her cigarette on to her lap. Trying to control the car, I pressed the head of my penis against the lower rim of the steering wheel. The car swept towards its first impact point with the central reservation. Marker lines unravelled diagonally below us, and a car's horn blared faintly from behind my shoulder. The drifts of broken windshield glass flashed like morse lamps in the sunlight.[23]

It is at this precise point that James Ballard orgasms. That the re-creation of his original, deadly crash with Helen Remington and her husband should prompt such a morbid and excessive physical response suggests an abnormal psychological state. Yet the passage is unusually precise and sensually rich in its descriptions of James Ballard's perceptions which, after the shapes of the plastics factory and Helen Remington's legs 'fused in [his] mind', become especially acute. The repetition of the word 'volumes', first used to refer to the white buildings, then to Remington's white legs, signals the conflation of the two in James' visual imagination. The pattern of prepositions, mapped from the first paragraph onto the second, describes a synaesthetic symmetry. The flyover rises *against*; the ground falls away *below*, in a simple sexual symbol of male ascendant and female compliant union. Helen Remington's legs are pressed *against* the seating; she leans *against* the pillar; James instinctively, unconsciously mimics her, sympathetically pressing his penis *against* the steering wheel. The car moves both *towards* the scene of their first meeting, and their crash; and in doing so, progresses in James' mind less *towards* the diagonals of the marker lines on the road than towards the diagonals of Helen Remington's crossed and uncrossed legs. The force of his 'direct sensuous apprehension of thought' is enough to produce his physical reaction.

Later in the novel, as James is once again driving whilst Vaughan has sex with a prostitute in the back seat, he begins to realize a degree of sympathetic union with others through his newly-reunified sensibility: 'I realized that I could almost control the sexual act behind me by the way in which I drove the car' (144). It is a moment of reflective and critical intensity, that which Eliot identifies as a 'dissociation of sensibility' affecting poetry in the seventeenth century and thereafter corresponds to what Laing diagnoses as a more widespread cultural malaise of the 'divided self' in the twentieth century. Ballard here addresses both of these alleged ruptures and attempts to propose a resolution. This attempt to reconnect with an immediate experience of thought in fact accords with Ballard's aforementioned scepticism about the value of the conventional Realist novel, a genre which coincides historically with the period Eliot specifies. *Pace* Eliot, it is the novel which is *the* dissociated genre. In *Crash*, Ballard is not only attempting to recuperate a lost manner of thought and feeling, but also trying to retrieve the novel-as-genre from its lack of poeticism. The key to identifying these moments in Ballard's fictions lies in isolating the material symbols – postures, gestures, and physical attitudes, whether of beings or objects – to which his prepositions refer.

However, fiction more generally employs physical symbolism as an adjunct to, or illustration of, an open display of social events. One exemplary instance occurs in Chapter 23 of *Persuasion* (1817): Jane Austen's careful and measured employment of Captain Wentworth's pen during the writing of his confession of love for Anne Elliot renders the physical object subordinate to the unfolding of the social drama; the dropped pen is the sole symbolic element in the episode. A more recent example would be the capture and slaughter of the sow in William Golding's *Lord of the Flies* (1954), in which the inchoate libidinal desires of the boys, and the secondary significance of the slaughter as a rape, is conveyed by the careful placement of remarkably few objects which the reader must track over the course of a few pages. Roger's spear, and its precise placement, is all that hints at more than an admittedly bloody hunt for food. All other elements of the scene – forest, butterflies, and flowers – are symbolically inactive, mere background to the psychosexual drama.

These two episodes are remarkable in their respective novels. Austen heralds the climax of her novel with the pen's symbolism; Golding presents the 'rape' of the sow as a pivotal moment in his. Both Austen and Golding decipher their own symbolism for us, within their own narratives, whether it be with the printing of a letter or by means of dialogue. Yet what is remarkable in these novels becomes merely part of the *mise-en-scène* in Ballard's fiction, and remains undeciphered within the narrative. *All* that exists has significance; no object is psychically inert. Every movement and posture holds *a priori* the level of significance granted to Wentworth's pen or Roger's spear; and all these movements, gestures and objects interact.

116   *'The Angle Between Two Walls': Sex, Geometry and the Body*

Perhaps the most complete example of this artistic method is to be found in Chapter 7 of *Super-Cannes*, in which Paul Sinclair brings the bullets he has found to his wife Jane's office. In reading this chapter, one must pay attention not to the dialogue but to these bullets. If we focus purely upon the diegetic narrative, without considering the contradictions expressed in the dialogue, we witness a distinct layer of signification from that which is apparent on first reading:

> 'Jane watched me as I leaned across her desk and placed the three bullets in her empty ashtray'...
> 'She touched the bullets with a pencil'...
> 'She prodded the bullets, moving them around the ashtray'...
> 'Jane played distractedly with the bullets, as if they were executive worry-beads supplied to all the offices'...
> 'Jane looked down at the bullets in her palm, seeing them clearly for the first time. She pressed them against her heart, as if calculating the effect on her anatomy, and with a grimace dropped them into the ashtray'...
> 'Jane held my wrist as I reached for the bullets.'
>
> (65–8)

In the second part of the chapter, on leaving Jane's office Sinclair witnesses a severe beating meted out by Eden-Olympia's security guards to a Russian and one of the Senegalese trinket-sellers in the clinic car park. After the security guards have departed, the entertainment over, Sinclair gets in his car to leave. The chapter concludes:

> I was tempted to run Halder [the security chief] down, but by the time I passed him the Russian and the Senegalese had gone, and the scattered beads lay blinking among the pools of blood.
>
> (74)

Here, the beads sold by the African are yoked via the violent bloodletting of the beating to the bullets in the ashtray. Whereas one would expect to find bullets in the pools of blood, the reader is obliged to observe a symmetry of displaced objects, so that the bullets do in fact become viewed as 'executive worry-beads', as they are earlier described. This violence is intended to serve the function of psychological release: a stress-reliever akin to but exceeding the purely personal remit of 'worry-beads'. The reader ought already to be aware of this violence-as-cleansing motif, before it actually occurs in the novel, from the gestural ballet of bullets in Jane's office. We should also be able to infer that Jane will reject the violence (she drops the bullets), though she knows Sinclair will become involved (she points the bullets towards him); he in fact is intrigued by the violence (he reaches for the bullets) but his relationship with his wife will restrain him (she holds his wrist to prevent him from taking them) although he will be infected by the desire for violence (he reacts to the beating with the impulse to run Halder down).

Such symbolism is in fact compounded, stratified into multiple layers. Objects connected with the bullets only in this scene acquire a transferred symbolic content: the pencil with which Jane stirs the bullets around the ashtray, as if apportioning them with a gun, is subsequently used to draw our attention to the computer, as 'Jane tapped a screen with her pencil' (67). The screen displays Greenwood's medical records of the Arab girls who have been abused. The pencil thereby symbolizes, in an entirely straightforward way, Jane's professional distance from these 'patients'; but it also, at a secondary stratum of symbolism, connects the girls with the bullets, and expresses an entirely different relation between the professional inhabitants of Eden-Olympia and the Arab locals. The bullets are placed in the ashtray both to connect them with the disposal of detritus – a connexion which implies that this 'detritus' is subject to ethnic 'cleansing' – and to indicate more literally that such bullets replace not only the stress-relieving worry-beads, but also stress-relieving cigarettes. This *motif* of cleaning and purging, which first appears in Ballard's fictions in his 1975 novel *High-Rise*, recurs offstage, in the background, throughout the chapter. The dialysis machine moving through its 'cleaning cycle', is a device for artificially drawing off the superfluous and unrequired waste products of the body. Eden-Olympia is full of such machines: in the car park, before the beatings, Sinclair considers some relatively mundane hypotheses to explain where he found the bullets: 'A nervy gendarme searching the garden might have fired into the pumphouse when the engine switched to detergent mode, startling him with its subterranean grumblings' (70). The physical aspect of Eden–Olympia is kept particularly antiseptic by these machines; its psychological condition is maintained in a corresponding manner by a mechanized system for purging its unconscious demons. Before the beating, Sinclair leans 'on the parapet, inhaling the scent of pines and the medley of pharmaceutical odours that emerged from a ventilation shaft' (71). But afterwards, 'The scent of disinfectant and air-conditioning suddenly seemed more real than the sweet tang of pine trees' (74), indicating (through Sinclair's unconsciously unified sensibility) that another of Eden-Olympia's automated self-cleaning processes has been at work, and at the same time hinting at the violence built in to the unnatural technologies of purification and decontamination.

The conclusion to which Ballard leads us in *Super-Cannes* – or one of the conclusions, at the least – is that in the socially-engineered Eden–Olympia, with its inversion of appearance and reality and its population of engineered psychotics, morality along with all other social entities becomes an automated process. Paul notes that there is an 'absence of an explicit moral order' (89); decisions about right and wrong emerge not from Eden–Olympia's society, but from its technologies. Penrose sees this as a kind of freedom, a freedom from morality, but Ballard's aim is surely rather to alert us to a new form of constraint: 'Civility and polity were designed into Eden–Olympia, in the same way that mathematics, aesthetics and an entire geopolitical world-view were designed into the Parthenon and the Boeing 747' (38).

Ballard's achievement is to go beyond Bateson, to reveal the meta-communicational contexts which we create, which conjoin inner space with the external world, and which imprison us. Ballard identifies a deep, intrinsic relation between technological contexts and the logic of the double bind, which results in a designed psycho-sphere in which the 'death of affect' is one of the consequences of the psychological *impasse* in which our technological environments place us.

What was originally absent from Bateson's theory was any awareness of the fact that, in evolving these literalizing strategies to deal with double binds, the schizophrenic assimilates and *mimics* the very form of the double bind. By confounding the literal with the metaphorical and vice versa, he contrives a discontinuity with his own metacommunicational system, turning the tables in an admittedly fantastic way not only upon the original instigator of the double bind, but in turn replicating its method in all his communications. Instigator and subject become reversed; hence the double bind at this point develops into a mimetic category of its own. Initially it describes a single act on the part of the instigator, but if it is successful in prompting a logical impasse, the double bind evolves into a closed context for communication between the instigator and the subject: a closed circuit, a self-perpetuating state. It is this state that Ballard depicts, both as psyche and as environment; and, as the modern cultural equivalent of the 'dissociation of sensibility', it is a divided state to which he proposes, in his poetic fictions, a radical resolution.

Notes

1. Martin Amis, *The War Against Cliché: Essays and Reviews, 1971–2000* (London: Jonathan Cape, 2001), pp. 101, 103, 106.
2. Colin Greenland, *The Entropy Exhibition: Michael Moorcock and the British 'New Wave' in Science Fiction* (London: Routledge & Kegan Paul, 1983), p. 99.
3. David Punter, *The Hidden Script: Writing and the Unconscious* (London: Routledge & Kegan Paul, 1985), pp. 9, 14.
4. Greenland, pp. 102, 99.
5. J. G. Ballard, *High-Rise* (London: Flamingo, 1993 [1975]), p. 40.
6. Peter Brigg, *J. G. Ballard* (Mercer Island, WA: Starmont House), p. 72.
7. J. G. Ballard, 'My Dream of Flying to Wake Island', in *The Complete Short Stories*, vol. 2 (London: Harper Perennial, 2006), pp. 330–41; first publ. in *Ambit* 60 (Autumn 1974).
8. Gregory Stephenson, *Out of the Night and into the Dream: A Thematic Study of the Fiction of J. G. Ballard* (London: Greenwood, 1991), p. 7.
9. Roger Luckhurst, *'The Angle Between Two Walls': The Fiction of J. G. Ballard* (Liverpool: Liverpool University Press, 1997), pp. 63, 62.
10. Luckhurst, *'The Angle Between Two Walls'*, p. 49.
11. Gregory Bateson, *Steps to an Ecology of Mind: Collected Essays in Anthropology, Psychiatry, Evolution and Epistemology* (St Albans: Paladin, 1973), p. 178.
12. Bateson, *Steps to an Ecology of Mind*, p. 182.
13. Bateson's original thesis is to be found in Gregory Bateson, Don D. Jackson, Jay Haley and John H. Weakland, 'Towards a Theory of Schizophrenia' in Gregory Bateson, *Steps to an Ecology of Mind: Collected Essays in Anthropology, Psychiatry, Evolution and Epistemology* (St Albans: Paladin, 1973), pp. 173–98 (first publ. in *Behavioural Science*, 1 (1956), pp. 251–64). Laing's re-examination of Bateson's theory may be found in R. D. Laing, *Self and Others* (London: Penguin, 1990 [1961]), pp. 144–50.
14. Though the question may be resolved to some degree by study of the J. G. Ballard archive now lodged at the British Library, London, yet to be catalogued at the time of writing.
15. In person at the Congress Centre, Great Russell St., London, 18 September 2003. See also 'Interview with JGB' by Andrea Juno and Vale, in *Re/Search: J. G. Ballard*, 8/9 (1984), 4–35 (pp. 8–9).
16. J. G. Ballard, *Running Wild* (London: Flamingo, 1997 [1988]), p. 7. Subsequent page references are given in the text.
17. I do not wish to suggest that Ballard anthropomorphizes the inanimate; indeed, I propose precisely the opposite. Rather, I use the word 'intentional' in Franz Brentano's philosophical sense of being *about* something, rather than in the sense of a thing being *purposive*.
18. J. G. Ballard, *Millennium People* (London: Flamingo, 2003), p. 23. Subsequent page references are given in the text.
19. Bateson, *Steps to an Ecology of Mind*, p. 180.
20. J. G. Ballard, *Super-Cannes* (London: Flamingo, 2000), p. 32. Subsequent page references are given in the text.

21. John Donne, 'To his Mistris Going to Bed', in *The Elegies and The Songs and Sonnets*, ed. Helen Gardner (Oxford: Clarendon Press, 1965), pp. 14–16.
22. T. S. Eliot, 'The Metaphysical Poets', in *Selected Essays*, 3rd edn. (London: Faber and Faber, 1951), pp. 281–91 (p. 286).
23. J. G. Ballard, *Crash* ((London: Vintage, 1995; first publ. London: Jonathan Cape, 1973), p. 74. Subsequent page references are given in the text.

Part III
'Babylon Revisited': Ballard's Londons

7
The Texture of Modernity in J. G. Ballard's *Crash*, *Concrete Island* and *High-Rise*

Sebastian Groes

J. G. Ballard is often considered to be a visionary, even prophetic, writer. Ballard's writing is indisputably avant-garde, but the subject matter of his work does not necessarily make him visionary in the 'predictive' sense, nor prophetic in the sense of causing future events by the power of invocation.[1] Joe Moran notes that: 'Ballard's torn feelings about the motorway [in *Crash* (1973) and *Concrete Island* (1974)] were really just a reflection of popular attitudes at the time.'[2] These novels were written years after the initial anxious wave of protest against the motorway revolution had subsided: 'we know that Ballard began writing about crashes just as public fears about them were beginning to recede'.[3] Similarly, *High-Rise* (1975) voices concerns about the utopian but misconceived and under-funded tower block projects in the 1950s and, in particular, 1960s, which had come to an abrupt halt with the partial collapse of Ronan Point on 16 May, 1968.[4] Iain Sinclair claims that Ballard's novel 'previewed the target towers of Canary Wharf' and so defined 'the psychic climate through which we are travelling'.[5] Yet, although the London Docklands Development Corporation (LDDC) was in control of the riverside only from 1981, the first Docklands redevelopment plans arrived as early as 1972, while earlier plans emerged during the Second World War, which saw the destruction of large parts of the docks during the Blitz.

It might be better to think of J. G. Ballard as a literary anthropologist whose work speculates on current social and cultural trends by imaginatively projecting them into extreme situations. In the early seventies, Ballard's work is not so much concerned with reading the surface appearance of the quotidian world in order to second-guess its future, rather it is an attempt to understand the ways in which contemporary social relationships are mediated and distorted by new forms of urban space at a highly specific moment in the post-war period. My reading of the urban disaster trilogy of *Crash, Concrete Island* and *High-Rise* historicizes these novels, suggesting that, although in the banal sense, they are 'about' cars, motorways, and apartment blocks, these novels are primarily interested in allegorizing the spatial impact of these phenomena upon modes of living, revealing late capitalism's brutal reshaping of the social and cognitive processes that determine everyday lives. These novels capture the texture of modernity – the distinct changes to the structure of feeling and aesthetic whereby language as a tool for meaningful communication becomes exhausted, and in which the dominating technology of concrete reshapes social structures and relationships in monstrous, dehumanized and Americanized ways. As Ballard puts it in *High-Rise*: 'this was an environment built, not for man, but for man's absence'.[6]

One way in which Ballard's trilogy can be read is as an attempt to translate postmodern spatiality into classical, human structures by inducing specific sensory reading experiences. Reading *Crash* certainly feels like traversing the elevated 'motion-sculpture of concrete that race[s]' through West London, giving us a sense of how speed and mobility are introducing horizontality and, perhaps, a feeling of emerging shallowness to the contemporary experience.[7] *High-Rise* takes us up into the life of a tower block for the well-off middle classes, a vertical city 'abandoned in the sky' (7); indeed, the original title proposed by Ballard for the novel was *Up!*. *Concrete Island*, meanwhile, takes us down in an equally vertiginous cognitive experience. The trilogy thus loosely but consciously re-enacts the classic Dantean structure of *The Divine Comedy*'s three canticles: *Inferno, Purgatorio,* and *Paradiso* (1314; 1315; 1321). *Crash* is a novel that discovers a new celestial city in the peripheral zones of the metropolis, where the protagonist observes how the minutiae of suburban life falter before 'the solid reality of the motorway embankments, with their constant and unswerving geometry, and before the finite areas of the car-park aprons' (49). Dr Robert Vaughan acts as James Ballard's Virgil – he hovers 'like an invigilator in the margins of [James] Ballard's life' (65), the 'aimless destinations' (17) have a distinctly purgatorial feel to them, and the fictional narrator/protagonist is given the name of the author. This connection is much more detailed than it at first seems, however. *Inferno* ends with Dante and Virgil climbing out of hell: 'I saw some lovely things / That are in the heavens, through a round opening / And then we emerged to see the stars again.'[8] *Crash* reworks this image, when, at the end of the novel Ballard and his muse, Catherine, stare at a car seat sprinkled with semen: 'watching these faint points of liquid glisten in the darkness, the first constellation in the new zodiac of our minds' (224). Just as Dante's trajectory is a mental journey through a city-as-hell, James Ballard's travels through London's peripheral spaces actually form an inward journey through the postmodern imagination towards a new kind of celestial city. And similar to the didactic nature of Dante's work, *Crash* is – Ballard would have us believe – a cautionary tale, 'a warning against that brutal, erotic, and overlit realm that beckons more and more persuasively to us from the margins of the technological landscape'.[9] Paradoxically, Ballard's novel points out the dangerous fissure between traditional humanist paradigms and postmodern psychopathologies as well as endeavouring to close the gap between them. This chapter explores the Dantean connection for *Crash*, *Concrete Island* and *High-Rise*.

During this particular period, Ballard's work connects these renegotiations of urban space to the social problems that were emerging as a result of more spare time – the direct product of increased individual wealth and the influence of the Welfare State. Ballard's exploration of what could be termed an 'anthropology of leisure' speculates on the emergence of new spatial configurations that reshape communities.[10] In 1930, John Maynard Keynes warned about the consequences of increasing affluence, which would result in more leisure time: 'Thus for the first time since his creation man will be faced with his real, his permanent problem – how to use his freedom from oppressing economic cares, how to occupy leisure, which science and compound interest have won for him, to live wisely and agreeably and well.'[11] Keynes warns of the negative effects occasioned by a lack of social structure and increasingly systematic labour; he also hints, however, that, in the light of more spare time, man will encounter new moral choices.

Literary obsessions with idleness hark back to Genesis; in *The City of God* Augustine notes that it is living without want that ensures 'perfect health in the body, entire tranquillity in the soul'.[12] In an English context, this tradition of laziness – *dolce far niente* [the sweetness of doing nothing] goes back to James Thompson's poem *The Castle of Indolence* (1748), which was an influence on Keats, whose 'Ode on Indolence' (1819) also celebrates the art of doing nothing. Oscar Wilde noted that: 'The condition of perfection is idleness; the aim of perfection is youth.'[13] For the Situationists in the France of the late 1950s and 1960s, who were a conscious influence upon Ballard's thinking,[14] leisure and laziness were key ideas that would be part of liberating man from the constraints imposed upon society by capitalism. Situationist thinking about work and 'free' time went back to the French Marxist writer Paul Lafargue's *The Right to Be Lazy* (1883), which attacked the working classes' 'love of work' as a 'mental aberration' and regarded 'the furious passion for work' as a Fall because the forced production after the Fall entailed a divorce of man from nature.[15] It is notable that most Ballardian protagonists are tempted in one form or another by a return to a prelapsarian state because they are forced, for various reasons, to stop working. In *Crash*, James Ballard's post-crash disability prevents him from working as a television producer and he spends much of his time driving around; in *Concrete Island*, Robert Maitland is marooned outside the professional fabric of society in a zone occupied by unemployed drop-outs; the tower block in *High-Rise* provides an apparently self-sufficient system that tricks its inhabitants into giving up work.

Ballard's novels show how the spatial organization of labour within society functions as an oppressive instrument. While, for Ballard, London is a space that represents the restrictions of labour and capitalist production, the suburbs are spaces of leisure, producing their own psychopathologies. The city represents Protestant tyranny, where one is not allowed to have fun but must work in order to rid oneself of one's sins. Ballard's rehabilitation of doing nothing is imbued with the revolutionary spirit of resistance that promotes our reclaiming of an authentic experience lost to those immersed in the capitalist teleology.

Yet, similar to the protagonist of *High-Rise*, Ballard is also 'aware of his ambivalent feelings for this concrete landscape' (25). Ballard's texts simultaneously warn against the paradoxes of leisure, and the danger of boredom and infantilism that comes with too much freedom and spare time. London's postmodern spaces turn into a middle-class playground for adults, where the unconscious drives of *homo ludens* are unleashed with often dangerous consequences. We can simultaneously see the transformation of London into a ludic city, a counter-cultural concept inspired by Johan Huizinga's *Homo Ludens* (1934) and Henri Lefebvre's *The Critique of Everyday Life* (1947), and developed by the Situationist International into a counter-space that resists the bourgeoisification and commodification of capitalist production. In Henry Lefebvre's words, when 'a community fights the construction of urban motorways or housing-developments, when it demands "amenities" or empty spaces for play and encounter, we can see how a counter-space can insert itself into spatial reality'.[16] Ballard's oppressive tower block is appropriated by its inhabitants and turned into a counter-space: a 'pleasant carnival atmosphere reigned' and 'on this Wednesday evening everyone was involved in one revel or another' (29). This ludic London works against the monotony of patterns and rhythms imposed by capitalism upon the urban environment and its inhabitants. In his book, *The Ludic City* (2007), Quentin Stevens also notes: 'Play also contains utopian impulses. It is non-exploitative and non-hierarchical. Play is subversive of social order and the mythologies which sustain it. The disruptive capacity of play is the opportunities it presents to unravel the mythic from within.'[17] At the most fundamental level, play is also an exercise of the imagination with sometimes benign and sometimes dangerous consequences. By hypothetically playing out narratives that take place at the level of representation, and not within the everyday, quotidian reality, we may gain new insights into ourselves while developing our capacity to empathize with others, but there is also the threat of regression into violence and chaos brought about by self-absorption.

Concrete Island: postmodern Crusoe in junk-city

In his travelogue, *America* (1986), Jean Baudrillard notes that, in contrast to the motorway systems of Europe, the American freeway system, and that of Los Angeles in particular:

> creates a new experience of space, and, at the same time, a new experience of the whole social system. All you need to know about American society can be gleaned from an anthropology of its driving behaviour. That behaviour tells you much more than you ever could learn from its political ideas. Drive ten thousand miles across America and you will know more about the country than all the institutes of sociology and political science put together.[18]

The idea of reading motorway behaviour anthropologically comes to Baudrillard via *Crash*, yet *Concrete Island* has equally interesting things to say about the changes to the psyche introduced by the experience of driving on motorways. In the novel, a 35-year-old architect, Robert Maitland, drives his Jaguar down the high-speed exit lane of the Westway interchange in west London when a blow-out makes him crash onto a patch of wasteland between and beneath the elevated motorways.[19] Despite his various attempts to make his way out of the concrete island, he is unable to escape from the hellish pit, and, after his messages for help are ignored, Maitland turns his attention to dominating the island itself. Besides meeting two social outcasts, the tramp Proctor and Jane Sheppard, a Beckettian 'logic' (the characters are locked inside their own consciousness; nothing happens) is taking its course, and by the end of the novel there is no resolution. This Beckettian influence also confirms Ballard's anthropological interest: *Concrete Island* mimics Beckett's short play 'Act Without Words I' (1956; 1957), a mime in which a man is flung into a pit in the desert from which he is, by some invisible power, unable to escape. This force also gives him tools for survival (a pair of scissors; a carafe of water; a palm tree; a lasso; cubes on which to stand), which the man uses in various configurations but is unable to resolve logically. Beckett's mime was inspired by anthropological research into monkeys, and Ballard's novel is asking similar questions about man's nature.[20]

Yet the presence of Beckett, whose work was profoundly influenced by his love for the *Inferno* and *Purgatorio*, also illuminates Ballard's reworking of Dante. Just as the eternal city, Rome, was central to Giambattista Vico's analysis of civilization, Ballard's investigation of London is central to his analysis of the condition of Britain in the post-war period. Vico's vision of history was based on the work of Dante whose 'conception of the city is linked to Virgil's celebration of the destiny of Rome; the ancient capital city provides an appropriate focus for his theological pattern of history'.[21] For Ballard this modern Rome is London, an ancient European city turned into a secular hell by the introduction of modern American landscape technologies, which makes it perfect to pinpoint the crisis of modernity in spatio-temporal terms.

The space we encounter in the novel is the result of the introduction of a distinctly American form of road building in a European capital city, leading to a rupture in the traditional way of experiencing the metropolis.[22] The American system of motorways is characterized by fluidity and movement and reduces space to a pure Idea, which is the opposite of the stasis of the European city, with its mass organized around the unity of a social centre. There is a paradox at the heart of driving an automobile: 'auto', etymologically derived from 'self', suggests that it is the subject who is in control of his or her mobility, but the opposite is happening. The autonomous subject is subjected to a process, a collective experience in which (s)he is a figure whose unconscious yields control. Maitland acknowledges this when he attempts to understand the reason for his predicament: 'Why had he driven so fast? . . . Once inside his car some rogue gene, a strain of rashness, overran the rest of his usually cautious and clear-minded character' (9). The potentially lethal power of the motorcar brings to the surface a curious urge normally buried within the unconscious: an escapist act of violence directed against the self.

Concrete Island presents us with a *topos* specific to postmodernity, namely spatial residue untended by its creators and ignored by its consumers: 'The compulsory landscaping had yet to be carried out by the contractors, and the original contents of this shabby tract, its rusting cars and coarse grass, were still untouched' (13). Andrzej Gasiorek offers an illuminating reading of this virgin wasteland:

> The concrete island on which Maitland crashes is not just a metaphor for his mind but also a symbol of the waste and destruction modernity leaves in its wake. It is a non-place in precise ways: it exists solely as a space left over and in between a series of interlocking highways, which define and isolate it; it is a forgotten patch of waste ground shaped by the discarded remnants of urban life; it is a habitus for the city's rejects, who are forced to live on its margins. This non-place functions as an abject, alienated microcosm, the darker other to mundane reality from which Maitland is so suddenly removed.[23]

Marc Augé's anthropological idea of 'non-space' is a suggestive one in this context, but Gasiorek's use of it does not quite fit with Ballard's island. Although Augé notes that 'a space which cannot be defined as relational, historical, or concerned with identity will be a non-place', it is nonetheless a real place, such as a motorway, an airport, leisure park or a shopping mall – neutral, public places with a social function – through which we travel: 'The traveller's space may thus be the archetype of *non-place*.'[24] Ballard's island is, on the contrary, a non-*space*, an unformed residue defined by the motorway non-place, not built with man in mind. It is Roger Luckhurst who points out the anthropological connection: 'Augé sketches a crisis in ethnology, which concerns itself with "anthropological place" as determining a referential grid for meaningful cultural inhabitation and act.'[25] Perhaps even closer to both Luckhurst's and Gasiorek's use of Augé in understanding the species of space that entraps Maitland is architect Rem Koolhaas, who, in his sprawling essay 'Junkspace' (2002), provides an illuminating idea:

> If space-junk is the human debris that litters the universe, junk-space is the residue mankind leaves on the planet. The built . . . product of modernization is not modern architecture but Junkspace. Junkspace is what remains after modernization has run its course, or, more precisely, what coagulates while modernization is in process, its fallout. Modernization has a rational program: to share the blessings of science, universally. Junkspace is its apotheosis, or meltdown . . .

Although its individual parts are the outcome of brilliant inventions, lucidly planned by human intelligence, boosted by infinite computation, their sums spell the end of Enlightenment, its resurrection as farce, a low-grade purgatory.[26]

Maitland's island is an example of Junkspace, the spatial fallout, or spillage, of motorway modernization, and the planned process of decorative landscaping as a form of farcical resurrection. Koolhaas's emphasis on 'purgatory' is also illuminating as it again reinforces the idea that Junkspace is an in-between space, whilst it also appropriates this new spatiality by reframing it in a classic humanist framework. The narrator tries to do something similar for Maitland's experience: 'The sequence of violent events only micro-seconds in duration had opened and closed behind him like a vent of hell' (8). Koolhaas's emphasis on the waning of Enlightenment thinking in the production of postmodern space also chimes with Ballard's spatiality. *Concrete Island* opens as follows:

Soon after three o'clock on the afternoon of April 22nd 1973, a 35-year-old architect named Robert Maitland was driving down the high-speed exit lane of the Westway interchange in central London. Six hundred yards from the junction with the newly built spur of the M4 motorway, when the Jaguar had already passed the 70 m.p.h. speed limit, a blow-out collapsed the front near-side tyre.

(7)

The density of details bearing down on the page is noteworthy: the exact date, age of the protagonist, location, speed, and the specification of the tyre's positioning all stress that London, as a triumph of modern civilization and product of Enlightenment thinking, provides too much fact, a reality far too dense for the narrator to escape from, until he is marooned and loses his sense of selfhood: 'More and more, the island was becoming an exact model of his head' (70).

London's social and cultural history – in the form of building foundations, an abandoned churchyard, a former art cinema, an air-raid shelter which are 'half-buried by the earth and gravel brought in to fill the motorway embankments' (38) – is literally covered up by concrete. Luckhurst notes aptly that Ballard's work in this period depicts 'the contemporary . . . projected as a ruin *of the future*',[27] but these novels also show how the present production of postmodern spatiality takes place on the ruins *of the past* which it abandons and suppresses. Again, the Dantean connection is present, as this repressed palimpsest, or texture, of London's cultural history also reminds one of Sigmund Freud's Rome analogy in *Civilization and its Discontents* (1930), where he imagines the superimposition of various forms of Rome throughout history in order to challenge the appropriateness of reading human consciousness, history and memory in spatial terms.[28]

Another way in which Ballard's text attempts to recuperate a human scale is through one of its key intertexts, Daniel Defoe's *Robinson Crusoe* (1719), in which the colonial master Crusoe is confronted with boredom after becoming marooned on an island. It is Crusoe's Protestant work ethic that provides a solution or, rather, a denial of his life of leisure. By cultivating and mastering the island, Crusoe is able to dispel the great nothingness that plagues him, whilst ensuring a place with the elect in heaven and promoting capitalism. Originally, the narrative about an empirical man stranded alone on a desert island can be read as an attempt to reinstate bourgeois urban civilization – a version of early eighteenth-century London with its coffeehouses and booming trade – in the wilderness, which he subdues to his control. The novel can be read as an investigation of freedom and personal relationships in the contemporary city in which Crusoe's contact with Friday stands for the alienating experience of encountering the Other, whilst it also symbolically adumbrates the paradox of the modern metropolis: being alone amongst the teeming millions.

Ballard's text simultaneously re-imagines and inverts *Robinson Crusoe*, and this helps us to sharpen our focus on Ballard's organization of this political geography. Defoe's attempted realism is significant because it inadvertently makes a statement about the condition of the author's understanding of 'the real' at a particular moment in history. In the case of Ballard, his use of factual realism (dense descriptions; close observations) in his urban disaster trilogy is important because it is a deliberate move away from the experimental, subversive phase of his early science-fiction writing and *The Atrocity Exhibition*, while his exploitation of the realist mode mocks its empirical underpinnings, suggesting that it is the conventional use of language and its supposed rationality which is no longer suitable to capture the late-twentieth-century experience. And, inversely, the novel shows that in the midst of civilization, there can be a new barbaric wilderness because the ideological foundations that make it possible for civilization to flourish are under constant threat.

The motorway and Junkspace are a-historical in impulse – they literally flatten our human experience. Maitland's initial resistance, through the rich archaeology of the unconscious and London's (cultural) history, to homogenization of the environment, echoes Lefebvre's comment on the acceleration of experience in the post-war period:

> History is experienced as nostalgia, and nature as regret - as a horizon fast disappearing behind us. This may explain why *affectivity*, which, along with the sensory/sensual realm, is referred to by a term that denotes both a subject and that subject's denial by the absurd rationality of space: that term is 'the unconscious'.[29]

Yet Maitland quickly realises that he is trapped within a secular purgatory: the self as constructed by one's own consciousness. In the absence of signifiers or markers that would give him some sense of history by which to sustain, or from which to derive, his identity, the emptiness of the island becomes a blank screen onto which he can project his self. Maitland soon discovers, however, that there is not much to project: 'He knew he was not merely exhausted, but behaving in a vaguely eccentric way, as if he had forgotten who he was. Parts of his mind seemed to be detaching themselves from the centre of his consciousness' (63). Maitland's loss of identity is directly connected to the image of postmodernity as producing spatial vacuity, signifying ambiguously both a liberation as well as spiritual emptiness.

Even language, one of the central modes of identification and meaning-giving tools within Western civilization, becomes useless. Throughout the novel, Maitland inscribes the landscape with messages addressed to the outside world: 'in wavering letters eighteen inches high, he marked up his message' in 'pieces of charred rubber: HELP INJURED DRIVER CALL POLICE' (62). Yet, it is the monstrous posthuman landscape which is unable to communicate human messages: 'He looked briefly back at the letters he had chalked on the embankment, but they were barely visible above the grass' (63). The texture of modernity shifts from linguistic sign-system to the dominant, abstract language of architecture which effaces history, memory and identity:

> Maitland found a last rubber marker in his jacket pocket. On the drying concrete he scrawled:
>
> CATHERINE   HELP   TOO   FAST
>
> The letters wound up and down the slope. Maitland concentrated on the spelling, but ten minutes later, when he returned after an unsuccessful attempt to reach the Jaguar, they had been rubbed out as if by some dissatisfied examiner.

MOTHER   DON'T   HURT   POLICE

He waited in the long grass beside the embankment, but his eyes closed. When he opened them, the message had vanished.

He gave up, unable to decipher his own writing.

(74–5)

This threat of regression, this loss of cognitive processes that help to keep a sense of identity for the subject – another Cartesian construct that emerged from Enlightenment thinking but which is crumbling as an unintended side-effect of postmodern spatiality – is particularly problematic in a society structured around identities that are created and mediated via capitalist modes of production.

Ballard approaches these various forms of regression by including the laws of thermodynamics in the rules of representation. As 'the island was sealed off from the world around it by the high embankments on two sides and the wire-mesh fence on its third' (13), it will be subject to a constant increase of forms of disorder and waste. Because the new, utopian schemes of the period are disconnected from, and radically different from, the organic structure of European cities, and London in particular, Ballard points out that the utopian and necessarily isolated nature of these schemes will lead to unintended side-effects. David Punter states that the trajectory of *Concrete Island* captures: 'a renunciation of the impulse towards the ideal society, and replaces it with a wish for abdication, yet in that act of abdication the self reasserts a useless sovereignty, apparently free from technological compulsion'.[30] Indeed, Ballard rejects the utopian aspiration that was part of the vision of urban planners in the 1950s and 1960s. Planning schemes and architectural innovation including the New Towns, the boom in high-rise office space, tower blocks, council housing, motorways, Brutalist architecture, and the vertical separation of cars and pedestrians by means of raised walkways set out to construct a society, which, if successful, would work well, yet much of the ideas turned out to be, in Arthur Marwick's words, ' "urban renewal" of the most disastrous sort'.[31]

High-Rise: the past as 'an unresolved mental crisis'

One of the sights that Maitland sees from his colonized piece of Junkspace in *Concrete Island* is that of tower blocks: 'Silhouetted against the evening corona of the city, the dark façades of the high-rise apartment blocks hung in the night air like rectangular planets' (23). One might imagine that it is the architect, Maitland, who actually designed the hypermodern tower block into which Dr Robert Laing moves in *High-Rise*. The high-rise is 'one of five identical units in the development project... [t]ogether they were set in a mile-square area of abandoned dockland and ware-housing along the north bank of the river' (8). When Laing looks at central London from his apartment on the 25th floor, he makes the following distinction: 'By contrast with the calm and unencumbered geometry of the concert-hall and television studios below him, the ragged skyline of the city resembled the disturbed encephalograph of an unresolved mental crisis' (9). London's physical structure embodies and induces an unhealthy state of mind; the city's spaces form a dense compression of Victorian architecture that leaves no room for the imagination, resulting in psychopathologies and violence. The tower block, on the contrary, gives a Godlike perspective whilst giving shape to a sedated, emotionless aesthetic that allows its materiality to be easily reduced to an idea: 'as if this huge building existed solely in his mind and would vanish if he stopped thinking about it' (34).

Gasiorek's historical framing of *High-Rise* is rather broad. His starting point is the Dwellings Improvement Act of 1875, yet Ballard's novel reacts against the rationalized, modernist planning project in and around London during the 1950s and 1960s; specifically, *High-Rise* projects into the future the influence of Le Corbusier's city *La Ville Contemporaine* (1922), with its tower blocks as machines for living. *High-Rise* mimics and mocks Le Corbusier's discourse, such as the architect's idea of the apartment as a 'the perfect human *Cell*, the cell which corresponds most perfectly to our physiological and sentimental needs. We must arrive at the "house-machine", which must be both practical and emotionally satisfying'.[32] The protagonist Laing's apartment is described as 'an over-priced cell': 'its studio living-room and single bedroom, kitchen and bathroom dovetailed into each other to minimize space and eliminate internal corridors' (9). Similarly, the high-rise is not a machine for living but a self-contained and self-sustaining organism divorced from community. Moreover, the description of the high-rise as a vertical city is a direct echo of Le Corbusier's utopian concept for a vertical garden city in Marseille (1946–52).

High-Rise speculates about the emergence of a new social ordering directed by postmodern spatiality, a tower block for the well-off middle classes 'abandoned in the sky' (7). At the same time, though, Ballard's novel anticipates the resurgence of gated high-rise living for the upwardly mobile individuals celebrated by the Thatcher doctrine. Joe Kerr states:

> The trend was started by Margaret Thatcher's flagship local authority of Wandsworth, who in the 1980s sold a public housing block into private hands. After a comprehensive refurbishment and the addition of a secure concierge entry system, various leisure facilities and carpets and potted plants for common areas, the flats were successfully marketed to young professionals, notwithstanding the tomato ketchup bottles periodically hurled at their expensive cars from the unmodernized council block next door. [33]

Indeed, *High-Rise* warns us that 'interdictory', or exclusionist, space which shuts out the working poor will remain intact because the assumed homogenization of the ingrained class system under late capitalism is a fantasy. Ballard explores the effects of such rationalization of space upon the human mind. The psychologist Laing, whose name may refer both to R. D. Laing as well as to the British motorway contractor, is basically the narrating vessel who diagnoses this process:

> A new social type was being created by the apartment building, a cool, unemotional personality impervious to the psychological pressures of high-rise life, with minimal needs for privacy, who thrived like an advanced species of machine in the neutral atmosphere. This was the sort of resident who was content to do nothing but sit in his over-priced apartment, watch television with the sounds turned down, and wait for his neighbours to make a mistake.
>
> (36)

The novel thus appropriates a sociological class observation that finds a newly arising socio-economic egalitarianism resulting from the socio-cultural revolutions of the sixties with their utopian, egalitarian goals, and it transplants these features to an artificial, vertical space, the apartment block. The tower block's 'two thousand tenants formed a virtually homogeneous collection of well-to-do professional people' (10) which manifests itself 'in the elegant but somehow standardized way in which they furnished their apartments, in the selection of sophisticated foods in the supermarket delicatessen, in the tones of their self-confident voices' (10).

Yet, there are various forms of interference that thwart the plans of the architect, Anthony Royal. Firstly, there is the transgression of social codes by people themselves: 'The mysterious movements of the air-hostesses as they pursued their busy social lives, particularly on the floors above her own, clearly unsettled Alice, as if they in some way interfered with the natural social order of the building, its system of precedences entirely based on floor-height' (14). More importantly, it is the new form of space itself that counters the intended effect: 'Their real opponent was not the hierarchy of residents in the heights far above them, but the image of the building in their own minds, the multiplying layers of concrete that anchored them to the floor' (58). Ballard's novel points out a simple, but insightful truth: one cannot translate the egalitarian impulses of the post-war period into practice by using vertical structures that (unconsciously) remind an already class-conscious people of the social hierarchies that are embedded within their national past. The name of the resident architect of the high-rise, Anthony Royal, already implies that his attempt at creating an egalitarian microcosm is a deluded one, and it does not take long before earlier hierarchies have reasserted themselves: 'In effect, the high-rise had already divided itself into the three classical social groups, its lower, middle and upper classes' (53).

Philip Tew states that, in *High-Rise*, the 'building is . . . a symbol of late capitalist modernity. Ballard's book can be read quasi-allegorically, conveying the theme of transition and change, of the innate and growing tensions in British culture, its intellectual and professional classes instinctively reaching for a new kind of "hierarchy"'.[34] Tew's ambiguous use of 'hierarchy' points exactly to the desire in Ballard's text to challenge and expose the replacement of former hierarchies of the Enlightenment with the blessings of the (late) capitalist consumer society. However, whether this reordering is directly attributable to capitalism is questionable as the high-rise operates outside the patterns of capitalism: 'The internal time of the high-rise, like an artificial psychological climate, operated to its own rhythms, generated by a combination of alcohol and insomnia' (12).

Indeed, *High-Rise* argues that, despite the apparent shift away from the rationality and trust in science associated with the Enlightenment, these 'new' modes of building are in fact an intensified perpetuation of such ways of thinking about the world. These postmodern modes are forms of hyper-rationalization that trigger their own revolt:

> Reasonably enough, the architects had zoned the parking-lots so that the higher a resident's apartment . . . the nearer he parked to the building. The residents from the lower floors had to walk considerable

distances to and from their cars each day – a sight not without its satisfaction, Laing noticed. Somehow the high-rise played into the hands of the most petty impulses.

(24)

High-Rise is an investigation and inverted criticism of the renegotiation of this drive for social homogenization on the grounds that it perpetuates the Hegelian pyramidal socio-economical structures that developed historically under the Enlightenment, due to unintended spatial manipulation of the unconscious. This is expressed by the narrator's comment on Anthony Royal, who realizes his project has failed:

> As for the new social order that he had hoped to see emerge, he knew now that his original vision of the high-rise as an aviary had been closer to the truth than he guessed. Without knowing it, he had constructed a vertical zoo, its hundreds of cages stacked above each other. All the events of the past few months made sense if one realized that these brilliant and exotic creatures had learned to open the door.

(134)

This is another lesson that *Concrete Island* teaches us: the replacement of one form of order by another may well have the opposite effect. When the residents realize that the new vertical structure forms yet another imposition of hierarchy, they rebel against the undelivered promise of equality until the project descends into anarchy.

High-Rise portrays the catastrophic consequences of an abundance of leisure, projecting a hyperactive society dominated by the Protestant work ethic, while its new spaces induce leisure and laziness: Laing 'without realizing why ... decided to take the day off' (27). Soon, a carnival atmosphere takes the tower block over, illustrated by the many parties being held, which again supports the idea that the high-rise works counter to the teleology of capitalism. The building induces a state of prelapsarian 'laziness' in the inhabitants, after which the degeneration of the architectural structure itself causes the occupants to collapse back into barbarism. In this sense, *High-Rise* is a criticism of Le Corbusier, whose manipulations of representational space included images of leisure that projected an utopian, Edenic society that was nothing more than a deceptive fiction.[35] The emphasis on play and play-acting, which are induced by the artificial surroundings, gives the events in this tower block both an infantile aspect, whilst making a serious claim for the importance of imagination.

Ballard's text plays the penitentiary logic of the tower block against the infantilizing and potentially liberating anthropology of leisure. The description of the high-rise as a zoo points to the idea of this kind of architecture as a social experiment that, paradoxically, has inhibiting as well as liberating effects. It also reminds one of Jeremy Bentham's panopticon which, as Michel Foucault speculates in his analysis of the history of the modern prison, *Discipline and Punish* (1975), was inspired by Le Vaux's menageries at Versailles, which contained every species of animal: 'The Panopticon is a royal menagerie; the animal is replaced by man, individual distribution by specific grouping and the king by the machinery of furtive power.'[36] For Foucault, the panopticon is a metaphor for the historical evolution of modern societies into disciplinary societies under permanent observation, yet the comparison of man to animals again links with Ballard's and Beckett's interest in anthropology. *High-Rise* can therefore be read as a fictional protest against the ways in which power is organised through architectural and geographical spatiality. The novel points out the unstated, implicit meaning of the codes of the geography and its architecture, and it suggests this kind of codification of authoritarian power can instigate the loss of democratic values. By comically transfiguring the authoritarian structure of the high-rise into a satirical image, Ballard's text translates postmodern spatiality back into human dimensions.

This is confirmed by a certain strand of Dantean images that are embedded within the novel. Anthony Royal has 'designed our hanging paradise' (15), the water 'too had made its long descent from the reservoirs on the roof . . . like ice streams percolating through a subterranean cavern' (48) and 'The carpets in the silent corridors were thick enough to insulate hell' (65). Similarly, Ballard's text emphasizes:

> the drama of confrontation each morning between these concrete slabs and the rising sun. It was only fitting that the sun first appeared between the legs of the apartment blocks, raising itself over the horizon as if nervous of waking this line of giants . . . Laing was the first to concede that these huge buildings had won their attempt to colonize the sky.
>
> (19)

Again, Dante provides Ballard's material here. In Canto XXXI of *Inferno*, as Virgil and Dante move from the eighth to the ninth Circle of Hell, Dante, blinded by sunlight, imagines he sees a city. Virgil explains to him: 'It happens that your imagination plays you false . . . You had better know that they are not towers, but giants'.[37] Although it seems that the sun, signifier of the natural world, has been defeated by the artifice of modernity, the description of the tower blocks as giants reduces their power by humanizing them, albeit in a monstrous form. Much of the narrative concerns the film director Wilder's quest to climb the high-rise to the very top of the structure, 'towards their new Jerusalem' (70), where the penthouse of its architect, Royal, is located: 'Wilder had imposed on himself a harder definition of ascent – he had to be accepted by his new neighbours as one of them' (114). This ascent counters the entropic decline that throws the enclosed space of the high-rise into chaos and regression.

Rather than engage in protest and direct action against the construction of urban motorways and housing developments, Ballard's texts have a genuine interest in the imaginative potential of these new spaces, while the trajectories of the novels themselves point out the futility and, more importantly, dangers of these utopian projects. Unlike the Situationists, Ballard avoids seeking alternative counter-spaces that work against the powers that create, (re-)organize and control space; instead, he criticizes spatial practices in the post-war period. His texts also show that the manipulation of spatial practices and the renegotiation of space by hegemonic powers are facilitated by manipulations of *representational* spaces. This is why the experience of social change in the post-war period takes place, first and foremost, in the imagination.

Notes

1. See Iain Sinclair's letter to Angela Carter reprinted in *Expletives Deleted* (London: Chatto & Windus, 1992), pp. 126–7 (p. 126).
2. Joe Moran, *On Roads: A Hidden History* (London: Profile, 2009), p. 44.
3. Moran, *Roads*, p. 191.
4. Andrzej Gasiorek notes that these two novels belong to 'the interregnum between the end of the "old Labour" project begun in 1945 and the beginning of the Thatcher era in 1979' but this is a rather broad periodization. See Andrzej Gasiorek, *J. G. Ballard* (Manchester: Manchester University Press, 2005), p. 107.
5. Iain Sinclair, *London Orbital* (London: Penguin, 2003 [2002]), p. 268.
6. J. G. Ballard, *High-Rise* (London: Triad/Panther, 1985 [1977]), p. 25. Further references are provided in the text.
7. J. G. Ballard, 'Shepperton Past and Present', *A User's Guide to the Millennium* (London: HarperCollins, 1996), pp. 183–4.
8. Dante Alighieri, *Inferno*, Canto XXIV, lines 137-39. In *The Divine Comedy*, trans. C. H. Sisson (Oxford/New York: Oxford University Press, 1998 [1980]), pp. 47–8.

9. J. G. Ballard, 'Introduction' to *Crash* (London: Vintage, 1995), p. 6.
10. Ballard develops this anthropology of leisure in his final phase (*Cocaine Nights* (1996), *Super-Cannes* (2000), *Millennium People* (2003), and *Kingdom Come* (2006)). See Sebastian Groes, 'A Zoo fit for Psychopaths: J. G. Ballard and London', in *The Making of London* (Palgrave Macmillan, 2011).
11. Cited in Peter Hall, *Cities of Tomorrow* (Oxford: Blackwell, 2001), p. 342.
12. Augustine, *Concerning the City of God against the Pagans*, trans. H. Bettenson. (Harmondsworth: Penguin, 1972), XIV, xxvi, p. 590.
13. Oscar Wilde, 'Phrases and Philosophies for the Use of the Young', *The Chameleon*, vol.1 (December 1894).
14. See Jeannette Baxter, *J. G. Ballard's Surrealist Imagination: Spectacular Authorship* (Aldershot: Ashgate, 2009), pp. 2–6.
15. Paul Lafargue, *The Right To Be Lazy*, trans. Charles H. Kerr (Chicago: Keer & Co, 1907), p. 9.
16. Henri Lefebvre, *The Production of Space*, trans. Donald Nicholson-Smith (Oxford: Blackwell, 1991), pp. 383–4.
17. Quentin Stevens, *The Ludic City* (London and New York: Routledge, 2007), p. 24.
18. Jean Baudrillard, *America*, trans. Chris Turner (London and New York: Verso, 1995), pp. 54–5.
19. J. G. Ballard, *Concrete Island* (London: Vintage, 1994 [1974]), p. 7. Further page references are provided in the text.
20. James Knowlson, *Damned to Fame: The Life of Samuel Beckett* (London: Bloomsbury, 1997), p. 419.
21. Mary T. Reynolds, 'The City in Vico, Dante, and Joyce', in *Vico and Joyce*, ed. Donald Phillip Verene (Albany: State University of New York Press, 1987), p. 111.
22. See Baudrillard, *America*, pp. 52–3.
23. Gasiorek, *Ballard*, p. 108.
24. Mark Augé, *Non-Places*, trans. John Howe. (London: Verso, 1995 [1992]), pp. 77–8 (p. 86).
25. Roger Luckhurst, *'The Angle Between Two Walls': The Fiction of J. G. Ballard* (Liverpool: Liverpool University Press, 1997), p. 129.
26. Rem Koolhaas, 'Junkspace', *October*, 100, 'Obsolescence' (Spring, 2002), 175–90 (175).
27. Luckhurst, *'The Angle Between Two Walls'*, p. 137.
28. See Sigmund Freud, *Civilization and its Discontents*, trans. James Strachey (New York: Norton, 1962), pp. 17–18.
29. Lefebvre, *Space*, p. 51
30. David Punter, 'J. G. Ballard: Alone among the Murder Machines', in *The Hidden Script: Writing and the Unconscious* (London: Routledge and Kegan Paul, 1985), pp. 9–17 (p. 17).
31. Arthur Marwick, *The Sixties* (Oxford and New York: Oxford University Press, 1998), p. 442.
32. Le Corbusier quoted in Peter Hall's *Cities of Tomorrow* (Oxford: Blackwell, 2002), p. 224.
33. Joe Kerr, 'Blowdown: The Rise and Fall of London's Tower Blocks', in Joe Kerr and Andrew Gibson, eds, *London: from Punk to Blair* (London: Reaktion Books, 2003), pp. 189–98 (p. 196).

34. Philip Tew, *The Contemporary British Novel* (London: Continuum, 2004), p. 33.
35. See J. R. Gold, 'A World of Organised Ease: The Role of Leisure in Le Corbusier's Villa Radieuse', *Leisure Studies*, 4:1 (1985), 101–10.
36. Michel Foucault, *Discipline and Punish*, trans. Alan Sheridan (London: Penguin, 1991 [1977]) p. 203.
37. Dante, *Inferno*, Canto XXXI, 24, 31.

8
J. G. Ballard and William Blake: Historicizing the Reprobate Imagination

Alistair Cormack

Introduction

This chapter will seek to investigate the points at which an imagination that struggles against the limits of material reality can usefully be historicized and to suggest the points at which that imagination might be argued to have genuinely broken free. The focus will be J. G. Ballard's *The Unlimited Dream Company* (1979) and, in particular, the many interesting intersections the novel has with the works of William Blake. The chapter will begin by acknowledging the novel's unique position in Ballard's *oeuvre* and, given this eccentricity, looking at ways it might be approached. It will also investigate two central questions. First, what are the implications of a writer such as Ballard – generally understood as, amongst other things, a high postmodernist – returning to a figure central to our understanding of Romanticism? Secondly, what are the implications for criticism of the replaying of tropes at different historical junctures, especially of tropes involving revolution, transcendence and transformation? Finally, by looking closely at Ballard's debt to Blake, it will make an argument about the nature of the revolution *The Unlimited Dream Company* envisages.

Is *The Unlimited Dream Company* Ballardian?

The place of *The Unlimited Dream Company* among Ballard's novels needs to be understood. In the early 1970s Ballard wrote his three devastating myths of the near future: *Crash* (1973), *Concrete Island* (1974) and *High-Rise* (1975). There was then a hiatus of four years before *The Unlimited Dream Company*.[1] Though in some ways consistent with its predecessors – there *is* a continuity in the depiction of central male figures single-mindedly pursuing their desires and fantasies – the novel marks a decisive move in a different direction. *The Unlimited Dream Company* is, frankly, not especially Ballardian, a term defined in the *Collins English Dictionary* as: 'resembling or suggestive of . . . dystopian modernity, bleak manmade landscapes & the psychological effects of technological, social or environmental developments'.[2] Compare this notion to the description of *The Unlimited Dream Company* offered by Andrzej Gasiorek:

> The novel's none too subtly named central protagonist, Blake,[3] crashes a light aircraft in [Shepperton] and, apparently passing through death back to a renewed life, emerges from the wrecked fuselage as a metamorphosing god. Shepperton is recast as a lush jungle paradise, a land of impossible tropical vegetation, joyfully sportive creatures, and strangely reinvigorated human beings. . . . the novel dreams a new life in which the sicknesses of a post-lapsarian realm are purged away through a rapturous fusion of all elements of the creation into a delirious unity. . . . *The Unlimited Dream Company* appears to set its face against the sordid realities of prosaic daily life anatomised in earlier works.[4]

Rather than being the representation of a dystopia and its effects on human psychology, *The Unlimited Dream Company* offers an investigation of the urge to escape the shackles of late capitalism. One might expect critics to fall upon such a work with fascination, keen to see what the writer who anticipates our contemporary landscape with such uncanny acuity might offer in the way of an answer to our malaises. Though initial responses to the novel, such as Malcolm Bradbury's (1979),[5] were very positive, it has since become virtually invisible in studies of Ballard; with the exceptions of *The Day of Creation* (1987) and *Rushing to Paradise* (1994) with which, as Gasiorek points out, it has some similarities – *The Unlimited Dream Company* is the least discussed of Ballard's novels.[6] It is likely that the reason for this is its distance from what is taken to be the core of Ballard's vision as expressed most fully in *The Atrocity Exhibition* (1970) and *Crash*. It seems that we have been far more comfortable with the 'Seer of Shepperton' when he is in his diagnostic mode. Instead of registering the ways in which *The Unlimited Dream Company* seriously might distort accepted views of Ballard, most critics have been content simply to pretend it does not exist.

It might seem that a certain blindness to the novel could be attributed to the conventional ways of reading Ballard which Jeannette Baxter has addressed in a compelling argument about the reception of his fiction:

> Following the Surrealists' visual investigations into latent and manifest forms of historical violence, Ballard's writings have staged a series of complex, and often ethically challenging, enquiries into contemporary representations of historical atrocity. As a result of this work, a tenacious critical perception of the author has become established which pictures him as a nihilistic and solipsistic historical voyeur whose writing is emotionally detached and morally vacuous.[7]

Baxter sees contemporary criticism on Ballard as 'responding to the current (re)turn to history in contemporary literature and criticism'; she offers a corrective of the view of Ballard as amoral through 'critical perspectives which reread Ballard's work as complex and controversial engagements with history, memory and trauma'.[8] However, *The Unlimited Dream Company* is not mentioned by any contributor to the collection, perhaps because it does not offer itself as an engagement with history in the same way as the accepted canon of Ballard's works. The reason for this can be seen in Gasiorek's perspicacious comment on the novel's vision of utopia which he understands is 'not . . . political at all; it hints at no programme of change within this world but rather envisages a mystical transformation that will take it into another ontological order altogether'.[9] Another way to say this is to point out that the novel imagines awakening from the nightmare of history, rather than providing a reflection of that nightmare. Thus, the novel does not fit comfortably into any available paradigm of reading Ballard's work: its utopianism renders it uninteresting to those who understand Ballard as nihilistically registering the death drive; the quasi-mystical nature of the revolution offered in the novel makes it very hard to map against any readily identifiable historical terrain. To begin reading the novel, other approaches need to be adopted.

'Blake' and William Blake (1): 'The Road of Excess Leads to the Palace of Wisdom'

Gasiorek's comment that Ballard's protagonist is 'none too subtly named' confirms that *The Unlimited Dream Company* invites us to read the works of William Blake as its most important intertext. Gasiorek, Bradbury and David Punter[10] have all referred to the poet in general terms when discussing the novel. As well as the pervasive comparisons suggested by the name, there are moments at which more specific parallels can be made. For instance, the response to capitalism offered by William Blake in 'London' can be likened to that of Ballard's Blake early in the novel. After his crash into the Thames, Blake tries to leave Shepperton and reflects on the 'stifling' nature of its bourgeois conformity: in shops 'customers moved in an abstracted way, like spectators in a boring museum'.[11] Seeing second-hand cars with 'numerals on their windshields' Blake understands them as 'the advanced guard of a digital universe in which everything would be tagged and numbered, a doomsday catalogue listing each stone and grain of sand, each eager poppy' (40).[12] When Blake envisages 'aerosoling a million ascending numbers on every garden gate, supermarket cart, and baby's forehead' (40) a further link can be made to the following stanza:

> I wander thro' each charter'd street,
> Near where the charter'd Thames does flow.
> And mark in every face I meet
> Marks of weakness marks of woe.[13]

William Blake's 'charter'd' world in which 'every face' is marked is similar to the digitalized suburban world of *The Unlimited Dream Company*. As E. P. Thompson has shown, there are a number of very specific meanings attached to 'charter'd' which arise from the debate between Thomas Paine and Edmund Burke concerning human rights.[14] That London is 'charter'd' means that it is a space which is entirely organized in terms of capitalist values and in which human freedom is bought and sold. The 'marks of woe' have, Thompson argues, a strong biblical resonance from the Book of Revelation; the Beast 'causeth all, both small and great, rich and poor, free and bond, to receive a mark on their right hand, or in their forehead . . . that no man might buy or sell, save that he had the mark'.[15] 'Marks of weakness, marks of woe' has the connotation of the mark of the Beast, which enables participation in capitalism. Just as Ballard's Blake realizes that the logical extension of the numerals on the car windows is a world in which everything – from poppies to the foreheads of babies – is marked according to the digital world of capitalism, in 'London' William Blake envisages humanity, chained in 'mind-forg'd manacles', marked and ensnared by commerce.

Ballard's return to William Blake seems straightforwardly to represent a visionary rejection of capitalism and, as the novel progresses, a replacement of it by the human world of the imagination. This is, indeed, the case; however, we must also take account of the ways in which these parallels are not so neat. The world of digitalized consumerism is a long way from William Blake's far earlier socio-economic formation. There is a common attitude to the dehumanizing effect of capitalism, but this does not lessen the distance between the different marks being described: one set are painted-on and only imaginary; William Blake's 'marks of woe', as well as being biblical and metaphorical, are the literal scars of war, disease and maltreatment notoriously absent from late capitalist Western suburbia. Indeed, there is a mildly comic bathetic effect generated from removing William Blake's 'London' – in all its urban centrality and apocalyptic force – to the suburban world of Shepperton. If William Blake represents a form of heroism then Blake represents a replaying of the tropes of imaginative resistance under the sign of postmodern irony.

Indeed, Gasiorek's view that the name is none too subtle reveals a danger; William Blake's works are remarkable in their complexity and the dialogic nature of their considerations of human social and psychic organization. There is a trap in viewing Ballard's use of Blake too simplistically, one fallen into by Bradbury in his review: 'Blake's name, presumably, is no accident. He opens the doors of alternative perception and evokes apocalyptic mirages of heaven and hell.'[16] In a newspaper review it is hard to offer anything particularly nuanced, but this remark encapsulates the dangers of reducing William Blake to the more memorable pronouncements from 'The Proverbs of Hell'. It is possible that the image of William Blake in this era – even in high-end literary discourse – was entirely conditioned by the fact that Aldous Huxley named the two accounts of his experiences of hallucinogenic drugs after the quotations from William Blake: *The Doors of Perception* and *Heaven and Hell* (1954); Jim Morrison's band The Doors famously named themselves after Huxley's memoir. What is interesting is that Ballard is a most careful reader of William Blake; however, he is also aware of less sophisticated appropriations that existed of the poet in the culture of the 1960s and 1970s. It is essential for critics to tease these two uses of William Blake apart and not reproduce a simplistic account of the poet; William Blake exists intertextually in *The Unlimited Dream Company* in a doubled form. Ballard's analysis of William Blake's carefully plotted utopianism is a strikingly original aspect of the novel, whereas the play with the peremptory and premature appropriations of him may be grasped as satire. William Blake becomes a symbol pointing in different directions, then, indicating the dangers and the possibilities of the counter-culture.

The Unlimited Dream Company begins, interestingly, with the character, Blake, analeptically describing an identifiable historical world. In Blake, Ballard presents us with a case study we might find in the works of R. D. Laing. Expelled from school for copulating with a cricket pitch, thrown out of university for trying to reanimate a cadaver, arrested for being 'overboisterous' in a playground near London Zoo, Blake is someone on the verge of being institutionalized, and, it is made explicit, whose pathology is due to, and possibly the liberating obverse of, the confinement and repression of bourgeois society. A more traditional creator of realist narrative might, at this point, seek, in Lukacsian vein, to examine the places at which this consciousness comes up against its brick walls – those points when even the most enterprising imagination presses against boundaries which signify real socio-historical limits rather than personal failure. Unsurprisingly, Ballard refuses this compromise and instead chooses to give his character's consciousness free reign as if to say: 'you delude yourself that you are the messiah: what might happen if you actually were?' The consciousness that had been repressed is subjected to a series of transformations. Now at liberty, Blake half perceives and half creates a world in which desire flows without restraint. Rejecting, defeating, seducing and consuming the boundaries made from the oedipal structures of the family and the exchange structures of capitalism, Blake takes us toward a vision of a form of utopia.

In the chapter titled 'The Remaking of Shepperton', Blake decides to create the suburb anew 'in my own image' (139). I will quote it at some length as the impression created by the passage is cumulative:

> I could smell Miriam's body ... Standing in the grass circle, I held my penis in my hand ... Semen jolted into my palm ... I threw the semen onto the cobbled pathway outside the vestry door. As I paused there ... green-fluted plants with the same milk-white blossoms sprang though the stones at my feet. ... At the filling station I ejaculated across the fuel pumps and over the paintwork of the cars standing in front of the showroom. Mile-a-minute vine hung in deep mists over the radiators ... Everywhere I went, scattering my semen on this dawn circuit of the town, I left new life clambering into the air behind me. Egged on by the rising sun, which had at last caught up with me, I moved in and out of the empty streets, a pagan gardener recruiting the air and the light to stock this reconditioned Eden.
>
> (141–3)

How a reader should respond to this passage is quite hard to gauge. Undoubtedly some sort of revolution is occurring and the enthusiasm of the first-person narrator is seductive. Bradbury is again instructive:

> Mr. Ballard invents a superabundant world for [Blake] to perform in. He dreams of birds, animals and fishes, and becomes them, moving through air, earth and water. When he spills his semen, exotic trees and flowers grow and wild animals and birds join him, along with the children, the old, the mothers, all of whom he manages to incorporate into his physical body and protect into flight.[17]

Equally, Gasiorek argues that Blake is 'a pagan god come to fecundate this pale copy of an animate world with his phallic power ... a Dionysian lord of misrule bent on unleashing the divine *energeia* that Shepperton has dammed up behind walls of social convention, sexual repression and horticultural order'.[18] Both critics read Blake's masturbation as a route to alternative perception and a means of reordering reality, and both seem to suggest that this process is – if not unequivocally in Gasiorek's view – endorsed by the novel. However, it seems unlikely that this is Ballard's intention. Neither critic registers the fact that the passage is very funny. Indeed, it would be hard to formulate a joke more obviously at the expense of the narcissistic and masturbatory tendencies of the untheorized egoistic revolutionary. The section's comedy is also registered at the level of style; the passage mixes the languages of mystical experience and pornography to bizarre and hilarious effect: one minute he is thinking of his paramour, holding his penis in his hand, at the next, he is ejaculating across fuel pumps, turning into a 'pagan gardener'. The world of Shepperton before Blake arrived is without doubt one of capitalist repression. But the transformation of the suburb through masturbation reflects the *subjective egoism* of a consciousness willing to transform any landscape it might happen upon into an unequivocal symbol of transcendence.

There is a much more evident problem with reading Blake as an unambiguously utopian figure. The scenes of free flight, which are the heart of the novel's vision of liberation, are punctuated by disturbing images of paedophilia and cannibalism. Initially, we are comforted by the notion that Blake is 'merging' with other people who lose their identity within his. His lover, Miriam, is engulfed, but soon after disgorged (172–3). Later, many children are taken into Blake's body but 'when their parents watched me anxiously I released the children from my body' (181). However, at the chapter's end we find two 'windswept mothers' searching for lost children and Blake reveals 'I had not released them when we landed' (184). Euphemistically, he comments: 'They would play with me forever, running across the dark meadows of my heart' (184). Shortly after, the pretence is dropped:

> ... as I sat in the rear seat of the limousine, I found a twelve-year-old girl peering down at me through the window. ...
>
> 'Blake, can I fly . . . ?'
>
> Ignoring the waiting sun, which I left to get on with the task of feeding the forest, I opened the door and beckoned the girl towards me. From her nervous hand I took her brother's model aircraft and placed it on the seat. Reassuringly, I helped her into the car beside me and made a small, sweet breakfast of her.
>
> (199)

Once again, it is possible to read this passage as Ballard's satire of the subjective tendencies of the romantic-individualist response to a world that is deformed through capitalism. As well as painting the world with our subjective imaginings, the logical result of a pure individualism is the sacrifice of the other. Blake's initial leap into free flight – a figure of transcendence and utopia – is only possible at the expense of a meaningful idea of the value of the independent lives of the inhabitants of Shepperton.

The Unlimited Dream Company and the counter-culture

The Unlimited Dream Company offers a fascinating insight into Ballard's slightly uncomfortable relationship with the counter-culture of the 1960s and 1970s. It is tempting to understand Blake as an entirely idiosyncratic invention of Ballard's; however, there were historical precedents surprisingly close to Blake and to whom Ballard had very easy access. Michael Moorcock, Ballard's close friend, was a long-time collaborator with the band Hawkwind. Ballard met the band at Moorcock's Ladbroke Grove home.[19] A survey of the biography of the band's most long-serving lead-singer – Robert Calvert – and a look through some of their songs would show that Ballard had plenty of readily available material upon which to base his character. Calvert had an interest in science fiction and published poetry in Moorcock's *New Worlds*. Like Ballard, he had a life-long obsession with aviation. After school he joined the Air Training Corps, but because of a hearing problem could not become a pilot. His solo concept album – *Captain Lockheed and the Starfighters* – explored both this obsession and his problems with mental illness. Calvert's highly theatrical performances with Hawkwind involved many changes of costume and identity, though his most familiar stage apparel was an airman's leather helmet and goggles. There is an obvious parallel here to Blake's early description: 'Only my compulsive role-playing, above all dressing up as a pilot . . . touched the corners of some kind of invisible reality' (11).

Blake's sexualized revolution has antecedents in the work of Wilhelm Reich about whose ideas Calvert wrote a song. Entitled 'Orgone Accumulator', it suggests, in its own gnomic fashion, the problems of a revolution based in sexual gratification; though the accumulator will stimulate the 'back brain' it will not serve social integration, but, instead, cause further isolation. Blake's revolutionary stance to society is reflected in Hawkwind's 'Urban Guerrilla', another track penned by Calvert. The lyrics reflect a proto-punk disenchantment with 'peace and love' hippie values and the change in political temperament towards a more violent expression of discontent that occurred in the early 1970s. Indeed the scene in Ladbroke Grove, from which the band emerged, always had a more political and urban flavour than much of the 'Flower Power' culture. The radical paper *Frendz*, an ethos of free gigs and festivals (including one under the Westway), combined with a strong dose of consciousness-altering drug-taking, made the scene the epitome of the more radical wing of the counter-culture. All the same, Hawkwind were not without their 'peace and love' elements and on the eight-sectioned fold-out design to their live album *Space Ritual*, which is covered with much cod-mystical material, Hawkwind quoted from William Blake's 'Auguries of Innocence': 'To see a World in a Grain of Sand / And a Heaven in a Wild Flower: / Hold Infinity in the palm of your hand / And Eternity in an hour'.[20]

Though there is no sense in which Ballard was writing about Calvert and Hawkwind directly, with such figures not only close at hand but making a substantial impact in the popular culture of the time, it is reasonable to assume that Ballard's vision was influenced by them and the scene from which they emerged. Blake is a figure representative of the psychological underpinnings of the counter-culture so totally embodied by Hawkwind. Ballard was sufficiently interested in this world to ask Moorcock for LSD – an experience which he did not enjoy and did not repeat. However, he was also unconvinced of its intellectual credentials. By making his character a bridge between Romanticism and the antipsychiatry movement, Ballard shows that the thinking borne by the counter-culture and also embodied by figures such as Laing and Reich always runs the risk of an overweening individualism: a celebration of the self as god. At the same time he saw that the world being made by the young radical friends of Moorcock was immensely preferable to the far more pathological world of consumerism.

'Blake' and William Blake (2): 'If the Fool Would Persist in His Folly He Would Become Wise'

The satire investigated above does not explain the sections of *The Unlimited Dream Company* looked at so far entirely. Indeed, it would be wrong to locate ourselves in total opposition to Blake, the sort of comfort in certainty Ballard always denies his readers. One way of understanding *The Unlimited Dream Company* is as a reading of the myths William Blake expounds in his prophetic books, especially *Milton* (1804 (c.1804–10/11)) and *Jerusalem* (1804 (c.1804–20)). In the latter work, the figure of Los – blacksmith and archetypal artist – represents the visionary attempt to maintain imaginative vitality during a period of the bleakest terror: he is a figure who has some common features with Blake. In *Jerusalem*, London is disintegrating because of the sleep of Albion. On Plate 10 Albion's sons, who now rule, are described as using reason to negate human life. Los rejects the ideology he finds all around him: 'I must create a System, or be enslav'd by another Man's. / I must not Reason & Compare: my business is to Create'.[21] It is only through an act of single-minded creativity that the power of the imagination can be maintained. Though not guilty of the egoism of Ballard's Blake, Los can allow no space to alternative argument or vision. If the fallen world is to be overcome it must be done without taking time to 'Reason & Compare'; there is always danger in subversive 'mental war' but it must still be enacted. The city of Golgonooza that Los forges is a redeemed London that returns it to its lost spiritual wholeness and weds its boroughs to locations in Jerusalem. On a beautiful page (Plate 27) of William Blake's illuminated book,[22] with the words on either side of a climbing plant, the following little song is inscribed:

> The Fields from Islington to Marybone,
> To Primrose Hill and Saint John's Wood:
> Were builded over with pillars of gold,
> And there Jerusalem's pillar stood.

. . .

> Pancrass and Kentish-town repose
> Among her golden pillars high:
> Among her golden arches which
> Shine upon the starry sky.
>
> The Jews-harp-house & the Green Man,
> The Ponds where Boys to bathe delight,
> The fields of Cows by Willan's farm:
> Shine in Jerusalem's pleasant sight.[23]

Los includes the particularities of London, down to individual pubs, within his vast mythical system. He and his 'golden builders' forge a renewed and vibrant city analogous to Blake's 'reconditioned Eden'. It is interesting to note that when still trapped in the fuselage of his aircraft Blake gazes at Shepperton and comments: 'I seemed to be looking at an enormous illuminated painting' (17). The vibrant world which the London suburb becomes owes much to the visionary transformations William Blake records in illuminated books such as *Jerusalem*. However, as before, we must register the differences. Shepperton has no place names and instead a series of identified generic features (shopping centres, car parks, car show rooms); the specificity of transformation in William Blake is thus changed. In *Jerusalem* a profoundly personal landscape is being redeemed through the imagination; in *The Unlimited Dream Company* it is the decathected architecture of late capitalist suburbia that is re-energized.

Ballard's Blake must also be understood as an interpretation of William Blake's figure Urizen; a mixture of the demiurge of Gnostic belief – he is a lesser deity but he believes himself to be God – and in part like the Old Testament Jehovah: the source of truth and morality and author of the book of the moral law under which this world is governed. In *Milton* and *Jerusalem*, William Blake calls him Satan, ('Then Los & Enitharmon knew that Satan was Urizen'),[24] but he first appears in the *Book of Urizen*. Here he separates himself from the rest of eternity and makes up his own laws to which he binds everyone. Because 'no flesh nor spirit could keep / his iron laws one moment'.[25] Urizen's religion becomes a savage sacrificial anti-human urge. In *Milton* this idea is returned to:

> And the Mills of Satan were separated into a moony Space
> Among the rocks of Albion's Temples, and Satan's Druid sons
> Offer the Human Victims throughout all the Earth[26]

Compare this with Blake after he has fecundated Shepperton and taken its inhabitants flying.

> Once I had devoured everyone in Shepperton I would be strong enough to move into the world beyond, through the quiet towns of the Thames Valley, a holy ghost taking everyone in London into my spirit before I set off for the world at large . . . Already I suspected that I was not merely a god, but the first god, the primal deity of whom all others were crude anticipations, clumsy metaphors of myself.
>
> (202)

William Blake views Urizen/Satan/God as a figure whose good will, whose desire for 'a joy without pain'[27] leads him to become a cannibalistic megalomaniac. Ballard, too, has created a being who, because of a rejection of the world he finds, has become a cannibalistic deity understanding himself to be the originary being.

The lesson that must be learned by Blake and by Los and Urizen is one of true visionary humanity and mutuality. As long as we view ourselves *as* selves we are condemned to an oscillation between a masochistic self-denial and sadistic self-assertion. This view of identity is brilliantly encapsulated by William Blake's the 'The Clod and the Pebble':

> 'Love seeketh not Itself to please,
> Nor for itself hath any care;
> But for another gives its ease,
> And builds a Heaven in Hell's despair.'
> So sang a little Clod of Clay,
> Trodden with the cattle's feet:
> But a Pebble of the brook,
> Warbled out these metres meet:
> 'Love seeketh only Self to please,
> To bind another to its delight;
> Joys in another's loss of ease,
> And builds a Hell in Heaven's despite.'[28]

A traditional Christian interpretation would endorse the Clod, but the poetic echoing of the first and last stanza indicates that the self is as insistently present in each. 'Another', the supposed object of love which the poem is ostensibly about is strangely absent, covered over by what the self asserts or denies. What appears to be an opposite point of view, the poet reveals to exist in the same wrong-headed moral universe, one in which love is always influenced by the controlling power of the self – pleasure in self-denial or self-assertion.[29] Instead the self must be done away with and replaced by imaginative mutuality. This idea reaches its culmination in William Blake's work towards the end of *Milton* where Milton – figure of the mistaken but well-meaning English visionary and revolutionary tradition – realizes he must destroy his 'self':

> All that can be annihilated must be annihilated,
> That the children of Jerusalem may be saved from slavery.
> There is a Negation, & there is a Contrary:
> The Negation must be destroyed to redeem the Contraries.
> The Negation is the Spectre, the Reasoning Power in Man.
> This is a false Body: an Incrustation over my Immortal
> Spirit: a Selfhood, which must be put off & annihilated alway. [*sic*]
> To cleanse the Face of my Spirit by Self-examination,
> To bathe in the Waters of Life, to wash off the Not Human,
> I come in Self-annihilation & the grandeur of Inspiration![30]

Binary thinking, reason and a belief in the self, end in the oppression so perfectly described in 'London'. Only an alternative vision, rejecting the self and accepting imaginatively the co-existence of a collective humanity, can make us human again. Blake's grand visionary humanism might seem to be precisely the sort of thing that Ballard is satirizing. However, as early as *The Crystal World*, Ballard has Sanders comment that: 'the gift of immortality [is] a direct consequence of the surrender by each of us of our own physical and temporal identities'.[31] Even the characters in *Crash*, *Concrete Island*, and *High-Rise* are fools persisting in folly in that their indulgence of what seems to be inhuman takes them out of the selfhood imposed on them. As Punter points out: 'the long tradition of enclosed and unitary subjectivity comes to mean less and less to [Ballard] as he explores the ways in which person is increasingly controlled by landscape and machine'.[32]

In most of Ballard's novels he shows that profound ambiguities lie at the heart of the problem of subjectivity. The Enlightenment – with its grand faith in human agency – has ended, but what has replaced it is usually represented by Ballard as dystopian. However, he also implies that the radical subjectivities discovered by figures such as Vaughan and James Ballard in *Crash* represent the advance guard of a new dispensation. William Blake was a thinker in open war with reason and the Enlightenment; for him Bacon, Newton and Locke were a trinity of utter wickedness who had cemented humanity's fall. Towards the end of *The Unlimited Dream Company* Ballard is closer to the poet's position than anywhere else in his work. Like William Blake, the redemption Ballard envisages is a passage through the actions of a Phallic God to a new idealism. This is shown by the plot of *The Unlimited Dream Company* in which the town rises up against Blake. Indeed, the Dionysian god is killed to be reborn in another form, a form whose identity is deliberately diffuse:

> I walked across the meadow, surrounded by a strange haze of light, as if my real self was diffusing through the air and lay with the bodies of all these creatures who had given part of themselves to me. I was reborn with them and within their love for me.
>
> (229)

Re-energized, Blake seeks escape from Shepperton and is sure he can achieve it. However, in the chapter titled 'I Give Myself Away', a moment of spontaneous affection makes him stop and give some of his new power to the trio of crippled children who have followed him around Shepperton throughout the novel preparing him for his death and rebirth (231-232). Once healed, *they* in turn lead him to an old people's home where Blake heals the sufferers from leukaemia and cancer:

> David calmly steered me among them as I handed out the gifts of sight and sense, health and grace, to these crippled people, dismantling pieces of my mind and body and passing them to anyone who clutched at my hands.
>
> 'Blake, you've been kind . . . ' Although David was at my right hand, his voice seemed to come from the far side of the park. I was unable to speak.
>
> Happily, I gave myself away.
>
> (235)

This, it seems convincing to argue, is the moment of Blakean annihilation of the subject, the final doing away with what William Blake, the poet, called the 'selfish centre'. In an act of both forgiveness and spontaneous affinity the townspeople then themselves bring Blake back to life again (237) and all eventually fly into the next world leaving him in Shepperton alone. The final paragraph of the novel adopts a purely Blakean register, bringing to mind the final plate of *Jerusalem*:

> Then we would set off, with the inhabitants of other towns in the valley of the Thames and in the world beyond. This time we would merge with the trees and the flowers, with the dust and the stones, with the whole mineral world, happily dissolving ourselves in the sea of light that formed the universe, itself reborn from the souls of the living who have happily returned themselves to its heart.
>
> (254)

> All Human Forms identified, even Tree, Metal, Earth & Stone. All Human Forms identified, living, going forth & returning wearied Into the Planetary lives of Years, Months, Days, & Hours; reposing And then Awaking into his Bosom in the Life of Immortality.[33]

Ballard adopts Blakean imagery and techniques very carefully. The similarity of the passages is striking and surely not coincidental. Both passages envisage a total dissolution of traditional subjectivity, not merely into other human subjects, but into the inhuman environment as well. Ballard wants to show how one might follow William Blake beyond the version of his politics encapsulated by such Proverbs of Hell as 'The road of excess leads of the palace of wisdom'[34] or 'Damn braces: Bless relaxes'.[35] Redemption is achieved through the annihilation of the self and a spontaneous imaginative engagement with the other.

The (re)turn to history

Returning to the questions with which this essay began, we may begin to make some concluding remarks about the status of William Blake and the notion of utopian revolution in *The Unlimited Dream Company*. Ballard is responding to the appropriation of William Blake in the 1960s and 1970s and rejecting the simplified version of visionary revolution he came to represent. However, there is another sense of William Blake in the novel; Ballard represents ideas explored in *Jerusalem* and *Milton*, and, indeed, specific sets of images, in order to show their urgent relevance to his contemporaries. Here there appear to be a set of ideas of transhistorical significance. A model for the notion of history relevant here is provided less by contemporary literary practice, than by the ideas put forward by Walter Benjamin in his 'Theses on the Philosophy of History'. Here Benjamin rejects the historian who tells 'the sequence of events like the beads of a rosary', and endorses one who:

> grasps the constellation which his own era has formed with a definite earlier one. Thus he establishes a conception of the present as the 'time of the now' which is shot through with chips of Messianic time.[36]

Ballard makes a constellation linking late capitalism with the era of the French revolution. In both times there are crushingly oppressive forces at work in the political world and within the subject, but there are also revolutionary possibilities that require vision to be realized. Through his engagement with William Blake, he re-energizes the present and reveals that it remains 'shot through with Messianic time'.

Ballard was by no means alone in turning to Blake at this time. If we agree a period called the long eighties – extending the decade to begin in the late seventies as the postwar consensus began to implode – it is certainly possible to argue that the three most significant works in British fiction from this time were Angela Carter's *The Passion of New Eve* (1977), Alasdair Gray's *Lanark* (1981) and Salman Rushdie's *The Satanic Verses* (1988). Though, doubtless, reflecting a certain taste – one partial to the magical, fantastical or surrealistic in fiction rather than more directly historical and realist modes – the choice could not be dismissed as entirely eccentric. It is incontestable that these novels engage with the most significant of questions: political and social revolution; gender; racial and national identity; and the nature, purpose and correct uses of artistic creativity. The confluence of fantasy and thematic seriousness is less coincidental when we notice that all of these novels self-consciously, and at some length, engage with the work of William Blake.

So why turn to Blake and why turn to him in the 'long eighties'? Perhaps it is because Blake's vision has much in common with socialism, but is in no way reducible to it. For the artist it offers a philosophy that valorizes the role of the imagination in the potential redemption of self and society. At a juncture when the left was uncertain and fragmenting, Blake offered a means of retaining a commitment to social revolution without appearing to endorse a variety of political and aesthetic positions that had become associated with authoritarianism or failure. He also offered a means of going beyond the overhasty insistence on the validity of individual rejections of inhuman social organization that characterized the movements of the late 1960s and early 1970s. *The*

Unlimited Dream Company needs to be understood as a careful working through of the fight against 'mind-forg'd manacles'.

Notes

1. Although he was producing short stories such as those collected in *Low-Flying Aircraft* (1978).
2. Quoted in Jeannette Baxter, 'J. G. Ballard and the Contemporary' in Jeannette Baxter, ed., *J. G. Ballard: Contemporary Critical Perspectives* (London and New York: Continuum, 2008), pp. 1–10 (p. 1).
3. In order to distinguish between them, Ballard's narrator will be referred to as 'Blake' and William Blake (1757–1827) as 'William Blake'.
4. Andrzej Gasiorek, *J. G. Ballard* (Manchester: Manchester University Press, 2005), p. 133.
5. Malcolm Bradbury, 'Fly Away: Review of *The Unlimited Dream Company*', *New York Times*, 9 December 1979, (Viewed at http://www.nytimes.com/books/98/07/12/specials/ballard-dream.html, accessed 25 June 2010.
6. Gasiorek, *J. G. Ballard*, pp. 134–6.
7. Baxter, *J. G. Ballard*, p. 7.
8. Baxter, *J. G. Ballard*, p. 7.
9. Gasiorek, *J. G. Ballard*, p. 138.
10. David Punter, 'J. G. Ballard: Alone Among the Murdering Machines' in *The Hidden Script: Writing and the Unconscious* (London, Boston, Melbourne and Henley: RKP, 1985). William Blake is referred to on pages 20, 21 and 23.
11. J. G. Ballard, *The Unlimited Dream Company* (New York: Washington Square Press, 1985 [1979]), p.40. Further page references are provided within the text.
12. We are alerted here by 'grain of sand' – a quotation from 'Auguries of Innocence' – to the Blakean context. The first two lines are: 'To see a World in a Grain of Sand / And a Heaven in a Wild Flower'. See William Blake, *Blake's Poetry and Designs*, ed. Mary Lynn Johnson and John E. Grant (New York and London: Norton, 1979), p. 209. Ballard's 'eager poppy' could be read as Blake's heavenly 'Wild Flower'.
13. Blake, *Blake's Poetry and Designs*, p. 53.
14. E. P. Thompson, *Witness Against the Beast: William Blake and the Moral Law* (Cambridge: Cambridge University Press, 1993), pp. 175–8.
15. *Revelations* xiii. 16–17.
16. Bradbury, 'Fly Away'.
17. Ibid.
18. Gasiorek, *J. G. Ballard*, p. 137.
19. I would like to acknowledge the generosity of Michael Moorcock for responding to me on the Research message board of Moorcock's Miscellany (www.mutiverse.org) and to Reinhart der Fuchs who runs the website, Accessed 17 July 2010 see string 'J. G. Ballard and Hawkwind'.
20. Blake, *Blake's Poetry and Designs*, p. 209.
21. Blake, *Blake's Poetry and Designs*, p. 316.
22. William Blake, *The Complete Illuminated Books* (London: Thames and Hudson, 2000), p. 324.
23. Blake, *The Complete Illuminated Books*, p. 321.

24. See Plate 10 of *Milton*, in *Blake's Poetry and Designs*, p. 251.
25. Blake, *The Book of Urizen* viii. 4, p. 156.
26. Blake, *Milton*, [Plate 11], p. 252.
27. Ibid ii. 4, p. 144.
28. Capitalization as published. Blake, *Blake's Poetry and Designs* 1979, p. 42.
29. See Heather Glen's exemplary reading of this poem in *Vision and Disenchantment* (Cambridge: Cambridge University Press, 1983), pp. 176–80.
30. Blake, *Milton* Plates 40–1, pp. 303–4.
31. J. G. Ballard, *The Crystal World* (London: Flamingo, 2000 [1966]), p. 169.
32. David Punter, 'J. G. Ballard: Alone Among the Murdering Machines', p. 9.
33. Blake, *Jerusalem*, Plate 99 in *Blake's Poetry and Designs*, p. 358.
34. Blake, *Marriage of Heaven and Hell*, Plate 7 in *Blake's Poetry and Designs*, p. 89.
35. Blake, *Marriage of Heaven and Hell*, Plate 9 in *Blake's Poetry and Designs* Plate 9, p. 90.
36. Walter Benjamin, 'Theses on the Philosophy of History', in *Illuminations*, ed. Hannah Arendt, trans. Harry Zohn (London: Fontana, 1992 [1968]), pp. 245–55 (p. 255).

9
Late Ballard
David James

There may be no clear rationale for turning to a writer's final work as a distinctive phase in its own right, an independent chapter of creativity. Yet it's equally tempting to make the case for the opposite: to reconnect that last body of writing with its younger corpus, maybe with the expectation of finding a certain self-consciousness in a writer's later style, or at least some sign of belated reflection on all that both precedes and informs his or her closing texts. Both approaches are viable and potentially revealing; both court the critical fetishization of lateness for its own sake. But what unites them is the supposition that we ought to grasp the essence of this culminating period from a readerly point of view, rather than from the writer's position of making new decisions as an elder technician looking back on all that has gone before. Endorsing this compositional perspective on the advanced years of a literary life, Martin Amis's 'impression is that writers, as they age, lose energy (inspiration, musicality, imagistic serendipity) but gain in craft (the knack of knowing what goes where)'.[1] Amis was speaking here of his disappointment with John Updike's late prose, which, for him, had become populated with infelicities, 'those rhymes and chimes and inadvertent repetitions', precisely the kind of 'excrescences and asperities that all writers hope to expunge from their work'.[2] Amis's preference for rhetorical economy is clear, and in turn typifies his own reviewing style as he works from the sentence out – reading for diction, cadence, and euphony before getting anywhere near matters of content. And to the extent that Amis's review of Updike's final short fiction offers something of a eulogy while fulfilling its more standard aims of evaluation, it bears comparison with his homage to Ballard himself some two months earlier in April 2009. In this instance, Amis also notes Ballard's influence in formal terms, especially the example left by the 'marvellous creaminess of his prose, and the weird and sudden expansions of his imagery'.[3] These adjectives of applause encourage us to ponder how Amis's rule-of-thumb about late style applies to Ballard in the case of *Millennium People* (2003) and *Kingdom Come* (2006). We might indeed ask whether any 'energy' is lost in these works only to be offset by a 'gain in craft', for it's a process that seems important to trace in the very texture of two novels whose prose appears paradoxically so anodyne for narrating their stories of revolt.

What follows is an attempt to make sense of this apparent disjuncture between mode and sentiment, between Ballard's dystopian vision – representing as it does an unequivocal continuity with his earlier work – and the mode of its articulation, which exemplifies a noticeable retraction from the qualities of metaphorical expansion and melodious phrasing that Amis praises in a writer's major (rather than 'late') phase. However, I want go a step further by complicating the symptomatology of stylistic old-age that Amis relies upon, by suggesting instead that the stylistic moderateness, and intermittent banality even, of Ballard's two final works is more purposive. It marks a re-inflection of a conscious kind, rather than a senescent lapse from form. Ballard develops, that is, a taut and unembellished register that not only forms a tonal kinship with the 'smothered unease' and deceptive 'balm' he attributes to the Metro-Centre in *Kingdom Come*,[4] but also with the kind of 'pointless' violence that *Millennium People* presents 'untouched by any emotions'.[5] More than this, Ballard exploits that symbiotic affinity between action and narrative discourse for a more daring purpose: risking simplicity (in syntax, vocabulary, and perspectivism alike) precisely as a way of *agitating* his reader. At best, the tedium of reading metaphorically restrained and dialogue-driven narration perpetually unsettles us, and dispels any comfortable reassurance that Ballard's newest prose will deliver recognizable pleasures by echoing his earlier *oeuvre*. However, my argument is that we should not simply characterize 'late Ballard' through tone, but show how his economy of expression might have a strategic purpose of its own. This is not to offer an apologia for the verbal coolness pervading Ballard's most recent fiction, but an attempt to explore the implications of responding to its reserved idioms and recursive plotting. If readerly agitation can be one reaction to the rhetorical *surface* of his last two novels, it simultaneously fulfils a more instrumental role in relation to what's happening *inside* both narratives, as the aggravating effects of style itself offer a counterforce to the endemic social monotony Ballard describes.

We might be inclined to draw a distinction, then, for Ballard's late writing between his style's interpretive effects and the affective impact of depicted events. Despite his preference for the enclosed mode of first-person retrospection in *Millennium People* and *Kingdom Come* alike, Ballard allows this perspectivism to assume a more critical force than both novels' functional descriptions might suggest. Ballard achieves this level of criticality despite his repetitive vocabulary, and also in the face of his impersonal characterization of questing or aggressive male protagonists. Thus my point here is not to rehearse this cursory list of the more compulsive structures of Ballard's fiction, so much as to emphasize, from a reader's phenomenological point of view, the various degrees of (dis)engagement that style itself elicits from his audience. In each novel, the deliberateness and frequent austerity of Markham's and Pearson's respective accounts seem to encapsulate the apathetic disenchantment of the communities they're drawn into. But in fact the rudimentary diction, the functional reiteration of atmospheric details, the aphoristic interjections about the portentousness of architectural form – such features work to unsettle the reading experience. That Ballard can leave us feeling distanced from the most intimate domestic episodes shows how he focuses our attention primarily on public space, to the extent that we come to find his built environments more immersive than his characters' private actions.

All of which hardly sounds new for readers of *High-Rise* or *Concrete Island*. But what *is* intriguing is the effect this depersonalizing impulse has had on Ballard's more recent technique – and the alienating, or at least emotively nullifying, effects for his twenty-first-century audience. Why should he have chosen, at this late stage in his career, to forego stylistic virtuosity in order to usher us into a more antagonistic relationship with his prose? Is he asking the reader to *do* something in response to what he formally leaves so diminished? To answer these queries, we have to entertain an understanding of what Ballard's narrative discourse activates, in addition to what it registers. We're familiar with the notion that a novel can formally incorporate its dramatic content, inasmuch as the picturing of a given scene and its very structural articulation may appear coeval, expressively intertwined. But Ballard takes this reciprocity of form and action further by reminding his reader that the 'level of style and syntax', as Richard Strier has observed, '*is* the level of "lived" experience'.[6] With this principle in mind, we can begin to appreciate why Ballard makes the grammatical, tonal and lexical decisions that he does in *Millennium People* and *Kingdom Come*, and in turn why he might *not* be aiming simply to mimic their bland settings through their dispassionate and deadpan narration. If Terence Hawkes is right to say that metaphor offers not simply a 'fanciful embroidery of the facts', but 'a way of experiencing the facts',[7] what does it mean for Ballard to restrain the metaphoricity of his writing or at least deploy analogies in a predictable fashion? What might his late turn to verbal economy be inviting us to experience? Indeed, could it be the case that he is asking us to do something other than merely admire his capacity to integrate style and content, and to respond less reverently but instead discontentedly, as the basis for adopting a more dissenting stance toward the events of eerie mass-indifference that Ballard unfolds?

Kingdom Come invites us to assume this combative stance, as Ballard plots Richard Pearson's journey – partly investigative, partly memorializing – through a depersonalized 'terrain of inter-urban sprawl, a geography of sensory deprivation', fringing the M25, whose lunar topography nurtures 'few signs of permanent human settlement' (6). Even as it moves into such identifiable settings, Ballard guards against the reader's absorption, involving us in the gradual atrophy of domestic and public spheres. Hopes of psychic redemption and collective rehabilitation previously trialled in *Millennium People* are cast aside in *Kingdom Come*; and the novel's language, in tempo and diction alike, mirrors this resignation. Dulled sequences of assertions stripped of ornament, matter-of-factly enunciated, establish a relation between vocabulary, inflection, and perception that prevails throughout. It's as though the paucity of expression correlates with the kind of cognitive desensitization that Pearson attributes to people living out predictable routines, ceaselessly purchasing more:

> History and tradition, the slow death by suffocation of an older Britain, played no part in its people's lives. They lived in an eternal retail present, where the deepest moral decisions concerned the purchase of a refrigerator or washing machine. But at least these Thames Valley natives with their airport culture would never start a war.
>
> (8)

The first two sentences of this passage are of comparable rhythm and clausal length; but lexically speaking, they're significantly different. They demonstrate a contrast between verb uses familiar to us if we recall how the high-rise or Chelsea Marina are described, in that Ballard reserves the more dynamic verbs for describing the condition of the built environment – or, as here, of generic, idealized categories ('History and tradition') – while invoking stative verbs for functionally relaying the actions of people, anonymous and homogenous in making their predictable 'moral decisions'. This contrary invocation of stative and active verbs as they are applied to 'people's lives' and generalized ideals, respectively, reveals the way Ballard makes rhetorical choices with the view to eviscerating all sense of agency from the community he surveys. Those 'Thames Valley natives' are consigned to stasis by the very diction in which they are addressed, as Ballard reinvests instead in 'the town' as an entity in its own right – lending it a sense of being, and evoking it in a more animated fashion than its population who remain in 'an end state of consumerism' (8).

Ballard's picture of suburban London famously integrates a hostility directed at mechanization, prophecies of Middle England's preparedness for uprising, and a lingering endearment toward places that seem immune from the most destructive communal unrest. Iain Sinclair uses this alternating posture in *Lights Out for the Territory* to characterize the historian Patrick Wright, in whose documentaries Sinclair infers a blend of 'scepticism, celebration of Englishness, the polemic that is half in love with the thing it denounces'.[8] Ballard's later style chimes with this tenor of irresolution, a tenor that becomes suspenseful in *Kingdom Come* as the 'entire defensive landscape was waiting for a crime to be committed' (7). And curious though the comparison may seem, Ballard's alternating rhetoric of prophecy and suspense sounds redolent, over a century on, of Thomas Hardy's contention that 'A writer's style is according to his temperament' – an assertion linking sensibility and syntax, insofar as Hardy implies that if a novelist 'has anything to say which is of value, and words to say it with, the style will come of itself'.[9] Certainly, Hardy remains one of Ballard's most unlikely precursors. But they do share something of a refusal to unite content and expression, offsetting as their respective novels do traumatic events against the impersonal manner of their treatment. Thus Hardy's pertinence can also be felt in the very tone of Ballard's address, especially in moments that take up Hardy's recommendation for 'getting a melancholy satisfaction out of life' by 'dying, so to speak, before one is out of the flesh; by which I mean putting on the manners of ghosts, wandering in their haunts, and taking their views of surrounding things'.[10] Ballard joins Hardy in compelling us to question the comfortable reciprocity of content and form, even as he writes in a style that seems to embody so completely the existential machinations of life in a 'defensive landscape'.

An incendiary late style

That Ballard has most recently displayed something of this combined approach – by writing prose whose sparseness seems at once withdrawn yet unnerving, reproducing a world-view that's both melancholic and seditious – typifies what Edward Said has called the 'experience of late style'. It expresses a 'type of lateness', comments Said, which 'involves a nonharmonious, nonserene tension, and above all, a sort of deliberately unproductive productiveness going *against*' the grain.[11] And what I want to outline here in respect to *Kingdom Come* are the ways in which Ballard develops his own version of that dissonant style, as he interrogates Middle England's social insularity and contented submission to consumerism. This preoccupation with the threatening nature of seemingly everyday routines returns in this final text, where suburbia itself provides a *'late* setting', in Said's phrase, a stage-set on 'which a crystallized, much-over-worked style conveys in itself' a 'parable' of that 'artistic/personal predicament of coming to a place, theme, or style at a late period in one's life'.[12]

For the Ballard of *Kingdom Come*, though, that predicament is shared purposefully with the reader, as though he wishes to rouse us from passive immersion in plot. In contrast to that 'rhetoric of regeneration' which Sinclair hears in Peter Ackroyd's vein of London writing,[13] Ballard develops what we could call a geometry of fear. He does this by making use of repetitive intimations of systemic collapse, intimations that keep returning to emphasize the Metro-Centre's macabre animism: 'Everything seemed dramatized, every gesture and thought. The enclosed geometry of the Metro-Centre focused an intense self-awareness on every shopper, as if we were extras in a music drama that had become the world' (41). Ballard's hyperbole is strategic, situating as it does the building as an anthropomorphic reference point against which new co-ordinates of human trepidation are plotted through the novel. Peter Turchi points out that 'geometry' as a critical term is most often invoked in accounts of emplotment: 'A plot is a piece of ground, a plan (as in the plan of a building), or a scheme; to plot is to make a plan or, in geometry, to graph points on a grid'.[14] Yet Ballard goes beyond plot. Gradually increasing, the novel's pulse of apprehensiveness is compounded, structurally speaking, by Ballard's programmatic organization of chapters—each bearing a title that figures literally, as a narratorial thought or spoken comment, in the ensuing episode it names. Offering its own proleptic sense of society's mechanization, Ballard's fascination with 'the geometry of the crowd' (as he titles Chapter 17) foregrounds why the modern city's crystallization in routines of its own making should occasion our collective panic. By arranging *Kingdom Come* so geometrically, then, Ballard creates a text that seems to want to systematize our responses to it – the predictability of its properties (diegetic and paratextual alike) intensifies the paranoid psychic landscape it charts. In turn, the novel's structural insinuation that our interpretive reactions are being contained, much like the Metro-Centre's automaton-like neighbours, plays an incendiary role: Ballard invites us to react *against* his novel's style when it works in sync with its setting, where the cumulative effect of simple declarative sentences matches the mall's capacity for 'smother[ing] unease' as it 'diffused its own threat and offered balm to the weary' (37).

Ballard implies that it's not enough simply to read about techno-modernity's ills. And it would seem that the success of a novel like *Kingdom Come* should be measured in its ability to refresh Brechtian lessons in spectatorial alienation, allowing us to stand back and claim some form of critical purchase on the scenarios it conveys and condemns. As I've suggested, that Ballard's style can become so restrained and mundane is purposive; it's a barometer registering the nullifying experiences he describes, showing syntactically how apathy eventually conditions his narrator's whole way of seeing. These sentiments are amplified when Pearson first meets his late father's solicitor. Ventriloquized through Fairfax, we hear Ballard's solemn pronouncements against that consumer pleasure-dome housed inside the Metro-Centre. The episode is worth quoting at length for the way it recalls the anthropomorphic setting of *High-Rise* as well, highlighting once again that primal desires can be reprogrammed by architectural design, perpetuating those desires while normalizing the part they play in everyday routine:

> 'It's a monstrosity'. Fairfax's voice had deepened, as if he was berating a parade ground of slacking troopers. 'The day they broke the first sod any number of people feared what it might do. We were right. This used to be a rather pleasant corner of Surrey. Everything has changed, we might as well be living inside that ghastly dome. Sometimes I think we already are, without realizing it'.
>
> 'Even so'. I searched for some way of calming him. 'It's only a shopping mall'.
>
> 'Only? For God's sake, man. There's nothing worse on this planet!'
>
> His temper up, Fairfax propelled himself from his chair, heavy thighs rocking the desk. His strong hands drew back the brocaded curtains.

> Beyond the leafy square and a modest town hall was the illuminated shell of the Metro-Centre. I was impressed that a suburban solicitor should give in to such a display of anger. I realized now why the curtains had been drawn when we arrived, and guessed that they remained drawn throughout the day. The interior of the dome glowed like a reactor core, an inverted bowl of light shining through the glass panels of the roof. A ten-storey building stood between the mall and Fairfax's burly figure, but the lights of the Metro-Centre seemed to shine through the structure, as if its intense luminance could penetrate solid matter in its search for this hostile lawyer squaring his shoulders.
>
> (31–2)

Fairfax and Pearson remain divided over whether this vast building is benign. And this division is reflected in the alternative lexicons of spatial description at work here. There's a gradual shift of emphasis across the passage from topographic reportage, through similes of iridescence, finally lending grammatical agency to the Metro-Centre as the determining presence of all those who dwell within its reach. This avid catalogue of analogies parallels Ballard's equally unending search for new discursive strategies, his persistent quest to expose our everyday complicity in embedded systems of exchange. Intoned by a shamanic voice, the passage imitates, if not embodies, the insistent blend of animism and argumentation that captures Ballard's critical pose. The ornamental use of anthropomorphisms does more to preserve a spectacle that should in fact be denounced.

Such an inadvertent manoeuvre of preservation betrays the implication that the Metro-Centre might be beautiful after all. Ballard, of course, means to conceal this level of enthralment, in order to defamiliarize the mall's vital status for the community it supposedly serves. This feels like a deliberate move, for sure; yet ultimately, Ballard leaves it to his reader to unpack the implication that Pearson's mindset is by no means unique. As with his underlying admiration of the Metro-Centre's structural perfection, there's something uneasy about the casual ease with which Pearson describes how 'Consumerism and a new totalitarianism had met by chance in a suburban shopping mall and celebrated a nightmare marriage' (189). Despite the running metaphor of connubial bliss – a metaphor that's initially inventive but ultimately predictable – the observation combines aphoristic panache with that simple resignation again, intoned by Pearson's willingness to accept that events are inevitable and public sentiment (like public space) is not open to change. Ballard thus expresses what should be seen as socially ominous in the language of witty aphorism, rendering the abnormality of totalizing consumerism more palatable. His implicit warning is that Pearson has, in effect, become a victim of his own stipulative grammar: a manner of speaking about an increasingly oppressive world that allows no provisional or qualifying clauses to invade its own rhetorical functionality; leaving no resources, in turn, to describe the grounds for redeemed urban futures. It's as if there's no space left to formulate democratic propositions, only further diagnoses of the unchanging present. And *Kingdom Come* encourages us to react to this acknowledgment, to remain watchful of the novel's own verbal mundanity, as Pearson proceeds to offer up his banal comparisons and recursive portents – as though the novel itself like the 'people of the retail city' were waiting with its reader 'for something violent to happen' (16).

Prophecies from a paranoid realist

Unlike the very literal scenes of carnality set in the tower block or motorway embankment of its 1970s predecessors, in *Kingdom Come* tell-tale signs that the Metro-Centre will play host to psychosocial perversions are largely implied, precisely because the physical and libidinal entrapments of this consumer-dome are so accepted. A monument to the most normal of routines, the mall is home to a consensual arena where the public actively sanction, and render conspicuous, their own allegiance to hours spent making endless purchases. Ballard is hardly partaking, therefore, in a vision of what social theorists like Ulrich Beck and Anthony Giddens have called our 'reflexive modernity'.[15] In Brooklands it's not that people are permanently 'condemned to individualization', as Beck might diagnose it,[16] so much as they maintain a communally endorsed exercise in self-satiation, where the uniqueness of one's personhood is, paradoxically, liberated rather than constrained within the carceral space of a mall. Preserving a sense of community here is nowhere near as futile as the familiar story of postmodern society's fragmentation would have us believe. The more sinister condition, as Ballard implies, is revealed by the way a population can become entirely unperturbed, spending their money and leisure time together so seamlessly as to no longer require any individual reflection about what they're doing.

By zeroing in on this communal picture of wilful blindness, *Kingdom Come* repeats *Millennium People*'s alignment with the genre of apocalyptic parable. Ballard has aspired to tell what is, in many ways, a moral story about a community that disowns the value of mutual responsibility and economic moderation. In so doing, his fable of a middle-class town evolving into a fascist stronghold warrants Peter Ackroyd's praise for writers who have shown the extent to which 'conventional wisdom is seen not to be wisdom at all'. Ackroyd maintains that:

> English novelists have assisted in this process by, as it were, stripping the veils of language – reality is now presented as uncomfortable, as being demanding, and as a result it has become less open to conventional habits of narration and description.
>
> That is why much recent fiction in England is filled with sporadic violence, with confrontation, with the harsh ironies which our social history has inflicted upon us ... we are continually being made aware of the oddness of the ordinary, the menace and brutality which lie behind the conventional political and social worlds. You might, I suppose, call it the new realism – paranoid realism.[17]

That 'confrontation' with 'sporadic violence' is hardly exclusive to Ballard's later phase. But what's useful about Ackroyd's coinage is that 'paranoid realism' not only specifies a mode of telling; potentially, it denotes both a thematic concern with the fear of unspecified threat *and* a series of stylistic commitments to less 'conventional habits of narration and description'.

It's in this dual-pronged fashion that Ballard could be said to have worked as a paranoid realist across his *oeuvre* of urban fictions, much like his contemporary visionary, Iain Sinclair. For both writers, paranoid ways of seeing manifest themselves in their narrative focus and timbre, allowing them to pay special attention to the architecture of unspecified menace. By approaching Ballard's prose at this level, we can see how he uses paranoia in *Kingdom Come* not only as a topic of discussion between characters or as a flickering narratorial speculation, but as an expression of the sentiments it embodies – a *poiesis* of paranoia, that is, whose interpretive effects may allow us to explore why Ballard should want to foster such an agitated reading experience.

Pearson has more than simply a propensity to hear that 'noise of conspiracy' beneath the verbal veneer of public announcements; he actively hunts down the sound of it wherever he moves. Mary Falconer, the Sergeant who soon dubiously quells the investigation into the shooting of Pearson's father, is described as 'a bundle of unease and disquiet wrapped inside an elegant blonde package' (25). Likewise, he searches too for what the distribution of inanimate objects might conceal, especially with respect to the consumer goods on which Brooklands sustains itself. Christie's free domestic appliances, for instance, given away as tokens of resistance to Metro-Centre purchase prices, shift from being 'familiar furniture' to 'something surrealist', a 'presence that unsettled the small crowd' looking on (89). Widening his remit for testing whether his suspicions of institutional tyranny are exaggerated or not, Pearson moves from the particular to the general condition. He does this by shifting from accounts of ordinary utilities made strange (as the description of Christie's fridges) to detecting a more diffuse – because all-pervasive – miasma of unsettlement, one that leaches into the lives of those who are most satisfied by the banalities of their shopping environment: 'A deep, convulsive chemistry was at work, waking these docile suburbs to a new and fiercer light' (152).

Working at the level of the community like this, Ballard revises Pearson's vocabulary in a fashion that reorients the novel's mode. The narrative modulates from retrospective testimony as Pearson begins to speak out and *for* the place he's so mistrustful of, preferring, accordingly, a more impersonal and aphoristic manner of address. Gnomic generalization thus becomes the chosen idiom for appeasing personal paranoia (the anxiety can be transplanted, shared out, when it's catalogued as a communal condition), but with the effect of flattening out the novel's narration: 'Like English life as a whole, nothing in Brooklands could be taken at face value. . . . Had I stumbled into a conspiracy that was now shaping itself around me? And had my father been one of its instigators?' (77). Such rhetorical questions struggle to intensify our sympathy for Pearson, because they simply rehearse the intimations of threat that he has been experiencing from the novel's outset, intimations that periodically return as he updates his descriptions of the dominance of a mall to which he himself is compulsively drawn. Indeed, for it to be effective, the dramatization of paranoia (whether as an intermittent feeling or as a collective malaise) relies on the writer evoking a sense of fear of unspecified peril. Given this proviso, there's only so far Ballard can have Pearson speak of paranoia in name without specifying its source and dissolving some of that anxiety of unknowingness which provokes someone to have delusions of persecution in the first place.

Formally speaking, we might say that Ballard's sequencing of paranoiac reactions ends up providing too deliberately – as exemplified by the ruminative rhetorical questions above – if not too rapidly an account of the way Pearson processes events. So functionally enunciated, Pearson's suspicions no longer seem warranted, giving little reason for us to be curious about his plight or to be enthralled by the imminence of the doom he predicts. Yet this is precisely the depletion of affect that Ballard wants us to experience. The narrative's steady dilution into long passages of dialogue, Pearson's recourse to frequent aphorism in place of scenic depiction, his perfunctory questions which at times don't even seem interesting to himself – these reveal Ballard's purposive deadening of his own style, making it as boring as the lives he describes, as he takes the risk of initially estranging us in order to draw us back in.

Against boredom

To return to that seemingly more implausible forebear: Hardy asserted in 1875 that 'The whole secret of a living style and the difference between it and a dead style, lies in not having too much style – being – in fact, a little careless, or rather seeming to be, here and there'.[18] While they certainly aren't haphazard, *Millennium People* and *Kingdom Come* do seem to demonstrate a deliberate reduction in stylistic flair on Ballard's part. With their economy, they signal a turn to spareness that compels us to ponder the relation between formal innovation and political critique. Did Ballard, in his final works, lose faith in the possibility that formally experimental novels might also have the capacity to articulate powerful social, polemical and philosophical interventions? Perhaps not. For to summarize: both *Millennium People* and *Kingdom Come* present alternative versions of suburbia while attenuating *on purpose* their own linguistic agility and tonal variety; they depict the lived environment with a functional syntax that emulates the monotony of what is outwardly described, detailing monotone sceneries where the predictability of public desires makes any idea of personal intervention seem redundant. With the repetition of these signature tropes, these texts are expressive of the kind of negativity that, for Said, is the hallmark of late style: 'where one would expect serenity and maturity, one finds instead a bristling, difficult, and unyielding – perhaps even inhuman – challenge'.[19] By allowing this furrowed brow of negative reflection to inflect his late writing, Ballard is reactivating a pervasive concern, stemming back to the early 1980s, captured in his 'fear' that 'the future' could well be reduced to 'one word: boring'. His worry 'that everything has happened', that 'nothing exciting or new or interesting is ever going to happen again', leads him to picture our urban 'future' as nothing but a 'vast, conforming *suburb of the soul*' – a region of apathy where 'nothing new will happen' and where 'no break outs will take place'.[20]

Two decades on from Ballard's admission, Maxted offers a mouthpiece in *Kingdom Come* for this worry about the prospect of the future's stultifying uniformity. ' "Boredom," ' declares Maxted, ' "and a secret pleasure in one's own malice. Together they can spur a remarkable ingenuity" ' (103). He reiterates his sentiments in the novel's climactic stages, taking in a whole population in starkly homogenous terms: ' "People are bored. Deeply, deeply bored. When people are that bored anything is possible. A new religion, a fourth reich. They'll worship a mathematical symbol or a hole in the ground. We're to blame. We've brought them up on violence and paranoia" ' (210). Similarly, Julia Goodwin, who might seem to be Pearson's only ally and source of affection, assures him that there's no way out, because the land over the horizon replicates what's here-and-now. If you feel trapped, she says, ' "You'll have to move. Just one problem: wherever you go you'll find nothing except a new kind of boredom" ' (67). Ballard's lasting 'fear' from the 80s, then, is revived in his last novel, to the extent that even Maxted's prophetic generalizations emulate Ballard's own: ' "The future is going to be a struggle between vast systems of competing psychopathies, all of them willed and deliberate, part of a desperate attempt to escape from a rational world and the boredom of consumerism" ' (105).

The insistent diction here (our 'future *is going to be* . . . '), uniting author and character, had previously been heard in *Millennium People*. With similar predictions of a horrific mass boredom that's yet to grip present London as extensively as it will, Gould tries to convince David Markham that he too is at once a passive and complicit inhabitant. Markham won't do justice to civic life, or reverse its delusions of contentment, until he admits his readiness to campaign against his own pacification. Ever drawn, as a charismatic orator, to the lilt of the spoken prognosis, Gould also insists that it has been Markham's destiny, as his 'disenchantment' grew, to join the anarchists after all, since his 'future' is already 'receding'. Gould characterizes Markham as 'a stage set, one push and the whole thing could collapse at your feet' (138). The 'stage set' is of course one of Ballard's favourite metaphors, one that works both ways: an analogue for the false trappings of middle-class contentment; and a cipher for implying that revolutionary action might come about when that 'set' is overturned by the very actors who occupy it. In *Millennium People* this vision of revolt is dispelled, as the 'kingdom' of the estate recovers its own sublime banality. As Ballard would later remark in *The Independent* around the release of *Kingdom Come* (echoing that attention to false appearances that underpins Ackroyd's formulation of paranoid realism): 'I realised that what we think of as conventional reality—this quiet suburban street, for instance—is just a stage set that can be swept away'.[21] Therefore his earlier lesson in *Millennium People* was clear: what if Middle England's self-legitimized stasis can't 'be swept away'? And in turn this question swivels round toward Ballard as an innovator: what might it mean to write a novel that is stylistically consonant with the (sub)urban blankness it condemns, a novel that barely modulates its own discourse in order to prompt us to engage more edgily with its implications?

It is this template for a suburban novel that *Kingdom Come* fulfils: a narrative that becomes what it shows, in the hope of antagonizing its readers and estranging them from passive evaluation. Ballard succeeds in doing this by following a similar arc of boredom-menace-revolt-restoration along which *Millennium People* tracks the Marina's path back to the status quo. After the bombing of the Metro-Centre, Pearson mirrors Markham's resignation that any further uprising would be quelled, remarking that 'It would soon be repaired' even though 'for the moment a section of space-time had been erased, exposing a deep flaw in our collective dream' (113–14). Likewise, even after its final destruction, seeming like 'a crashed airship', Pearson notes that 'in other ways it resembled the caldera of a resting volcano, still smoking and ready to revive itself. One day it would become active again' (279). The Zeppelin analogy is familiar to us by this point; but so is the rather hyperbolic simile of the recent eruption, as though Ballard is evoking—through Pearson's compulsive reaching for larger and more catastrophic analogues – how the desire to equate the Metro-Centre with something far more than it actually is remains not simply symptomatic of the substitution of boredom for paranoia. It also reveals that to re-describe this environment is far more interesting than living in it; that to inflate the scale of events with personal prophecies of apocalypse is more rewarding than harnessing the collective power of discontentment; and that, by implication, the actuality of uprising is less stimulating for a daydreamer like Pearson than violence as an unrealized prospect. He seems more eager to defer the onset of the community's self-destruction in order to preserve it as a thought experiment – the kind of event that exists only to be endlessly re-envisioned, an event whose efficacy is measured not against how it might reform social space, but against the hypothetical possibilities of its occurrence. Such is the compromise that *Kingdom Come* captures, where the libidinal satisfactions of re-imagining violent futures far and away surpass the more rigorous, if laborious, work of realizing instrumental change. The novel thus closes with a knowingly passive prospect of the Metro-Centre's self-recuperation.

And in this finale Ballard is deliberately running the risk of aestheticizing the perception of an animistic environment – aligning it with Pearson's viewpoint as a character whose watchfulness rarely elicits our sympathy – at the expense of addressing a more proactive (and less paranoid) vision of environmental reform, a vision in which place itself, in Sinclair's words, might become 'more than a metaphor'.[22]

What I've suggested, then, is that our estimation of the distinctiveness of Ballard's late phase involves not so much a decision about whether to opt for praise or disappointment – to applaud the perfection of his earlier fiction or indict him for the loss of a previously impressive aesthetic. Rather, it takes on a more dialectical guise: we must negotiate between the idea that Ballard allows the *form* of his fiction to embody what it shows, and our own acknowledgement that his decision to write so colourlessly at times may *not* in fact be such a conscious one. Certainly, as Martin Amis would have it, the ambiguity surrounding whether Ballard intended to pare things down as he did epitomizes the senior writer losing that 'knack of knowing what goes where'. But to follow Amis's model would be to mistake the challenges involved in reading late Ballard, for there's something else afoot aside from mistakes in craft. To what extent his retracted and sometimes monotone narration is intended to encapsulate the dystopian sensibility that underlies it – syntactically incorporating the torpid suburban realm it describes – is the open-ended question that's posed to us after engaging with *Millennium People* and *Kingdom Come*. It's an all the more pressing question to address once we accept the level of uneasy participation they invite from us, especially when 'to read and look at Ballard's work', as Jeannette Baxter has contended, 'is to be an active producer of the textual spectacle'.[23] In this dynamic way, Ballard not only offers two climactic parables of paranoia, or indeed the exhaustion of paranoia under the shadow of conspicuous consumption, where everyone seems to condone each other's self-deceiving complicity in lifestylization as a new shared faith. More so, the critical efficacy of both novels is extradiegetic, rather than simply contained in sociological lessons we draw from their plots. That is to say, they create a peculiar set of interpretive conditions, as our alternating admiration of, and resistance to, Ballard's psychopathological vision is mediated by style itself – particularly, as we've seen, when his relatively impassive, figuratively uninventive use of pictorial space becomes entirely appropriate to the ennui of Markham's and Pearson's reactions to material space.

It's tempting to see these ruptures in register as a literary correlative to Ballard's own prediction that urban life as a *'graspable'* or *'central experience*' will be dissolved in the near future from within, just as 'Sections of the landscape will have no connection whatsoever with each other'.[24] But, again, that would be to assume that Ballard's formal contortions respond mimetically to the world—merely mirroring, rather than offering a way of reading that's critically distanced from, the familiar picture of postmodernity's social derangement. What I've been arguing is that form, depicted environment, and reader are triangulated in a deceptively dynamic fashion, whereby Ballard's effort is not merely to allow scenery and style to infuse one another, but also to engage us viscerally with the way style *behaves* in situations where characters face the nullification of creative thinking and resistance. While tracing the submission of individual will to the consumer's virtualized needs, he came to regard his late fiction less as an instrument flatly tuned to the chord of dystopian boredom, than as a catalyst for interpretive interaction. By being so poised it leaves us wanting disquietude: Ballard's composure simulates what he condemns, precisely in order to incite unsettling responses to the most accustomed lifestyle ideals.

Notes

1. Martin Amis, 'The Master's Voice', rev. of *My Father's Tears and Other Stories*, by John Updike, *The Guardian*, Review, 4 July 2009, p. 6.
2. Amis, 'The Master's Voice', p. 6.
3. Martin Amis, 'From Outer Space to Inner Space', *The Guardian*, Features & Reviews, 25 April 2009, p. 2.
4. J. G. Ballard, *Kingdom Come* (London: Fourth Estate, 2006), p. 37. Subsequent page references are given parenthetically in the text.
5. J. G. Ballard, *Millennium People* (London: Flamingo, 2003), p. 176. Subsequent page references are given parenthetically in the text.
6. Richard Strier, 'How Formalism Became a Dirty Word, and Why We Can't Do Without It', *Renaissance Literature and Its Formal Engagements*, ed. Mark David Rasmussen (New York: Palgrave, 2002), p. 212 (my emphasis).
7. Terence Hawkes, *Metaphor* (London: Methuen, 1972), p. 69.
8. Iain Sinclair, *Lights Out for the Territory* (London: Granta, 1997), p. 303.
9. Thomas Hardy, 'The Art of Authorship' (1890), repr. in *Thomas Hardy's Public Voice: The Essays, Speeches, and Miscellaneous Prose*, ed. Michael Millgate (Oxford: Clarendon Press, 2001), p. 103.
10. Hardy, *The Life and Work of Thomas Hardy*, ed. Michael Millgate (London: Macmillan, 1984), p. 218.
11. Edward S. Said, *Late Style: Music and Literature Against the Grain* (New York: Pantheon, 2006), p. 7.
12. Said, *Late Style*, p. 157.
13. Iain Sinclair, 'Upriver', rev. of *Thames: Sacred River*, by Peter Ackroyd, *London Review of Books* 31.12, 25 June 2009, p. 6.

14. Peter Turchi, *Maps of the Imagination: The Writer as Cartographer* (Texas: Trinity University Press, 2004), p. 188.
15. See Ulrich Beck, Anthony Giddens, and Scott Lash, *Reflexive Modernization: Politics, Tradition and Aesthetics in the Modern Social Order* (Stanford: Stanford University Press, 1994).
16. Beck, Giddens, Lash, *Reflexive Modernization*, p. 114.
17. Peter Ackroyd, 'The English Novel Now', *The Collection: Journalism, Reviews, Essays, Short Stories, Lectures* (London: Chatto & Windus, 2001), p. 326.
18. Hardy, *The Life and Work*, p. 108.
19. Said, *Late Style*, p. 12.
20. J. G Ballard, 'Interview with J. G. Ballard', by Andrea Juno and Vivian Vale, *RE/Search*, 8.9 (1984), p. 8.
21. Marianne Brace, 'J. G. Ballard: The Comforts of Madness', *The Independent*, 15 September 2006. http://www.independent.co.uk/arts-entertainment/books/features/j-g-ballard-the-comforts-of-madness-415967.html, accessed 8 August 2010.
22. Iain Sinclair, *The Verbals: Kevin Jackson in Conversation with Iain Sinclair* (Kent: Worple, 2003), p. 76.
23. Jeannette Baxter, *J. G. Ballard's Surrealist Imagination: Spectacular Authorship* (Farnham: Ashgate, 2009), p. 2.
24. Ballard, 'Interview with J. G. Ballard', by Juno and Vale, p. 29.

Part IV

'The Personal is Political': Psychology and Sociopathology

10
Empires of the Mind: Autobiography and Anti-imperialism in the Work of J. G. Ballard

David Ian Paddy

> Let us go forward in malice to none and good will to all. Such plans offer far better prizes than taking away other people's provinces or land or grinding them down in exploitation. The empires of the future are the empires of the mind.
>
> Winston S. Churchill, 'Anglo-American Unity', 6 September 1943

A ludicrous offer

In 2003, J. G. Ballard was offered one of the highest honours a citizen of his nation can receive, the Commander of the Order of the British Empire (CBE). It was an honour he refused. Long-time readers of Ballard's work were surely more surprised by the offer than the refusal. That Britain's answer to William S. Burroughs and Jean Genet was now deemed significant and respectable enough to be given a royal award was a strange turn of events; it was as if one of the most notorious criminals were being given the keys to the city. Ballard's anti-conventional disposition meant that he would reject the award, and his reasons were clear: 'as a republican, I can't accept an honour awarded by the monarch. There's all that bowing and scraping and mummery at the palace. It's the whole climate of deference to the monarch and everything else it represents'.[1] By refusing the CBE, Ballard reaffirmed his status as a writer who bucks convention and as a public persona who wryly dismisses accepted wisdom.

Still, something else resides within his reasons for rejecting the CBE that shines light on a significant undercurrent of Ballard's work (and persona). Ballard's resistance was not just against class, authority and tradition. He was similarly repelled by the award's imperial ramifications: 'A lot of these medals are orders of the British Empire, which is a bit ludicrous. The dreams of empire were only swept away relatively recently, in the 60s. Suddenly, we seem to have a prime minister who has delusions of a similar kind.'[2] The medal embodied aspects of British culture and heritage that Ballard spent his lifetime challenging. In a career that began in the 1950s, Ballard had long been writing counter-myths, works that aim to dismantle, deconstruct and destroy accepted ideologies and worldviews, and while these counter-myths can be read with broader application, it is clear that Ballard's perspective is rooted in the context of a Britain coping with the fading legacy of its Empire. A British child born in Shanghai, Ballard waged war, implicitly and explicitly, on the insularity of post-war England and its archaic imperial dreams in their many variegated forms. At the heart of Ballard's resistant work is a resistance to imperialism.

It is perhaps surprising, then, that few critics have examined the imperial or postcolonial dimensions of Ballard's body of work at length. Roger Luckhurst's seminal study, *'The Angle Between Two Walls'* (1997), offers tantalizing suggestions, but the politics of Empire are not his primary concern.[3] More recently, Jeannette Baxter in *J. G. Ballard's Surrealist Imagination* (2009) has offered a postcolonial reading of *The Crystal World* within the framework of Surrealism, as well as accounts of Ballard's take on globalization in *Cocaine Nights* and *Super-Cannes* in her essay 'Visions of Europe' (2008).[4] And although other critics, such as Dennis A. Foster, Liam McNamara, and Andrzej Gasiorek, touch on colonial or imperial issues, these are not, again, their primary focus.[5] Too often critics have examined Ballard's work within generalities about violence or 'the social', but such concepts need to be placed within a particular frame and context. My goal in this chapter is to give greater prominence to the study of nation and imperialism within Ballardian criticism.

If a resistance to Empire is at the heart of Ballard's work, then what form does this resistance take? Ballard's writing, for the most part, does not take the shape of an overt critique of real-world political dramas; he is less interested in depicting the history of Empire or examining how it functioned at an institutional level, in the way one might expect in the work of Joseph Conrad, V. S. Naipaul or J. G. Farrell. Nor does Ballard's speculative fiction amount to an elaborate allegory about the end of the British Empire, as Fredric Jameson once claimed: 'Ballard's work is suggestive in the way in which he translates both physical and moral dissolution into the great ideological myth of entropy, in which the historic collapse of the British Empire is projected outwards into some immense cosmic deceleration of the universe itself as well as of its molecular building blocks'.[6] So, how to make a case for J. G. Ballard, post-imperial writer?

Starting with an analysis of his first published story, 'The Violent Noon' (1951), a story that has received virtually no attention but one that contends with the politics of colonial struggle in Southeast Asia, I illustrate how imperial and postcolonial issues were there from the start of Ballard's writing career. Quickly rejecting the overt colonial politics of his first story, Ballard moved toward the 'New Wave', or inner-space science fiction he first became well-known for, but rather than abandon his interest in imperialism his particular brand of science fiction in the 1960s offered a means of examining imperialism from a new angle. Not only did the traumatic legacies of imperialism require a more nuanced literary methodology, but by the 1960s new forms of cultural imperialism and social control were also coming to the fore through forces like advertising and electronic media. Ballard's psychologically inflected science fiction provided a means for engaging with what I will refer to as psychic imperialism. To illuminate this turn in Ballard's work, I make reference to the psychoanalytic literature of Jacques Lacan and Slavoj Žižek. In the final section of this chapter, I turn to *Super-Cannes* (2000), to examine how his later work presented globalization as a new, post-war form of imperialism, which makes coolies of the human mind.

'The Violent Noon': anti-imperialist beginnings

Ballard's childhood in Shanghai was clearly of great importance to him, and in stories, novels, essays and interviews he made much of this most colonial and international of Chinese cities, with its European architecture and skyline, alive with European nightlife, cinemas and clubs. He also drew attention to the surreal qualities of his home on Amherst Avenue as a bit of England dropped in the middle of Chinese rice paddies. Equally important to his self-narrative was the destruction of all this in 1941, when the Japanese seized the International Settlement, and in 1943, when Ballard's family was placed in the Lunghua internment camp.

Despite the radical disruption of his colonial life and the grimness of a childhood lived out in war, Ballard consistently conveyed the experience of destruction as productive. Think of how he portrays young Jim in *Empire of the Sun* (1984), breaking out of his stereotyped and contained world of mock Englishness (such as the pretend Eton of the

Cathedral School) into new realms of possibility and toward a new identity. In this we see Ballard constructing (or looking back on how he constructed) a worldview in which the destruction of a simulated England was traumatic yet liberating because, psychologically, trauma exposed social illusions; in this case, the illusions of a mock England built on Chinese terrain. As the narrator of *Empire* says, 'The years in Lunghua had not given Jim a high opinion of the British'.[7] Yet, again, the loss of faith in a narrative of national identity is presented not entirely as loss, but as a revelatory new freedom.

In his autobiographical accounts, Ballard goes on to describe his move to England as his second great experience of alienation and disruption. Leaving behind the colonial dreamscapes of Shanghai, he found himself completely at odds with the strangeness that was England: 'Coming to England in 1946 was a shock that I've never recovered from . . . . English life as a whole in '46 seemed enormously detached from reality'.[8] Like so many other writers raised in Britain's colonies, from E. R. Braithwaite to V. S. Naipaul, Ballard found the reality of the 'motherland' to be sharply in contrast with the picture imprinted from British literature: 'the England I had been brought up to believe in—A. A. Milne, *Just William*, *Chums* annuals—was a complete fantasy'.[9] In his numerous autobiographical pieces, Ballard constantly presents England and its extension into the world through imperialism as a kind of flimsy fiction.

Importantly, an imperial imagination was forged in the literature of his childhood. In 'Pleasures of Reading', he discusses his early love of *Robinson Crusoe* and *Treasure Island*, and elsewhere comments on his steady diet of adventure comics, Charles Kingsley and G. A. Henty's books for boys.[10] In *Miracles of Life*, he emphasizes his love of American comics, such as *Buck Rogers*, *Flash Gordon* and especially *Terry and the Pirates*, since it was set in the Far East, but also the English boyhood staples of the era, *Chums* and *Boy's Own* annuals. The war's disruption unsettled Ballard's familial and personal life, but it also disturbed the mental template forged by English education and colonial reading. Ballard summarizes this when he says of the invasion of Shanghai:

> So was nailed down the coffin of the British Empire, though the corpse was the only one not to know it was dead, and continued to kick for too many years to come. The myth of European invincibility had died, something that an eleven-year old brought up on G. A. Henty and tales of derring-do on the north-west frontier found

hard to accept. The British Empire was based on bluff, in many ways a brilliant one, but that bluff had been called.[11]

In *Miracles* he puts this more succinctly; reflecting on the sinking of the HMS *Petrel, Repulse* and *Prince of Wales*, Ballard says: 'Despite my admiration for the Japanese soldiers and pilots, I was intensely patriotic, but I could see that the British Empire had failed. I began to look at A. A. Milne and the *Chums* annuals with a far more sceptical eye' (56). With this background in mind, it is no surprise that a critical attitude toward nation and Empire would inform Ballard's writing.

A reader familiar with Ballard's work might find something remarkable about his first published story, 'The Violent Noon', a contest winner in the Cambridge student paper, *Varsity*. Written when Ballard was twenty-years old, four years after he had first arrived in England, it foreshadows forthcoming Ballardian concerns in protozoan form, yet, in its overt topicality it is notably atypical. Ballard's career begins with a piece that addresses imperial politics in a quite direct and realistic manner that he would soon abandon.

'The Violent Noon' is set in Malaya during the so-called Malayan Emergency, when Chinese guerrilla fighters fought for independence from the British colonial government between 1948 and 1960. The story begins with two English colonials, Hargreaves and Michael Allison, disagreeing over the fate and benefits of the Empire. As seen by the Malayan driver, Hargreaves is a 'pompous manicured idiot' who 'talks of fighting and defending the Empire and doesn't even know which end of his machine gun to hold'.[12] In contrast, Michael Allison is a 'slim understanding man' who is 'so sympathetic and intelligent and genuinely wants Malay to be free', yet, he 'exploits its people for the greed of others, working them to disease and early death on the plantations' (9). The English group comes under fire by guerrilla fighters, and ironically it is Michael Allison, defender of Malayan freedom, and his daughter who are the victims of violence in the struggle for independence.

The second half of the story concerns the show trial of innocent Chinese men, the result of a 'justice of vengeance', as Hargreaves and Mrs. Allison convince themselves of the rightfulness of their lies in court for the preservation of imperial civilization. The story ends with the bitter taste of institutional corruption so familiar to readers of Joseph Conrad and Graham Greene, as well as George Orwell's writings on Burma; the hypocrisy of the 'white man's burden' is exposed, yet the judicial, military and police forces of the Empire carry the day. The resemblance to the work of these other authors also makes the story subject to the same types of criticism of imperial duplicity that Edward Said makes of Conrad in 'Two Visions in *Heart of Darkness*',[13] for the story clearly intends to reveal the lies behind the invading culture's claims to ethical superiority, but the colonized subjects of Malaya remain simplified subjects, given no real voice and are of not much interest.

Even at this early stage, 'The Violent Noon' works with that familiar Ballardian territory where an act of violence disturbs the sanctity of the real world and unveils unseemly desires and motivations. Yet, what is most striking about the story is how overt it is as a piece of political and, specifically, imperial criticism. This is Hargreaves:

> Look at India, Burma, Ceylon. Just given away. Given away. And we've collapsed like a pricked balloon. There used to be a lot of rubbish shouted about the Empire. Heroics and drum-pounding. But no one ever really believed all that. The Empire is built on purely economic foundations. Without the colonies England ceases to have any actual existence. She's just a minor geographic location. You don't find the Dutch listening to all this talk about self-government and independence.
>
> (9)

Less than six years since his departure from Shanghai, Ballard clearly had the East on his mind, yet the parade of stories and novels that begins to emerge five years later contains little of this sort of content.[14] While *The Drowned World* (1962) and *The Crystal World* (1966) resonate with colonial themes (for instance, the latter is placed in a corrupt French diamond town in the African republic of Cameroon), they do not use the raging battles of contemporary political events as the central point of narrative interest, as does 'The Violent Noon'.[15] These works point us in a new direction.

In an interview with Mark Pauline, a few years after the release of *Empire of the Sun*, Ballard noted that he had 'always wanted to write a book about my China background', while claiming that *Empire* wasn't 'all that different from most of my other writing; it's just that my other fiction doesn't have *the reassurance of the familiar*'.[16] He continues:

> But I've been writing about it all the time—I just wrote about it *in disguise*. . . . As I was writing *Empire of the Sun* I was constantly seeing bits of my other novels coming up. It was like an assembly kit made

up of bits of my other novels set not in the near-future, but in the 1940's.

(138–9)

Such statements reveal that *Empire* was not a naturalistic digression from the rest of Ballard's *oeuvre* and that something of his interest in international politics, found in 'The Violent Noon', was at work in his more 'imaginative' novels and stories.

Still, Ballard's notion that he began working 'in disguise' requires commentary. Rather than a confession that his fictions are in fact allegories, Ballard implies that the dark realities of twentieth-century history resist the kind of transparent representation hoped for by naïve realism. Like many postwar authors, Ballard reckoned with the limits of realism, and in particular with the representational challenges of contemporary history. Linda Hutcheon sees the highlighting of the narrative dimensions of history to be central to postmodern fiction, while Jago Morrison argues that traumatic events like the Holocaust and the dramatic disruptions of colonial independence movements have challenged faith in a singular, direct and authoritative telling of history.[17] Speaking of his childhood experiences of war, Ballard himself claimed: 'Reality, I was fast learning, was little more than a stage set whose actors and scenery could vanish overnight'.[18] If war could so quickly undo Shanghai's European facades, then what would a stable sense of reality or narrative look like?

In *Miracles* Ballard offers a tantalizing anecdote that illustrates the problems of finding a singular, stable meaning in any narrative account. In the anecdote, he writes about the drained swimming pools he began to encounter in the gardens of English expatriates after the invasion of the Japanese in 1937. As the drained swimming pool has been one of the most common images in Ballard's *oeuvre*, the attempt in *Miracles* to 'explain' the origin behind it is certainly a tease:

In the coming years I would see a great many drained and half-drained pools, as British residents left Shanghai for Australia and Canada, or the assumed 'safety' of Hong Kong and Singapore, and they all seemed as mysterious as that first pool in the French Concession. I was unaware of the obvious symbolism that British power was ebbing away, because no one thought so at the time, and faith in the British Empire was at its jingoistic height.

(26–7)

That Ballard offers the drained pool as 'obvious symbolism' of British imperial decline is enticing, especially for this reading, but the obvious must be met with caution. Has the pool always meant this? Or should the emphasis be on Ballard's prefatory 'I was unaware', the significance being imparted now by the Ballard of the present writing the memoir? In this passage, Ballard draws our attention to the changing meaning of his past.

After writing 'The Violent Noon', it would seem he became quickly dissatisfied with the conventions of realist storytelling and would need to find new means to cope with the complexities of reality and the instability of meaning. Yet it is equally important that in the years after *Empire*, Ballard consistently gave his work and his past a new signification that placed greater stress on national and imperial meanings for his works than had been the case prior to *Empire*. Between 'The Violent Noon' and *Empire* his interest in his 'China background' and international themes went 'in disguise'; a new direction in fiction became necessary.

The conquest of inner space: psychic imperialism

In the early 1960s, Ballard began speaking of his writing as a form of 'inner-space' fiction, and this clearly became the literary method whereby he took the familiar and worked it 'in disguise'. Luckhurst has traced the history and development of 'inner space', looking to usages by J. B. Priestley and R. D. Laing, and he shows the term to be more than a mere reversal or inversion of science fiction's 'outer space'.[19] While inner space generally appears as an externalization of a character's inner turmoil onto the surrounding landscape, Luckhurst observes that Ballard kept refining and redefining the term as his fiction evolved (51). With this in mind, Ballard's genesis of inner-space fiction should be understood in a particular literary context.

When Ballard began writing in earnest at the end of the 1950s, the dominant mood of English writing was one of quiet parochialism. After World War Two, many writers, notably Philip Larkin, Kingsley Amis, John Braine and Barbara Pym, turned away from large themes and global visions toward intimate portraits of provincial life. Often nostalgic in tone, their works looked to the past to note the qualities of English life that were disappearing in the years of postwar austerity and welfare state modernization. Ballard felt no affiliation to this mode of writing, in either its middle-class or supposedly Angry-Young-Man variety, perhaps because he knew nothing of the England these writers were lamenting.

In 'Memories of Greeneland' (1978), Ballard argues, 'Parochialism seems to me to be the besetting sin of contemporary English fiction', stating further that for many English writers, 'concentration on the life of their own country seems invariably to lead them into all the worst defects of provincialism'.[20] For him, books by these authors were small in scale, small in imagination. In contrast, his respect for Greene, Anthony Burgess and Lawrence Durrell stems from their emigrant interest in the broader world (137). The future, for Ballard, had to be found outside England and the English imagination.

As Ballard began to develop his aesthetics and aesthetic strategies, his inspirations were to be found elsewhere, notably in the continental avant-gardes, as well as in the iconography of American Pop Art. In 'The Pleasures of Reading', he also notes that writers like William S. Burroughs 'restored my faith in the novel at a time, the heyday of C. P. Snow, Anthony Powell and Kingsley Amis, when it had begun to flag' (181–2). Ballard consistently equates English fiction with a narrow parochialism, joined to realism as its tiresome bedmate. In contrast, science fiction offered the potential to open up fiction to new realms of the imagination against such limiting provincial realism.

Yet, in the essay 'Which Way to Inner Space?' (1962), Ballard also expresses concern for the potentially juvenile and generic limitations of much contemporary science fiction.[21] Too often it is locked in an interest in outer space, and ignores new concepts when it should take on an experimental spirit. Ballard's resultant development of inner-space fiction was intended as a rejection of English realism and conventional science fiction. He looked to Surrealism and Futurism especially, for their use of startling dream imagery, emphases on mechanism and movement, and foregrounding of the means of representation. Inner space, then, simultaneously troubled English realism, with its unquestioning acceptance of the world as it is and faith in literary transparency, as well as conventional science fiction for its uninterest in the contemporary world and experimental form.

Significantly, Ballard's own accounts of inner space, primarily in 'Which Way to Inner Space?' and 'Time, Memory and Inner Space' (1963), do not describe a purely abstract form of avant-gardism. Rather the notion of inner space is never entirely divorced from an autobiographical or mimetic impulse. In 'Time, Memory and Inner Space', he asks: 'How far do the landscapes of one's childhood, as much as its emotional experiences, provide an inescapable background to all one's imaginative writing?'.[22] He goes on to discuss how the imagined terrain of his novel *The Drowned World* was generated from a merging of his memories of Shanghai floods and his first impressions of London. Furthermore, as Baxter has carefully elucidated, Ballard's notion of inner space extends the theory and work of the Surrealists, not simply by borrowing a stylized arcade of fantastic imagery, but by building on Surrealism's exploration of history's unconscious to produce a politically motivated artistic method for presenting the traumas of World War Two and its aftermath.

Thus, Ballardian inner space is not a solipsistic retreat into the human mind. Ballard's extension of Surrealism has autobiographical and historical foundations, and it is an attempt to engage with the world along an indirect course. Realism relies on a clean line between inner and outer worlds, but Ballard asked what to make of a modern world in which our human-built environments have our unconscious desires designed into their very fabric, where the inner and outer ceases to be clearly delineated. Similarly, as his disillusioning experience of his childhood literature revealed, the imagination surely does the ideological work of transforming the world we live in.

The limiting aspect of 'The Violent Noon' is that it dealt too directly with reality, and, thus, hadn't gone far enough. This can be clarified by the psychoanalytic theories of Jacques Lacan. In *The Four Fundamental Concepts of Psycho-Analysis* (1973), Lacan says: 'it is in relation to the real that the level of phantasy functions. The real supports the phantasy, the phantasy protects the real.'[23] Lacan is making a crucial distinction between the terms 'reality' and the 'Real'. 'Reality' is a socially-inherited fantasy that screens us from the traumatic Real: 'Reality prevents us from encountering the Real: Reality itself is for those who cannot endure (the Real that announces itself) in their dreams.'[24] We wake up from our dreams to go to reality because reality is a fantasy that is easier to cope with than the traumatic Real of our desires. The Real exposes the lie of reality.

Though 'The Violent Noon' looked abroad, away from a provincial English landscape, its method was still realist. In the story, Ballard tries to deal too directly with a political reality akin to the one he knew in Shanghai, but as Lacan and a later Ballard would argue, such reality is a false screen, it is a safety net for avoiding a deeper trauma. Ballardian inner space, rather than an evasion of realism's supposed real-world subject matter, becomes a means of going all the way to the unconscious, to encounter the Real that reality masks.

A story like 'Manhole 69' (1957), published six years after 'The Violent Noon', displays a shift from reality to the Real, from political realism to a politics of the mind. It is noteworthy that the story shares a structural continuity with 'The Violent Noon'. 'Manhole 69' begins in much the same way but instead of Hargreaves and Michael Allison debating the pros and cons of the Empire, 'Manhole 69' begins with Dr Neill and Morley debating the pros and cons of Neill's experiment in severing the conscious mind from its primitive unconscious twin, to rid the mind's waking factory of its inefficient sleeping and dreaming partner. Illustrating Lacan's notion that we wake from our dreams to escape the Real, 'Manhole 69' shows a speculated world in which the characters 'couldn't go to sleep now if [they] tried'.[25] The test subjects are forced to live entirely in reality, but they come to suffer from a madness of total consciousness; blocked from the Real, they nevertheless experience the hell of total reality. Dr. Neill's attempt to keep them from sleep's 'eight-hour peepshow of infantile erotica' (51) fails when he realizes they 'could no longer contain the idea of their own identity. But far from being unable to grasp the idea, I'd say that they were conscious of nothing else' (66). The ego's sense of stability and total control collapses. More importantly, 'Manhole 69' and 'The Violent Noon' are both tales about a battle for control, and in both cases the desire and rationale for control are ultimately undermined by a Freudian return of the repressed. Clearly the end result of Neill's experiment in mental control is bound to the logic of capitalism, for without the wastefulness of the dreaming mind, the never-sleeping brain would guide an always-working, productive body.

As his fiction developed throughout the 1960s, it became more clearly oriented toward inner space. With this development, Ballard shifted the tension from an earlier colonial model of the struggle between the corrupt forces of rational civilization and the wild brute forces of the repressed to a series of fictions in which a character's stable division of inner and external reality collapses. This traumatic disturbance reveals for the character the ways his or her mind has been manipulated and constructed by the forces of a consumerist ideology promulgated by a media landscape. Here we see the development of what I refer to as Ballard's interest in psychic imperialism. One of the first places this vision can be encountered is in 'The Subliminal Man' (1963). Although Dr Franklin initially regards Hathaway as psychopathic, he realizes that this rogue figure sees through the false veneer of quotidian reality, which consists of activities built solely around conspicuous consumption, and sees behind it an omnipresent subliminal advertising. Franklin's wife, Judith, blithely concedes to the mental control: 'Advertising is here to stay. We've no real freedom of choice, anyway.'[26] It is a short jump from here to Ballard's final novel, *Kingdom Come* (2006), where a new form of shopping-mall nationalism funnels sports fanaticism into consumer fascism.

Ballard's most extreme examination of consumer culture as a form of psychic imperialism is *The Atrocity Exhibition* (1970). This dense, deliberately difficult work employs a variety of avant-garde techniques of fragmentation, condensation and collage to force the reader to face the existential challenge of making meaning of a fragmented universe that encourages passivity. It performs for the reader the instability of identity and desire in a turbulent consumerist era when assassination and war wrestle with toothpaste and car commercials for space on billboards and the television screen. The fragmentation of Ballard's hero acts as an iconic representation of the technological schizophrenia induced in every citizen of postmodern culture. The notion first tested in the story 'The Terminal Beach' (1964), that a third world war would take place in the mind, becomes the central idea for *The Atrocity Exhibition*:

> 'Dr Austin may disagree, but it seems to me that his intention is to start World War III, though not, of course, in the usual sense of the term. The blitzkriegs will be fought out on the spinal battlefields.'[27]

In a world where 'the nervous systems of the characters have been externalized' (44), the characters' most private desires and thoughts have been scripted for them in advance by a commodity and media culture, while their environments of cement and television are the concrete realization of their unconscious sexual and aggressive drives. In short, the apocalyptic psychological battle of *The Atrocity Exhibition* is Ballard's attempt to update such anti-imperial novels as George Orwell's *Burmese Days* and Anthony Burgess's *The Long Day Wanes*, to address a form of psychic imperialism in which a new empire of signs and commodities colonizes and conquers the mind.

Super-Cannes: globalization and the new world order of enjoyment, or Winston Churchill with the Marquis de Sade

A further change in Ballard's writing since *Empire* reveals a different strategy for resisting English parochialism and examining new forms of imperialism. With *Empire* we begin to see what might be regarded as an internationalist turn in Ballard's work. After working with the Chinese setting of *Empire*, he went on to write of central Africa (*The Day of Creation* (1987)), the Pacific atoll of Saint-Esprit (*Rushing to Paradise* (1994)), Gibraltar and Costa del Sol in Spain (*Cocaine Nights* (1996)), and the southern coast of France (*Super-Cannes* (2000)). Ostensibly this interest in international settings and global politics would seem to be a return to the terrain of 'The Violent Noon', and in some ways these novels bear more of that story's surface realism, but these works are clearly built upon the foundations of inner-space fiction and its exploration of psychic imperialism. Furthermore, the globe-hopping of Ballard's later novels does not simply produce a form of vicarious travel literature, but becomes a way for Ballard to examine globalization as a new form of international imperialism.

In his autobiographical writings, Ballard not only emphasized the importance of Shanghai to his life and work, but he would frequently insist that, 'Shanghai was not a British colony.'[28] In doing so he corrected a misperception (Shanghai was a zone of imperialism, but it was not solely a British one), but the assertion was also important to Ballard's self-portrait because the trauma of his arrival in England is largely written as the trauma of losing a dynamic international community for what he regarded as a parochial and monochromatic one instead. Thus, it is telling that in an interview, he made this claim about one of the purposes of his fiction: 'I've tried to change the world to be like Shanghai of the 1930s.'[29] Shanghai as an international, vibrant, forward-looking centre acted as the positive counter to an England imagined as homogenous and backward looking.

Ballard's adoration of Shanghai's internationalism, however, becomes troubled in later novels like *Cocaine Nights* and *Super-Cannes*. The latter, with its idealized multi-national corporate campus, Eden-Olympia, 'an Eden without a snake',[30] represents what Baxter has called 'a fictional remapping of continental Europe' that engages with:

> the impact of global capitalism on physical and psychological landscapes, the transition of a Federalist Europe into a neo-imperial 'super-state', the resurgence of racist and political extremism, the rise in immigrant labour forces and the rapid growth of the sex industry within Europe's markets of 'free-trade'.[31]

As his fictional settings became increasingly international, the celebratory quality of Shanghai's dynamic internationalism, once set against English parochialism, was now also being set against the flattening, homogenizing practices of multinational capitalism.

In a pristine environment of 'simulated nature trails' (37), the resident head psychologist, Wilder Penrose, is quick to point out that Eden-Olympia's ideal business complex has rid itself of the kind of bad politics associated with an earlier model of expansionist capitalism: 'Companies here aren't involved with the Third World. None of them are sweating rubber or bauxite out of a coolie workforce. The raw material processed at Eden-Olympia is high-grade information' (29). Furthermore, he claims with unintentional irony: 'There's nothing racist, by the way. We're truly multinational – Americans, French, Japanese. Even Russians and east Europeans' (19). However, despite Penrose's cheery utopianism, Eden-Olympia is simply a research base founded on neo-liberal economic principles, which, 'holds that the social good will be maximized by maximizing the reach and frequency of market transactions, and it seeks to bring all human action into the domain of the market'.[32]

In his investigations, the protagonist, Paul Sinclair, discovers that a secret world of violence governs this idyllic business camp. In a world where work has replaced leisure, where everyone has become 'too sane' (248), Penrose believes the citizens of Eden-Olympia need a necessary venting of more primal urges to maintain their high level of productivity. Sinclair becomes fascinated by Penrose's theories. He comes to believe the notion that places like Eden-Olympia are truly Nietzschean realms beyond good and evil, where, as Penrose claims: 'A giant multinational like Fuji or General Motors sets its own morality... We've achieved real freedom, the freedom from morality' (95). Gasiorek notes that Ballard's late novels all feature Nietzschean guru figures, but in *Super-Cannes*, Penrose gives 'an ironic twist to Nietzsche's stress on self-overcoming' by making 'the corporation, not the individual... the higher entity' (194). Such an emphasis on the corporation over the individual stems implicitly from Penrose's free-market ideology.

Sinclair, however, starts to become wary of a world in which: 'representative democracy had been replaced by the surveillance camera and the private police force' (38). He comes to realize that the real danger of Penrose's ideas is not the exercise of violence itself, but the way it has been systemized and controlled. This overlaps with Žižek's observation that visible, or 'subjective' acts of violence, are perhaps less troubling than 'systemic' violence, 'the often catastrophic consequences of the smooth functioning of our economic and political systems'.[33] While true, it is still important to point out that Penrose's reign of violence is aimed at France's immigrant communities and is built on the extreme grounds of National Front sentiments. One of the first acts of violence in the novel, for instance, is staged against a 'Senegalese trinket salesman' (71). This is not a vaguely cathartic expression of violence, but an outpouring of rage within a politically ethnic and national context.

The novel begins with Sinclair's wife, Jane, coming to the corporate park to replace David Greenwood, who had taken Penrose's ideas too literally, becoming a sniper who killed several colleagues and himself. However, it turns out that the real trouble that Greenwood posed for Eden-Olympia was that his violence was of an unproductive variety; it did not replenish the system to allow for greater productivity. Far from subverting multinational capitalism, Penrose's form of violence proves to be the very engine of its power, which is why Sinclair can conclude: 'The Adolf Hitlers and Pol Pots of the future won't walk out of the desert. They'll emerge from shopping malls and corporate business parks' (256). Ballard's late fiction is intent on showing the malevolent political forces at work in the antiseptic, seemingly non-ideological spaces of contemporary business and consumption.

From *The Atrocity Exhibition* to *Super-Cannes*, Ballard has charted how the modern nation state has been trumped by the postmodern corporation and media industry as the dominant modes of social order. What is clear from the trajectory of these books is that Ballard did not believe the whiff of imperial sulphur had evaporated in this transition. For Ballard, the mode may have shifted from national to global, but the repressive mechanism of civilization outlined by Freud in *Civilization and its Discontents* remains the same. But where Freud argued that civilization is always a tentative contract because 'instinctual passions are stronger than reasonable interest',[34] the Ballard of *Super-Cannes* complicates this. While the nation-state in its imperial phase may have used a more overtly repressive mechanism, multinational consumer capitalism is still a form of imperialistic civilization that seems to encourage the indulgence of primal passions. It does so, however, in a controlled way and on its own terms, since it manufactures the desires.

The writings of Lacan might once again offer a helpful parallel in thought. In an article intended as a preface to an edition of the Marquis de Sade's *Philosophy in the Bedroom* (1795), Lacan proposes a compelling comparison of Sade's work with the philosophy of Immanuel Kant. His claim is not simply that Kant's rationalist worldview is secretly stained by a dark, perverse, irrational unconscious, but, more daringly, that the work of the Marquis de Sade shares more in common with Kant's reason than Freud's irrational mind.[35] Addressing this article, Žižek argues:

> Lacan does not try to make the usual 'reductionist' point that every ethical act, as pure and disinterested as it may appear, is always grounded in some 'pathological' motivation . . . the focus of Lacan's interest, rather, resides in the paradoxical reversal by means of which desire itself . . . can no longer be grounded in any 'pathological' interests or motivations, and thus meets the criteria of the Kantian ethical act, so that 'following one's desire' overlaps with 'doing one's duty'.[36]

For Lacan, Sade's works do not embody a Bacchanalian world of erotic frenzy and freedom. Rather, sexuality in Sade's world is routinized, rationalized and mechanized, and it is primarily concerned with imperatives and rules. For Lacan, desire does not thwart the law; it comes from the law and supports it. In other words, 'desire is the Other's desire'; that is, our desire is not our own but comes from the symbolic order of authority and law (658).

In *Super-Cannes*, Ballard explores a similar idea, but he grounds this idea in the particular historical development of globalization. Yet Lacan's arguments provide an insight for thinking about changes that occurred in Ballard's fiction since the 1960s. A work like *The Atrocity Exhibition* attempts to expose the irrationality of rationality, which can be felt in the work's very form where seemingly schizophrenic discourses permeate blocks of texts that mimic the abstracts of scientific journals. It is possible to look back to the 1960s inner-space fictions as works that still conceived of the unconscious as a wild brute force waiting to be unleashed. But if this is the case, then Ballard's vision at that point had not departed so radically from the imperialist literature of his childhood. In this mode, a figure like Vaughan in *Crash* (1973) can still stand as a crude model of 1968-style liberation: fight oppressive civilization by acting out your real desires. Later works, like *Super-Cannes*, however, seem to reverse such a tactic. Wilder Penrose is not Vaughan. Rather than violating the rules of civilization, Penrose's demand of his clients to liberate themselves, and act freely on their desires, works instead as a compulsion for them to do their duty. The rules of the new Empire, the new regime of neoliberal consumer capitalism, demand that we enjoy ourselves, to enjoy desires that are not our own.

In 1943, Winston Churchill gave a speech at Harvard in which he sought to establish commonalities between the British and American peoples. In the epigraph to this chapter, a passage from this speech, Churchill hopes to banish to the past the image of Empire as a kind of looting disguised as government building, 'taking away other people's provinces or land or grinding them down in exploitation'.[37] Instead, the prime minister appeals to something seemingly more benign in its abstraction, 'The empires of the future are the empires of the mind'. J. G. Ballard, who was interned at Lunghua at the time of the speech, might have agreed with Churchill's phrase, but his writing gives a darker inflection to the sentiment. Ballard's Shanghai childhood attuned him to an international world, while the war and his subsequent move to England helped generate a critical and anti-imperial outlook in his work. Like Churchill, Ballard saw a new imperialism coming into shape in the postwar years, a new empire of the mind. Unlike Churchill, Ballard envisioned nightmares in the new powers coming to work in our psychic colonies. After the ebbing of the British Empire, Ballard gave dramatic witness to what Angela Carter called the 'colonialisation of the mind'[38] shaping the late twentieth century. As a writer who held the imagination to be humanity's last great resource against powers of control and boredom, Ballard was a modern William Blake worrying at the 'mind forg'd manacles' of our globalized days.

Notes

1. J. G. Ballard in conversation with Tania Branigan, 'It's a pantomime where tinsel takes the place of substance', *Guardian*, 22 December 2003, http://books.guardian.co.uk/departments/generalfiction/story/0,6000, 1111871,00.html, accessed August 2010.
2. Branigan, 'It's a pantomime'.
3. Roger Luckhurst, *'The Angle Between Two Walls': The Fiction of J. G. Ballard* (New York: St. Martin's Press, 1997).
4. Jeannette Baxter, *J. G. Ballard's Surrealist Imagination: Spectacular Authorship* (Farnham: Ashgate, 2009); 'Visions of Europe in *Cocaine Nights* and *Super-Cannes*', in Jeannette Baxter, ed., *J. G. Ballard: Contemporary Critical Perspectives* (London: Continuum, 2008), pp. 94–106.
5. Dennis A. Foster, 'J. G. Ballard's Empire of the Senses: Perversion and the Failure of Authority', *PMLA* 108.3 (May 1993), 519–32; Liam McNamara, 'The Ruse of the Social: Human Waste and the Gated Community', *Reconstruction: A Cultural Studies eJournal* 2 (Summer 2000). http://www.reconstruction.ws/ 023/mcnamara.htm; Andrzej Gasiorek, *J. G. Ballard* (Manchester: Manchester University Press, 2005).
6. Fredric Jameson, 'World Reduction in Le Guin' [1975], in *Archaeologies of the Future: The Desire Called Utopia and Other Science Fictions* (London: Verso, 2005), p. 269.
7. *Empire of the Sun* (New York: Simon and Schuster, 1984), p. 174.

8. 'From Shanghai to Shepperton', *Re/Search 8/9: J. G. Ballard*, ed. V. Vale and Andrea Juno (San Francisco: Re/Search, 1984), pp. 112–24 (p. 114).
9. *Miracles of Life: Shanghai to Shepperton: An Autobiography* (London: Fourth Estate, 2008), p. 124.
10. The Pleasures of Reading' [1992], in *A User's Guide to the Millennium: Essays and Reviews* (New York: Picador, 1996), pp. 178–82.
11. 'The End of My War' [1995], in *A User's Guide to the Millennium*, pp. 283–94 (p. 289).
12. 'The Violent Noon', *Varsity* (Saturday, May 26, 1951), p. 9. http://www.jgballard.ca/uncollected_work/uncollected_art/jgb_violent_noon.pdf
13. Edward W. Said, 'Two Visions of *Heart of Darkness*', in *Culture and Imperialism* (New York: Vintage, 1994), pp. 19–31.
14. The next story to be published is 'Prima Belladonna' in *Science Fantasy* (1956).
15. See Baxter, *J. G. Ballard's Surrealist Imagination*, pp. 38–52.
16. Mark Pauline, in *J. G. Ballard: Conversations* (San Francisco: Re/Search, 2005), pp. 127–58 (p. 138).
17. Linda Hutcheon, *A Poetics of Postmodernism: History, Theory, Fiction* (London and New York: Routledge, 1988); Jago Morrison, *Contemporary Fiction* (London and New York: Routledge, 2003).
18. Ballard, 'The End of My War', p. 288.
19. Luckhurst, *'The Angle between Two Walls'*, p. 48.
20. 'Memories of Greeneland' [1978], in *A User's Guide to the Millennium*, pp. 137–9 (p. 137).
21. 'Which Way to Inner Space?' [1962], in *A User's Guide to the Millennium*, pp. 195–8.
22. 'Time, Memory and Inner Space' [1963], in *A User's Guide to the Millennium*, pp. 199–201 (p. 199).
23. Jacques Lacan, *The Four Fundamental Concepts of Psycho-Analysis* [1973], trans. Alan Sheridan (New York: W. W. Norton and Company, 1981), p. 41.
24. Slavoj Žižek, *How to Read Lacan* (New York: W. W. Norton and Company, 2006), p. 57.
25. 'Manhole 69' [1957], in *The Complete Short Stories* (London: Flamingo, 2001), pp. 50–67.
26. 'The Subliminal Man' [1963], in *The Complete Short Stories*, pp. 412–25 (pp. 424–5).
27. *The Atrocity Exhibition* [1970] (San Francisco: Re/Search, 1990), p. 12.
28. Ballard, *Miracles of Life*, p. 4.
29. Marianne Brace, 'J. G. Ballard: The comforts of madness', *The Independent*, 15 September 2006, http://www.fpmrecords.com/miscdoc/jgballard_interview.html, accessed 9 August 2010.
30. Ballard, *Super-Cannes* (London: Flamingo, 2000), p. 258.
31. Baxter, 'Visions of Europe', p. 96.
32. David Harvey, *A Brief History of Neoliberalism* (Oxford: Oxford University Press, 2005), p. 3.
33. Slavoj Žižek, *Violence* (New York: Picador, 2008), p. 2.
34. Freud, Sigmund, *Civilization and its Discontents* [1930], trans. James Strachey (New York: W. W. Norton and Company, 1989), p. 69.
35. Jacques Lacan, 'Kant with Sade' [1963], in *Écrits*, trans. Bruce Fink (New York: W. W. Norton and Company, 2006), pp. 645–68 (p. 645).

36. Slavoj Žižek, 'Kant with (or against) Sade', in *The Žižek Reader*, ed. Elizabeth Wright and Edmond Wright (Oxford: Blackwell, 1999), pp. 283–301 (p. 288).
37. Winston Churchill, 'Anglo-American Unity' (Speech at Harvard University, Boston, 6.9.1943), in *Winston S. Churchill: His Complete Speeches 1897–1963*, ed. Robert Rhodes James, vol. 7: 1943–1949 (New York and London: Chelsea House Publishers, 1974), pp. 6823–7 (p. 6826).
38. Angela Carter, 'Notes from the front line' [1983], in *Shaking A Leg: Collected Writings*, ed. Jenny Uglow (London: Penguin Books, 1997), pp. 36–43 (p. 38).

11
'Going mad is their only way of staying sane': Norbert Elias and the Civilized Violence of J. G. Ballard

J. Carter Wood

Introduction

How should we evaluate J. G. Ballard's fiction as social commentary? There have been a range of answers to this question. Many analyses of Ballard's writing – inspired not least by the author's emphasis on exploring the psychological terrain of 'inner space'[1] – have focused on the unconscious and symbolic or emphasized the transcendence of materiality rather than engagement with social life itself.[2] Others have stressed Ballard's attention to the media-constructed simulacra of reality: 'a concern with the material conditions of production and consumption of mass-media artefacts', Michel Delville claims, is 'conspicuously absent' from Ballard's work.[3] But Ballard commented on numerous political and aesthetic topics, and developed a reputation for perceptive, even prophetic, analysis of social change, a view perhaps more reflected in recent criticism. Andrzej Gasiorek has referred to Ballard as both 'a historian of the post-war era, who is interested in the unfolding of social developments over time' and 'a cartographer of the contemporary period'.[4] Dominika Oramus sees in Ballard's later work a chronicle of the 'twilight of the West'.[5] Iain Sinclair even suggests that sociology has triumphed over literature in Ballard's recent work, remarking that the novel *Kingdom Come* (2006) 'could have been stripped down to be a series of savage essays or presentations about the motorway corridor with dramatised events happening in the middle'.[6]

In my view Ballard's writing – however idiosyncratic and experimental – offers an insightful understanding of psychology, social life and historical change that extends well beyond the post-war period. The importance of an innate human nature has long been a key interest of his. In a 2005 interview with the German newspaper *Die Zeit*, he observed:

> All of my books deal with the fact that our human civilization is like the crust of the lava discharged from a volcano. It looks stable, but when you put your foot on it, you feel the fire.

Asked about the apocalyptic tone in some of his writing, he responded, that the 'worst' type of 'war and terror':

> is the subtle way that violence fascinates us. If we want to successfully work against it, we have to finally admit that human beings are not completely capable of being civilized. Regrettable but true.[7]

Ballard's contrasting of civilization's *potential* with its *limits* recalls a methodological approach that has yet to be connected to his writings: Norbert Elias's theory of the 'civilizing process', which has become influential in the historiography of violence.[8] Without suggesting a specific adoption (whether conscious or not) by Ballard of Elias's ideas, I do think they have had overlapping insights into the human condition. Some of Ballard's novels, for example, can be seen as staging fictional crises in the historical and sociological processes that Elias explained. From this perspective, I will examine *High-Rise* (1975) and *Super-Cannes* (2000), which, although separated by a quarter century, reflect different aspects of the author's recurring interests in social alienation, violence and human psychology. Their distinct emphases also recall different aspects of Elias's thinking: 'de-civilization' and the 'quest for excitement in unexciting societies'. I present, first, a brief summary of the theory of the 'civilizing process'.

A crash course in civilizing processes

In 1930s Germany, Norbert Elias began developing an innovative historical sociology that focused on manners, emotions, and self-restraint. Painfully aware of the fragility of modern civilization (as he watched it being destroyed by Nazism), he nonetheless explored the profound historical developments that had reshaped everyday human life. Elias saw the social and the self as inseparable: society and psyche advanced (or retreated) together, with a particular 'balance of tensions within the personality' being influenced by innate psychology, socialization and day-to-day interaction.[9] The 'tensions' are primarily between 'affects' – emotions or drives toward pleasure – and the psychological mechanisms that rein them in. Elias's emphasis on the unconscious and on an internal conflict between drives and self-control was clearly influenced by Freud.[10] However, his use of such notions was rather vague and selective. Elias ignored, for example, the central Freudian emphasis on childhood sexual development, and he avoided speculations – such as those Freud made in *Civilization and Its Discontents* – about a 'death drive'; moreover, he distanced his historical analysis from what he saw as Freud's static and ahistorical psychology.[11] (Elias's Freudian inheritance is thus less direct and more ambiguous than Ballard's.) In Elias's theory, a particular psychological 'balance of tensions' derives from a 'drive and affect-economy'[12] that varies across different times and places, shaped by social relationships that Elias called 'figurations'. Post-medieval figurations in Western Europe were mainly characterized by rising self-control, expanding foresight, and a growing restraint of emotions and impulses, what he called a 'civilizing process'. He later spoke of *processes* that might run at different rates, such as the enforcement of a monopoly on legitimate violence by increasingly powerful states; lengthening chains of interdependence through trade and production; shrinking power differentials among social groups (i.e. 'functional democratization'); growing refinement of and subtlety in manners; growing pressure to restrain emotional, sexual and aggressive impulses; and a greater role for 'conscience' in regulating behaviour.[13]

Social interdependence and the monopolization of violence were most significant. Interdependence referred to trends – trade, division of labour, urbanization – compelling individuals to regulate their conduct in an increasingly differentiated, subtle, consistent and restrained manner.[14] He used automobile traffic as one metaphor to explain this relationship:

> Cars are rushing in all directions; pedestrians and cyclists are trying to thread their way through the *mêlée* of cars; policemen stand at the main crossroads to regulate the traffic with varying success. But this external control is founded on the assumption that every individual is himself regulating his behaviour with the utmost exactitude in accordance with the necessities of this network. The chief danger that people here represent for others results from someone in this bustle losing his self-control.[15]

He also focused on the state enforcement of 'pacified social spheres', in which violent acts were criminalized and alternative means of dispute settlement were provided, making private vengeance – previously common – less necessary. Thus, the 'moulding of affects' and the 'standards of the economy of instincts'[16] develop historically, through social processes interacting with innate psychological capabilities.

Elias was acutely aware that European society after the Second World War presented a historical anomaly. He resisted – in contrast to some of his contemporaries – an anti-modernist perspective, and instead highlighted the real benefits that a large portion of the population of modern societies enjoyed. 'In the more developed nation-states,' he observed in one of his later works, 'people's security, their protection against the more brutal strokes of fate such as illness and sudden death, is much greater than in earlier periods, and perhaps greater than at any time in the development of humanity.'[17] This echoes a comment by Ballard:

> Many people have said to me, 'What an extraordinary life you've had', but of course my childhood in Shanghai was far closer to the way the majority of people on this planet, in previous centuries and in the 20th century, have lived than, say, life in Western Europe and the United States. It's *we* here, in our quiet suburbs and our comparatively peaceful cities, who are the anomalies.[18]

Perhaps because of his comparatively positive view of modern life, Elias has been misunderstood as positing an optimistic and naively progressive view of historical development. However, like Ballard, he had painful personal experiences in the Second World War[19] and was well aware of the contingency of (and tensions within) the process he described. These points lead us to *High-Rise* and *Super-Cannes*, which dramatize two aspects of the civilizing process: its *potential reversal* and its *susceptibility to producing psychological dissatisfaction*.

Tower, infernal: dismantling civilization in *High-Rise*

One of Ballard's consistent themes has been the social and psychological dimensions of the 'gated enclave'; he is fascinated by 'worlds within a world' where the physical environment distorts human nature into an *'asocial* habitus'.[20] In several of his novels, characters revert to more impulsive and primal forms of behaviour, a process often accompanied by cruelty and/or violence. Here, Ballard's interest in the darker side of human psychology combines with an awareness of the fragility of civilized social relationships. Ballard himself often suggested that this theme originated in his own life experiences as a boy in Shanghai, particularly the Japanese conquest of the city and his internment with his family in a prison camp. From that, he gained 'the sense that reality itself was a stage set that could be dismantled at any moment, and that no matter how magnificent anything appeared, it could be swept aside into the debris of the past'.[21] The inherently unstable nature of civilized life is a consistent theme across Ballard's *oeuvre*.

Social disintegration plays an often underestimated role in Elias's theories. While he has been accused of describing social change as automatic, inevitable and one-directional, Jonathan Fletcher rightly argues that he saw the civilizing process as 'never completed and constantly endangered'.[22] Indeed, as Abram de Swaan observes, he came to believe that civilization 'is not a permanent state but rather a precarious process, that may very well reverse itself'.[23] Despite increasing self-control, 'cruelty and joy in the destruction and torment of others' continued: 'affective outbursts may still occur as exceptional phenomena, as a "pathological" degeneration, in later phases of social development'.[24] In crises, the 'armor of civilized conduct' could 'crumble very rapidly',[25] and Elias drew attention to the conditions required to maintain an even relatively pacified society, observing dryly: 'Classes living permanently in danger of starving to death or of being killed by enemies can hardly develop or maintain those stable restraints characteristic of the more civilized forms of conduct'.[26]

Fletcher summarizes Elias's three main symptoms of de-civilization: a shift from *self*-control toward *externally enforced* limits; increasingly *unstable* patterns of self-restraint; and 'a contraction in the scope of mutual identification between constituent groups and individuals'.[27] These have tended to occur where 'there was a decrease in the (state) control of the monopoly of violence, a fragmentation of social ties and a shortening of chains of commercial, emotional and cognitive interdependence'. Such a society would be characterized by:

> a rise in the levels of fear, insecurity, danger and incalculability; the re-emergence of violence into the public sphere; growing inequality or heightening of tensions in the balance of power between constituent groups; a decrease in the distance between the standards of adults and children; a freer expression of aggressiveness and an increase in cruelty; an increase in impulsiveness; an increase in involved forms of thinking with their concomitantly high fantasy

content and a decrease in detached forms of thought with an accompanying decrease in the 'reality-congruence' of concepts.[28]

These factors might 'trigger' each other in a 'mutually reinforcing spiral'.[29] Such a de-civilizing 'spiral' is vividly enacted in *High-Rise* within a single, massive residential complex that descends into a conflict characterized by all the de-civilizing criteria Fletcher describes.

Elias saw increasing social interdependence as a key civilizing factor. In *High-Rise*, the titular setting of the novel is an isolated (and isolating) structure: a world unto itself.[30] With few exceptions, the lifestyle of one of the book's protagonists, Dr. Robert Laing, is 'as self-contained as the building itself' (9). Residents have few traditional community ties. As conflict among them intensifies, their already weak interdependencies – both external and internal – break down further. Ever fewer residents go to work (98), and even those who maintain some pretence of normality become increasingly focused on events *within* the building. Later, telephone lines (both public and private) are disconnected, externally resident building workers stop showing up, and shipments to the supermarket and restaurant cease. The residents, effectively, 'were cutting themselves off from the outside world' (102).

The residents disperse into increasingly fragmented warring factions and a creeping 'separation of loyalties' occurs as three 'classes' emerge based on different groupings of floors (53). Minor conflicts turn into violent disputes and group identities coalesce around new 'established' and 'outsider' groups distinguished by floor, 'clan' (65) and 'small scale tribal enclaves' (70).[31] Those groups deemed to be 'lower' in status are denigrated: residents of lower floors, for instance, are referred to as a 'band of migrant workers' (25) or as 'animals' (27). Eventually, even the clan-system breaks down, and people begin 'retreating into their own apartments' and 'barricading themselves away' (120).

These trends are accompanied by a 'renascent barbarism' (79) that recalls an important principle for Elias. Human affects form a unified 'whole':

> We may call particular instincts by different names according to their different directions and functions, we may speak of hunger and the need to spit, of the sexual drive and of aggressive impulses, but in life these different instincts are no more separable than the heart from the stomach or the blood in the brain from the blood in the genitalia.[32]

Changes in the self-control of impulsive acts in different areas, he suggests, are mutually influencing. In *High-Rise*, declining restraint with regard to noise (84), sexual inhibitions ('blue movies', 31) and outward aggression (the 'grilling' and 'slapping' of a woman identified as a 'vagrant', 33) are connected at an early stage, with one of the protagonists, Richard Wilder, exemplifying the turn to impulsivity. Wilder commits the novel's first act of violence when, during a power outage, a 'cruel but powerful impulse' (48) drives him to drown an Afghan hound in one of the complex's swimming pools. In the novel, growing impulsivity regarding sex and violence is connected to decreasing restraint with regard to bodily functions, recalling Elias's linking of changing standards of restraint regarding acts such as spitting, the revealing of nakedness, vomiting, flatulence, urination and defecation. *High-Rise* emphasizes its characters' reversal of such trends, resulting in a marked decline in hygiene – whether personal[33] or public[34] – and a 'falling interest in civilized conventions of any kind' (100). Wilder succinctly exemplifies the *interconnected* nature of impulsivity when he breaks into the flat of his neighbour Charlotte Melville: he trashes it, urinates into the bath, exposes himself, lies in a drunken stupor recording his own belches and, when she returns, rapes her (128-30). While the interconnections between different kinds of impulsive behaviour are complex, a recent survey of the history of murder highlights the possibly significant 'relationship between levels of aggression and of hygiene'.[35]

As Fletcher notes, the relaxation of restraints also reduces the differences between adult and child behaviour, a tendency exemplified at various points in *High-Rise*. Having had the 'longest possible childhood' (47) that his mother could arrange for him, Wilder allowed his childlike impulsiveness to continue, resulting in the 'childish [sex] games' (48) that he (unsuccessfully) attempted to play with his wife early in their marriage. Other residents are compared to children in various contexts. Wilder's wife refers to the growing conflict in the tower as 'a huge children's game that's got out of hand' (57). 'For the first time since we were three years old', says one resident to Laing, 'what we do makes absolutely no difference' (40). The growing conflict brings out the 'childish strains' (71) in Anne Royal, wife of the complex's architect. As one resident tells Laing, 'everyone's working off the most extraordinary backlog of infantile aggressions' (109). Wilder observes the shrinking difference in behavioural standards from another direction, when he considers that the 'civil war' in the building had made the children 'as combative as their parents' (116). He also tries to dissuade two airline pilots from the 'childish act' of 'raiding' the upper floors with the ultimate goal of urinating in the pool (58), combining the themes of childishness, aggression and bodily functions.

The tower's decivilizing spiral is most vividly signalled by violence. Elias highlighted a historical process he called the 'courtization of warriors', which made social advancement and power *less* dependent on brute force during the early-modern period. This process is vividly reversed in *High-Rise*, where a process that we might call 'warriorization' sees the re-emergence of violence into formerly pacified public spaces. These processes are signalled by the book's first (human) death: the plunge of a resident known as 'the jeweller' from a fortieth floor window (41) causes no change in everyday life. Wilder's comment to Laing that the death would make 'a good starting point' (55) for a television documentary on the conflict in the building is entirely appropriate, as more episodes of violence and counter-violence follow. The building residents' increasing alienation from the state monopolization of force is made clear by an exchange between Anne and Anthony Royal:

'Anne, we're *leaving* . . . '

'At last – and why has no one called the police? Or complained to the owners?'

'We are the owners.'

(71)

But even the Royals' internalized control wanes. The tower's authorities (e.g. the building manager or the pool attendant) have abandoned their posts (43, 55), and the public spaces of this 'unpoliced city' (40) – such as its hallways and elevator lobbies – become arenas of disorder.

De Swaan has analysed incidents of modern mass-slaughter, arguing that brutal emotionality and cool, calculating restraint can coexist when the 'barbarity' is 'compartmentalized'.[36] He refers specifically to the use of terror in Bosnia by Serb paramilitary units: 'Here, the wildness and brutality are let loose, or maybe even instilled, and at the same time instrumentalized, for specific purposes, within demarcated spaces at an appointed time: an archipelago of enclaves where cruelty reigns while being reined in all the while.'[37] In *High-Rise*, similarly, the broader society seems untouched – and unaware – of the savage descent of the complex into disorder. De Swaan's analysis focuses on the large-scale violence of totalitarianism or war, but he makes clear that the '*modus operandi* of compartmentalization need not be so extreme' and might function in social conditions that are, at least on the surface, far more normal and 'innocuous'.[38] Although *High-Rise* does not offer a strictly *realistic* scenario, some American inner-city areas, Loïc Wacquant has argued, have had rates of violence that meet or exceed those of warzones; these islands of extreme violence have existed in an otherwise orderly society.[39]

Ballard, of course, is not simply dramatizing a particular sociological or historical model, and *High-Rise* exhibits classic Ballardian idiosyncrasies and interests. Rather than Elias's emphasis on the crumbling of refined behavioural standards resulting from a sudden catastrophe, for instance, Ballard depicts a wilful – and oddly fulfilling – dismantling of civilizing mechanisms. Whereas Elias saw (correctly) that increasingly restrained, stable interdependencies within effectively pacified social spaces tend to produce stronger levels of self-control and reduced violence, Ballard suggests (not implausibly) how intensely controlled societies might generate new forms of 'psychopathology'. While important, these differences do not prevent seeing important connections between the two authors. Elias was not only aware that the civilizing processes he theorized could be *reversed* in a total fashion, he also believed that civilization bred its own more chronic dissatisfactions. This point leads us to Ballard's novel *Super-Cannes* which makes use of a similar assumption.

At play in the garden of the gods: *Super-Cannes* and the quest for excitement in unexciting societies

Ballard's observations about the double-edged nature of modern life – that its unprecedented levels of comfort and security may lead to new forms of frustration and discontent – have been reiterated throughout his fiction and non-fiction. In a 2004 interview, he doubted that new technologies – such as the Internet – could 'halt the slide into boredom and conformism', speculating:

> the human race will inevitably move like a sleepwalker towards that vast resource it has hesitated to tap – its own psychopathy. This adventure playground of the soul is waiting for us with its gates wide open, and admission is free.[40]

This tension between strict discipline and the emotional extremity that Ballard has often referred to as 'psychopathy' is indeed at the centre of his 2000 novel, *Super-Cannes*, set in a French business park (modelled on the real-world Sophia Antipolis) on the Mediterranean coast.[41]

Although Elias's overall perspective was in many ways different from Ballard's, he similarly emphasized that the significant benefits of the civilizing process (such as greater security) had a psychological 'price': 'it requires and instils greater restraint in the individual, more exact control of his affects and conduct, it demands a stricter regulation of drives and – from a particular stage on – more even self-restraint'.[42] Spontaneous actions, strong emotions and even violent acts, he believed, were sources of pleasure and satisfaction; their constraint, however, increased across history, restricting a person's conduct 'like a tight ring' and causing 'a more steady regulation of his drives according to the social norms'.[43] Elias explored these themes with Eric Dunning in a 1967 essay originally titled 'The Quest for Excitement in Unexciting Societies'.[44] 'Civilized' societies are 'unexciting' in that they prohibit extremes of the 'spontaneous, elementary and unreflected type of excitement, in joy as in sorrow, in love as in hatred' (71); here, work discipline extends into everyday life.[45] Even elites 'can never release the circumspection and the foresight which are the concomitants of emotional restraint without endangering their position in society'.[46] A long historical process developed individual *self*-control until it had become 'second nature'.[47] The continuing need for excitement, however, drove the parallel rise of 'mimetic' leisure activities – such as sport: a 'change of gear which concerns the whole organism on all levels'.[48] Activities were 'mimetic' in that they produced affect-laden reactions *like* those of earlier, less restrained ages; rather than a 'liberation from tensions', they aimed, Elias and Dunning argued, to *restore* 'that measure of tension which is an essential ingredient of mental health'.[49] (It has recently been suggested that the 'optimal level of anxiety and aggression in human societies – that is the level at which peaceableness is maximized – may not be zero').[50] Most people find the release offered by well-defined 'mimetic' activities to be sufficient; but, not all of them do. *Super-Cannes* explores these tensions.

Indeed, the main setting in *Super-Cannes*, the business park 'Eden-Olympia', can be seen as a zone of hyper-civilization where the main psycho-social processes Elias concentrated upon operate in heightened form: the vast *interdependencies* of global capitalism, the *monopolization of physical force* by bureaucratized authorities and the *internalized restraint of emotions* demanded by high-pressure work routines. The theme of impulsivity – and Eden-Olympia's hostility to it – is repeatedly raised, particularly by the narrator, Paul Sinclair. Paul accompanies his wife Jane to the park, where she has taken up the job formerly belonging to David Greenwood, a doctor who had gone on a deadly shooting spree for reasons that – until the end of the novel – are unclear. The park seems to epitomize restraint, work discipline and order.

Upon arrival, Jane remarks upon the incongruence between the park's appearance and Greenwood's bloody rampage. ' "It all looks very civilized, in a Euro kind of way" ' she notes, ' "Not a drifting leaf in sight. It's hard to believe anyone would be allowed to go mad here" ' (9).[51] One of the park's psychologists, Wilder Penrose, introduces the pair to their new environment and praises the predictable and planned 'intelligent city' designed for maximum productivity and devoid of traditional community identity or interaction. Instead, an 'invisible infrastructure' ensures a smoothly running, thoroughly pacified environment with 'no parking problems, no fears of burglars or purse-snatchers, no rapes or muggings' (38).

Paul resists the park's 'ceaseless work and its ethic of corporate responsibility'; the 'civility and polity' that had been 'designed into' it, he notes, leave him feeling 'deeply bored' (38). He later identifies the park as an 'outpost of an advanced kind of puritanism, and a virtually sex-free zone' (155). Not that there is *no* sex in the park: television pornography is plentiful and Paul has glimpses of furtive, intense sex among his neighbours; however, that activity seems carefully channelled, having little connection with spontaneous desire. He watches through his married neighbours' window as the husband returns from what – we later discover – is likely to have been an evening of organized brutality: Paul sees his animated recounting of the night's violence segue into lovemaking (76). Paul too begins to link sex to other forms of illicit impulsivity. During a jaunt in Cannes, Jane nonchalantly shoplifts a magazine. She and Paul make love upon their return ('a rare event after her long working days') after Jane 'had been excited by the illicit pleasure of leaving for Cannes on the spur of the moment. An impulsive decision ran counter to the entire ethos of Eden-Olympia' (77). She had smiled after the theft:

> accepting that a benign lightning strike had illuminated our excessively ordered world . . . The emotion had been draining from our lives, leaving a numbness that paled the sun. The stolen magazine quickened our lovemaking.
>
> (77)

As Jane loses herself in work discipline, Paul not only investigates Greenwood's rampage but is also drawn to impulsive acts: he damages Penrose's car (90–91) and, on the spur of the moment, steals a BMW (118-19). The latter belongs to Frances Baring, an Eden-Olympia executive who plays a key role in Paul's introduction to the park's seamier side.

In *Super-Cannes*, as in *High-Rise*, many links are drawn between impulsivity, violence, crime and sex; this recalls Elias's emphasis on impulsivity and self-control being part of 'the personality structure as a whole'.[52] Paul, for instance, finds that in the wake of the impulsive Cannes daytrip, his relationship becomes enervated: 'Jane and I rarely made love', he notes, their passion 'smothered by a sleep of eye-masks and sedatives, followed by cold showers and snatched breakfasts' (155). Jane, Paul states, 'moved naked around our bedroom, in full view of [their neighbours] Simone Delage and her husband, flaunting not her sex but her indifference to it'; Cannes offers 'an antidote to this spartan regime' (155), to which Paul continues to flee. Distanced from his wife (who develops an oddly affectless sexual relationship with the Delages) Paul sadly observes that their marriage 'had been the last of her hippie gestures, the belief that impulsive acts alone gave meaning to life' (272).

There is, however, another side to impulsivity in Eden-Olympia. In a lengthy conversation with Penrose, Paul discovers that the furtive criminality he has become aware of is one element of a 'controlled and supervised madness' the psychologist has organized to help 'cure' a crippling 'malaise' previously apparent among the park's hard-working professionals. Recalling Paul and Jane's own experience, Penrose observes:

> They weren't having sex at all . . . The adult film channel, hours of explicit hardcore, did no better. People watched, but in a nostalgic way, as if they were seeing a documentary about morris dancing or roof-thatching, an old craft skill popular with a previous generation . . . Short of making sexual intercourse a corporate requirement, there was nothing we could do.
>
> (257–58)

The decline in sex was emblematic of a broader crisis: the park's executives suffered from 'an inability to rest the mind, to find time for reflection and recreation' (251) due to the high degree of 'self-restraint' (256) in their work. The 'malaise' recalls Elias's suggestion that emotional restraint – 'affect-inhibition' – might make an individual 'no longer capable of any form of fearless expression of the modified affects, or of direct gratification of the repressed drives'.[53]

But Penrose found fantasies 'filled with suppressed yearnings for violence, and ugly narratives of anger and revenge' in the 'strange dreams' of the 'highly disciplined professionals' (258). Seeing these as remnants of a long historical process of psychological repression, he identifies a solution: 'Small doses of insanity are the only solution. Their own psychopathy is all that can rescue these people' (251). Based on his theory, he had developed a 'therapeutic' regimen beginning with theft, drug-taking and sexual perversion and ending with organized violence: so-called 'special actions' (349) involving attacks on the immigrant and petty-criminal underclass near the business park. As a senior security officer says to Paul, 'Going mad is their only way of staying sane' (202).

There are elements here of the compartmentalized 'de-civilizing process' found in *High-Rise*; however, *Super-Cannes* also highlights a different aspect of Eliasian sociology, one that, curious as it may seem, involves sport. Throughout *Super-Cannes*, the violent 'special actions' are referred to – in many contexts and by different characters – in terms of leisure activities, 'games' or sports. They are, for instance, carried out by men in 'bowling jackets' organized like sports teams. Frances Baring refers to some of the more 'fun' actions as 'rugger club japes' (307). Penrose compares them to an 'adventure-training course' or a 'game of touch rugby' (259), and he refers to 'a voluntary and elective psychopathy, as you can see in any boxing ring or ice-hockey rink' (264). He tells Paul that the original notion of using violence to restore people to health occurred to him through boxing (242-43). (Elias also made use of boxing as an important example of the civilization of impulsive violence into rule-bound enclaves.)[54] Referring to a brutally executed crime that Paul had witnessed, Penrose states, it 'was really a kind of sporting event. The film was a record of a successful hunting party. In fact, all the crimes are somehow . . . recreational' (247).

The connection between sport and violence – which recurs even more directly in Ballard's novel *Kingdom Come* (2006) – brings us back to the 'quest for excitement'. Elias, too, claimed that *excessive* self-control caused 'constant feelings of boredom or solitude'; the internalized struggle caused by civilizing pressures did not always find 'a happy resolution', leading to 'perpetual restlessness and dissatisfaction' since 'inclinations and impulses' could only be indulged in limited form.[55] Excessive self-restraint might prevent even the satisfactions of these 'modified affects'.[56] Elias and Dunning emphasized that 'mimetic' activities had become central to advanced human societies, providing the refined, controlled and spectatorial joys of, for example, sport, film, fantasy and mild perversion. Penrose's 'therapy' in *Super-Cannes*, of course, involves brutality and fascistic political extremism. It is, as Paul recognizes, 'deranged' (360) and hardly a fictional application of Elias's figurational sociology. However, the same social and psychological tensions

Elias and Dunning addressed are vividly dramatized in Ballard's novel, and the whole notion of Penrose's violent, therapeutic 'games' recalls the 'controlled decontrolling of emotional controls' explored by the two social psychologists.

Conclusion

Ballard offered no comprehensive analysis of real-world violence, most of which – in whatever time or place – can be explained without reference to middle-class psychopathology. However, whether in the context of acute social breakdown or chronic psychological dissatisfaction, his fiction provides vivid insights into the operation of, and limits to, civilizing processes. Both Elias and Ballard considered the difficult interaction between human nature and changing social and technological environments. To some extent, Ballard's fictional approach to 'civilization' begins where Elias's ends: Elias sought to understand systematically how it increased (even if he warned of its fragility) while Ballard focused his gaze on its shadowy borders, limits and failures. The social collapse dramatized in *High-Rise* is hardly 'realistic'; however, it draws on the main elements of the social and psychological reality Elias analysed. By dismantling a society, Ballard, in effect, reverse-engineered the processes through which it was built.

In *Super-Cannes*, Frances Baring refers, accurately enough, to Penrose's 'lunatic ideology' (350). But it was Ballard's talent to use such madness so lucidly. It *is* mad, but it fascinates *because* it appeals to deep-seated motivations. Asked about violence in 2004, Ballard suggested his novels offer 'an extreme hypothesis' about the future:

> As I've often said, someone who puts up a road sign saying 'dangerous bends ahead' is not inciting drivers to speed up, though I hope that my fiction is sufficiently ambiguous to make the accelerator seem strangely attractive.[57]

Although rather more staid, Elias's theories offer some similar insights into psychology. If Ballard explored what we are and where we are (possibly) going, Elias confined himself to understanding how we got here. Ballard the novelist, of course, had far more freedom to produce variations on the possibilities of human life than Elias the sociologist. While there is no coherent Ballardian 'theory of violence' which extends throughout his work, I suggest that the framework of recurring assumptions about human psychology he developed has some parallels with Elias's more systematic view. Such parallels are one reason that, to answer the question I posed at the opening of this essay, I think we should take Ballard's role as a historical sociologist – his warnings about the 'dangerous bends' ahead – rather seriously indeed.

Notes

1. See, for example, 'Which Way to Inner Space?' (1962) and 'Time, Memory and Inner Space' (1963), reprinted in J. G. Ballard, *A User's Guide to the Millennium: Essays and Reviews* (London: HarperCollins, 1996), pp. 195–8 (pp. 199–201).
2. See many of the essays in a special edition of *Science Fiction Studies* 55 (Nov. 1991), esp., Jean Baudrillard, 'Ballard's *Crash*', trans. Arthur B. Evans, *Science Fiction Studies* 55 (Nov. 1991), 313–20; Nicholas Ruddick, 'Ballard/*Crash*/Baudrillard', *Science Fiction Studies* 58 (Nov. 1992), 354–60.
3. Michel Delville, *J. G. Ballard* (Plymouth: Northcote House/British Council, 1998), p. 89.
4. Andrzej Gasiorek, *J. G. Ballard* (Manchester: Manchester University Press, 2005), p. 5.
5. Dominika Oramus, *Grave New World: The Decline of the West in the Fiction of J. G. Ballard* (Warsaw: University of Warsaw, 2007), p. 14.
6. Tim Chapman, 'When in Doubt, Quote Ballard: An Interview with Iain Sinclair', *Ballardian*, 29 August 2006, http://www.ballardian.com/iain-sinclair-when-in-doubt-quote-ballard/, accessed 24 Nov. 2010.
7. 'Gewalt ohne Ende', *Die Zeit*, 8 Sept. 2005, p. 43. My translation. Original quotes: '*All meine Bücher handeln ja davon, dass unsere humane Gesittung wie die Kruste über der ausgespienen Lava eines Vulkans ist. Sie sieht fest aus, aber wenn man den Fuß daraufsetzt, spürt man das Feuer.*' '*Es gibt viele Arten von Krieg und Terror, aber das Schlimmste ist, dass Gewalt einen unterschwelligen Reiz auf uns ausübt. Wenn wir sie erfolgreich bekämpfen wollen, müssen wir endlich zugeben, dass der Mensch nicht komplett zivilisierbar ist. Bedauerlich, aber wahr.*'
8. For a summary of this historiography in a British context, see J. Carter Wood 'Criminal Violence in Modern Britain', *History Compass* 4, no. 1 (2006), 77–90.
9. Eric Dunning, 'Preface', in Norbert Elias and Eric Dunning, *Quest for Excitement: Sport and Leisure in the Civilizing Process* (Oxford: Basil Blackwell, 1986), pp. 6–7; Jonathan Fletcher, *Violence and Civilization: An Introduction to the Work of Norbert Elias* (Cambridge: Polity, 1997), p. 22.
10. E.g. Norbert Elias, *The Civilizing Process: The History of Manners and State Formation and Civilization* (Oxford: Blackwell, 1994 [1939]), p. 249.
11. As Alan Sica has put it with reference to the *Civilizing Process*, the use of Freud 'does not make or break the book': cited in George Cavalletto, *Crossing the Psycho-Social Divide: Freud, Weber, Adorno and Elias* (Aldershot: Ashgate), p. 174. Chris Rojek criticises Elias for being inattentive and 'overcomplacent' about the miseries caused by civilization which Freud highlighted: *Decentring Leisure: Rethinking Leisure Theory* (London: Sage, 1995), p. 54. Fletcher argues that 'by historicizing Freud's basic categories Elias thus releases himself from Freud's reductionist and static notions' (Fletcher,

Violence and Civilization, p. 26). Steven Pinker has recently observed that Elias's emphasis on 'increases in self-control, long-term planning, and sensitivity to the thoughts and feelings of others' are 'precisely the functions that today's cognitive neuroscientists attribute to the prefrontal cortex'. Steven Pinker, 'A History of Violence', *The New Republic*, 19 Mar. 2007, and available at http://www.edge.org/3rd_culture/pinker07/pinker07_index.html, accessed 24 Nov. 2010.
12. Elias, *Civilizing Process*, p. 452.
13. Dunning, 'Preface', p. 13.
14. Elias, *Civilizing Process*, p. 445.
15. Elias, *Civilizing Process*, p. 446.
16. Both citations, *Civilizing Process*, p. 165.
17. Norbert Elias, *The Loneliness of the Dying*, trans. Edmund Jephcott (New York: Continuum, 2001 [1985]), p. 7.
18. J. G. Ballard, from the voiceover of the television documentary 'Shanghai Jim' (BBC Bookmark, 1991; produced by James Runcie). Transcript: http://www.ballardian.com/shanghai-jim-voiceover-transcription, accessed 24 Nov. 2010.
19. Elias, who was Jewish, fled Germany in 1933, coming to Britain in 1935. Because he was a German, however, he spent several months in internment camps near Liverpool and on the Isle of Man after the outbreak of war. His mother is thought to have died in Auschwitz. Norbert Elias, Stephen Mennell and Johan Goudsblom, *Norbert Elias on Civilization, Power and Knowledge: Selected Writings* (Chicago: University of Chicago Press, 1998), p. 10.
20. Gasiorek, *J. G. Ballard*, pp. 25, 110.
21. Quoted here from J. G. Ballard, *Miracles of Life: Shanghai to Shepperton* (London: Harper Perennial, 2008), p. 58.
22. Fletcher, *Violence and Civilization*, p. 178.
23. Abram De Swaan, 'Dyscivilization, Mass Extermination and the State', *Theory, Culture & Society*, 18, nos 2–3 (2001), 266, referring to Norbert Elias, *The Germans: Power Struggles and the Development of Habitus in the Nineteenth and Twentieth Centuries*, trans. Eric Dunning and Stephen Mennell, ed. Michael Schroeter (New York, 1996).
24. Elias, *Civilizing Process*, pp. 158, 159.
25. Elias, *Civilizing Process*, p. 253.
26. Elias, *Civilizing Process*, p. 506.
27. Fletcher, *Violence and Civilization*, p. 83.
28. Fletcher, *Violence and Civilization*, p. 83.
29. Fletcher, *Violence and Civilization*, pp. 84–5.
30. J. G. Ballard, *High-Rise* (London: Harper Perennial, 2005 [1975]). Further page references are provided within the text.
31. For a real-world sociological examination of this sort of pattern partly based upon Eliasian concepts, see Abram de Swaan, 'Widening Circles of Disidentification: On the Psycho- and Sociogenesis of the Hatred of Distant Strangers; Reflections on Rwanda', *Theory, Culture and Society* 14, 2 (1997), 105–22.
32. Elias, *Civilizing Process*, pp. 156–7.

33. E.g. 'The sweat on Laing's body, like the plaque that coated his teeth, surrounded him in an envelope of dirt and body odour, but the stench gave him confidence, the feeling that he had dominated the terrain with the products of his own body.' Ballard, *High-Rise*, p.107.
34. Exemplified by the piling up of rubbish in the hallways and apartments.
35. Pieter Spierenburg, *A History of Murder: Personal Violence in Europe from the Middle Ages to the Present* (Cambridge: Polity Press, 2008), p. 206.
36. De Swaan, 'Dyscivilization', p. 268.
37. De Swaan, 'Dyscivilization', p. 269.
38. De Swaan, 'Dyscivilization', pp. 270–1.
39. Loïc Wacquant, 'Decivilizing and Demonizing: The Social and Symbolic Remaking of the Black Ghetto and Elias in the Dark Ghetto', in Steven Loyal and Stephen Quilley, eds, *The Sociology of Norbert Elias* (Cambridge University Press, 2004), pp. 95–121 esp. pp. 88–9.
40. Interview by Jeannette Baxter, 'Age of Unreason', *Guardian*, 22 June 2004, http://www.guardian.co.uk/books/2004/jun/22/sciencefictionfantasyandhorror.jgballard, accessed 18 May 2009.
41. Alexander Gutzmer, 'Wer Alles Sieht, Wird Traurig', *Welt Online*, 3 June 2007, http://www.welt.de/wams_print/article916363/Wer_alles_sieht_wird_traurig.html, accessed 24 Nov. 2010. Available in translation as 'Seeing Everything Makes You Sad', *Ballardian*, 7 Dec. 2007, http://www.ballardian.com/seeing-everything-makes-you-sad, accessed 24 Nov. 2010.
42. Elias, *Civilizing Process*, pp. 506–7.
43. Elias, *Civilizing Process*, p. 452.
44. First presented at the Annual Conference of the British Sociological Association in 1967, the essay was published two years later in *Sport and Leisure* as 'The Quest for Excitement in Leisure' and reprinted in Norbert Elias and Eric Dunning, *The Quest for Excitement: Sport and Leisure in the Civilizing Process* (Oxford: Basil Blackwell, 1986).
45. Elias and Dunning, 'Quest for Excitement', p. 71.
46. Elias and Dunning, 'Quest for Excitement', p. 70.
47. Elias, *Civilizing Process*, pp. 450, 447.
48. Elias and Dunning, 'Quest for Excitement', p. 76.
49. Elias and Dunning, 'Quest for Excitement', p. 89.
50. Nancy Dess, 'Violence and Its Antidotes: Promises and Pitfalls of Evolutionarily Aware Policy Development', in Richard W. Bloom and Nancy Dess, eds, *Evolutionary Psychology and Violence: A Primer for Policymakers and Public Policy Advocates* (Westport, Conn.: Praeger, 2003), pp. 239–68 (p. 262).
51. J. G. Ballard, *Super-Cannes* (London: Flamingo, 2001 [2000]). Further page references are provided within the text.
52. Elias, *Civilizing Process*, p. 157.
53. Elias, *Civilizing Process*, p. 454.
54. Elias, *Civilizing Process*, p. 166.
55. Elias, *Civilizing Process*, pp. 453–4.
56. Elias, *Civilizing Process*, p. 454.
57. Baxter, 'Age of Unreason'.

12
The Madness of Crowds: Ballard's Experimental Communities

Jake Huntley

In J. G. Ballard's last four novels, vermilion sands have been swept from the esplanades, petrified forests cleared for development, and the concretized wastelands subjected to thoroughgoing urban regeneration. Instead, there is the artist's impression of Estrella de Mar (*Cocaine Nights*, 1996); Eden-Olympia (*Super-Cannes*, 2000); Chelsea Marina (*Millennium People*, 2003); and the Brooklands Metro-Centre (*Kingdom Come*, 2006). Glossy as a sales brochure designed for the property-obsessed, these developments become locations for social experiments, vast Petri-dishes where weird cultures are allowed to thrive. Ballard scrupulously constructs his Ideal Home exhibition, seditiously pops the stopper from a phial of something rather nasty, and then cheerfully steps back to record in what pattern it spreads. Cults of willed madness; the health benefits of controlled violence; middle-class revolutionaries exploring the potential of untargeted terrorism; and consumer values exaggerated into a healthy-option fascism have all emerged from the Shepperton laboratory in Ballard's latter phase. They are almost as insistent and pervasive as the fucked-up, fucked-in American cars, grounded pilots and those ubiquitous, drained swimming pools that furnish so much of Ballard's earlier output. Within these gated communities, psychological enclaves become unlocked. Ballard has commented that: 'Pearson (in *Kingdom Come*) follows the same trajectory as the narrators of *Cocaine Nights*, *Super-Cannes* and *Millennium People*, outsiders beguiled into serving a regime that they dislike but which appeals to unsatisfied needs that they have long repressed.'[1]

This essay aims to outline the symptoms and sketch the dynamics of these crowds, but not as expressions of masses or groups, the mob or *la canaille*, responding to the call of a demagogue or cresting the wave of a received opinion. Similarly, Sigmund Freud's attention to group behaviour cannot offer full insight here, resting as it does on similar concerns from the perspective of psychological desire. As Paul Connerton explains in 'Freud and the Crowd', Freud sees an 'asymmetric' relationship: 'he does not examine leaders as such but offers a psychology of the ruled'.[2] Instead of an emphasis on leadership, these Ballardian crowds are composed of a more ambiguous and fluid set of relations, resulting from subtler, superfluous poisons and can be better examined through the work of Elias Canetti, who seeks, in *Crowds and Power* (1962) to break any assumed link between crowd and leader. This will further be pursued in relation to Gilles Deleuze and Félix Guattari's notions of order-words and assemblages, explored in *A Thousand Plateaus: Capitalism and Schizophrenia* (1991), to suggest that the repressed needs are for the most inimical forms of social cohesion.

Misdirection

A particularly vivid and unnerving expression of crowd trouble occurs in *Kingdom Come*, when a car bomb at the Metro-Centre draws a mass of onlookers. Whilst the material damage to the shopping centre is limited, the several thousand people gathered together are agitated by the attack, somehow sensitive to the shockwaves and left teetering on the brink of action yet without knowing what to do. Brief eddies of activity occur as elements of the crowd turn their gaze and attention from the Metro-Centre to their fellow spectators and the effect is random and unconscious movement, a kind of externalized neural feedback pattern or like the magnetized dance of iron filings. Pearson, the narrator, here to investigate his father's death in an earlier shooting at the same mall, inadvertently finds himself briefly elevated to the position of a group leader:

> When I turned to avoid a traffic sign the entire column swung after me. I stopped to pick a strip of burnt rubber from my shoe, and they marked time without thinking, then resumed their strolling pace when I set off again . . . The unique internal geometry of the crowd had come into play, picking first one leader and then another. Apparently passive, they regrouped and changed direction according to no obvious logic, a slime mould impelled by gradients of boredom and aimlessness.[3]

The curious mycological metaphor, spores of which can be identified in *Cocaine Nights* where the residents of Estrella de Mar have been rendered equally inert and passive in 'a special kind of willed limbo',[4] extends further back, however, to Elias Canetti's *Crowds and Power*. Canetti analogizes upwards from the congested, contested space at the level of the microbe to distinguish the salient features of the singularly particular noun of assemblage: *the crowd*. In distinction from Plato's *Republic*, Canetti seeks to reduce the necessity and significance of a leader figure or demagogue, the 'tyrant' for whom the mob will do anything they are told.[5] For Canetti, the relationship between crowds and power is subject to subtle exchanges of command; power does not flow straightforwardly *from* a crowd to a leader, nor is a crowd ever easily led. Flows of power and influence should not be mistaken as causal. Instead, the superfluous poison of power drifts and eddies, determined by occult currents, in precisely the fashion Pearson witnesses and, briefly, experiences. Crowds display various attributes and characteristics and should certainly not be assumed to be mindless. As if to emphasize the shift in the terms of his argument, Canetti deliberately uses the plural to break from the convention of an anonymized, atavistic mob regurgitated throughout history. The distinction Canetti proposes might be deemed an epistemological move as much as a contingent one. John McClelland sums up how 'by the time of Freud and Hitler, crowd theory had effectively become leadership theory. "No leader, no crowd" is the motto of almost all crowd theory up to Canetti'.[6] Distinct from a swarm; party; cluster; congregation, or any other form of collective, crowds come into being precisely as a result of a loss of inequality that Canetti calls the *discharge*: 'Before this the crowd does not actually exist; it is the discharge which creates it. This is the moment when all who belong to the crowd get rid of their differences and feel equal.'[7] The crowd, then, is not merely a group of people in close proximity; there is a subtler circuit in operation. (Rather in the manner that Leibniz discusses substances and relations where numerous sheep may be scattered over a hillside but only some belong to the flock of an individual shepherd.) It is a point reiterated by John McClelland: 'A crowd does not become a crowd until its members lose their "burdens of distance", differences in rank, status and property . . . [Canetti] means us to take very literally his assertion that the crowd is not a crowd until the discharge happens.'[8] Crucially, however, the assumption of equality is in fact false: 'It is based on illusion; the people who suddenly feel equal have not really become equal.'[9] Only a small number of people are irreversibly affected by the discharge, and these Canetti refers to as 'crowd crystals'.[10] It is precisely this that causes the milling masses to swing behind Pearson for a few unsettling moments before 'the crowd, as such, disintegrates'[11] into onlookers, bystanders and frustrated shoppers who continue to roam aimlessly. The threat of violence might be on a hair-trigger, and the question should be: which hidden hand has the gun?

Within Ballard's work, the answer is that the discharge is generally caused by the character keen to get the social experiment underway, the character with the psychological starting pistol. Amid 'the memory-erasing white architecture; the enforced leisure that fossilized the nervous system' (34) of *Cocaine Nights*, the residents of Estrella de Mar are anaesthetized by ennui and indolence, a blank, homogenous collective, dormant and waiting for just such a crowd crystal or (top) seed. The arrival of the charismatic tennis coach, Bobby Crawford, changes things when he attempts to revive the inhabitants and re-establish social connections. His catalyst for community regeneration is crime. The burdens of distance are done away with through making everyone a potential target of criminal acts, thereby establishing an equality of victimhood. When Charles Prentice, the narrator, arrives at the resort to discover why his brother has pleaded guilty to a deadly arson attack, he too is quickly beguiled by Crawford. For the individual, Crawford claims his doses of criminality will 'quicken the nervous system, and jump the synapses deadened by leisure and inaction' (180). On a larger scale, meanwhile, he insists: 'A real community has created itself here. It rose spontaneously out of people's lives' (260). Ever the corrupted philosopher warned of by Plato,[12] Crawford dupes the crowd, persuading them against their own interests:

> People are like children, they need constant stimulation. Without that the whole thing runs down. Only crime, or something close to crime, seems to stir them. They realise that they need each other, that together they're more than the sum of their parts. There has to be that constant personal threat.
>
> (260)

Criminal behaviour or taking the law into one's own hands ('something close to crime') functions as the discharge. Here too, what is most apparent is that the vitalizing force is not a clear exchange, with Crawford orchestrating events, but, again, it is more like a circulatory flow – after receiving an initial prompt, the residents wind themselves up.

Revived by acts of vandalism, burglary and petty arson, the community's creativity begins to flourish – ballet classes, tea dances and an impromptu arts festival result from Crawford's intervention. As Jeannette Baxter explains:

The secret behind Estrella de Mar's cultural cohesion resides in the controversial thesis that criminal violence is a legitimate corrective to social and psychological inertia. Beneath the polite surface of school festivals, tea parties and tennis club luncheons lurks a far less palatable reality.[13]

It is only at the end of the novel that Prentice learns how Crawford has been acting in conjunction with a number of other prominent residents and how they all bear responsibility for the devastating fire at the Hollinger house. When Crawford is shot, Prentice is framed for the killing, just as his brother has been. The interchangeability is as much role-playing as anything staged by the resort's Marina Players, as if Charles has merely been his brother's understudy throughout. This highlights how Ballard's attitude to the conventions of the detective genre is at least the equal of his disregard for standard SF fare. As a whodunit, *Cocaine Nights* is as innovative as Cluedo. But that is not the point of it; *what* is being done remains the issue.

In *Super-Cannes*, Paul Sinclair moves with his wife to the Eden-Olympia business park, which psychiatrist Wilder Penrose refers to as: 'an ideas factory for the new millennium'.[14] Penrose's particular idea is to explore the health benefits of bouts of madness in a community where perpetual work has replaced leisure and the notion of a Puritan work-ethic has collapsed in on itself. As he explains: 'Small doses of insanity are the only solution. Their own psychopathy is all that can rescue these people' (251). Violent attacks prescribed as part of a therapeutic programme act as a 'forcing house designed to expand the psychopathic possibilities of the executive imagination' (261) and the result is a remarkable rise in health levels. Working over a mugger, prostitute or immigrant cleaner does wonders for executive blood pressure or middle-management dermatitis. The containment of the microbe also has relevance at the corporate, as well as corporeal, level: 'A voluntary and sensible psychopathy is the only way we can impose a shared moral order', Penrose insists to Sinclair: 'Here at Eden-Olympia we're setting out the blueprint for an infinitely more enlightened community. A controlled psychopathy is a way of resocializing people and tribalizing them into mutually supportive groups' (264–5). The smooth management-speak makes this all sound like role-play, but the key point is, rather, that everyone is in on the act.

Again, as with Prentice, there is a deception being played on the newest member of the community. Sinclair's wife has been taken on as replacement paediatrician after her predecessor, David Greenwood, went on a shooting spree. Whilst Jane adopts the professional role of the paediatrician, Sinclair is forced to increasingly identify with Greenwood, effectively becoming his understudy in a similar narrative manoeuvre to Charles' interchangeability with Frank. He learns that ' "Penrose and Professor Kalman and Zander decided to conduct an experiment. They ran a special trial to explain what went wrong with David. You were their laboratory rat" ' (335). This experiment within an experiment is significant. Sinclair is essentially set up to present the symptoms of the wider community, to represent the *assemblage* and be treated in the manner of a scapegoat. Such is the state of Eden-Olympia that Sinclair's response to this revelation is to reach for a shotgun and Greenwood's hit-list.

In *Millennium People* it is Dr Richard Gould, a suspended paediatrician, who foments unrest among the bourgeoisie of Chelsea Marina, encouraging them to see Twickenham as 'the Maginot Line of the English class system'.[15] His reference to the failed fortifications along France's Eastern border is significant because his strategy is to target, breach and infiltrate at unpredictable points of English life. Whilst the rebellion in the Chelsea Marina sees rioting where skips have thoughtfully already been ordered for the subsequent clear-up, Gould's project is staging senseless attacks. His band of bourgeois renegades bomb Heathrow, the National Film Theatre and that crucible of all their cultural values, Tate Modern. The method of insurgency is equally significant. Gould claims: 'The attack on the World Trade Centre in 2001 was a brave attempt to free America from the 20th Century' (139). Gould believes the twentieth century itself to be a 'malaise'. The manifesto behind these absurdist percussive aftershocks is explained by the narrator, David Markham, after his investiture in the protest movement:

> It isn't a search for nothingness. It's a search for meaning. Blow up the Stock Exchange and you're rejecting global capitalism. Bomb the Ministry of Defence and you're protesting against war. You don't even need to hand out the leaflets. But a truly pointless act of violence, shooting at random into a crowd, grips our attention for months. The absence of rational motive carries a significance of its own.
>
> (194)

The rioting within the Chelsea Marina is effectively nothing more than disturbance, cultural white noise, much like the demo held to protest about Radio 4, behind which the real insurrectionary activity can be achieved. After Gould is betrayed by his co-conspirators and another smoking gun is placed in the hand of another guileless narrator, revolutionary fervour calms and house prices stabilize. The crowd, as theorized prior to Canetti, from Gustave Le Bon to Freud, is a rebellious, primitive mass, King Mob, a repeating, atavistic entity. As such, it is an act the middle classes cannot hope to pull off successfully:

> But even Chelsea Marina helped to prove Gould's point. As he soon realized, the revolution was doomed from the start. Nature had bred the middle class to be docile, virtuous and civic-minded. Self-denial was coded into its genes. Nevertheless, the residents had freed themselves from their own chains and launched their revolution, though now they are only remembered for their destruction of the Peter Pan statue in Kensington Gardens.
>
> (292)

Here, too, earlier thinking on the crowd does not quite explain the occurrences. The bombing of the Stock Exchange or MoD uses explosive power to challenge systemic power and is loud and clear for everyone; the cause is identifiable, as is the effect. The assault on Frampton's statuary in Kensington Gardens, however, 'says' nothing, it registers power and protest liberated from even rational motive. These crowds have the power to cause damage – and the more significant power of threatening whatever they choose.

In returning to the Metro-Centre of *Kingdom Come*, it is here that the crowd comes into its own. Swept along in 'an intense transactional present' (46) created by the mall, the inhabitants of Brooklands reconfigure their community to reflect consumer standards projected beyond the shop doors. A resident explains the influence of the Metro-Centre to Pearson: 'It's an incubator. People go in there and they wake up, they see their lives are empty. So they look for a new dream . . . ' (59). The new dream is a sports community, uniformed in St George's vests and baseball caps, prone to racist violence after weekend league games, a sort of Burberry fascism, where the *blut und boden* mythopoetic of Nazism is upholstered in the jangled class signifiers of aspirational antagonism and exclusive-gym thuggery. The social spaces of Brooklands, and indeed all the M25 towns, are constantly occupied by crowds, and Pearson's brush with demagoguery is perhaps inevitable as he cannot avoid these massed gatherings. Even his desire for an empty space in which to think is thwarted. The previously abandoned racing track he heads for is filled with one of Freud's examples of a primitive crowd, the army.[16]

As ever, there is a psychiatrist, Dr Maxted, on hand to provide a diagnosis: 'The suburbs are the perfect social laboratory. You can cook up any pathogen and test how virulent it is. The trouble is, they've waited too long. The whole M25 could flip and drag the rest of the country into outright psychopathy' (210). The consumer-crowds of *Kingdom Come* are maintained even when people are away from the mall as the flow of commodity-desire-as-social-desire is continually broadcast through the exclusive (to everyone) shopping channel. Pearson, an ex-advertising executive, helps to shape this new social phase with the star of the mall's cable channel, David Cruise. Together they inspire a consumer-cult, making a celebrity of Cruise and producing oblique advertising designed to cajole and perplex viewers into becoming better consumers in the face of a non-specific enemy connoting materialistic satiety. The effect of this retail shock therapy exacerbates the madness of crowds, leading to a siege of the Metro-Centre with the hostage-takers descending into a paramilitary state inflected with religiosity. The death of Cruise leads to the most explicit example of this when his disciples place his body in front of the Metro-Centre's three bears, hoping for a fairy-tale resurrection. Amid the satirically scrambled symbolism of this act it is possible to read Canetti's notion that crowds can be seen as victims of the illness of power. They are herded into the margins of maddened behaviour by the intervention of Pearson and Cruise and are judged to have 'flipped' – completing a revolution – when they chain Maxted to one of the bears, sacrificing him in the final inferno.

As far as they are inspirers of the crowds, what Crawford, Penrose, Gould and Maxted represent is a compulsion within these micro-communities to establish a way of talking about what is occurring. They are the theorizing wing of the revolution, mixing the fizzier bits of medical discourse, anthropology and pop psychology into an effervescent, rhetorical cocktail and persuading the narrator to swallow it.

Assemblage

But it is not just the specific formulation of these crowds as chance gatherings which adequately explains their intensive derangement, their piquantly Ballardian psychopathology. To account for their special madness it is necessary to explore Deleuze and Guattari's notion of assemblages. The assemblage is an elaboration upon the earlier formulation (principally proposed by Guattari) of the 'machinic' organizing flows and it remains *in nuce* far more than any of the other adapted, updated or recomposed concepts that they employ: 'The assemblages are in constant variation, are in themselves constantly subject to transformations.'[17] Despite this unfixed, indeterminate quality (what Jean-Jacques Lecercle identifies as a lack of specific explanation),[18] the assemblage can be understood through an outline of the essential features.

An assemblage consists of 'a *machinic assemblage* of bodies, of actions and passions, an intermingling of bodies reacting to one another; on the other hand it is a *collective assemblage of enunciation*, of acts, statements, of incorporeal transformations attributed to bodies'.[19] Related to this on a perpendicular axis is the reterritorializing aspect and the deterritorializing or cutting edge, which constitutes a line of flight 'that carries away all of the assemblages'.[20] The canonical example (examined in *A Thousand Plateaus*) is the feudal assemblage with its bodies (lords and vassals); locations; functional relations (knight-stirrup-horse) intermingling to form 'a whole machinic assemblage', and then the expressed statements – 'oaths and their variables' – that enunciate this. Deleuze and Guattari state:

> On the other axis, we would have to consider the feudal territorialities and reterritorialisations, and at the same time the line of deterritorialisation that carries away both the knight and his mount, statements and acts. We would have to consider how all this combines in the Crusades.[21]

As this indicates, the assemblage is in perpetual and reciprocal motion, expression and content interrelating to constitute the 'variables of the assemblage'.[22] In short, as Ian Buchanan notes: 'The assemblage replaces and reconfigures that staple sociological and philosophical concern, the relationship between man and his world . . . Composed of its own relations, the assemblage is not, however reducible to them, it has its own vitality. It also has its illnesses.'[23] Buchanan's cautionary conclusion is a point about the assemblage that should not be overlooked – it contains a potential for excess, an indirect flow that can elude containment and may flip from positive vitality towards something sickening.

Among Deleuze and Guattari's postulates of linguistics is the emphasis upon the primacy of *indirect discourse*, the 'constellation of voices' from which one draws a singular voice.[24] From Estrella de Mar to Eden-Olympia and the Metro-Centre 'mere' conversation is frequently too narrow an option or even somehow awry, deemed less successful, as the following examples from *Super-Cannes* show, than 'semaphore between distant peaks' (38), or a character trailing off in mid-sentence, 'unaware that her lips were moving' but communicating 'a sub-vocal message across the void' (112). Baxter, in relation to *Cocaine Nights*, explains one particular way in which this indirect, collective enunciation operates:

> Crawford wields an enormous amount of influence over the community of Estrella de Mar. His provocative language is seldom articulated in any explicit way, for instance, rather it is disseminated second hand through the resort's discursive networks – a veritable tissue of quotations drawn from Crawford's manifestos for socio-cultural transformation.[25]

Yet the collective assemblage extends beyond simple community buzz words (like the 'ratissages' of *Super-Cannes*) that may be heard or spoken subliminally. Deleuze and Guattari note how: 'one is necessarily led to treat nonlinguistic elements such as gestures and instruments in the same fashion, as if the two aspects of pragmatics joined on the same line of variation, in the same continuum'.[26] The lines of flight that link these collective assemblages call through the most oblique of elements. Thus, in *Cocaine Nights*, Prentice's response to the firebombing of his rental car is to observe without perturbation: 'Fires are the oldest signalling system' (156). It is as if the scorched metal and charred dashboard, fusing primitive order-word with vatic warning, confirms something for Prentice in a way he understands yet does not consciously know. (And the signal proves to be both prophetic and well-spoken indeed.) Similarly, after the cremation of his first wife, killed in the Heathrow bomb at the start of *Millennium People*, David Markham notes: 'I watched the smoke rising, a series of bursts as if this dead woman was signalling to me' (35). In both instances the imperative impulse of the communication is acknowledged since, as Canetti cautions: 'Commands are older than words.'[27]

Perhaps unsurprisingly, Sinclair also comes to view his investigation into Greenwood's rampage in *Super-Cannes* as deciphering a trail of signs or a signifying assemblage replete with breaks: 'It's as if someone is flashing a torch in the dark, sending a message we should try to decode' (105). This series of bursts (or perhaps jolts) is a constitutive aspect of the functioning of the assemblage, where the flow is brought to attention and made apparent through interruption (the flickering of the torch-beam), or the meeting of associative flows (the rail-flow suspended by the traffic-flow at a level crossing). As Deleuze and Guattari observe: 'A machine may be defined as a *system of interruptions* or breaks (*coupures*).'[28] An early warning of the problems to come is in the propensity of these social and cultural (that is, machinic) assemblages towards dramatic, violent or explosive expression.

Gould, in *Millennium People*, offers the most complete analysis, encouraging Markham to see in even a meaningless attack: 'a crazy gesture that signals some kind of message' (139). He later elaborates upon this: 'We can't see the road for all the signposts. Let's clear them away, so we can gaze at the mystery of an empty road' (249–50). Just like the liberation of the irrational act, going off-message deviates flows that are in danger of becoming predictable and sluggish.

Similarly, in *Kingdom Come*, the bomb at the Metro-Centre is intended to be another signal, the trigger to a general uprising. Realizing the ambiguous signalling power of the Metro-Centre, Pearson devises an advertising campaign to feed into this. Pearson outlines his approach to his collaborator David Cruise by saying: 'There is no message. Messages belong to the old politics . . . Your role is to empower them. You don't tell your audience what to think. You draw them out, urge them to open up and say what they feel' (146). This dissolving of the speaker-message-addressee produces a new assemblage within which 'subjects (both the speaker and the grammatical subject, *'sujet de l'énonciation'* and *'sujet de l'énoncé'*) are replaced by collective assemblages of enunciation'.[29] Not forgetting the interconnectivity of assemblages – what Lecercle neatly explains as 'the abstract materiality of utterances and institutions and the concrete materiality of objects'[30] – it is possible to identify the unhealthy lurch that propels these communities into their collective psychopathology. As Deleuze and Guattari warn: 'Anybody can shout, "I declare a general mobilisation," but in the absence of an effectuated variable giving that person the right to make such a statement it is an act of puerility or insanity, not an act of enunciation.'[31]

The effectuated variable is precisely where the fault lies: amid the interminable flicker of messages, the confused, scattered media and the subliminal and overhead order-words (all those advertisements and planes hauling advertising pennants), the process, in Penrose's words, of 'resocializing people and tribalizing them into mutually supportive groups' (26) renders them acutely vulnerable to a sickening *static*. Merged into the collective, these people experience not the deterritorializing 'cutting edges' of the assemblage which allows the free flowing of 'lines of flight' but rather the stultification of reterritorialization where lines of flight have become crushingly re-grounded: '*R*eterritorialisation occurs when this free movement is subjected, or falls back on, one of its components as a grounding territory.'[32] The point being made by Deleuze and Guattari is both blunt and bleak: sometimes trying to escape one routine merely results in falling into another. Ballard provides an illustration of this as assiduous middle-managers and their families turn their diligent attention to the routines of office- or housework and redirect it elsewhere: 'Crime could flourish at Eden-Olympia without the residents ever being aware that they were its perpetrators or leaving any clues to their motives' (89). The blocking, or seizing up of the assemblage, the decline into stratification, is evident in Penrose's minatory diagnosis in *Super-Cannes*: 'If you don't keep busy it's easy to find yourself in a state close to sensory deprivation. All kinds of chimeras float free, reality becomes a Rorschach test where butterflies turn into elephants' (246). The machinic assemblage, collective assemblage of enunciation and potential de- and re-territorializations become forces of attrition, grating against each other so that, in Buchanan's phrase: 'stratification refers to any type of obstruction to a clear view of the assemblage'.[33] Deleuze and Guattari are quick to emphasize the danger of being locked into an inimical circuit such as this: 'You will be organised . . . You will be signifier and signified . . . You will be a subject, nailed down as one, a subject of the enunciation recoiled into a subject of the statement.'[34] Of course, remaining caught in this situation simply results in a case of galloping stultification (as it were); in each of the four examples an uneasy and unhealthy equilibrium has been established: 'Staying stratified – organised, signified, subjected – is not the worst that can happen; the worst that can happen is if you throw the strata into demented or suicidal collapse, which brings them back down on us heavier than ever.'[35] Thus, the luxury apartments and dedicated retail spaces succumb to conflagrations while staccato retorts of gunfire echo from Mediterranean shores to the tidied malls of the Metro-Centre: as Maxted puts it: 'Consumerism is running out of road, and it's trying to mutate. It's tried fascism, but even that isn't primitive enough. The only thing left is out-and-out madness . . . ' (242).

Impulse

> The suburbs dream of violence. Asleep in their drowsy villas, sheltered by benevolent shopping malls, they wait patiently for the nightmares that will wake them into a more passionate world . . .
> (3)

The *incipit* to *Kingdom Come* (and our introduction to the thinking of narrator Richard Pearson) suggests the essence of the quartet of Ballard's texts and indicates the pervasive nature of the collective enunciation. In its metonymy and reliance on the non-personal pronoun, the *'machinic assemblage* of bodies, of actions and passions' is also in evidence: what is waiting to wake? Not just the residents, but the gathering together of social effects; cultural codes; markers of proximity and contiguity; attitudes and shared interests. A snowballing of everything that constitutes the suburban.

Throughout the four texts, the impulse is to provide a way of sharpening consciousness, quickening the vital reactions and rejuvenating life. In considering this, the comparison with the assemblage can be concluded. The impetus for Deleuze and Guattari's construction of the concept of the assemblage is best understood not as *signifying* ('Yes, it's all very cleverly complicated, but what does it *mean*?') but as *producing* ('What is it for?'). As with much of Deleuze and Guattari's thinking, it facilitates their account of the perpetual flow of desire, the circulatory system of their philosophy: 'Desire causes the current to flow, itself flows in turn, and breaks the flows.'[36] The desire to awake to a more passionate world, revivifying existence, restoring vitalism in place of banal routine is the central premise of Ballard's texts. The prescription for this – such as the doses of 'structured violence' (147) dished out in *Millennium People* – can in its turn be read as 'symptomal', in Fredric Jameson's phrase, exposing 'discontinuities, rifts, actions at a distance'.[37] The instances of violence, *ratissages*, bombings or 'games' of sexual assault, serve as fault lines where desire surfaces, erupting through the breaks in social-machines and emerging like pressured lava.

Deleuze, in particular, is not opposed to a little violence as a way of inciting or jolting fresh thought, yet in these texts the closeness between revolutionary and fascist assemblages (warned of especially in *Anti-Oedipus*) seems particularly pertinent. The potential for dream merges apparently seamlessly with nightmare: '(I)f it is true that all assemblages are assemblages of desire, the question is whether the assemblages of war and work, considered in themselves, do not fundamentally mobilize passions of different orders.'[38] From the Brooklands suburbs to Eden-Olympia, these different orders may enact Mackay's predictions and take us out of our course towards something hideous and frightening indeed.

Notes

1. 'Kingdom Come: An Interview with J. G. Ballard', in Jeannette Baxter, ed., *J. G. Ballard Contemporary Critical Perspectives* (Continuum: London, 2008), pp. 122–8 (p. 127).
2. Paul Connerton, 'Freud and the Crowd', in Peter Collier and Edward Timms, eds, *Visions & Blueprints: Avant-Garde Culture And Radical Politics In Early*

228 'The Personal is Political': Psychology and Sociopathology

     Twentieth Century Europe (Manchester University Press: Manchester, 1988), pp. 194–207 (p. 197).
3. J. G. Ballard, *Kingdom Come* (Fourth Estate: London, 2006), p. 120. Further page references are provided within the text.
4. J. G. Ballard, *Cocaine Nights* (Flamingo: London, 1997 [1996]), p. 34. Further page references are provided within the text.
5. Plato, *The Republic*, trans. Desmond Lee (Penguin Books: London, 2007), *ix*, *vii*, §565e).
6. John S. McClelland, *The Crowd And The Mob: From Plato To Canetti* (Unwin Hyman: London, 1989), p. 297.
7. Elias Canetti, *Crowds & Power*, trans. Carol Stewart (Gollancz: London, 1962), p. 17.
8. McClelland, *The Crowd And The Mob: From Plato To Canetti*, p. 296.
9. Canetti, *Crowds & Power*, p. 18.
10. Canetti, *Crowds & Power*, p. 18.
11. Canetti, *Crowds & Power*, p. 19.
12. Plato, *The Republic*, vii, vi, §492–3.
13. Jeannette Baxter, *J. G. Ballard's Surrealist Imagination: Spectacular Authorship* (Ashgate: Aldershot, 2009), p. 99.
14. J. G. Ballard, *Super-Cannes* (Flamingo: London, 2001 [2000]), p. 16. Further page references are provided within the text.
15. J. G. Ballard, *Millennium People* (Flamingo: London, 2003), p. 85. Further page references are provided in the text.
16. Sigmund Freud, 'Chapter/Paper', in *Standard Edition* vol 18, trans. James Strachey (Hogarth Press: London, 1964), pp. 93–9.
17. Gilles Deleuze and Félix Guattari, *A Thousand Plateaus: Capitalism and Schizophrenia*, trans. Brian Massumi (University of Minnesota Press: Minneapolis 1991), p. 82.
18. Jean-Jacques Lecercle, *Deleuze And Language* (Palgrave Macmillan: Basingstoke, 2002), pp. 190–1.
19. Deleuze and Guattari, *A Thousand Plateaus*, p. 88.
20. Deleuze and Guattari, *A Thousand Plateaus*, p. 89.
21. Deleuze and Guattari, *A Thousand Plateaus*, p. 89.
22. Deleuze and Guattari, *A Thousand Plateaus*, p. 91.
23. Ian Buchanan, *Deleuzism* (Duke University Press: Durham, 2000), p. 120.
24. Deleuze and Guattari, *A Thousand Plateaus*, p. 84.
25. Baxter, *J. G. Ballard's Surrealist Imagination*, p. 99.
26. Deleuze and Guattari, *A Thousand Plateaus*, p. 98.
27. Canetti, *Crowds & Power*, p. 303.
28. Deleuze and Guattari, *A Thousand Plateaus*, p. 36.
29. Lecercle, *Deleuze And Language*, p. 25.
30. Lecercle, *Deleuze And Language*, p. 185.
31. Deleuze and Guattari, *A Thousand Plateaus*, p. 82.
32. Claire Colebrook, 'Gilles Deleuze and Félix Guatarri', in Julian Wolfreys, ed., *Modern European Criticism and Theory* (Edinburgh University Press: Edinburgh, 2006), pp. 301–9 (p. 305).
33. Buchanan, *Deleuzism*, p. 123.
34. Deleuze and Guattari, *A Thousand Plateaus*, p. 159.
35. Deleuze and Guattari, *A Thousand Plateaus*, p. 161.

36. Gilles Deleuze & Félix Guattari, *Anti-Oedipus*, trans. Robert Hurley, Mark Seem, Helen R. Lane (Athlone Press: London, 1984), p. 5.
37. Fredric Jameson, *The Political Unconscious: Narrative As A Socially Symbolic Act* (Cornell University Press: New York, (1981), p. 57.
38. Deleuze and Guattari, *A Thousand Plateaus*, p. 399.

13
'Zones of Transition': Micronationalism in the Work of J. G. Ballard

Simon Sellars

'The collapse has begun'

Consider the spatial imagery in Ballard's work. It is often predicated on a vocabulary of secession, a quasi-revolutionary zeal mediated not so much by hard rhetoric or ideology, but by a concealed network of colonies, anomalous regions and virtual city-states, often metaphoric in nature and analogous to the mind-state of Ballard's deracinated characters. Examples are found across all phases of his career: the counterfeit spaceship in 'Thirteen to Centaurus' (1962); the abandoned New York in 'The Ultimate City' (1976); the gated community in *Running Wild* (1988); the ecotopia in *Rushing to Paradise* (1994); the overtly secessionist movement in *Kingdom Come* (2006). Ballard's fabled vision of suburbia is similarly detached, defined as the psychological catchment area of the built environment: 'In the suburbs you find uncentred lives. The normal civic structures are not there.'[1] In addition to its psychosocial character, there is an anarcho-libertarian slant underpinning this spatial logic that is of particular interest, since its structure and complex interaction with the outside world strongly parallels the successes and failures of the real-world phenomenon of micronations: small, often ephemeral 'nations', sometimes without land, but occasionally claiming the type of physical space Ballard describes. Micronations can be satirical or a component of an art project, but occasionally they can have political motives. Micronations are sometimes called 'model nations', since they are often hobbyist exercises that mimic the structure of independent nations and states, but are not recognized as such by established states.[2]

There is a further correspondence with what Marc Augé has identified as 'non-place'. According to Augé, in the era of 'supermodernity' (the 'obverse [of] postmodernity'), our perception of time has altered due to 'the overabundance of events in the contemporary world', so that history loses its authority and becomes non-functional, collapsed into an eternal present where 'the recent past – "the sixties", "the seventies", now "the eighties" – becomes history as soon as it is lived'.[3] This contraction of time and space necessitates an 'anthropology of the near', a discipline no longer focused on archaeo-exotic locales but on the immediate, urban present, where we are 'even more avid for meaning'[4] due to our inability to invest much substance in the recent past. For Augé, this produces: 'a world thus surrendered to solitary individuality . . . a communication so peculiar that it often puts the individual in contact only with another image of himself'.[5] The physical manifestation of this is 'non-place': 'Spaces which are not themselves anthropological places [but] instead . . . are listed, classified, promoted to the status of "places of memory", and assigned to a circumscribed and specific position.' This is a 'world where people are born in the clinic and die in the hospital, where transit points and temporary abodes are proliferating under luxurious or inhuman conditions'.[6]

This terrain of transport systems, airports, supermarkets, hospitals, holiday resorts and hotel chains (overlaid with the virtual topography of super-compacted communications networks) is also rich Ballardian territory. According to Roger Luckhurst, *Crash* (1973), for example, portrays a 'suspended state of duty-free malls, a zone at once inside and yet outside the legal parameters of the country it exists in . . . [where the characters] experience the motorways as weirdly detached from an embedded culture or history or morality'.[7] The peculiar qualities engendered by Ballard's suspended zones, amplified by the spatial and temporal vectors of Augé's map of non-place, echo the odd limbo that many micronations inhabit. These qualities transform into explicitly micronational movements in Ballard's later work, typified by *Millennium People* (2003), with its 'anomalous enclave'[8] of middle-class discontents, and *Kingdom Come*, in which a shopping centre is overrun by consumers, sealed off by an ad-hoc paramilitary force and declared a 'micro-republic'.[9] But the micronationalism always follows a particular trajectory, devolving into an act stripped of rebellion and recycled into a self-reflexive game that is always bested by the super-absorbent properties of consumer capitalism. In Ballard, when the chosen model replicates global, national and militaristic modes, micronational alternatives fatally collapse, and his failed secessionaries, trapped in this synchronic feedback loop, have no choice but to integrate back into the system, which, as explained in *Millennium People*, is 'self-regulating. It relies on our sense of civic responsibility.

Without that, society would collapse. In fact, the collapse may even have begun'.[10] Where, if at all, might viable models of resistance be found in Ballard?

'Inverted Crusoeism'

Born in Shanghai in 1930, Ballard lived there until 1945, entirely within a mesh of parallel worlds: first in the privileged expatriate community in Shanghai's International Settlement, which was under British and American control but on Chinese sovereign territory then, when war broke out, under Japanese military occupation, and finally in the Lunghua civilian camp, where he and his family were interned in March 1943. He has described Shanghai's wartime limbo as a 'strange interregnum' when 'one side in World War II had moved out and the other had yet to move in'.[11] Subsequently, he elaborates, 'zones of transition have always fascinated me',[12] and his writing would consistently explore this fascination. According to Andrzej Gasiorek, Ballard's characters pursue a 'flight from anything that might disturb the safety of an alienated habitat . . . [a] retreat from the beckoning light into the darkness of the cave [sounding] the death-knell of all politics'.[13] Although this analogy refers to the later novels, an anti-political retreat seems to have been a driving motivation right from the start of Ballard's career. Ballard has said that his earliest literary influences were: *'The Ancient Mariner* . . . *The Tempest* . . . *Robinson Crusoe* . . . *Gulliver* . . . even the *Alice* books to some extent. One reads them at a very early age, and they shape one's view of "alternative" fiction: non-naturalistic fiction that creates a parallel world which comments on our own'.[14] The Crusoe metaphor, the potency of being cut off from civilization (wilfully, in the Ballardian universe), testing reserves of inner strength in order to build a new world of the senses, is a motif he would return to repeatedly.[15]

Tentative attempts to document this strange slipstream can be found even in his first published story, 'The Violent Noon' (1951). It is set during the Malayan Emergency, which lasted from 1948 to 1960, when the National Liberation Army guerrillas battled British, Malayan and Commonwealth forces. The story portrays that extraordinary stasis when the locus of power is undecided, or is being usurped by something unknown, resulting in a moment of suspended time, an interzone where accepted laws and morals cease to apply.[16] This peculiar sense of alienation is more clearly essayed in his early science fiction work, where the narratives would betray a consistent fascination with escaping the strictures of chronological clock time. 'The Day of Forever' (1966), for example, is about a future when the Earth has stopped rotating and time literally stands still. A young man, Halliday, haunts the abandoned hotels in an African town, scavenging food and supplies, and hoping to rediscover his ability to dream, which he has somehow lost when world time had stopped. Previously, he had lived in 'the international settlement at Trondheim in Norway',[17] an obvious reference to Ballard's childhood. In his semi-fictionalized account of his war years, *Empire of the Sun* (1984), Ballard's avatar, young Jim, imagines Shanghai's International Settlement as life lived 'wholly within an intense present',[18] a comment on the unreality of the expatriate experience, where class and privilege shelter Jim and his family from both the past – Shanghai's relationship to its Chinese history – and the future: the spectre of impending war. Unsurprisingly, given this biographical connection, Ballard has described 'The Day of Forever' as a 'favourite story of mine . . . Perhaps the young man running around those abandoned hotels reminds me of my own adolescence, and that strange interregnum in Shanghai'.[19]

But both stories also recall Augé's non-functionality of the past and non-existence of the future, and yet this 'intense present', free from both historical consequences and future implications, also liberates Jim when it is transferred to the stasis of Lunghua: 'For the first time in his life Jim felt free to do what he wanted. All sorts of wayward ideas moved through his mind, fuelled by hunger and the excitement of stealing' (120). In *The Drowned World* (1962), a subtly revolutionary flavour underwrites this liberation, hinting at micronational themes to come. The character Kerans holes up in the crumbling penthouse suite at the abandoned Ritz Hotel, in exile from the scientific party he was working with:

Sometimes he wondered what zone of transit he himself was entering, sure that his own withdrawal was symptomatic not of a dormant schizophrenia, but of a careful preparation for a radically new environment, with its own internal landscape and logic, where old categories of thought would merely be an encumbrance.[20]

There is a palpable sense that the vestiges of the old world are being destroyed before this 'radically new environment' can be ushered in, which will finally free Kerans to test and live off his mental and physical reserves without the deadening aids of civilized society: 'This inverted Crusoeism – the deliberate marooning of himself without the assistance of a gear-laden carrack on a convenient reef – raised few anxieties in Kerans' mind' (47).

Ballard's 'inverted Crusoeism' is also on display in *Concrete Island*, which again takes the familiar narrative shape of the robinsonade. The architect, Robert Maitland, crashes his Jaguar, stranding himself on 'a small traffic island, some two hundred yards long and triangular in shape, that lay in the waste ground between three converging motorway routes'.[21] Maitland's interior thoughts make the connection explicit: ' "you're marooned here like Crusoe – If you don't look out you'll be beached here for ever" ' (32). Alone, feverish and injured, and therefore unable to leave the traffic island, which is invisible to passing motorists, he imagines the wasteland reshaping itself into 'an exact model of his head . . . moving across [the island], he seemed to be following a contour line inside his head' (69, 31). Although this suggests that the entire narrative might be taking place in Maitland's mind, perhaps in the split seconds flashing through consciousness as he dies on the island from his injuries, the scenario can be read as more than simply a literary conceit.

Ballard wrote *Concrete Island* at a time when the real-world potential of micronations was beginning to be explored. The best-known example, Sealand, was founded in the late 1960s by the pirate-radio DJ, Paddy Roy Bates, who took over an abandoned WWII gun platform in the North Sea and declared it an independent state. In Western Australia in 1970, a wheat farmer outraged at government production quotas formed the Hutt River Province Principality. Styling himself as 'Prince Leonard', he declared 'war' on the Australian federation, a non-violent, three-day conflict that resulted in the 'secession' of his farm. In the same year, a drifter named El Avivi founded another micronation, Akhzivland, by claiming a small town in Israel that had been evacuated after the War of Independence, a typical zone-within-a-zone operating to this day, as does Sealand and Hutt River, under a cloud of dubious legality. Maitland replicates these overt acts of reclamation, recovering and recycling of territory. Although he does not go so far as to declare war or overt sovereignty, Maitland nonetheless 'psychically' claims the island, which, like Sealand and Akhzivland, is a liminal region, an adjunct to civilized society, forgotten and discarded: ' "I am the island" ' (71).

During the 1980s and 1990s, there were several further instances of individuals forming micronations in their homes and declaring their real estate as sovereign territory, either as a joke[22] or due to some kind of dissatisfaction with the outside world. This tendency finds a striking echo in 'The Enormous Space' (1989), where the character Ballantyne is demoralized by a serious car crash, a painful divorce and the incessant demands of his job. He decides to shut himself off from the world and his problems, never to leave his house again, a decision rendered in explicitly micronational terms:

> I sat at the kitchen table, and tapped out my declaration of independence on the polished formica.
>
> By closing the front door I intended to secede not only from the society around me. I was rejecting my friends and colleagues, my accountant, doctor and solicitor, and above all my ex-wife. I was breaking off all practical connections with the outside world. I would never again step through the front door.[23]

Having seceded into willed social isolation, Ballantyne collapses the outside world into a fatally narrow inner perspective: 'I would eat only whatever food I could find within the house. After that I would rely on time and space to sustain me' (698). With that, he convinces himself that he is free to do as he pleases, to the exclusion of all others, since he is supposedly acting true to his imagination, a point Ballard makes by reintroducing the Crusoe metaphor:

> In every way I am marooned, but a reductive Crusoe paring away exactly those elements of bourgeois life which the original Robinson so dutifully reconstituted. Crusoe wished to bring the Croydons of his own day to life again on his island. I want to expel them, and find in their place a far richer realm formed from the elements of light, time and space.
>
> (700)

In fact, Ballantyne becomes crazed with delusions of immortality, referring to himself in the third person and believing he can detach himself from the physical plane: 'I am no longer dependent on myself. I feel no obligation to that person who fed and groomed me' (701). Ostensibly outside of morality, he survives by trapping and eating neighbourhood pets. He even resorts to cannibalism, killing and eating the TV repairman after animal stocks are exhausted. His narration describes chronological and spatial dimensions expanding away from him, as they do in *Empire of the Sun*, when young Jim, his senses similarly deranged by hunger and the dislocation of war, hallucinates that the interior of his house is withdrawing from him. After a colleague calls on Ballantyne, he admits her to the house and then watches her 'walking towards me, but so slowly that the immense room seems to carry her away from me in its expanding dimensions. She approaches and recedes from me at the same time, and I am concerned that she will lose herself in the almost planetary vastness of this house' (708). By the final scene, she too has been killed and is lying in state in his freezer, where he is soon to join her in a planned suicide.

'The Enormous Space' frames a consistent theme in Ballard's work: the concept of a neural freezone as a 'morally free psychopathology of metaphor, as an element in one's dreams',[24] although it pushes this to the extreme: total immersion into the realm of the imaginary and a fatal disengagement from reality. As such, it is a virtual retelling of 'The Overloaded Man' (1961), in which the character Faulkner attempts to disassociate objects from their cultural meaning by 'training his ability to operate the cut-out switches'.[25] Faulkner tells his friend Hendricks that he might 'actually be stepping outside of time', explaining that it is difficult to invest conscious recognition in objects 'without a time sense' (334) and drawing us once again into the time-slippage characterizing the archetypal Ballardian interzone. Faulkner continues with the experiment until objects and structures appear as pure geometric shapes, 'armchairs and sofas like blunted rectangular clouds' (337). He even perceives his wife as an angular collection of planes, which he attempts to smooth into a more rounded form. When he has finished with her, she falls to the floor, 'a softly squeaking lump of spongy rubber' (343). Faulkner has murdered her without even realizing it, a victim of his own internalized messianic complex, and the story ends with his understanding that what he desires most is 'pure ideation, the undisturbed sensation of psychic being untransmuted by any physical medium' (343). Reaching this state would at last allow him to 'escape the nausea of the external world', which he achieves by drowning himself in his backyard pond, '[waiting] for the world to dissolve and set him free' (344).

Both 'The Overloaded Man' and 'The Enormous Space' represent the outer limits of Ballard's longstanding project to map inner space, a concept he has defined as: 'an imaginary realm in which, on the one hand, the outer world of reality and, on the other, the inner world of the mind meet and merge . . . a movement in the interzone between both spheres'.[26] For Ballard, the existence of this 'imaginary realm' is a response to the all-invasive media and communications landscape, and its inexorable collapsing of time, space and consciousness into hyperreality:

> We live in a world ruled by fictions of every kind . . . the increasing blurring and intermingling of identities within the realm of

consumer goods, the pre-empting of any free or original imaginative response to experience by the computer screen . . . The most prudent and effective method of dealing with the world around us is to assume that it is a compete fiction – conversely, the one small node of reality left to us is inside our own heads.[27]

But the oscillating 'movement between spheres' from the earlier definition is critical: once the balance favours irreversibly either side of the spectrum, the consequences prove fatal, as Hendricks warns Faulkner in 'The Overloaded Man', 'By any degree to which you devalue the external world so you devalue yourself' (334). In later years, Ballard would explore the obverse of this equation, but with the same result, as his characters drag their psychopathologies, kicking and screaming, into the outer world of reality, which they attempt to reshape in accordance with their degraded inner maps. This is a notable development in *Rushing to Paradise* (1994), which signals in Ballard's work the stirring of a sense of entrapment within late capitalism, manifest in a much harder version of micronationalism. The echoes of real-world enclave-cults such as Jonestown are apparent in *Rushing to Paradise*, and its central character, the charismatic Dr Barbara, seems modelled on religious-utopian gurus like Waco leader David Koresh. Dr Barbara builds an isolated community on an abandoned Pacific island, and, like Koresh, coerces others into joining her through sheer force of personality and rhetoric, before destroying almost everyone and everything as the authorities move in. In so doing, she provides, as Gasiorek suggests: 'a darker account of the megalomania that may be productive when confined to the autonomous imagination . . . but that is so cataclysmic when unleashed upon the world . . . for, as Ballard has rightly noted, the "history of [the 20th] century is the history of a few obsessives, some of the most dangerous men who have ever existed on this planet, being allowed to follow their obsessions to wherever they wanted to take them" '.[28]

'Gated communities, closed minds'

The urge to form micronations, whether as a joke, an experiment or a religious utopia, can in some ways be attributed to globalization and the failure of political action to ignite the mass imagination. As Ballard once put it, the 'overriding power of the global economy threatens the autonomy of the nation state, while the ability of politicians to intervene as an equalizing force has faded'.[29] In this vacuum, micronational enclaves thrive. Sealand and Hutt River are benign examples, but there are other more aggressive templates, as documented in Erwin S. Strauss's incendiary handbook, *How to Start Your Own Country* (1984), and in the research of sociologist Judy Lattas.[30] These include model nations formed as scams to lure unwary investors, right-wing communes promoting racial purity, and hardcore anarchist anomalies concerned with the violent carving out of patches of turf in thrall to utopian ideals. Strauss even outlines various methods for those wishing to form their own micronation, such as the 'mouse that roared strategy',[31] which involves getting hold of small, 'cheap weapons of mass destruction', finding a patch of unclaimed, disputed or forgotten territory (such as Sealand's gun platform), occupying this interzone, and threatening to use the weapon against any superpower that tries to evict you.[32] Strauss justifies this in 'libertarian moral terms', arguing that 'whoever (through the initiation of force) puts a victim in the position of having to choose between his own life and freedom, and the lives of others, is morally responsible for whatever the victim must do to protect his own life and freedom'.[33] With a similar agenda, the self-styled 'anarcho-leftoid' Keith Preston predicts that the 'empire' of the United States, like the Soviet Union before it, will at some near-future point cease to exist, broken down by market forces into smaller, self-governing entities. Gangs led by drug warlords will prove the true power base, forming provisional governments and controlling micro city-states in a grassroots structure embodying 'different values, beliefs and customs . . . sovereign in their own enclaves, federated with others when necessary for joint purposes'.[34] Preston looks to various historical models to justify his prediction, such as ancient Greek republics, medieval city-states, traditional tribal networks, early American pioneer societies and micronations, concluding that sovereign enclaves are 'the only possible approach to avoiding either chaos or tyranny'.[35]

While either solution might seem radically implausible, there are clear antecedents in the phenomenon of gated communities. The infrastructure of these micro-worlds is predicated on the unease that particular groups feel regarding a certain quality of life and welfare that they believe governments cannot guarantee, but that can nonetheless be bought via sealed-off suburban areas guarded by surveillance technology and private security firms. In *Running Wild*, the gated community, Pangbourne Estate, is essentially a micronation, one of many similar estates in the area housing thousands of urban professionals and their families: 'Secure behind their high walls and surveillance cameras, these estates in effect constitute a chain of closed communities whose lifelines run directly along the M4 to the offices and consulting rooms, restaurants and private clinics of central London.'[36] But Pangbourne Estate is also an archetypal non-place. Although it takes its name from the nearby town, it 'has no connections, social, historical or civic, with Pangbourne itself' (15), echoing Augé's description of transient urban environments that are neither 'relational, historical or concerned with identity', but that are connected instead, via the high-speed technology of the motorway and networked surveillance, to 'transit points and temporary abodes'[37] – the offices, consulting rooms and private clinics of the Pangbourne universe.

For Ballard, globalization's mediation, consumption and broadcasting of experience produces a paradoxical effect that gives the illusion of connectedness, but in fact creates withdrawal, a regression into disparate, private worlds, culminating 'in the most terrifying casualty of the century: the death of affect . . . [the] demise of feeling and emotion'.[38] The result, in micronational terms, is what a character in *Super-Cannes* (2000) describes as: 'the ultimate gated community . . . a human being with a closed mind'.[39] Corroborating some of Preston's more extreme arguments, Ballard's late-period work, beginning with *Rushing to Paradise*, renounces the preoccupation with temporality that was the hallmark of his earlier work in favour of an obsession with defending physical space from outside forces.[40] This shift reaches its apex in *Cocaine Nights* (1996) and *Super-Cannes*, which provide unambiguous examples of the professional middle classes retreating into fortified enclaves, bulwarked not so much by weaponry as by the switching off of the sensory reach of the human nervous system and its replacement by a technological exoskeleton of CCTV, satellite dishes and triple-security locks. Reading Ballard, Augé (if not Preston) would surely recognize his own conclusion:

> In one form or another . . . some experience of non-place . . . is today an essential component of all social existence. Hence . . . the fashion for "cocooning", retreating into the self: never before have individual histories (because of their necessary relations with space, image and consumption) been so deeply entangled with general history, history *tout court*.[41]

In *Millennium People*, this commingling of individual and general histories is explicitly generated, even actively encouraged, by capitalism's tight control of space, image and consumption. The novel charts an uprising in Chelsea Marina, an exclusive gated community in London, where middle-class citizens, rejecting their perceived role as a type of 'new proletariat', revolt against what they see as a meaningless society, turning their community into a miniaturized war zone. But the action is doomed to fail, since the revolutionaries are too indoctrinated in consumerism to push the boundaries completely:

> I tripped on the kerb and leaned against a builder's skip heaped with household possessions. The revolutionaries, as ever considerate of their neighbours, had ordered a dozen of these huge containers in the week before the uprising. A burnt-out Volvo sat beside the road, but the proprieties still ruled, and it had been pushed into a parking bay. The rebels had tidied up after their revolution. Almost all the overturned cars had been righted, keys left in their ignitions, ready for the repossession men.[42]

The revolt that almost causes Chelsea Marina to secede is swiftly absorbed back into the system, an act of rebellion finally remembered more for a childish, tabloid act of violence than any sustained programme of social change. Inevitably, the authorities move in as martial law is declared and Chelsea Marina becomes 'an anomalous enclave ruled jointly by the police and the local council' (256). The transgression of meaningless violence is usurped by the more powerful intervention of state violence, the Simulated State absorbing and repackaging rebellion in an unequivocal demonstration of the futility of performing actions that can be broken down and reabsorbed as news bites, as spectacular entertainment. For John Gray, this is an important dynamic in *Super-Cannes*, where it is threaded throughout the narrative as 'part of a new industry [that feeds us] with brilliant, violent, strange, surreal imagery, but with the goal not of emancipating us, but of keeping us at the job, keeping us working . . . the liberation that comes with wealth, affluence, freedom of choice can be used as a tool of social control'.[43]

This insidious current also powers *Kingdom Come*. Its narrator, Richard Pearson, a former adman, is bored, jobless and disaffected. He travels to the London satellite town of Brooklands to investigate the death of his father, killed in the Metro-Centre shopping complex by an unknown gunman opening fire on the lunchtime crowds. He becomes embroiled in the dark undercurrents of Brooklands' sport-and-product obsessed social strata, where fiercely nationalistic, violent mobs wear shirts emblazoned with the St George's Cross. He meets David Cruise, a forgotten actor now the host of the Metro-Centre's cable-TV channel. Drawing on his advertising experience, he reboots Cruise's image, portraying him as the tortured *noir* hero of billboard campaigns and TV spots in a notable inversion of Cruise's blow-waved idol persona. These inflammatory mini-narratives spark the imaginations of the Brooklands residents, bonding them into a tightly controlled mass that hangs on Cruise's every word. Swept away with delusions of grandeur, Pearson pulls the strings of this 'smiley, ingratiating, afternoon TV kind of führer' (258), stage-managing Cruise's overwhelming popularity with the Metro-Centre crowds, and, incredibly, the actual secession of the Metro-Centre itself.

'Greater autonomy'

Kingdom Come reads like the fictional companion to the *Harvard Design School Guide to Shopping* (2002), an initiative of the architect Rem Koolhaas, and among the most exhaustive analyses of the phenomenon of consumerism. A central focus of the guide is how the traditional idea of the suburban mall, as a distinct, clearly delineated entity, is disappearing, rendering meaningless the old demarcation between urban and suburban space. Shopping becomes 'urban' and the city becomes the mall:

> Shopping, after decades of sucking the public away from the urban centers, has proven to the city that it can now create all the qualities of urbanity – density of activity, congestion, excitement, spectacle – better than the city itself has been able to do in recent memory. Once, shopping needed the city to survive. Now, the urban has been reduced to a theme of shopping.[44]

Analogously, *Kingdom Come* portrays Brooklands as simply an extension of the Metro-Centre, a mere sideline on the way to the main event:

> The traffic into Brooklands had slowed, filling the six-lane highway built to draw the population of south-east England towards the Metro-Centre. Dominating the landscape around it, the immense aluminium dome housed the largest shopping mall in Greater London . . . Consumerism dominated the lives of its people, who looked as if they were shopping whatever they were doing.
>
> (15)

In Ballard's new metropolis, shopping has so invaded the urban that it fulfils all civic and social functions, becoming a virtual city-state far more influential than standard institutions. *Kingdom Come* argues that the distinction between religion and consumerism becomes blurred when the globalized economy erodes faith in institutions and governments, so that the only thing left is 'a cathedral of consumerism whose congregations far exceeded those of the Christian churches' (15). The *Harvard Guide* concurs, although it notes the process in reverse: in the US, churches model themselves on malls to become 'megachurches', featuring bowling alleys, aerobics classes and counselling services.[45] Functioning like megastores, these new entities are armed with enough economic and emotional capital to completely obliterate all competition, 'function[ing] suspiciously like the category killer . . . for every megachurch that pops up, one hundred churches fold'.[46] Not only is 'shopping melting into everything, but everything is melting into shopping', with governments 'no longer willing or able to support . . . institutions' in their original state.[47] Traditional social and civic structures must either face the threat of obsolescence or remodel themselves after the consumerist model, as indeed happens when the Metro-Centre dismantles traditional conceptions of the city to redefine urbanity, then religion, as itself:

> [He described] the huge dimensions of the Metro-Centre, the millions of square feet of retail space, the three hotels, six cineplexes and forty cafes.
>
> 'Did you know,' he concluded, 'that we have more retail space than the whole of Luton? . . . The Metro-Centre creates a new climate, Mr Pearson. We succeeded where the Greenwich dome failed. This isn't just a shopping mall. It's more like a . . . '
>
> 'Religious experience?'
>
> 'Exactly! It's like going to church. And here you can go every day and you get something to take home'.
>
> (40)

According to the *Harvard Guide*: 'shopping has created its own interior realms – the bazaar, the arcade, and the shopping mall all exist in a lineage of greater control and greater autonomy from exterior conditions'.[48] In *Kingdom Come*, the logical extension of this 'greater autonomy' is the Metro-Centre's secession from Brooklands, which begins when a group of residents see the inherent worship of shopping as a way to instil political control: 'The micro-republic would become a micro-monarchy, and the vast array of consumer goods would be [the] real subjects' (222). Ballard's revolutionaries are so in thrall to consumerism that they no longer wish to live within the terms and values of the real world. Secession of the consumer state seems the commonsense solution, yet they fail to see, as the *Harvard Guide* demonstrates, that consumerism is already autonomous, and that it is everywhere, limitless and relentless, redefining the world as itself, even the acts of transgression enacted in its name. As in *Millennium People*, the revolution becomes an act of empty symbolism as the authorities again move in to drive the rebels from the mall they had occupied for two months.

As to where a workable model of resistance might lie, answers can be found in Ballard's assertion that true revolution can only occur through imaginative means, a revolution of aesthetics rather than political ends: preserving the sovereignty of the imagination as if it is, as he puts it in *Super-Cannes*, the 'last nature reserve' (264), but without the fatal inversion that beset Faulkner and Ballantyne. For Ballard, politics is a subset of advertising. Politicians sell personal style rather than govern objectively, resulting in a complete invasion of the political realm by consumerism and aesthetics. Because 'world economic systems are so interlocked . . . no radical, revolutionary change can be born anymore . . . It may only be from aesthetic changes of one sort or another that one can expect a radical shift in the people's consciousness'.[49] In *Kingdom Come*, the explicitly micronational elements in the narrative are easily recouped by consumer capitalism. What is not so easily absorbed is Pearson's new sense of worth, the sense that he has found himself in a confrontation with the forces of consumerism and has summoned the nerve to walk away, resisting what the *Harvard Guide* terms the 'psychoprogramming' of end-state consumerism. Pearson, alone, sees the folly of the Metro-Centre micro-republic, predicting how the consumer landscape, which has now expanded to become the State itself, will always renew itself:

> One day there would be another Metro-Centre and another desperate and deranged dream. Marchers would drill and wheel while another cable announcer sang out the beat. In time, unless the sane woke and rallied themselves, an even fiercer republic would open the doors and spin the turnstiles of its beckoning paradise.
>
> (280)

In his analysis of *Kingdom Come*, Benjamin Noys highlights its 'self-criticism' of Ballard's late-period work and the fascination with transgression: 'While Ballard traces how such a "revolution" flirts with fascism the end of the novel traces the descent of the revolution into the kind of inertia that was found in his earlier fiction'[50] – indeed, the inertia of 'time slippage' that was paradoxically revealed to be liberating in stories like 'The Day of Forever'. Pearson broadcasts his creations to the world, but when they reach peak capacity he disengages, refusing to follow the logic of transgression – the cycle of action-reaction-destruction – to its bitter conclusion, a trajectory that destroys the characters Prentice in *Cocaine Nights* and Sinclair in *Super-Cannes*. Both literalize their unconscious roles as switches in a perpetual relay of destruction. Prentice willingly substitutes himself for his brother Frank as perpetrator of a fatal, mysterious house fire, while the real crime of consumer capitalism – the selling of transgressive acts as entertainment, leading to the fire – reforms around him, forever evading detection. Sinclair takes his place as the death angel of the novel's anomie-infested business parks, avenging another character's death, yet undermined by the knowledge that his rebellion will inevitably be soaked up as more balm for violence-hungry consumers. Contrary to this, Pearson enacts an alternative that Noys, taking his cue from Baudrillard's early work, terms 'becoming banal':

> The account that . . . Ballard give[s] of simulated alterity suggests that transgression is not actually transgressive; it is rather that transgression is boring . . . To play the game of transgression is to fall within an unacknowledged banality, as well as to continue to sustain the dead forms of contemporary culture. Therefore it is a matter of pushing through and completing the banality of transgression . . . Contrary to the desire to find a real future crime we might follow Baudrillard's previous suggestion for a fatal strategy: becoming-banal.[51]

Pearson's actions suggest that remaining anonymous, withdrawing and embracing obscurity could well prove to be the most radical strategy of all. But the point would not be to disengage completely, lest Ballantyne's fate be visited, but in knowing when to stop, to withdraw, to resist classification, to exercise choice, to reform; and when to re-emerge.

Within this fluctuation, there is a final connection with micronationalism. In 2003, the Amorph!03 conference was held in Finland, gathering together delegates to discuss the future of micronations. Many of the 'nations' represented were based on the NSK model, a template that marked a shift away from the traditional claiming of physical space.

According to NSK, a Slovenian art collective,[52] their micronation is in fact a 'state in time', which 'claims no territory, but rather confers the status of a state not to territory but to mind, whose borders are in a state of flux, in accordance with the movements and changes of its symbolic and physical collective body'.[53] For the 'NSK State in Time' – informed by the breakup of Yugoslavia, the subsequent reorganization of geographical boundaries and the re-emergence of Slovenia – the process of globalization has changed forever the role of the nation state. Therefore, time, as an aggregation of individual experiences, becomes the only productive way to measure, and inhabit, space, which has now become a commodity, fought over for inscrutable nationalistic or consumerist purposes. Movement for NSK creates subjective time, and therefore new experiences, recalling Halliday in 'The Day of Forever', who, moving from town to town, attempts to restart his imaginative inner life in a global era where time has stopped completely.

Ballard's characters, to varying degrees of success, have been claiming allegiance to their minds – to the sovereignty of their imaginations – since the very beginning of his career, and the message appears more pertinent today:

> The consumer conformism – 'the suburbanization of the soul' – on the one hand and the gathering ecological and other crises on the other do force the individual to recognize that he or she is all he or she has *got*. And this sharpens the eye and the imagination. The challenge is for each of us to respond, to remake as much as we can of the world around us, because no one else will do it for us. We have to find a core within us and get to work.[54]

But it is his final words that are particularly worth remembering. Here, we find a genuine call to arms that puts his failed revolutionaries – Faulkner, Ballantyne, Prentice, Sinclair – to shame. Instead, Ballard points towards the future and to Pearson: 'Don't worry about worldly rewards. Just get on with it!'[55]

Notes

I would like to acknowledge the assistance of a Monash Postgraduate Publications Award with the initial research phase of this essay.

1. Quoted in Iain Sinclair, *Crash: David Cronenberg's Post-mortem on J. G. Ballard's 'Trajectory of Fate'* (London: British Film Institute, 1999), p. 84.
2. See John Ryan, George Dunford and Simon Sellars, *Micronations: The Lonely Planet Guide to Home-made Nations* (Footscray: Lonely Planet Publications,

2006); Erwin S. Strauss, *How to Start Your Own Country* (Port Townsend: Loompanics Unlimited, 1984 [1979]); Judy Lattas, 'DIY Sovereignty and the Popular Right in Australia', in *Mobile Boundaries/Rigid Worlds* (Sydney: Centre for Research on Social Inclusion, 2005). <http://www.crsi.mq.edu.au/documents/mobile_boundaries_rigid_worlds/lattas.pdf >, accessed 18 July 2010; and *Cabinet*, issue 18 (Summer 2005). <http://www.cabinetmagazine.org/issues/18/toc.php>, accessed 18 July 2010.
3. Mark Augé, *Non-places: Introduction to an Anthropology of Supermodernity*, trans. J. Howe (London and New York, Verso, 1995), pp. 30, 26.
4. Augé, *Non-places*, pp. 7, 29.
5. Augé, *Non-places*, pp. 78, 79.
6. Augé, *Non-places*, p. 78.
7. Roger Luckhurst, *'The Angle Between Two Walls': The Fiction of J. G. Ballard* (Liverpool: Liverpool University Press, 1997), p. 129.
8. J. G. Ballard, *Millennium People* (London: Flamingo, 2003), p. 265.
9. J. G. Ballard, *Kingdom Come* (London: Fourth Estate, 2006), p. 222.
10. Ballard, *Millennium People*, p. 104.
11. J. G. Ballard, 'J. G. Ballard's comments on his own fiction', *Interzone* (April 1996), p. 23. Here, Ballard clarifies that the 'strange interregnum' refers to two periods: the time between Pearl Harbour, in December 1941, and internment at Lunghua in March 1943; and the end of the war in 1945, when American forces took control of Shanghai. He revisited the phrase to describe the latter in his autobiography, *Miracles of Life*: 'August 1945 formed a strange interregnum when we were never wholly certain that the war had ended, a sensation that stayed with me for months and even years. To this day as I doze in an armchair I feel the same brief moment of uncertainty.' J. G. Ballard, *Miracles of Life* (London: Fourth Estate), p. 104.
12. Ballard, 'J. G. Ballard's comments on his own fiction', p. 23.
13. Andrzej Gasiorek, *J. G. Ballard* (Manchester: Manchester University Press, 2005), p. 188.
14. David Pringle, 'J. G. Ballard Interviewed by David Pringle', *Interzone* (April 1986), pp.12–16 (p. 12).
15. In the introduction to *Concrete Island*, Ballard writes: 'The day-dream of being marooned on a desert island still has enormous appeal, however small our chances of actually finding ourselves stranded on a coral atoll in the Pacific.' J. G. Ballard, *Concrete Island* (London: Vintage, 1994 [1974]), p. 4.
16. The character Hargreaves finds himself, despite his reservations, caught up in a narrative of revenge that frames innocent men for the murder of a British officer, the implication being that during war, normal ideas of reality are suspended. J. G. Ballard, 'The Violent Noon', *Varsity*, 26 May 1951, p. 9.
17. J. G. Ballard, 'The Day of Forever' (1966), in *The Complete Short Stories: Volume 2* (London: Harper Perennial, 2006), pp. 136–54 (p. 137).
18. J. G. Ballard, *Empire of the Sun* (London: Grafton Books, 1988 [1984]), p. 27.
19. Ballard, 'J. G. Ballard's comments on his own fiction', p. 23.
20. J. G. Ballard, *The Drowned World*, (Harmondsworth and Ringwood: Penguin, 1974 [1962]), p. 14.
21. Ballard, *Concrete Island*, p. 11.

22. It is actually remarkably easy to treat micronations as a joke, given that adolescent boys often tend to form them. See Ryan, Dunford and Sellars, *Micronations*, pp. 56–7.
23. J. G. Ballard, 'The Enormous Space' (1989) in *The Complete Short Stories: Volume 2* (London: Harper Perennial, 2006), pp. 697–709 (p. 698).
24. Graeme Revell, 'Interview with JGB by Graeme Revell' (1984) in V. Vale and Andrea Juno, eds, *RE/Search #8/9: J. G. Ballard* (Re/Search Publications: San Francisco, 1991), pp. 42–52 (p. 47).
25. J. G. Ballard, 'The Overloaded Man' (1961) in *The Complete Short Stories: Volume 1*, pp. 330–44 (p. 334).
26. Brian Wood, 'Munich Round-Up: Interview with J. G. Ballard', trans. Dan O'Hara, *Ballardian*, 15 March 2008, <http://www.ballardian.com/munich-round-up-interview-with-jg-ballard>, accessed 13 July 2010.
27. J. G. Ballard, 'Introduction to the French edition of *Crash!*' (1974), *Foundation: The Review of Science Fiction*, 9 (November 1975), pp. 45–54 (p. 48).
28. Gasiorek, *J. G. Ballard*, p. 139.
29. J. G. Ballard (1996), quoted in V. Vale and Mike Ryan, eds, *J. G. Ballard: Quotes* (San Francisco: RE/Search Publications, 2004), p. 37.
30. See Lattas, 'DIY Sovereignty'.
31. This gambit is named after *The Mouse that Roared*, a 1955 novel and 1959 film adaptation about a fictitious European country, the Duchy of Grand Fenwick, which inadvertently captures the American government's experimental doomsday device, leading to the USA's defeat in an accidental war.
32. Strauss, *How to Start Your Own Country*, pp. 18–19.
33. Strauss, *How to Start Your Own Country*, p. 21.
34. Keith Preston, 'When the American Empire Falls: How Anarchists Can Lead the 2nd American Revolution', *Attack the System*, 2005, <http://attackthesystem.com/when-the-american-empire-falls-how-anarchists-can-lead-the-2nd-american-revolution>, accessed 13 July 2010.
35. Preston, 'When the American Empire Falls'.
36. J. G. Ballard, *Running Wild* (London: Arrow Books, 1989 [1988]), p. 16.
37. Augé, *Non-places*, p. 78.
38. Ballard, 'Introduction to the French edition of *Crash!*' p. 45.
39. J. G. Ballard, *Super-Cannes* (New York: Picador, 2002 [2000]), p. 256.
40. Gasiorek, *J. G. Ballard*, p. 186.
41. Augé, *Non-places*, pp. 119–20.
42. Ballard, *Millennium People*, p. 8.
43. John Gray, 'Interview with J. G. Ballard' [transcript], BBC Radio Four, 2000, <http://groups.yahoo.com/group/jgb/message/1137>, accessed 13 July 2010.
44. Sze Tsung Leong, ' . . . And There Was Shopping', in Chuihua Judy Chung, Jeffrey Inaba, Rem Koolhaas, Sze Tsung Leong, eds, *Harvard Design School Guide to Shopping* (Cologne: Taschen, 2002), pp. 128–55 (p. 153).
45. 'One megachurch in Houston even designed its entertainment schedule in consultation with Walt Disney World.' Sze Tsung Leong, 'The Divine Economy', *Harvard Design School Guide*, pp. 298–303 (p. 302).
46. Leong, 'The Divine Economy', p. 302.
47. Leong, ' . . . And There Was Shopping', p. 129.

48. Sze Tsung Leong and Srdjan Jovanovic Weiss, 'Air Conditioning', *Harvard Design School Guide*, pp.92–127 (p. 93). In addition, as the developer of the Bluewater shopping centre, a complex with rich Ballardian significance, says: 'We have never seen [a shopping mall] as the last regional centre, but as the first stage of a city' (Chuihua Judy Chung and Juan Palop-Casado, 'Resistance', *Harvard Design School Guide*, p. 640).
49. Revell, 'Interview with JGB by Graeme Revell', p. 52.
50. Benjamin Noys, 'Crimes of the Near Future: Baudrillard/Ballard', *International Journal of Baudrillard Studies*, vol. 5, no. 1, January 2008 <http://www.ubishops.ca/baudrillardstudies/vol5_1/v5-1-article8-Noys.html>, accessed 18 July 2010.
51. Noys, 'Crimes of the Near Future: Baudrillard/Ballard'.
52. NSK (Neue Slowenische Kunst) is perhaps most famous for its 'music branch', the group Laibach.
53. Eda Cufer & Irwin quoted in Ryan, Dunford and Sellars, *Micronations*, p. 129.
54. Jonathan Cott, 'The Strange Visions of J. G. Ballard', *Rolling Stone*, 19 November, 1987, pp. 76–80 (p. 127).
55. Cott, 'The Strange Visions of J. G. Ballard', p. 127.

Index

Ackroyd, Peter, 165, 169, 172
Adams, Parveen, 92
Adorno, Theodor,
 'The Essay as Form' (1958), 53
Akhzivland, 234
Aldiss, Brian 22, 24, 25, 30
 'Danger: Religion!' (1969), 25
Amazing Stories, 36
Amis, Kingsley, 23–4, 186, 187
 The Golden Age of Science Fiction (1981), 6, 23
Amis, Martin, 1, 105, 160–1, 174
Antonioni, Michelangelo
 Blow-Up (1966), 74
Archigram (1961), 37
Artaud, Antonin, 78, 83
 'An End to Masterpieces' (1936), 83
 theatre of cruelty, 83–5
Augé, Marc, 13, 129, 230–1, 233
Augustine, St,
 The City of God, 125
Austen, Jane
 Persuasion (1817), 115
avant-garde, 72, 187, 190
Axell, Albert and Kase, Hideaki
 Kamikaze: Japan's Suicide Gods (2002), 62–3

Bacon, Francis (seventeenth-century thinker), 154
Bacon, Francis (twentieth-century artist), 1
Ballard, J. G.
 'Alphabets of Unreason' (1969), 64
 The Atrocity Exhibition (1970), 3, 6, 7, 8, 29, 35–46, 71–85, 88–102, 143, 190, 193, 194
 'Chronopolis' (1960), 4
 'The Coming of the Unconscious' (1966), 54
 'The Concentration City' (1957), 4
 Cocaine Nights (1996), 6, 12, 191, 215, 216–17, 218–19, 224, 239, 244
 Concrete Island (1974), 10, 13, 105, 123–33, 137, 142, 154, 162, 234
 Crash (1973), 5, 6, 8, 9, 11, 25, 29, 73, 74, 77, 88–102, 113–15, 123–5, 142, 143, 154, 231
 The Crystal World (1966), 31, 154, 184
 The Day of Creation (1987), 191
 'The Day of Forever' (1966), 232–3, 244, 245
 'The Day of Reckoning' (2005), 63
 The Drowned World (1962), 184, 187–8, 233–4
 Empire of the Sun (1984) 3, 6, 60, 181–2, 184–5, 190–1, 233, 235
 'End-Game' (1963), 52
 'The End of My War' (1995), 57, 59, 61
 'The Enormous Space' (1989), 3, 13, 234–6
 Hello America (1981), 105
 High-Rise (1975), 10, 12,105, 123–6, 133–9, 142, 154, 162, 199, 201–6, 209, 210, 211
 The Kindness of Women (1991), 60
 Kingdom Come (2006), 3, 6, 12, 13, 161–75, 189–90, 198, 210, 215, 216, 221–2, 225, 226–7, 230, 231, 240–5
 'The Man on the 99th Floor' (1962), 52
 'Manhole 69' (1957), 28, 188–9
 'Memories of Greeneland' (1978), 187
 Millennium People (2003), 6, 12, 110–11, 161–3, 171, 172, 173, 174, 215, 220–1, 225, 227, 231, 239–40, 243

Ballard, J. G. – *continued*
  Miracles of Life (2008), 182–3, 185–6
  'My Dream of Flying to Wake Island' (1974), 106, 108
  'Myth Maker of the C20th' (1964), 53, 54–6
  'Myth Maker of the Twentieth Century' (1996), 53, 54–6
  'Notes From Nowhere: Comments on Work in Progress' (1966), 54
  'The Overloaded Man' (1961), 13, 236–7
  'The Pleasures of Reading' (1992), 182, 187
  'Prima Belladonna' (1956), 4
  Project for a New Novel (1958), 2, 78
  Running Wild (1988), 6, 108–10, 230, 238–9
  Rushing to Paradise (1994), 6, 13, 191, 230, 237, 239
  'Sinister Spider' (1992), 57–8
  'The Subliminal Man' (1963), 78, 189
  Super-Cannes (2000), 6, 12, 112, 116–18, 181, 190–4, 199, 201, 206–11, 215, 219–20, 223–4, 226, 239, 240, 244
  'Survival Instincts' (1992), 57, 58
  'Terminal Documents' (1966), 53, 54–6
  'Time, Memory and Inner Space' (1963), 11, 187–8
  'The Terminal Beach' (1964), 29, 190
  'Thirteen to Centaurus' (1962), 3, 230
  'Track 12' (1958), 30
  'The Ultimate City' (1976), 230
  'The Ultimate Sacrifice' (2002), 62
  The Unlimited Dream Company (1979), 6, 11, 142–58
  'Unlocking the Past' (1991), 57, 59–61
  A User's Guide to the Millennium: Essays and Reviews (1996), 50, 53, 65
  'The Violent Noon' (1951), 6, 11, 181, 183–4, 185, 186, 188–9, 191, 232
  Vermilion Sands (1971), 39

'The Voices of Time' (1960), 6, 19–34
'Which Way to Inner Space?' (1962), 11, 22, 54, 187
'Zone of Terror' (1960), 29
Barthes, Roland
  punctum, 84
Bataille, George
  Story of the Eye (1928), 2
Bates, Paddy Roy, 234
Bateson, Gregory, 9
  'double bind', 107–9, 110, 111, 112, 113, 118
Baudrillard, Jean, 92, 244
  'Ballard's *Crash*' (1991), 93, 96, 99, 101
Baxter, Jeannette, 36, 72, 144, 174, 180, 188, 191, 218–19, 224
Beck, Ulrich, 168
Beckett, Samuel, 127–8
  'Act Without Words' (1956; 1957), 128
Bellmer, Hans, 2, 72
Benjamin, Walter, 78, 82
  critical montage, 7, 39
  photography, 73
  self-alienation, 81
  'Theses on the Philosophy of History' (1940), 156–7
  'The Work of Art in the Age of Mechanical Reproduction' (1936), 80–1, 83
Blake, William, 10, 142–58, 195
  'Auguries of Innocence', 150
  The Book of Urizen (1794), 10
  'The Clod and the Pebble', 153
  Jerusalem (c.1804–20), 10, 151–2, 156
  'London', 145, 146
  Milton (c.1804–10/11), 151, 152, 154, 156
  'The Proverbs of Hell', 146, 156
Boyd, William, 1, 6
Boy's Own Paper, 182
Bradbury, Malcolm, 143, 144, 146, 148
Bradshaw, Peter, 2
Braine, John, 186
Braithwaite, E. R., 182
Brigg, Peter, 106

Briggs, Robin, 26
Buchanan, Ian, 223
Buck Rogers, 182
Buck-Morss, Susan, 81, 82, 83
Buddhism, 28
  anâtman, 28
  nirvâna, 28
Burgess, Anthony, 187
  The Long Day Wanes (1956–9), 190
Burgin, Victor, 88, 90
Burial, 4
Burke, Edmund, 145
Burroughs, William, 35, 51, 54–6, 179, 187
  The Letters of William Burroughs: 1945–59 (1993), 55
  Literary Outlaw: The Life and Times of William Burroughs (1991), 55
Butterfield, Bradley, 93, 94

Cabaret Voltaire, 4
Calvert, Robert, 149–50
Campbell, John W. Jr, 22, 23
  Astounding Science-Fiction, 22, 23
  'Twilight' (1934), 22
Canetti, Elias, 13, 224
  Crowds and Power (1962), 216, 217, 221
Carnell, E. J., 20
Carroll, Lewis
  Alice books, 232
Carter, Angela, 195
  The Passion of New Eve (1977), 157
CBE (Commander of the Order of the British Empire), 179
Chalk, Warren,
  Living City Survival Kit (1963), 38
Chang, Jung
  Wild Swans (1992), 57, 58
Chemistry and Industry, 20, 52
Chums, 182, 183
Churchill, Winston S., 179, 190, 194–5
Clear, Nic, 37
  Architectural Design, 4, 37
  Unit 15, 3
Cokliss, Harley, 3

Coleridge, Samuel Taylor
  The Rhyme of the Ancient Mariner (1798), 232
Comsat Angels, The, 4
Connerton, Paul
  'Freud and the Crowd', 216
Connor, Bruce, 7
  assemblage, 35–46
  'Black Dahlia', 40
  Canyon Cinema, 42
  Cosmic Ray (1961), 40, 42
  The Child (1959–60), 40
  Crossroads (1976), 43
  Marilyn Times Five (1968–73), 43
  A Movie (1958), 40, 41–42
  Report (1963–7), 43–5
  Television Assassination (1963–95), 44
Conrad, Joseph, 180, 183–4
'*Crash!*' (BBC film, 1971), 3
'*Crash*: Homage to J. G. Ballard' (2010), 1–2
Cronenberg, David
  Crash (1996), 2, 92
Curson, Richard
  'Home' (2003)

Dali, Salvador, 1, 36
Dante, Alighieri
  The Divine Comedy (1314; 1315; 1321), 124–5, 128, 138–9
Dean, Tacita, 2
death of affect, 9, 74, 81, 88, 89, 93, 94, 95, 118, 239
Debord, Guy, 38
  The Society of the Spectacle (1967), 76, 81
Defoe, Daniel
  Robinson Crusoe (1719), 131, 182, 232
Deleuze, Gilles and Guattari, Félix, 8, 13
  Anti-Oedipus: Capitalism and Schizophrenia (1972), 79
  assemblage, 222–7
  A Thousand Plateaus: Capitalism and Schizophrenia (1980), 216, 223
Delville, Michel, 198

Derrida, Jacques,
　Specters of Marx, The State of Debt, The Work of Mourning and the New International (1994), 61, 62
Dick, Philip K., 24
Disch, Thomas M., 22
Donne, John
　'Elegie: To His Mistres Going to Bed', 113
Doors, The, 146
Drake, Gabriella, 3
Duchamp, Marcel, 40
Dunning, Eric, 207, 210–11
Durrell, Lawrence, 187
Dwelling Improvements Act (1875), 134

Eisenstein, Sergei, 40
Elias, Norbert, 198–212
　'civilizing process', 12, 199–201
　'The Quest for Excitement in Unexciting Societies' (1967), 207, 210–11
　sport, 210
Eliot, T. S., 20, 29
　Burnt Norton (1935), 29
　Four Quartets, 29
　'dissociation of sensibility', 113, 115
Eno, Brian, 4
entropy, 21–4, 30–1, 180–1
Ernst, Max, 36
Evans, Dr Christopher, 108

Farrell, J. G., 180
Flash Gordon, 182
Fletcher, Jonathan, 202, 203
Foster, Dennis A., 180
Foucault, Michel
　Discipline and Punish (1975), 138
Frendz, 150
Freud, Sigmund, 6, 24–6, 28, 189, 215–16, 221
　Beyond the Pleasure Principle (1920), 25
　Civilization and Its Discontents (1930), 62, 131, 193, 200
　the death drive, 25, 28, 29, 62, 200
　'The "Uncanny" ' (1919), 7, 50–66
　the Zuider Zee, draining of, 25–6
Futurism, 72, 187

Gasiorek, Andrzej, 72, 129, 134, 143, 144, 146, 148, 180, 192, 198, 232, 237
Genet, Jean, 179
Giddens, Anthony, 168
Ginsberg, Alan
　'Howl' (1955), 55
Godard, Jean-Luc
　Alphaville (1965), 38
Golding, William
　Lord of the Flies (1954), 115
Gray, Alasdair
　Lanark (1981), 157
Gray, John, 240
Greene, Graham, 183–4, 187
Greenland, Colin, 105, 106

Haffner, Sebastian
　Germany: Jekyll and Hyde (1940), 63, 64, 65
Haneke, Michael, 2
Hardy, Thomas, 164, 171
Harvard Design School Guide to Shopping (2002), 241–3
Hawkes, Terence, 163
Hawkwind, 149–50
Henty, G. A., 182
Hillers, Martha
　A Woman in Berlin (1954), 63–4, 65
Hinduism, 28
　Absolute Reality (*Brahman*), 28, 31
　âtman, 28
Hitler, Adolf, 193
　Mein Kampf (1924), 64–5
Hostel (2005), 92
Hostel Part II (2007), 93
Huizinga, Johan
　Homo Ludens (1934), 126
Hurst, Damien, 2
Hutcheon, Linda, 185
Hutt River Province Principality, 234, 238
Huxley, Aldous
　The Doors of Perception (1954), 146
　Heaven and Hell (1954), 146

Independent Group, 36
　Alloway, Lawrence, 36
　Banham, Reyner, 37
　Hamilton, Richard, 36
　'This is Tomorrow' (1956), 36
Inner Landscape, The (1969), 25
inner space, 9, 12, 88–91, 93–4, 186, 187–9

Jackson, Rosemary,
　Fantasy: The Literature of Subversion (1981), 30–1
Jameson, Fredric, 6, 180–1, 227
　Postmodernism, or the Cultural Logic of Late Capitalism (1991), 36, 75
Joy Division, 4
Jung, C. G., 6, 11
　Archetype, 26, 29
　collective unconscious, 26
　individuation, 24, 27–9, 31
　mandala, 19, 24, 26–31
　Memories, Dreams, Reflections (1963), 27
　The Red Book: Liber Novus (2009), 27
　Self (*âtman*), 27–9, 31
Just William, 182

Kant, Immanuel, 193–4
Keats, John,
　'Ode on Indolence' (1819), 125
Kerr, Joe, 135
Kennedy, J. F.
　Zapruder film, 43–4
Keynes, John Maynard, 125
Kingsley, Charles, 182
The Klaxons, 4
Kode9, 4
Koolhaas, Rem, 241
　Junkspace, 10, 129–30
Koresh, David, 237
Kracauer, Siegfried, 8
　'The Mass Ornament' (1923), 76–7
　The Tiller Girls, 75–6, 78, 80
Kristeva, Julia
　abjection, 8, 88–95, 97, 99, 101

Lacan, Jacques, 91, 92, 181, 193–4
　The Four Fundamental Concepts of Psychoanalysis (1973), 188

Lafargue, Paul
　The Right to Be Lazy (1883), 126
Laing, R. D., 9, 11, 27, 35, 106, 107, 108, 115, 135, 147, 151, 186
　The Divided Self (1960), 108
　The Politics of Experience (1967), 107
Larkin, Philip, 186
Lattas, Judy, 238
Lawson, Mark, 3
Le Bon, Gustave, 221
Le Corbusier
　La Ville Contemporaine (1922), 134
Le Guin, Ursula, 24
Lecercle, Jean-Jacques, 223, 225
Lefebvre, Henry
　The Critique of Everyday Life (1947), 126
　The Production of Space (1991), 126, 132
Leibniz, Gottfried, 217
Lessing, Doris, 24
Litt, Toby, 1
Locke, John, 154
London Docklands Development Corporation (LDDC), 123
LSD (drug), 150
Luckhurst, Roger, 26, 29, 50, 72, 99, 107, 129, 180, 186, 231
Lynch, David, 2

Manaugh, Geoff
　Bldgblog: Architectural Conjecture, Urban Speculation, Landscape Futures (2009), 4
Manic Street Preachers, The, 4
Marcuse, Herbert, 35
Marey, E. J., 98
Marinetti, F. T., 81
Marker, Chris
　A Grin Without A Cat (1977), 38–9
　La Jetée (1962), 38
Marwick, Arthur, 133
McClelland, John, 217
McEwan, Adam
　'Honda Team Facial', 2
McLuhan, Marshall, 35, 38, 46
McNamara, Liam, 180
Melchior, Dan
　'Me and J. G. Ballard' (2002), 4

Milne, A. A., 182, 183
Mondo Cane, 39
Moran, Joe, 123
Moorcock, Michael, 19, 22, 24, 35, 72, 149–51
Morrison, Jago, 185

Naipaul, V. S., 180, 182
Newton, Helmut, 1
Newton, Isaac, 154
'New Wave' (in SF), 6, 19, 22, 23, 24, 28, 181
New Worlds, 19, 20, 22, 24, 35, 36, 38, 42, 72, 149
Nietzsche, Friedrich, 192
Normal, The, 4
Noys, Benjamin, 94, 243–4
NSK (Neue Slowenische Kunst), 244–5

Oramus, Dominika, 198
Orwell, George, 183–4
   Burmese Days (1934), 190
Oswald, Lee Harvey
   assassination of 44–5

Paine, Thomas, 145
Parrinder, Patrick, 26
Paolozzi, Eduardo, 36–7
   Bunk!, 36–7
   General Dynamic F.U.N, 37
Pauline, Mark, 184
Plato
   Republic, 217
Pop Art, 36, 72
Pot, Pol, 193
Potter, Peter,
   'Thirteen to Centaurus' (1965 adaptation for BBC)
Powell, Anthony, 187
Preston, Keith, 238, 239
Priestley, J. B.,
Pringle, David, 26
Punter, David, 105, 133, 144, 154
Pym, Barbara, 186

Radiohead, 4
Réage, Pauline (Anne Desclos/Dominique Aury)
   Story of O (1954), 30

Reich, Wilhelm, 150, 151
Rushdie, Salman
   The Satanic Verses (1988), 157

Sade, Marquis de, 190
   Philosophy in the Bedroom (1795), 193–4
Sage, Vic, 99, 101
Said, Edward, 165
   'Two Visions in *Heart of Darkness*', 184
Saw (2004), 92
Sawyer, Andy, 20
Science Fantasy, 20
Seagrave, Sterling
   Dragon Lady: The Life and Legend of the Last Empress of China (1992), 58–9
Sealand, 234, 238
Seitz, William. C, 39–40
Self, Will, 1
Sellars, Simon, 37
Seltzer, Mark, 92
Shakespeare, William,
   The Tempest (1611), 232
Simmell, Georg
   phenomenology of money, 79
Simon, Art, 43
Simpson, Dave, 4
Sinclair, Iain, 1, 165, 169, 198
   Lights Out for the Territory (1997), 164
Situationism, 125
Snow, C. P., 187
Sobchak, Vivian, 99
Spenser, Edmund
   'Two Cantos of Mutabilitie' (1609), 21, 31
Spielberg, Steven
   Empire of the Sun (1987), 2
Stephenson, Gregory
   Out of the Night and Into the Dream (1991), 26, 98, 107
Stevens, Quentin
   The Ludic City (2007), 127
Strauss, Erwin S.
   How to Start Your Own Country (1984), 238
Strier, Richard, 162

Sudijc, Deyan, 4
Surrealism, 36, 72, 144, 187, 188
Swaan, Abraham de, 202, 205
Swift, Jonathan
　Gulliver's Travels (1726), 232

Tarkovsky, Andrei
　Stalker (1979), 31
Terry and the Pirates, 182
Tew, Philip, 136
Thatcher, Margaret, 135
Thomas, D. M., 24
Thompson, E. P., 145
Thompson, James
　The Castle of Indolence (1748), 125
Tubb, E. C., 19
　'Memories are Important' (1960), 23
Turchi, Peter, 165

Updike, John, 160

Van Sant, Gustav, 2
Varsity, 183
Vico, Giambattista, 128

Waquant, Löic, 206
Warhol, Andy, 36
　Death and Disaster, 36
Weiss, Jonathan
　The Atrocity Exhibition (2006), 2, 46
Wells, H. G., 21, 22, 26
Wexler, Haskell,
　Medium Cool (1969), 2
Whiteread, Rachel, 2
World Trade Centre,
　attacks on 9/11, 62–3, 220
Wright, Patrick, 164
Wells, H. G.
　The Time Machine (1895), 21

York, Thom, 4

Zelazny, Roger, 24
Žižek, Slavoj, 92, 181, 192, 194
Zoline, Pamela
　'The Heat Death of the Universe' (1967), 22–5
　'The Holland of the Mind' (1969), 25

CPI Antony Rowe
Chippenham, UK
2018-09-10 13:44